The Witch is Dead: Dark Oz Book 2 by Geneva Monroe
Copyright © 2024 by Geneva Monroe
Paperback ISBN: 978-1-960352-17-0
Published by Purple Phoenix Press LLC

Published by Purple Phoenix Press
Book Cover by Stella Nova, Geneva Monroe
Illustrations by Geneva Monroe
Author Portrait Photography by C.D. Redman

THE WITCH IS DEAD

AUTHOR OF THE SUN SERPENT SAGA

GENEVA MONROE

The Witch is Dead

Geneva Monroe

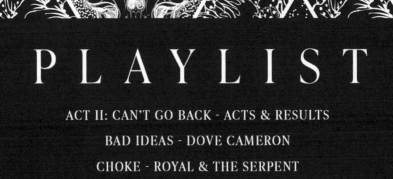

PLAYLIST

ACT II: CAN'T GO BACK - ACTS & RESULTS

BAD IDEAS - DOVE CAMERON

CHOKE - ROYAL & THE SERPENT

WICKED WAYS - EVERYBODY LOVES AN OUTLAW

I'M A SUCKER FOR A LIAR
IN A RED DRESS -ADAM JENSEN

TOXIC - 2WEI

NICE GUY - PAIGE GOLD

WOLVES - SAM TINNESZ, SILVERBERG

LOSE CONTROL (STRINGS ED.) - TEDDY SWIMS

DEEPER - VALERIE BROUSSARD, LINDSEY STIRLING

DEAD TO ME - CHLOE ADAMS

QUEEN - LOREN GRAY

I'M SO SORRY - IMAGINE DRAGONS

STOLEN MEMORIES - GABRIEL SABAN

WICKED AS THEY COME - CRMNL

SUPER VILLAIN - STILETO, SILENT CHILD, KENDYLE PAIGE

PASS THE KNIFE - NO/ME

SHARKS - IMAGINE DRAGONS

THE BEAUTIFUL LETDOWN - SWITCHFOOT, JONAS BROTHERS

JUST MY TYPE - JEREMY RENNER

SPIDER IN THE ROSES -
SONIA LEIGH, DAPHNE WILLIS, ROB THE MAN

IN THE AIR TONIGHT - NATALIE TAYLOR

SAVAGE (BITMASTER REMIX) - BAHARI, BITMASTER

Content Warning

The Witch is Dead: Dark Oz Book 2 is an adult, why choose retelling, with darker elements, where the main character has multiple partners. **It is not intended for minors.**

Triggers include: human trafficking, abuse, discussion of on and off-page rape, sexual assault, child abuse and neglect, torture, electrocution, murder, graphic violence, drug overdose, forced drug use, somnophilia, grief, loss of a parent and sibling, dubious consent, explicit and graphic sexual content, sexual content with multiple partners, explicit and graphic language, graphic gore, bondage, mature language, and bullying.

Reader discretion is advised.

Your mental health matters.

Hotline Numbers

The main character of this novel has a history with human trafficking. There are several characters in the book who have been trafficked. While it is a major component of this story, and Dark Oz is a work of fiction, human trafficking is not.

If you or someone you know is a victim of human trafficking please call the number below. Every call is confidential and they are available 24/7.

National Human Trafficking Hotline
1-888-373-7888

No one should ever struggle alone. Your mental health matters. You matter.

National Sexual Abuse Hotline
800.656.HOPE (4673)

National Domestic Violence Hotline
800.799.SAFE

National Center for Missing and Exploited Children
800.THE.LOST (843-5678)

Suicide and Crisis Lifeline
988

The Italian Lines

In L. Frank Baum's Oz, before the Tin Woodsman was made of tin, his name was Nick Chopper, short for Niccolo. Thus, Nick and his entire family are Italian. Crowe also dabbles in the language, having grown up among the Ciopriani family. Most of what Nick says is in English, but when he feels particularly angry or vulnerable, the Italian tends to find its way out. You'll also find Italian phrases from his entire family peppered throughout the book.

As a tip: Kindles and the Kindle apps will translate the Italian lines for you with almost perfect accuracy. Occasionally, the translation software misses the nuance of context. However, it's still convenient when you want to know exactly what flavor of swearing Nick's slinging...and the swoony lines...those too.

There is also a list of all Italian phrases and their translations at the back of the book.

Happy reading.

To those needing a reminder:

No one gets to tell you what you deserve.

–1–
NICK

The hard knuckles of Crowe's fist slammed into my cheekbone. I welcomed the pain that shot straight through the back of my eye socket. I deserved it and more. Once he figured out what happened, Danny would probably be taking a swipe at me, too.

I fucked up. I regretted my choice before I'd even made it.

"Explain to me, you son of a bitch, why Thea seems to think it was you who sold us out?" His next hit landed with a thud against my side, driving the oxygen from my lungs in a *woosh*.

"Or why you're letting him hit you?" Danny added coldly, knowing my refusal to defend myself was as much of an admission of guilt as the words themselves.

"Because I did," I said with as little emotion as possible, spitting a wad of blood onto the pavement.

The words hadn't fully left my lips before Crowe drew his Desert Eagle and pointed it at my chest. The gold titanium gleamed in the green-tinted street lights.

"Say that a-*fucking*-gain." He pulled back on the slide of the pistol. The snapping sound of the gun cocking sliced bone deep. A normal man would have flinched. But there wasn't anything left of the man in me anymore. The little bit of humanity I'd held on to ran out the back of that bank.

Regret wasn't a big enough word to explain the emotion barreling down on me. Crowe's eyes were blazing with rage, and it was entirely possible he was about to shoot me. Fuck, I would shoot me. That was the problem. I was ready to sacrifice anyone for our girl. We all were.

The shot didn't come. Instead Danny's fist knocked me to the ground, followed by his boot colliding with my side.

"Do you have any idea what you did? What you could have done?" The heat of Danny's rage was at such odds with the cold fury pouring from Crowe. "Fuck, Nick. Fuck!"

I pushed onto my knees, giving Crowe's gun a long look. It shook in his hands. Crowe's hands never shook. I stared down the barrel, trying to reach past it to the brother I'd grown up with. He had to understand. Crowe knew better than anyone the depth of what I endured. Eastin took everything, replacing it piece by piece until I was hollow, not even flesh and bone anymore, just a tin can forgotten like rusted scrap metal. If anyone understood that I couldn't afford this kind of vulnerability anymore, it was him.

"It wasn't supposed to go down this way."

"Exactly what fucking way was it supposed to go down?" Danny asked, moving to hit me again but spinning back at the last second. At least he was reigning in some form of control. For now.

"Once I realized what was happening, all I saw was the hurt in her eyes, the confusion, the fear. I tried to double back, except, fucking Thea took off."

It killed me when she'd barred that door and refused to let us through it. I'd wanted her gone, and she was running—dodging bullets as she went. Bullets I was responsible for. Thank Ozma none of them hit her.

"She took off because you sold her out to Emily Oz damn Rosen!" Crowe nearly screamed the words at me, little bits of spit flying with them. "Fucking hell, Nick. I told you what she'd already done to Thea. Do you have any idea what Emily would have done if she actually caught Thea?"

"I didn't sell her to Emily!" I snapped back, regret be damned. "I gave up the emerald's location to Westin. I don't know how Em's Wolves got on the scent."

"Because that's somehow better," Danny fumed, matching every bit of Crowe's intensity. "You were going to hand over our only leverage to the supreme bitch of Oz, and what, hope that she also didn't try to take her pound of flesh while she was at it?"

"Nothing went down like it should have. If it had been right, you would have your answers, and Thea would be long gone on her way to a new life by now. Thea would be safe and happy. Westin would be one shiny emerald richer and wouldn't give a fuck about the rest of us anymore."

When Danny's pacing quickened, his fingers tapping out his thoughts on his thighs, I knew he was hearing me out. If they would slow down and see reason, they would understand.

"The second you two walked out of the vault, I knew the whole thing had gone sideways. The Wizard didn't hold up his end of the bargain. Thea locked the emerald in the vault, and then Em's people showed up. By the time Crowe told us we had company, I was already trying to cut our way out of that bank."

"I can't process this bullshit," Crowe said, holstering his gun. "If you say anything else right now, I swear to fucking Oz, I'm going to shoot you."

Nodding, I climbed onto my feet. Fair enough. I'd shoot me, too.

Crowe spun to Danny. "What does he mean Thea locked the emerald in the vault?"

"Exactly what it sounds like. The Wizard demanded that we take down Westin and bring him her emerald, too. They refused to give us more than fuck-all until we did."

"Sly motherfucker. Of course one priceless gem isn't enough. Don't get me wrong, I hope Westin chokes to death on her own damn ego, but what is he expecting? That we're going to waltz into that fortress she calls a pleasure yacht and snip-snap take her out?"

"Pretty much. When The Wizard was done with us, Thea locked the necklace back in the vault and pocketed the key. I was too..." A flash of pure remorse sank his features. "...distracted to realize what she was doing until it was done."

"That's actually fucking lucky." Crowe ran his hand through his hair. For the first time since Thea ran, he looked like his typical, carefree self.

"How do you figure?"

"Because I embedded a tracker in the key."

I blinked in disbelief, then blinked again. "Sorry. You had a priceless key, and despite the bank killing people over even a whiff of tampering, thought it wise

5

to pop a tracker in it?" I shouldn't be criticizing poor choices right now. *Però cazzo,*[1] he wasn't the one who walked into that bank.

"Give me a little credit. I'm not an amateur. Your pa didn't make me take all of those classes for me to fuck up jobs." He walked back to where he'd left the cab, the rest of us following after him. "I didn't know what was going to happen today, and it felt like a good idea to make sure we could recover that key if it went missing. So say, 'Thank you, Crowe.' Because finding her again is the only thing keeping me from putting a bullet in that empty fucking chest of yours."

I followed behind the guys, the slap of our footsteps echoing off the brick buildings. Crowe practically jogged to the cab. It had been a long time since I'd seen him unhinged like this. Anger plumed off of Crowe in waves. I wouldn't be surprised if he started scorching footprints into the concrete.

He would understand. They both would.

Thea was a liability to us all. I realized that day in the kitchen that nobody thought clearly where she was concerned, myself included. I spent too damn long cauterizing the nerve endings of my heart to allow her to make me feel things again.

It couldn't happen. Never again. I had to do something.

They would understand— eventually.

Crowe tore open the back door. Bullets were sunken into the side of the car, buckling the paneling and splintering the glass.

"Fucking asshole, Nick. Fucking. Asshole." He spun, pulling his gun from the holster. Aiming it at the sidewalk, he pulled the trigger over and over. A dull ringing filled my ears until I could barely tell the difference between the ignition of each bullet, the exploding concrete, and Crowe's feral roar of anger. When he finally emptied what was left of his clip, he stared at the chasm cut into the sidewalk. His chest heaved as he tried to catch his breath. None of the pent-up emotion seemed to have ebbed from the outburst. If anything, he seemed to be wound even tighter.

---

1. But damn,

"Crowe, man, I—" He cut me off with a snarl.

"You're doing all the bodywork to fix this car."

"It would have been me doing the bodywork anyway."

Crowe glared at me, making the tattoo along his temple flex with the pulsing vein.

I held up my hands in supplication. He was right. A bit of axle grease was a small price to pay for betraying them.

He stepped over a dead body to climb into the car. The man's hands were a blackened, charred mess. Crowe must have triggered the security system, hitting the attacker with a more than lethal level of electricity. It was the same system we had on the house. If anyone were stupid enough to put a hand to the car, they wouldn't live long enough to debate that choice. The backseat was still converted into Crowe's surveillance setup.

The cab was the brainchild of all three of us. I engineered the seats to convert and flip into anything we needed, from a mobile command unit to a triage surgical center. I refused to think of the hours Thea and I spent lounging in the backseat together. Or the way she looked out the window like endless opportunity was held back by a single pane of bulletproof glass. *Fuck.*

Crowe slid into the backward facing passenger seat, clicking at the controls built behind the seat back. Four monitors showed what remained of the bank feeds and the carnage within. He pulled up a satellite map of Ozmandria, typing in long strings of code into the window at the bottom.

I leaned against the wall of the neighboring building, watching his progress through the window and using the corner of my sleeve to dab at the split under my eye. I should be grabbing some med supplies from the car and cleaning this up, but for now a bit of space between us was probably wise.

"There," Crowe said with finality. "That pretty little dot is her."

Danny leaned into the car. "She didn't make it very far."

"Lucky for us." Crowe twisted to look me straight in the eye. "This conversation isn't over, but I want Thea here when you explain your stupid fucking rationalization for all of this. Then she can decide which part of your body the bullet goes in."

7

"Stop being dramatic. It's not like you," Danny said, pulling on his shirt to get him out of the car. With the push of a button, the car rearranged itself back into your average shitty cab. "Let's go. I can't wait to see the furious look on her face when we show up. That woman is smoking hot when she's pissed."

–2–
THEA

"No. No. No. No. No," I pleaded with the car as it shuddered to a stop. I hadn't even made it out of town. Instead, I was stalled out in the middle of the road a mile from the W7 on-ramp. Figures I would steal a shitty car with barely a quarter tank of gas in it.

I got out of the compact sedan and slammed the door shut, kicking the wheel for good measure. A car laid on his horn and blared by me.

"Don't bother seeing if I need help or anything, douche waffle," I shouted back at him, throwing up a cathartic middle finger.

The pavement was cold on my bare feet. They were sore from the pounding I'd given them getting out of the bank. I knew that I'd never be able to run in the outrageous heels Danny had picked for me, but I was seriously wishing for them now that I was dragging my ass down cold, wet asphalt.

A drizzle of icy rain was falling, coming down harder by the minute. It instantly soaked through my thin blouse, rinsing my skin of the blood coating it. I wrapped my arms tight around myself in a feeble attempt to stay warm.

What the fuck was I going to do? I had no money, no contacts, and no plan. I was screwed. No, I was worse than screwed. Maybe I could steal another car and, in a stroke of luck, some person stashed money in the glove compartment, or a sandwich. One thing was for certain: I couldn't stay here. How long would it take for Em's people to catch up with me? I needed to get out of sight.

A fluorescent sign flickered through the haze of rain: Revolt. I didn't know what it was, but it was better than freezing in the middle of the road. The second I pushed open the glass door, I was hit by a wave of warmth, sending a wave of tingles down my limbs until my fingertips and feet felt like they were on fire.

I stomped on the worn entry carpet of the lobby, brushing the excess water off my body and squeezing out my hair.

"You look like a drowned cat."

I spun towards an old, dingy concierge desk. The hotel looked like it hadn't been updated in the past forty years. The once green silk couches were threadbare, their cushions lumpy on the edges and sunken in the center, and the wood trim was discolored from where the varnish was worn away.

"Sorry, I... my car ran out of gas and..." I brushed my wet hair from my eyes and instantly forgot everything I was saying. "Toto?"

Familiar flowing red hair shook with laughter. Her nose wrinkled as she laughed, a lovely pink flooding her cheeks and setting off her many freckles. Even her eyes seemed a brighter shade of green now that we weren't prisoners in the back of a truck.

"How are you here?" I asked, trying to keep my jaw from hanging open.

"You mean, how did I get out of the back of a shipping truck, in a locked parking garage, all the way back in Kinland, to be managing a run-down hotel on the west end of Emerald City?"

"Yeah, that?" I was so shocked that I'd even forgotten how cold I was.

"Well. Turns out that someone" --she held her hand up in a mock stage whisper-- "murdered Eastin Witcher. They were too busy chasing down some cab to care about a bunch of homeless girls running loose." She gave me an exaggerated wink and giggled with such effervescence that it made the room brighter. I couldn't help but smile. In another life, I think we would have been best friends. "The others from the truck went running in all directions. I don't know what happened to them. I managed to find a service hatch that followed the building's wiring and used that to scramble back to the surface that way."

She tossed a blazer that was hanging on the chair back at me. "Thanks," I said gratefully.

"I was trying to hitch a ride to anywhere when Ginger found me. She set me up here."

"She just gave you a job, a stranger?"

"Seeing as I haven't had papers in a long time, courtesy of The Farm, I wasn't going to be able to do *regular* employment. Ginger finds girls like us and gives them a chance to earn their keep."

"So she's your pimp?"

"No, no, nothing like that," Toto laughed. "She owns several of these hotels around the EC. She plants girls in all of her establishments to help her find her next mark, men who seem gullible and easily swayed by a pretty face. She wouldn't be able to successfully con them if they'd met her already, so she has an army of scouts who find her marks for her. She'd never admit it, but I think she's secretly trying to take over OZ by taking down one man at a time."

"Wow."

"Ginger's different. I've never known anyone like her. She gave me a room behind the office and decent enough pay. It beats literally everything I've ever done before this, and she's never once asked for anything in return. I bet I could convince her to find a place for you, too."

"I can't stay that long. There are people after me." I sat down on the edge of the couch. A pang of loss for a life and a friendship I could never have swelled in my stomach. "I wouldn't say no to a dry change of clothes if you have them." I added with a laugh, "Or a car."

"I might know of a car that nobody is using at the moment."

"One that isn't stolen?"

"I didn't say that, but it's not currently in use. I have a bit of money saved that I can give you, too."

I was already shaking my head, no.

"I owe you, Thea. You tried to free me, and it got you thrown in beside me. Then, you could have left us in that truck, but you didn't. For the first time in my life, I'm truly free." Toto tossed a "back in 5 minutes" sign on the desk and gestured for me to follow her. "Come with me. I'll find you something to change into."

"It won't be a problem leaving the desk?"

"Nah, nobody ever stops in. We haven't had anyone check-in for over a week now. The entire hotel is empty. To be honest, I think Ginger only gave me this as a pity position. I'm pretty sure she uses it as a front to launder money. But you didn't hear that from me."

"Who would I tell?"

The outer door opened, bringing with it a blast of cold air. I shivered, instantly recognizing the three men who stumbled over each other into the lobby.

"Damn it."

I frantically scanned the room, looking for any way out. If I was smarter, I would have scouted for exits when I came in. Nope, now I was sprinting for a door that could be a broom closet, for all I knew.

"Thea, don't run," Crowe yelled.

But I wasn't waiting around to hear what he had to say. Thundering steps closed in behind me. Just as I made it to the handle, two strong arms wrapped around me. One arm banded around my chest, pinning my arms to my sides. The other hooked my hips and hauled me backward. My bare feet squeaked as they fruitlessly fought against the tile floor.

"Put me down, you backstabbing brute." I tried to angle my head down to bite at his meaty, tattooed arm. Nick spun me around to face the others.

"Only if you promise to be a good girl and stay put," Danny said, smug as ever. He walked over to us like he had all the time in the world. "But, Princess, I don't actually think you know how to behave."

Crowe's face was a mix of relief and straight-up rage. He could get in line because those emotions had been warring inside me since the day I got in his cab.

Toto barreled into Danny, knocking him on his ass. She didn't slow down at all. The too-thin girl was a wild creature, swinging a fireplace poker like a bat straight at Nick's head. It connected with a loud crack, making Nick's eyes roll in his head. Releasing his grip on me, he crumpled to the ground like a bag of cement.

"Run, Thea. I've got these guys."

I turned straight into the unforgiving wall of Crowe's hard body. His arms latched around me, firmly holding the back of my neck, so I was forced to look at him.

"Stop," he growled at me through clenched teeth. Then his voice melted into something softer, smoother. "I'm not gonna hurt you. I'm never going to let anyone hurt you." His eyes flicked to Nick's unconscious body. "I would kill any man who did."

I tried to look away from him, weakly fighting against the arm snaking tighter around my waist. The problem was, I didn't want to fight him off. Not really.

He whispered low in my ear. "If you want to run, Beautiful, I'll run with you. But don't you ever run from me again." Before I could fake a protest, he was kissing me soft, deep, and so damn tenderly that my heart throbbed like it might explode. Tears pricked at the corners of my eyes, and as each one fell, my resolve crumbled just a little bit more.

Toto jumped on Crowe's back, pulling on his arms and punching at his shoulders.

"Let her go! Get your big ape hands off of her!"

His grip tensed, holding me closer and refusing to acknowledge the hundred pounds of woman that was beating at his back.

"Daffodil?" Danny said in almost a whisper but loud enough to draw everyone's attention to him. "Holy fuck. It is you."

Toto jumped down from Crowe's back, pushing us sideways and stumbling over us for Danny.

"Dandy?" Her voice broke at the end of his name, sounding smaller and more childlike than I had ever heard her sound.

He dwarfed her small frame, pulling her into a massive hug. "I thought you were dead. I thought... I thought... I can't believe you're here."

Tears fell from his still-shocked eyes. *Tears.* I couldn't tell what was more shocking, that Toto was his sister or that Danny was capable of crying.

"Dandy, you have to let me go. I can't breathe."

He released Toto, holding her at arm's length but still running his hands over her shoulders like he couldn't believe she was real.

15

"Wait. You're his sister?" Crowe said, still confused.

"Oh my god." Realization dawned on me. *Daniel Kalidah.* "That's why I recognized the name you gave at the bank. It was on the missing person's report."

"Yeah, I filed a report twice a year for each of my sisters. Just in case."

I felt so daft for not connecting the dots sooner, smacking Danny on his shoulder, "I was trying to get a hold of *you* when Em figured out what I was doing." Laughter bubbled out of me, inappropriate for sure, but the irony was too much. "Shit, I was one keystroke away from emailing you."

"Fuck." Danny's expression twisted with a baffled mix of emotions. "I'm sorry, Thea."

"Don't be." He looked so much like Toto did that day in the truck. He had the same downward tilt of his lips and the same tightness in the brows. "Like I told your sister, if it wasn't her, it would have been someone else. I was always headed to East—"

"Wait," Crowe interrupted, pointing at Toto. "But you're that girl in the back of the Cyclone truck. The one Thea freed before we left Kinland."

"For OZ sake. Catch up, Crowe. Toto is Daffodil. Daffodil is Toto. I met her at The Farm. I tried to tell Danny where she was being sent, but Em found out, sold me to Eastin, and shipped me to OZ. Then, I killed Eastin and freed Toto. Now she's here." I spit the entire long chain of events out in one breath, leaving me gasping.

"Toto?" Crowe said, even more confused.

"When my kid sister was a toddler, she couldn't say Daffodil. It was the D and all those syllables; it always came out Toto. It kind of stuck," she said, shrugging her shoulder. "I haven't heard anyone call me Daffodil in so long. I almost forgot it was my name."

"Oh," he said, still looking dazed.

Toto leaned over Danny's arm to look down at Nick. "I'm sorry I knocked out your friend."

"Don't be," I said before either of them could speak. "That asshole sold me out to Em. So he deserved it. Feel free to hit his deceiving ass again if you feel like it."

"At least it's a hot ass. I mean, look at that muscle tone," Toto bent over and spanked Nick's right butt cheek with the full force of a woman who'd been spanking men all her life. "Look, hardly any jiggle."

-3-
THEA

C rowe's fingers trailed down my neck. Pausing on each individual finger-print purpling along my throat. The muscles and vocal cords were still sore from being choked, but they were nothing compared to the alternative. If Crowe hadn't blown Albert's face off... I shivered. Without Crowe, I never would have made it off the sidewalk alive. From the look on his face, he knew it too.

For the past thirty minutes, Crowe refused to let me out of arm's reach. He wore down my defenses in a laughably short amount of time. I wasn't entirely sure I liked this foreign feeling of dependency. I'd never been a slave to my heart before, but there was no denying that driving away from Crowe felt like drinking battery acid. I instantly regretted it; it left me raw, and I still felt sick from my choices.

As much as I wanted to purge myself of the feeling, leaving was the right thing to do. I couldn't trust any of them, not anymore. Even knowing all of that, it took Crowe calling me *"Darling Thea"* once, and I let him walk all his charm right back in. It was hard to deny him when those blue eyes were so obviously shaken.

Toto tossed a change of clothes at me. She eyed Crowe suspiciously. As she left the tiny apartment, she made several not-so-veiled threats about all the ways she could skewer his dick and roast it should any harm befall me. The vague sounds of Danny dragging Nick's unconscious body floated in from the lobby.

Crowe insisted on helping me with my clothing after I visibly grimaced. The tumble I'd taken when I was tackled hadn't done me any favors. I was covered in a new series of bruises, and I was fairly certain a few of the deeper lacerations on my lower back had reopened.

We hadn't discussed what happened at the bank yet. Of the three men, Crowe seemed the most genuinely unnerved by how things played out. All of his normal playfulness had evaporated, and what was left was unusually serious.

More and more, I believed that he hadn't known what was happening. That didn't mean he would side with me on any of it. Despite his declarations, he, Danny, and Nick were brothers in all but blood. I wasn't fooling myself into believing that his allegiance somehow lay with me.

"These make me want to put another bullet in his brain," Crowe said, softly pressing a kiss to the highest mark and then moving lower to give the same attention to each blemish and cut.

I should have pulled away, but instead of stepping back, I closed my eyes and let my body fall into his gravity. The image of Albert's grotesque dead eye staring at me was seared into my subconscious, haunting me whenever my mind drifted too far. I could still feel the sticky warmth of his blood on my palms.

"I've never been so terrified," he continued, voice so soft I could barely hear him. "When I saw your body go limp beneath that Wolf. I was afraid that I was too late." He kissed the side of my temple. "I should have known you'd never give up so easily."

He was right, and a bit of comfort wasn't going to make me give up now, either. I pushed out of his grip. "Good, then you'll understand why I can't leave here with your merry band of backstabbers."

The second I was out of his arms, his hand latched onto mine, reeling me backward. "Nick betrayed us both. Thea, I—"

The bedroom door pushed open, propped by Toto's hip. "The big tattooed hunk of man meat is waking up. He keeps gibbering on in some nonsense language. The only thing I can make out is your name. He seems to have plenty to say about you. Sexy as sin accent, but if you don't get out there soon, I'm pretty sure my brother is going to knock him back out again."

"He'd be doing us all a favor," I grumbled. A sour lump formed in the back of my throat. I thought things with Nick had been...something. I didn't have a word to describe it, but there was *something,* and the loss of whatever it was stung.

I stepped away from Crowe, shrugging off his concern and lengthened my spine. Strapping on my best boss bitch expression, I followed Toto back into the lobby.

"I don't think he likes the tie-up job I did on him." She gestured to the raging man in the center of the room. Red, smooth rope laced around his torso in intricate patterns and knots. If I wasn't still so pissed, I might have been able to appreciate just how mouth-watering Nick was. The muscles of his tattooed arms strained against the chair's back. They were pinioned in place by the broom handle resting in the crook of his arms. The wood creaked each time he pulled, but it prevented him from being able to twist free of his bindings.

"Seriously, it's some of my best work," Toto said proudly, slapping at where his thighs were restrained spread eagle to the chair legs. It was amazing how confident she had become. The transformation was truly astounding. Was the meek girl I'd seen at The Farm an act, or had freedom agreed with her so much that she'd blossomed into this striking woman?

"Why do you know how to do shibari?" Danny asked hesitantly, distracting himself from the obvious answer by poking Nick in the cheek with the same fireplace poker Toto had knocked him out with.

A litany of Italian curses spilled from the asshole's mouth. I had to bite down on my lip to keep from smiling. I was still pissed at Danny too, but that shit was funny.

"Nevermind. Don't tell me," Danny added quickly, looking at his feet with what I could only describe as shame.

"Dandy, it's been fifteen years. I don't fear my past, and neither should you."

I tugged against Crowe's vice-like fingers, "You're worse than a boa constrictor. I promise not to bolt for the door. You can let go of me."

Unease flitted across his face, that same flicker he'd given me when I put the car into drive. The hurt shifted into something far more sinister. For the first time, I could see a shadow of The Scarecrowe filling the space around him. This was the man who took people apart piece by piece, and all of his attention was aimed directly at me.

"Go ahead and make *your promises*, pretty girl. If you run, *I promise,* next time, the version of me that catches you won't be this nice guy." He gestured with a swirly motion at his stone-cold face. "I'm barely holding on to him right now."

"That's almost enough of a threat to make things interesting." I winked.

The corner of his lips lifted. It wasn't a lie. I loved how he cared for me. Nobody had ever treated me with such reverence, but the promise of an unhinged Crowe was hotter than a bonfire in hell. There was a brutality simmering under the surface of his playful smiles. I'd always known it was there, even before he told me about his demons. A very reckless part of me wanted to see what happened when he finally snapped.

Nick's eyes bore into me as I walked to him. I bent over until I was level with him. Even though he was sitting, I didn't have to bend far. I plucked at the rope suspended between his biceps and the lattice work running down his torso. It vibrated in the air. The knots were beautiful; even more alluring was the fact that Nick was completely at my mercy right now. It was a type of power I'd never experienced before, and I liked it.

"Could you teach me how to do this?" I asked, continuing to slide my fingers along the loops pressed into his ribs. Nick shivered.

Crowe's icy composure finally cracked. Behind me, he breathed an amused laugh. "I volunteer."

I looked over my shoulder at him. "I bet you do."

"It's easy enough to learn," Toto replied, grabbing a handle built behind Nick's neck. His head was forced up with a gagged cough. She patted the top of his head like a dog. "Good boy."

There was no stopping the snort that bubbled out of me this time. If murder had a look, Nick was giving it.

She continued, "These knots are more of an intermediate level, but I could show you some much simpler configurations. I have a spare rope in the cabinet here. Dandy, turn around. I'll demonstrate on you."

"Fuck no." He shot up, holding his hands out like he feared she might charge him. "This is *not* a thing that's happening."

I sighed and poked at Nick's purple cheekbone. From the broken knuckles on Crowe's hand, this was probably his doing. I wish I'd been there. "Then, I guess it's your turn, *cazzo*. Explain."

When it was the boys poking at him, Nick was all rage. But when his focus shifted to me, his expression was devastatingly void of all emotion. They say to kill them with kindness, but nothing kills you like indifference.

"Fiore Mio..." His tone was placating. It made me want to tear his tongue out, if only so I never had to hear him say anything so sinfully beautiful again.

"Don't '*Fiore Mio*' me. You're not going to wave a magic sexy accent wand at me and expect all to be forgiven."

"You wouldn't understand, and anything I said wouldn't matter anyway."

I spun, grabbing the knife on Crowe's belt, and leapt at Nick. Landing on his lap, I gripped a fistful of his lazily tousled hair and flicked open the blade. A small trickle of blood leaked around the edge of the blade and over his Adam's apple. "Try. Fucking. Harder."

Nick gritted his teeth, the rope creaking as he strained against his bindings.

Toto leaned toward Crowe, talking in a hushed whisper, "I should have made him shirtless. This would be so much hotter."

"Ew. Please stop." Danny shuddered.

"It's impressive how you got the rope to frame his package like that. It's practically a gift-wrapped dick," Crowe added.

"Oh, it really is. That knot at the top is perfectly placed to rub against—"

Danny pinched the bridge of his nose, squinting. "Please, please stop."

Without meaning to, my eyes dropped down to the knot resting above the zipper of his pants. It really would rub all the right things when you were grinding down. Just the idea of riding Nick while he was trussed up was enough to make my heart start pounding hard.

Damn it. Focus, Thea! This was not the time for my mind to start wandering.

Nick's eyes tightened on the necklace of bruises scattered around my throat. His voice was uncharacteristically low, accent thick as he said, "You weren't supposed to be hurt."

That was all it took to bring all of my rage and focus slamming back. I snapped in front of his vision to bring his eyes back to mine. "You traded me to The Farm and thought I'd somehow make it out of that scenario unscathed? My bitch of an aunt has done *nothing* but hurt me my entire life!"

"See this." I pulled on the collar of my shirt, showing him the scar on my shoulder. "This was from when she whipped me with a dozen long-stem roses. The thorns tore open a gash big enough to need five stitches. I was seven."

Nick swallowed, the bloody lump of his Adam's apple dragging over the blade.

"And these—" I lifted the hem of my shirt to show where five small white dots freckled my abdomen. "Are from when they had to remove my appendix after she caned me hard enough to make it rupture. So, tell me *A-FUCK-ING-GAIN* that I wasn't supposed to be harmed!"

Angry tears burned the backs of my eyes, and my chest heaved as I struggled to draw in a full breath. I could feel the embers of my rage sparking, tearing me apart from the inside out. If I could, I would let it demolish this entire hotel, taking us all down with it.

Nick pulled at the ropes, his own restrained breaths fighting to match mine. "I didn't trade *you*, Fiore Mio. I traded the emerald to Westin. You were never part of the bargain."

Like that somehow made it better? "Those weren't Westin's bullets aiming for me. It wasn't Westin's man strangling me in the parking lot."

"They were *Wolves*," Crowe hissed, drawing all of our attention. Toto took a step back, stumbling into Danny. Even I wanted to recoil, and I'd grown up around them my entire life. Mentioning the Wolves was like summoning the boogeyman.

"You're sure?" Danny's expression was colder than I'd ever seen it. The entirety of that intensity focused on Nick, making my skin prickle in warning.

Toto wasn't wrong. Danny might very well kill Nick tonight—Which was a devastating realization. This whole time, I'd assumed Danny was pulling Nick's strings, but if Nick had really acted alone, then what did that mean?

Crowe nodded. "The man I shot in the parking lot and the man at the cab both had the wolf's head branded into their necks."

"The Wolves raided my family's commune."

Danny pushed Toto back, but she shoved past him, surprising us all by clocking Nick hard in the jaw and barely missing me on the recoil. The hit jarred my arm, slicing deeper into his throat than I'd intended. The gash wasn't deep enough to sever anything important, but blood freely flowed from the wound.

I dropped the knife, terrified of what I had almost done.

"Fiore Mio..." he mouthed, whispering low enough I couldn't actually hear the words.

Nausea turned in my stomach as Nick's black shirt became glossy with blood. I was pissed and hurt, but I didn't want him dead. I may have thought I did before, but my foolish heart cared too much to end his life.

"Ow." Toto shook her hand out. "What the hell are you made from, metal?"

Crowe gently closed the blade and put it back onto his belt. "I think that's enough playing with stabby things for a little while."

I nodded and climbed off of Nick's lap, putting some very necessary space between us.

Nick stretched his jaw, making a slight popping sound. He glared back at Danny. "I told you already. I tipped off Westin on when and where she could snatch the emerald. It was a routine drop. She was never supposed to get near Thea. I don't know how Em's Wolves caught the scent. That's the truth."

I shook my head. It didn't make sense. Nick seemed to care about so little. What could Westin have dangled before him to make betraying everyone he cared about worth it?

"Why?" It was a simple word, but so much emotion was wrapped around that single syllable. I tucked my arms around my middle. "The least I deserve is to know what you got for it."

His accent thick, Nick said, "Rid of you."

He might have driven a knife into my chest from how sharply the pain radiated from it.

"Rid of the way you drag up every emotion in me."

Like I could escape the raw cut of them, I backed away a step with every word until my legs hit the edge of the armchair, and I fell into it.

He didn't relent, every scathing word hitting deeper than the last. "I can't stand it. I've had every bone in my body broken, all of them." Nick's expression finally broke. The placid indifference shifted into an honest mix of pain and fury. His hands pulled at their bonds. His legs strained until a crack ran down the center of the chairleg. "I've had pieces of my flesh filleted away. None of it hurts the way feeling this emotion does. You don't understand. I can't allow myself to be that man again, Thea."

I couldn't breathe. The room closed in, the moldering walls seeming to shrink with each passing second.

"Nick, that's enough," Danny barked, like somehow he might be able to stop the truth filling the room like gasoline waiting for a match.

"That day in the kitchen, you smiled at me so purely. Your pretty eyes blinked up at me like you saw beneath all of the scars to the man I used to be—and he made you happy. It reignited something I hadn't felt in a long time. The truth hit me like an axe to the heart. I wasn't chasing pussy like the rest of these idiots. It was so much worse. I was falling in love with you."

"What did you just say?" My heart pounded in my ears, my lungs screamed for breath. The only thing my brain could compute was the way the room was beginning to spin.

"Since I obviously wasn't strong enough to resist you, the only option was to ensure you never set foot in Oz again. The Wizard would give you a new life, a good life with a new identity."

I shook my head, unable to process what he was saying.

"But you'd already sunk your hooks in deep with those two." He lifted his chin to Danny and Crowe. "I've known them my whole life. For as long as you allowed it, they would never let you go, especially if they knew Westin was gunning for you. If you thought you'd been betrayed, that would ensure you stayed gone. Handing the emerald over to Westin solved both problems."

"You unbelievable asshole. You just went ahead and made that decision for us. You couldn't stand that you're missing a heart, so you had to burn what was left of mine." The violence shifting around Crowe swelled so much I could feel the intensity of it from across the room. His fists tightened until they were trembling at his sides. "You have no fucking idea, Nick."

"No idea? Vin…"

Crowe lunged for Nick, pulling his knife from its sheath. Danny barely managed to intercept him before the knife on his belt was fully unsheathed. Even though Danny was holding Crowe back, Nick kept going. "*You* were so blinded by her that you got captured by Monkeys. Fucking Monkeys, Crowe. When was the last time any of us were pinched? Even Danny managed to get himself drugged, trying to prove that he wasn't affected by her. Thea changed all of us."

"I'm the problem, so remove me from the equation." The ringing in my ears turned into a roar, loud enough I couldn't hear myself when I spoke. "It was that simple."

The entire room shifted its attention back to me.

Nick looked pale. Maybe the ropes were cutting off circulation, maybe I had cut him too deep after all, or maybe he felt enough remorse that it was draining him.

"Why not kill me?" I stood up, forcing myself to be as tall as I could manage. "That'd be the simplest option."

Both Crowe and Danny barked angry retorts so vehemently it was impossible to tell what they were saying. Something about death and burning the world, blah blah blah. I was over this entire conversation. If I wasn't worth his compassion, then why was I bothering to listen at all?

Nick paid no attention to their proclamations, keeping his unflinching stare for me alone. "I would never jeopardize your safety. There was no other way. I didn't care if The Wizard came at me for double-crossing him. If I took a bullet to the brain for it, at least I would die knowing I hadn't allowed myself the weakness of loving you."

Raped. Beaten. I'd almost died. Twice. I took my hits in stride, enduring enough pain to last me two lifetimes. None of it compared to this. Just as I was beginning to know what kindness felt like, it turned on me, and then I turned my back on the only man to ever treat me like I mattered.

I was done being tossed around to suit the needs of other people.

"You want rid of me?" I turned and walked straight for the door, holding my middle finger high. "How's this?"

"Thea!" Crowe bellowed.

The room filled with static, it buzzed in my head like a swarm of hornets. I was barely seeing straight, the edges of my vision narrowing on the door. It didn't matter where I was headed so long as it was far away from this building.

Plowing through the door, I ran into the pouring rain. The drops felt like tiny blades pelting down on me. What had I done to deserve any of this? Was this what breaking felt like? My soul stretched so far the spider web unraveled.

I lifted my face to the sky and screamed.

-4-
THEA

My vocal cords were still raw from screaming when Crowe burst through the hotel door. Hauling me back, his fingers dug into my skin, pinning my shoulders to the door hard enough to make the glass vibrate.

My aching body screamed in protest, but I didn't feel an ounce of the pain. I was too stunned by the man before me for there to be anything but him.

Rain skimmed over his sharpened features, the grey world around us making the blue of his eyes blaze. There were barely words beneath his growl. "You promised."

I thrashed wildly in his grip, futilely bucking my body against miles of hard muscle. "You expect me to stay after what he just said?"

"No. I expect you to listen when I tell you that being with you is the only thing holding me together right now." He slammed me harder into the glass, one hand sliding up my throat and angling my face up to him. "Danny doesn't want to admit it, but he's mad for you, too. He'll probably follow you wherever you go like the sad little kitten he is, and Nick..." Some of the ferocity behind his grip eased. "I hate what happened to you. I hate that he abandoned everything on the fool's notion that he could ever ignore the way you permeated every part of this group. But Nick... You don't know the whole story."

"I don't want to know the whole story. I want to be done with all of this." I pounded my fists as hard as I could against his chest. "I have a heinous bitch to kill and a Wizard to appease." I fought against the wet glass. My bare feet slipped on the cold pavement, allowing Crowe to press more of his body against mine. "Let me go, and I'll be nothing more than a bad memory. Then you can have your precious lives back."

"You're still not listening." Crowe leaned in low, the bristly edge of his jaw brushing against mine as he spoke. "You'll never be done with us. Where you go, I go, Beautiful. Go ahead and leave, but you're lying to yourself if you think I won't chase you all the way to Westin's doors."

We lingered for several long seconds, drowning in icy rain. The storm roared, pelting the cement in a cadence that sounded more like the executioner's drum roll than an act of nature. The longer I met Crowe's stare, the harder it beat down on us until my heart thrummed against his fingers in time with the storm.

Crowe's chest heaved against my breasts, each breath warming my rain-chilled cheeks. He sank his hand into my hair, clamping around the drenched strands and pulling down until my lips hovered under his. "Darling Thea, you will never be free of me because I've already given all of myself to you."

Maybe there was truth to what Nick had said. Maybe love was a weakness because I could feel my strength leaving me. Our lips collided in a savage clash, his mouth moving against mine like he was drawing my soul into him with each pass of his lips. I surrendered to it without an ounce of protest.

With Crowe claiming each of my breaths, it took longer than it should have to process the cold press of a knife against my stomach. As the panic set in, Crowe's body surged harder against me, stealing my ability to speak.

"Don't move," he commanded. The sound of shearing fabric mixed with the din of the storm until rain sluiced down my bare chest in glacial torrents. I shivered when the heat of his tongue met chilled skin, moving along my breasts with angry nips.

Releasing my throat, Crowe sawed at the waistband of my leggings. The blade's edge glimmered deep crimson in the tinted light of the hotel sign, Nick's blood tainting the steel and staining the pale blue cotton with each swipe.

"What are you doing?" I asked, watching as he destroyed what little was left of my borrowed clothes.

"Making sure you never forget your promises again."

The elastic snapped, and he tore the fabric down the center. My underwear followed closely after until only ribbons remained. Rain slid over my exposed skin, painfully cold compared to the raw heat pluming from Crowe's body.

There was no playful preamble and nothing nice about the way he touched me. Dropping the knife to the ground, his fingers dragged over my body before plunging in deep enough that my feet lifted off the ground.

I cried out, my head smacking into the glass door. He didn't stop, didn't slow even as his other hand began undoing the fly of his pants.

"Crowe, we're outside," I said, staring at the headlights streaming down the road. "There are people driving by."

"Then they'll know exactly what it looks like to be claimed by someone." Crowe slid his fingers free, leaving me empty and bare to the elements. Taking my wrists in hand, he wrapped my arms around his neck, saying, "Hold on, Gorgeous, because this isn't going to resemble anything close to gentle."

Crowe grabbed my ass, lifted me up, and slammed his cock into me hard enough the door rattled. The metal hinges creaked in protest of the pummeling. Linking my ankles, I held on, sinking my head into his neck so that it didn't slam against the glass with each punishing hit.

"I'm not something that can be owned," I said through gritted teeth, holding on to my rage like it was a lifeline. When would these boys understand that I belonged to no one but myself?

Crowe's teeth dragged over my skin like he could hardly restrain himself from devouring me whole. "I wasn't talking about you, Darling Thea."

My entire body trembled, comprehension driving my ecstasy higher. Nothing had ever been mine before. With the way Crowe was fucking me now, there was no doubt.

I would never be free of him.

Just as I was sure my sanity was about to explode into tiny bits of confetti, Crowe dropped me back on my feet. The cold pavement tore at the still bare soles of my feet, but I was provided with no time to cope. Giving me a hard tug and twist on my hips, Crowe pushed me forward. My palms hit the glass, barely supporting my body, before he drove back into me.

His fingers bit into the sides of my hips, pressing on the large bruise from my fall to the pavement. Pain mixed with cold, contrasting against the heady rush of blood and making my skin feel like it was on fire. My nipples pressed against the cold surface until no part of me wasn't assaulted by sensation. I kicked my head back, rolling my body with his thrusts and reveling in the brutality of Crowe's passion.

I gasped, pushing against his grip and getting nowhere. "Fuck, Crowe, point taken. You're mine,"

He grabbed my throat, arching me back and growling into my ear, "Say it again."

"You're mine," I choked out the words, emotion cutting at my throat as much as his grip did.

Turning my face so that he could kiss me, Crowe rumbled, "Glad you've finally caught on. Now come for me. I want Nick to see exactly what he's forsaking."

The storm of emotion outside was so overwhelming that I hadn't even registered there was an audience on the other side of the rain-streaked glass. Nick wore a gloriously tortured expression. Still tied to the chair, he had no option but to watch as Crowe took everything, and he got nothing. He'd chosen this. The bitter sadist in me wanted him to choke on that regret.

Thrilled, I pushed my ass into each of his thrusts, meeting him hit for hit. "Harder. Shatter me."

Crowe hummed in approval. "Whatever my girl wants."

I stared Nick down, meeting his metallic eyes with unflinching confidence. Beside him, Danny watched with nearly the same level of tormented need. Toto sat in an armchair to the side, grinning like she was watching a Sunday matinee. I wouldn't be surprised if she had popcorn somewhere.

One hand gripping mine, our fingers curled together, forming a fist against the glass. The other hand sank low to stroke against my clit. Instantly, a familiar charge built, my entire being seizing around Crowe's cock.

With the added weight of Nick and Danny's glares, causing my emotions to spin in a cyclone, I came hard. Harder than I knew a woman was capable of. My vision splintered, their faces fading in and out with each of Crowe's finishing strokes. My muscles seized with the tiny aftershocks rocketing down my spine.

Crowe turned me to face him. His forehead dropped to mine, his breaths mingling with mine in tiny puffs of air. I closed my eyes as we slowly caught our breath. His fingers drifted over the bruises along my neck, noting that an entirely new set was decorating my skin.

"Fuck, Thea." He sounded just as broken as Nick looked. "I'm sorry. I shouldn't have."

I cupped his cheek, the hurt in his eyes nearly breaking me, too. "Did you hear me telling you no?"

Crowe kissed me so damn softly it threatened to break my heart. It felt like goodbye, despite his vows and how he clung to me. "It's unacceptable. I *never* should have lost control like that." He kissed a bruise that was low against my collarbone.

Long pieces of his hair had fallen free of the elastic, obscuring his crow tattoo. I brushed them back, pressing my rain-soaked lips to the bird and the scars masked beneath the feathers. "I love every part of you, Vincent Crowe..."

He sucked in a sharp breath through his teeth.

"...and if this is what loving the darkness looks like, then, Pretty Boy, I want it all." The words tumbled from me without any thought. That didn't make them less true. I didn't know what love looked like, but no other word could describe this messy emotion. It was terrifying and consuming, and I'd felt wrong every second since I'd left him on that street—until right now.

"I'm not all darkness." Crowe tucked his face into the crook of my neck, tightening his arms like a vice around my lower back. It was unexpectedly vulnerable, reminding me of how I'd once clung to my mother after surviving a nightmare.

He continued, his lips moving against the slick skin of my shoulder, "I worked hard to wall this part of me away, but losing you fractured something. No matter how hard I tried, I couldn't stop it from leaking out and taking over. I nearly killed Nick twice. My brother. I would have in there, too, if Danny hadn't held me back. But, Thea, being with you felt like I was finally the man I was supposed to be. When you left, a piece of me left with you. I can't do that again. I'll never come back from it. I don't *want* to be that man." Straightening, he brushed the rain from my cheeks and the hair clinging to my lashes. "I only want to be the man that loves you the way you deserve."

"This is the way I deserve."

"No, you deserve better..." His hand drifted down to lightly graze the bruises. "But I'm too selfish to let you have anything else."

-5-
DANNY

Watching Crowe rail Thea against the door was the most excruciating thing I've ever had to watch. Or so I thought, until we had to watch the slow way they'd spoken to each other afterward. She touched his face with tender adoration, even after he'd fucked her so violently there were probably stress fractures in the door frame. To know she accepted him, even after showing her his truth. Not just accepted it but wanted more.

Thea was amazing.

Would she choose Crowe, like everyone else always chose him over me? He'd obviously gone all in with her, but Thea was impossible to predict. I'd found the one person in the world who understood me, the real me...then royally fucked it up by treating her like she was nothing more than a warm body—when she was so obviously more. The memory of all I'd said to her in the bank was sour in the back of my throat. I didn't know what I'd do if she chose to put Yellow Brick behind her.

I wasn't the only one conflicted by the tenderness happening amidst the deluge outside. Moments after what had looked a fuck of a lot like the word "*love*" falling from Crowe's lips, Nick broke the broomstick pinning his arms, the leg, and one arm of the chair. The ropes unraveled, hanging loosely around his blood-soaked collar. Every muscle in his body strained, filling the room with the gentle sound of his joints popping.

The bitter breeze and smell of wet asphalt followed them into the lobby. Crowe had wrapped his shirt around Thea. It wasn't any drier than her clothing, but it managed to cover most of her with the illusion of decency. Of course, it wouldn't have been necessary if Crowe hadn't cut them off her to begin with, a detail that hadn't gone unnoticed by any of us. It was hard to miss the way her tits pressed into the glass with every thrust.

Thea stumbled in with Crowe's arms protectively around her. I wasn't the least bit surprised that she was having trouble walking. Her skin had a freshly fucked glow, and tender marks were littering her body, including a second set of bruises along her throat. The unmistakable bite marks against her upper breast made heat rise along the back of my neck. Fuck. With smudged blotches of color everywhere, the girl looked like an impressionist painting.

"I've got to say. I really like your friends, Dandy. Top rate entertainment." Daffodil snatched a blanket and wrapped it around Thea while Nick and I stood like fools in the center of the lobby. I didn't know what to do with myself. So much had flipped and changed in such a short period of time. It left me with an acidic feeling of helplessness, like the entire world had shifted off-kilter.

"So what now?" my sister asked, reaching for another blanket to give to Crowe.

Thea eyed Nick's loose ropes with distrust, then eased herself into the armchair. Crowe's face twisted, watching the ginger way she lowered herself onto the cushions. He was way too rough with her. From the state she was in when we arrived, the Wolf that attacked her had already chewed her up and spat her out—and that was before being pounded into the door by a six-foot bird of prey.

"Em's Wolves will still be looking for me."

I walked to the window, peering down the road at where she'd abandoned the red sedan in the middle of the road. "You barely made it to the edge of the city, although nobody would be looking for you here," I said cautiously.

"Unless someone knows what kind of car she drove off in," Nick remarked with just as much trepidation.

"No doubt someone has checked the surveillance cameras around the bank by now. It's what I would do." Crowe slid his arms beneath Thea, settling her on his lap. It seemed tender and sweet, but I knew him better than that. He was still terrified she'd bolt for the door. We all were. "It's only a matter of time before someone notices the broken-down car out there and connects the dots."

Thea looked down at her nails. If she was going to tell the rest of us to fuck off, now would be the time. "We need to get to Westin's."

"Witcher?" Daffodil asked. "Escaping one Witcher wasn't enough for you?"

"I don't have a choice. If we want The Wizard's cooperation, killing Westin is his price. It's the only way to find out what happened to your sister."

I released the breath I was holding, relief rolling through me like a cold drink of water. Until I saw Daffodil's face.

"What do you mean find my sister?" Daffodil twisted her hair around her finger, just like when we were children. It was what she did anytime she knew we were going to be in trouble.

"I asked The Wizard to help me take down The Farm and locate your family."

"But you said sister, singular. Shouldn't we be looking for both of them? Have you already found one of the others? Was it Daisy?"

Thea's eyes flicked to me. The image of Didi's lifeless body, marks from the autopsy still penned against her flesh, lingered too fresh in my mind. "Didi is dead."

Crowe sat up, causing Thea to shift with a groan. His hand soothingly skated up and down her arm. "How do you know?"

Thea twisted to address her directly. "As a sign of good faith, The Wizard gave Danny her bill of sale and autopsy record." She rested her hand on the arm of the obviously heartbroken Daffodil. "I'm so sorry, Toto. She's been gone for a long time now."

"How long?" she choked out. "How long did she last?"

I tried to say something, but when I looked at my sister, all I saw was the terrified face she'd made the day the Wolves dragged her away and the pattern my mother's blood had made against her pale yellow dress. It made it impossible to speak, to think, to want to do anything but rage.

"Dandy, how long?"

I was drowning in guilt, and there was no surface, no way to break out from under it. How had I thought that I was anything but a coward? I was afraid of everything. I couldn't even look my sister in the eye.

"Breathe, Danny." Thea's soft hand cupped the side of my face, knocking me from my spiraling thoughts. "One moment of fear doesn't mean you deserve a lifetime of guilt."

I blinked. I hadn't seen her get up or walk over, but here she was, touching me with a tenderness I hadn't earned. I'd been so cruel in the bank, fucked her, and tossed her aside for my own rage like it cost me nothing. "How would you know what I deserve?"

The empathy in her eyes threatened to break me.

"Your past only defines you if you let it." She brushed her lips to the side of my mouth, not a kiss but something akin to it. This was almost more intimate.

I tilted my face towards hers, knowing how she'd feel in my hands and wanting to disappear into it. Thea was yanked out of my reach just as my fingers skimmed her jaw.

"Hey!" she squealed.

"Give me this," Crowe said, sitting her firmly back in his lap, one arm banded around her waist so she couldn't escape again. I'd seen this kind of display countless times when we were kids. When he set his eyes on something, he didn't give a fuck who or what had laid claim to it first. What I couldn't believe was that Thea was letting that shit stand. If it had been me doing that, her knee would have connected with my balls the second I put a hand on her.

"Two years," I said to Daffodil, trying to ignore the others. It didn't matter if Thea was choosing Crowe. "She died two years after we were taken, thanks to a soon-to-be dead man by the name of Deveaux."

"Sylvan Deveaux?"

"You know him?" I tamped down my panic and forced myself to meet the green eyes that matched my own perfectly. Had she been sold to him? Had he hunted her like he'd hunted Didi? Abused her? Worse? A thousand horrific scenarios played out in my mind.

"He used to come into the Chateau. Shibari was never his flavor. He didn't strike me as the kind of guy who liked losing control."

How was she so calm? I just told her that our sister was dead, and she spouted the murderer's name like it was nothing.

"I already regret asking this question, but Chateau?" The unknown hanging over me like a guillotine was worse than knowing the truth. I pinched the bridge of my nose against the oncoming migraine.

"Have to admit, little brother, you held out longer than I was expecting," Daffodil said, kicking her feet onto the coffee table. "Most people want to know immediately."

I hated this. I hated that the girl who would make me crowns of dandelions was talking so casually of her enslavement like it wasn't of any more concern to her than what we would be having for dinner.

"I've had two placements. First was in a home doing mostly manual labor, 'small hands in small spaces' kinds of things. That was until the owner died, and his son sent everyone back to The Farm. Since I was older the second time around, I was sent to Chateau d'Coeur. The Chateau was a renovated hotel of sorts, way out in the countryside, where people could book a cultivated experience."

"A brothel," I growled.

"Not really. Sometimes there was sex, but it was more than that," she said with a dismissive wave.

Sometimes there was sex? The idea made me see red, but she tossed it out there like being coerced into the sex trade wasn't a critical part of her life.

"Clients might stay anywhere from a day to a week, or some stayed for a considerably extended period of time. I was groomed to be the resident shibari specialist, entertaining guests who wanted to know the kind of freedom that comes with a complete loss of control."

"I bet you understand." Daffodil winked at Nick, who had started winding his former restraints around his fists like a boxer wrapping his knuckles for a fight.

"I understand that it's easier to tie someone up than to endure being tied to something."

Daffodil shucked off his comment, "Sure, baby, keep believing that. Denial almost looks as good on you as those ropes did."

"Maybe that's because you haven't tried tying yourself to the right thing," Crowe quipped, nuzzling Thea's neck and making her hum in satisfaction.

Nick looked away from them. "Or maybe one man's gift is another man's curse."

Crowe grinned. "And she's the gift that keeps giving." He whispered something into Thea's ear that made her turn bright red. His hand slid up the length of her thigh and between the folds of the blanket. Thea's lips parted, and the toes peeking from beneath the edges of the blanket curled.

"This is hell." I scrubbed at my face. "I always knew I was headed here. I just figured the devil would wait until after I died to start my torment."

Daffodil giggled like I'd just told a joke. But I wasn't joking. The entire room was making my palms itch.

"I loved the Chateau," she continued. "Ya know, once I accepted my fate."

Accepted her fate. My stomach turned. What exactly did it take to accept one's fate in a glorified brothel?

"Sometimes I'm even a bit homesick for it. There was a sense of community. We were almost family."

"But then?" Thea asked, thinking what I was thinking. If this Chateau was so great, then how did she end up back at The Farm?

"The Northern Syndicate shut it down. I don't know what happened to everyone else. I was sent separately to The Farm."

"Wait, *The Syndicate* sent you to The Farm?" I said, thoroughly confused.

Picking up my line of thinking, Crowe added, "That doesn't make sense. Why would you shut down one brothel just to return them to the very people who sold them into the skin trade to begin with?"

Daffodil shrugged. "I don't know. I was standing in line with the other girls, waiting to be loaded onto a bus, and this woman pulled me from the group."

A clanging of awareness went off in my head, like a fire alarm pulled in a crowded theater. A woman had singled out Daffodil. There was only one woman I knew cutthroat enough for a place on the Northern Syndicate, and I was willing to bet it was the same one that had hand-selected my sister. But why?

"I was dropped at The Farm. She made a point of telling the guards that I needed a decon, so I was placed apart from the rest of the captives. That was lucky, though, because otherwise, I don't think I'd have met Thea."

"What are you thinking?" Crowe asked. His fingers were combing through Thea's wet hair, the same hand I knew had just been stroking her beautiful pussy. It was distracting how at ease they looked together.

I gritted my teeth. I could only manage one emotional crisis at a time, and there wasn't any room for jealousy right now.

"I'm thinking we're stuck in the middle of someone else's long game, and I don't like it."

-6-
NICK

The broken fluorescent light over the bathroom mirror flickered. The discarded ropes and stained shirt lay in a heap of black and crimson against the dingy linoleum. I ran a thin washcloth over the dried blood coating my neck. The almost too-deep gash on my neck throbbed. It was close, the closest I'd come in a long time to kissing death.

Thea had actually cut me. Straddling my hips, she ground down on my cock, brandishing that dagger with a level of fury that made my blood rise to her siren call. If I hadn't already been sinking in deep with that girl, then this was the coffin nail sealing my fate. She wasn't scared of pain. She bared her teeth and stared her fear straight in the eyes. It was possible that I'd found the one person who wouldn't break when she crashed against the rocky edges of my soul.

I bet if I'd been the one with the knife, she would have presented her throat to me and offered up the first cut. Just the idea of it made me hard. Like that night in the construction yard, Fiore Mio blazed, never looking back at the trail of destruction behind her. Except that wasn't entirely true. This time, she was mortified by the damage she'd dealt as if my life actually mattered to her. Somehow, she still cared.

And now Thea was out there, curled in Crowe's lap. That was if he hadn't coerced her into riding his cock while they waited. I thought I knew what regret was before, but I landed on a whole other plane the second I hung up the phone with Westin. I knew there would be consequences for my actions. I just hadn't expected those consequences to be ridden hard against a pane of glass so that I was forced to witness every single blissed-out expression.

That demonstration had brought one fact into startling clarity. I wanted to be the one pressing her tits into the door and yanking back on her hair with savage finality. I wanted to claim her screams as my own. It didn't matter that she was going to destroy whatever was left of me, that she would tear apart the only family I cared about, or that she was a liability none of us could afford. I hungered for her—and I hated it.

I tore open a tiny alcohol swab from the hotel's first aid kit. The burn of the antiseptic zinged my senses. I breathed it down, letting it remind me that I wasn't the man who loved things, even her. *Especially* her. Crowe could have Thea, and when he decided to share again, Danny too. I wouldn't allow myself to fall back into that beautiful trap.

Thea was a lethal injection straight into the vein for someone like me. The scar I'd surely get from this cut was all I'd be taking from Dorothea Rosen. It wasn't like I had a choice anyway. Thanks to my deceit, she would never trust me or touch me again. It was better this way. Crowe was good to her, or at least better than I could ever be. I wasn't good for anyone.

"I'm not going." Toto's muffled yelling filtered through the closed door. Her apartment, if you could call it that, was small. The main room was barely large enough to hold the futon in it. There was a small kitchenette and an even smaller bathroom. You could hear everything in the lobby as though you were still standing at the desk. Maybe that was the point. Toto and Danny had been battling it out for the past half hour.

"I've spent my entire life looking for you. I'm not leaving you to rot in this mold farm."

"Oz damn, when did you grow up to be such a drama king?"

Tossing the scraps of suture tape and gauze into the trash, I pulled the bedroom door closed behind me. The stale air of the lobby had permeated every facet of the hotel. Toto's summation that this was only a front was probably a sound one. It didn't look like a paying guest had entered these doors in a long time.

"I have a job to do, Dandy. I can't just leave because you finally decided to show up and save the day." Toto stomped her foot like a petulant child. She was cute, in a waifish kind of way, and scrappy. Toto reminded me of one of those dogs you saw women carrying around in purses, but when you got close, they'd try to bite your ankles. She was perceptibly adaptable, too. I'd seen her shift her demeanor depending on how she thought each person wanted to be handled. It was probably how she'd survived in the feeding tank for as long as she had.

"Finally showed up?" Danny really sounded angry now. I'd heard that tone from him more times than I could count, the same one he used on Crowe when his shenanigans got out of control.

I lazily flipped through the register. There were printouts from dozens of daily records. Times of arrival and check out. If anyone decided to show up and asked for records, she'd be able to show them. It was a bit outdated, but it looked complete. From the looks of it, a fair amount of money funneled through the hotel. Whatever scam Ginger was running, it seemed to be booming. But, she would need someone here to man the desk and keep up the facade of a running hotel. It was the perfect place to stick a nobody like Toto.

I scanned the lobby for Thea. The resident temptress was nowhere to be seen, and neither was Crowe. Curling my hand into a fist, I took a long, slow breath. It didn't matter where they were or what they were doing.

"You're coming with us, and that's final."

Toto growled in frustration. "You're a stubborn ass. No wonder Thea was running away."

That was a low blow, one we all deserved, but still low. Danny took a slow step back. Toto grabbed a raincoat sitting on the back of a chair, shooting me dagger eyes in the process.

"Dick."

"What did I do?"

A grumbled slew of curses followed her across the lobby. With a middle finger flying high, she stomped out the door.

Danny bent over the counter and banged his head repeatedly on the surface. "What did I do to deserve this?"

"You really have to ask that? We're not good men, Dan. What made you think we'd ever deserve a happy ending?"

His sad eyes lifted, but he didn't bother raising his head. He looked like a man on the chopping block, waiting for the axe to fall.

"I waited my whole life to find my sisters. I finally find one of them, and she won't listen to reason. Plus, to no one's surprise, Thea picked Crowe...again. Then, the two of them fucked off out the door like they were eloping or some shit."

"Seriously?" My long-since atrophied heart galloped out of control, kick-starting with such ferocity I seriously considered that I might be having a heart attack. Flashes of the two of them settling into a picture-perfect life flickered through my mind. None of it matched either of them, but that didn't stop a nightmare of picket fences and white dresses from unfolding before me.

"No." Danny snorted. "Shit, look at your face."

"I don't make faces. Where did they go?"

He ambled into Toto's apartment. "Do you think there's any booze in this death trap of an apartment?"

"Dan, where are Crowe and Thea?" I said with more urgency. He couldn't just drop a bomb like that and ignore me.

"Fucking hell, this place is such a shit hole. I can't believe she wants to stay." Danny flung open the few cabinets in the kitchenette.

"Dan!"

"I know you broke an entire chair in rage, but that display they put on really rattled you, huh? You can take your panties out of a twist, Priscilla."

I made a disgusted sound in the back of my throat. I hated when he pulled that patronizing shit.

"They're siphoning some gas and moving the stolen car out of the middle of the road. I've got a crisp hundred-dollar bill that says he fucks her twice in the process. Ozma knows I would."

Like summoning the devil, Thea burst through the door. Her long auburn hair was slick with rain. The shirt Toto had given her was plastered to her chest, becoming transparent enough that I could make out the dusty hue of her nipples beneath the cotton.

"I should have taken that bet," I mumbled. Something was making her rampage across the lobby, and Crowe's noticeable absence meant it was probably him.

Danny poked his head out the apartment doorway. "What's the point of getting dry clothes if you're just going to soak them again? At this point, you might as well go naked." He ran his thumb over his lower lip. "I know I wouldn't mind."

"First of all, fuck you, Danny." She shifted and pointed directly at me. "Fuck you, too."

I did a double blink. How was she continuing to shock me?

"I didn't say anything."

Thea narrowed her eyes. "You don't have to. Even your effortlessly sexy hair makes me want to tell you to fuck off."

"And that's a bad thing?" I replied with a shrug.

She held up a hand, blocking me from her view and choosing instead to address Danny directly. "Police were already checking out the car."

"Shit. We need to get going."

"It's fine. Crowe said he was dealing with it."

"Did you see my sister? We have to go."

"But, Crowe said—"

"Crowe dealing with things just means we'll have to leave sooner. He isn't exactly good at subtlety. So, Thea, my sister? Where is she?"

With a relenting sigh, she gestured to the door. "Smoking on the curb."

He started moving for the exit, but as he passed Thea, she snagged his arm. "Danny, I know you want to force the issue, but you can't make her come with us. Westin isn't her fight."

"Daisy is her sister, too. You'd think that would be reason enough."

Thea put her hands on her hips and leveled a glare sharp enough to cut stone. "Or maybe she finally knows what it's like to be free and doesn't want an overbearing asshole making decisions for her."

"She has you there," I said.

"Shut up," they replied in eerie unison.

51

"You have to give her space." Thea's hand gently stroked his arm. Danny's breathing halted, ceasing every tiny bit of movement like she'd paralyzed him with a single touch. "You're not loving her by acting like another owner."

Danny's expression crumpled, shooting a look of regret and longing towards the windows.

"She's not yours to control." Thea continued, "Toto is her own person. Let her figure out who that is."

Danny turned back to Thea, taking the time to study her expression before speaking. "What about you, Firecracker?" He ran his fingers through her hair, trailing them down the side of her throat when the strands pulled free. "Do you need space?"

Slowly, they turned into each other, like they didn't realize they were caught in each other's gravity. Danny was my brother, not in blood but born of the blood we'd shed together. I loved him more than I loved myself. He'd been there during my darkest days, but that didn't mean I wasn't imagining breaking every single finger caressing her skin.

"I don't know what I need," Thea said in a barely audible whisper, like the words themselves scared her. This was the girl who laughed in the face of villains, and she was terrified by the strength of her own emotions. Maybe we had more in common than I realized.

I hated that, too.

"We *need* to get the hell out of here," I said loudly enough to dispel whatever was brewing between them. Thea and Crowe were bad enough, but something would die if I had to listen to the three of them all night again. It was torture when I didn't have a heart capable of caring; now I wouldn't be able to stay away.

"Problem, Nick?" Danny's eyes cut sideways to me, a demonic smirk on his lips that I'd seen too many times. That look warned of the days, maybe even weeks, of torture ahead of me. I'd revealed my weak point and managed to piss everyone off enough to have them apply pressure all at once.

"You're probably right. I'm sure Crowe has it handled." Danny's fingers toyed with the hem of her shirt while he nuzzled his nose into the space behind her ear. The murmur of whispers filtered over to me, promises of things he would do to her.

"I'm still angry with you," she protested, despite the way her spine arched when the back of his hand brushed her stomach.

The deep tones of his voice were muffled against the skin of her neck. "Then stop me."

The knuckles in my fists popped, the reassembled joints protesting from how hard I squeezed them. An ache radiated into my wrists, throbbing in time with the one forming in the center of my chest.

Fuck him for forcing this emotion on me.

Fuck her for creating it.

Fuck me for craving it.

I wanted her body to bend the way it was bending to him now. I wanted to take, and take, and take from her until she no longer existed on this plane. I was not a man who allowed the weakness of wanting anything. Danny fucking knew that and was flashing it in my face like a laser target from that rifle he loved so damn much. Each swipe of his hands along her hips threatened to pull the trigger and destroy me.

"I'm not some toy you can play with when it suits you, then toss back to the ground when you're done." Her words were sharp, edged to cut deep, like he deserved to bleed for her. She was definitely angry about something more than my betrayal. Thea turned abruptly, like she'd rather be anywhere but with him.

Hooking her around the waist, he hauled her back. "Who said anything about being done?" He hissed into her ear, hand splaying possessively against her stomach. "I wasn't the one who put a bolted door between us, Princess."

Slowly, her shirt lifted to reveal the bare skin just below her breasts. My heart rate picked up, mocking me with just how affected it was by this display. I couldn't look away. All I could do was stay rooted to the spot, holding my breath to keep from screaming a mantra of insults.

The subtle curve of her abdomen stopped at the line of pale pink panties peeking above the low-slung yoga pants. Her stomach was pebbled with goosebumps, interrupted along the sides by small purple bruises that were most definitely left by Crowe's fingers. A single beauty mark lingered to the right of her navel. Nonna Lucia used to say that birthmarks were a sign of being kissed by angels. It made me want to kiss it, too, if only for a taste of that heaven.

Danny's index finger dipped beneath the elastic, tracing that small strip of pink, at the same time his other hand firmly tilted her chin to look back at him.

"If you ever pull a stunt like that again—"

"You'll what, Danny? What can you do to me that hasn't already been done?"

Fearless. The harder he pushed, the more viciously she pushed back. Thea could break him. I knew she could. She'd nearly broken Crowe. In the five years since we'd left my father, I'd never seen him resemble the man he'd once been—except for when the barrel of his gun pointed at me and her body slammed against the glass. It was then I saw the darkness he pretended wasn't there anymore.

Thea struggled to pull her chin from his grasp, "If I want a hundred locked doors between us, then that's what I'll get."

His other hand pushed lower, disappearing entirely. The tang of copper coated my tongue as my teeth ground against the inside of my cheek to keep from shouting. Thea's breath hitched, and despite her rage, her eyes drifted shut the moment Danny dipped low to press a kiss to her jaw.

"Then I will spank that perfect ass so red you won't be able to walk, let alone run for a door again."

Thea cried out from whatever Danny was doing with the hand not pressing tiny white marks into her chin. I was going to implode, and I'd welcome it, knowing it'd cease this reality.

The outer door swung open, a draft sweeping across the lobby, right along with Crowe. His eyes widened as he took in the scene before him.

I readied myself for the tantrum, knowing Crowe wouldn't be in the mood to share after the scare Thea had given him. He might have been fine with it before, but now? Things were changing for all of us. Crowe's need to protect had gone into overdrive, much like Danny's need to control. The two would clash, and the collision would be catastrophic, with Thea right in the middle of the carnage.

I could see it all playing out, like watching a movie in slow motion. He walked straight to her with his arms outstretched like a kid standing before an entire pile of presents at a birthday party. His fingers flexed over and over with impatience.

"Gimme."

He tore Thea from Danny, managing to simultaneously push our brother away and dip her into an overly dramatic kiss. Thea's squeal of protest shifted into a sigh, making my teeth grind until pain bloomed behind my eyes. Before Crowe could tip her upright, Danny scooped Thea into his arms and tossed her onto the settee.

"Fuck," Thea cried, gripping the armrest above her to slow the obvious dizziness she was fighting from being spun, tossed, and kissed in a matter of seconds. "Wait...just..."

Crowe moved, either to pummel Danny or, from how he looked at Thea's arms stretched above her, join them.

"No." The sound involuntarily barked out of me. I punched the armchair, driving my fist into the lumpy cushion hard enough to tip the chair on two legs before slamming down again. All three of them stopped. Thea propped herself up on her elbow, twisting so that she could see me clearly.

"There is a time and a place for this. Neither is here." I added beneath my breath, "And preferably when I am far, *far* away."

Thea opened her mouth to argue, the curving lines of her face going hard and preparing for a fight. "You don—"

"No," I cut her off before she could start. "We need to leave."

"I handled it," Crowe said, tugging off her bunched shirt and tossing it behind him in one smooth motion.

"Hey!" Thea yelled, trying to smack his hands away. Crowe slid his grip down the length of her arms, lifting them over her head and pinning her wrists to the armrest with his hips.

"I'm still mad at you," she grumbled as he leaned over her for a sinful upside-down kiss. Thea tried to continue ranting against his mouth. I knew her well enough to know that if she really wanted to fight him off, she'd be trying a whole lot harder.

Danny moved into position at the end of the lounge, their Thea tug-of-war apparently forgotten. Grabbing the waistband of her yoga pants, Danny pulled them and her underwear free of her legs.

Tearing her mouth from Crowe's, she snapped at Danny, "I'm mad at you, too."

"You keep saying that…" He lifted one knee over his shoulder, never once breaking eye contact with her. "Except we both know the truth."

Dragging a finger through the wetness gathering between her spread thighs, Danny smiled with predatory glee. *Fuck.* Her bratty mouth might be protesting what they were doing, but that dripping cunt told an entirely different story. Even more so when her hips bucked into the touch with a soft moan that sounded a hell of a lot like yes.

"That's what I thought." Not pausing his descent, Danny ordered Crowe, "Keep her still."

"No," I said again, firmer this time. The deep tones of my voice reverberated around the room.

Nobody stopped.

I might as well have ceased existing for all they acknowledged my protests. Danny closed his mouth over her clit, one hand pressing her hips firmly into the threadbare cushion, the other teasing at her entrance. The noises she made went from grumbles to gasps, to an all-out moan when Crowe palmed her breast.

I was wrong before. This would be what killed me.

"Fuck, Danny," Thea cried out when he shoved two fingers deep into her pussy.

I was an asshole. I sold them out and deserved a healthy dose of retribution, but this was taking things further than I could handle. The red that had already been bleeding into my vision coated it entirely.

I grabbed the back of Danny's collar and hauled him off of her. He stumbled backward, tripping over an end table, sending it and him to the ground in pieces.

"What in the fuck, Nick?"

"I said, no. We need to leave. We're not doing this here. Your fucking sister is right outside. Do you really want her to see that this is how you treat women, fucking them with your friend in the middle of a lobby?"

Crowe snickered.

I turned on him. "You're not any better."

"Me?" A mix of amusement and astonishment flickered over Crowe's expression.

"Yes, you, *cazzo*.[1] Thea deserves better than being fucked in the rain where anybody driving by can watch."

Crowe stood to his full height, abandoning the curve of her waist. I still had several inches on him, but that didn't stop him from looking down his nose at me. "Don't lecture me about treating her better. She nearly died because of you." He shoved my shoulders. "One minute."

He shoved them again, this time forcing me back until I was up against the front desk. "If I had been one minute later, that Wolf fucker would have strangled her to death. Raped her and strangled her in the middle of the street." Crowe punctuated his words like they could take a chunk of me with them. "Like you have any idea what it means to treat someone right. You haven't cared for something in six years. Cat fucked you up, and now the rest of us are paying for it. *Thea* is paying for it. You're just like your fucking father, *Niccolo*."

"Fuck you, *Vincenzo*."

He wasn't wrong. What did I know? Nothing. *Niente*.[2] Not an Oz damn thing.

---

1. Yes, you, fucker.

2. Nothing.

I turned for the door. "Do what you want. I'm leaving, and I'm taking the cab. Whether or not you're in it is up to you."

"Don't turn your back on me, asshole."

The rumble of thunder echoed outside, just as Toto ran face-first into me. Rain streamed off her, the ashen color of her skin setting off every one of my alarms.

"*Wolves!*"

With that one word, chaos erupted around us.

—7—
THEA

I rolled off the couch while Crowe and Danny jumped to their feet. The bright streaming light of dozens of headlights stopped in front of the glass doors to the lobby, along with a rolling thunder that I had mistaken for the storm and realized now was the roar of engines.

Yanking my leggings back up, Crowe threw my still-wet shirt back to me. He double-checked the gun from his holster and cursed.

"Everything I have is back in the Oz damn cab."

Danny shook his head. "I emptied mine in the lobby of the bank. I have maybe one shot left."

"*Fottuti idioti.*"[1] Nick walked to a security hatch in the wall, cracking the glass with his elbow and pulling free an axe. "You couldn't have reloaded on our way here?"

"I would have a full clip, but I fired it into the cement in an attempt not to kill your ungrateful, dumb, backstabbing ass," Crowe seethed.

"You're so eloquent when you're angry," Nick chided.

Crowe pointed his gun directly at Nick, pulling the trigger with an empty click repeatedly. "Next time, I won't aim at the sidewalk."

Danny smacked the back of Crowe's head. "If you're done bickering, we need to figure out an exit plan. Because it's not going to be out the front door."

The glass at the front of the hotel crashed, and several silver canisters flew into the room. One of the tubes rolled across the worn carpet, coming to a stop when it bumped my toes.

"Fuck, Thea, get the hell out of here."

"What the hell is—" The canister popped, thick grey smoke spewing from one end.

Crowe hauled me backwards, tugging the bottom of my shirt to cover my mouth and nose. The wet fabric clung to my nostrils as I tried to inhale.

"This way." Toto rushed to the door in the corner, holding it open and coughing on the already cloudy air. "If we can get to one of the upper hotel rooms, then we can go down the fire escape to the alley."

Crowe made a face, scrunching his nose and eyeing the door wearily. "I don't like the idea of going up. It feels like we're asking to get cornered. There's no back door?"

"That's a serious safety violation," Danny grumbled at his sister, "Another reason you shouldn't stay. What if there was a fire?"

Toto scoffed, "Or a pack of wolves breaks down the front door in search of my dumb fuck brother and his so-called gang?"

"Hey," we all said in unison.

The door slammed open, and six men wearing gas masks shaped like the muzzle of a wolf stepped into the room. Behind them, dozens more men waited for their turn to take a bite. Em must have sent every one of her attack dogs after us.

"You guys have fun talking it out," I said, pushing past them, "I'm going with Toto's route."

Crowe and Toto were close behind me as we crested the first landing. I wasn't surprised that Crowe followed the second I decided to leave. Good or bad, the decision didn't matter—that man promised to follow me wherever I went, and right now, I was headed up. I tugged on the door labeled with a big number two. It was locked.

"Not that one," Toto panted, bounding up the stairs two at a time. "The only accessible floor is the fourth. The rest are locked. Well, and the roof."

"You've got to be kidding," Danny balked from below.

"Shove your criticisms straight up your unnecessarily commanding ass," she shouted back down. I had a momentary vision of what they must have been like as bickering children.

The door to the stairwell slammed open.

Nick gave me a solid push up the next flight of stairs. "Go. I'll take care of these guys and buy you some time."

I leaned over the railing, seeing the mass of black leather working their way up the spiral of stairs. "Nick, you're not the hero. Don't start acting like one now."

"You're right, Fiore Mio. I'm a villain, and you've gotta stop caring about me." He set the axe against the railing, making sure it was at the ready for when his clip ran out. "Dying to keep you alive is the only good I'll ever be for you."

"There must be fifty men down there. You can't—you're not even wearing a shirt." I wasn't speaking in full sentences; my fractured emotions pouring out in the form of words. "You're not made of metal, Nick. If a bullet hits—YOU'LL DIE!"

"I'll be fine. It's been a long time since I've had what felt like a fair fight." He aimed the gun down the stairs, popping off a shot. The crack of the gun echoed around the concrete walls, splitting apart my ears. The man dropped to the ground, the wolf mask torn and brain matter spraying the wall behind him.

Crowe urged me further up the stairs. "We don't have time for this." I could barely hear him over the ringing in my ears. "He'll be okay, but we need out of this stairwell yesterday. So, start moving that fine ass to the next floor."

"Come on, Princess, Nick will catch up," Danny added.

Following Danny, I sprinted as fast as I could, using all my willpower to keep from leaning over the railing to see what was happening to Nick. All the while, a war zone echoed in the stairwell. Making it to the fourth floor, Toto threw herself at the door. Screaming when it wouldn't open, just like all the others.

"That's it. You're not going back to Ginger," Danny shouted.

Toto swiveled, cocking back like she was about to push him down the steps. "You don't make decisions for me. You're not the King of the Forest. You can't just roar and expect me to bow at your feet."

"Figure it out later," I shouted. Fuck. Nick was sacrificing himself, and these two were still arguing. "How many more floors to the roof?"

"Six."

"Fucking hell, okay." Crowe grabbed my hand, pulling me higher. "Nick is only going to be able to hold them off for so long."

By the time we made it to the tenth floor, the possibility of throwing up was very real. My chest burned and my legs throbbed, all echoed by the steady ring in my ears.

"That's the roof access," she said, pointing to a small set of stairs. Danny shoved Toto out of the way, turning the latch and lifting the small door. With a quick scan, he waved us on, and we all spilled back into the pouring rain.

The rooftop wasn't sizable, there was only a large silver vent, an electricity panel...and no ladder.

"Son of a bitch. I knew it. I fucking knew going up was a bad idea." Crowe quickly ran from corner to corner, "There's no fire escape."

"Of course there isn't," Danny barked. "This hotel is a *death trap*."

"It's only about fifteen feet." Toto scanned the skyline. The alley separating the buildings wasn't terribly wide, but it was too far to jump.

Crowe shook his head. "Thea isn't jumping over a ten-story drop."

"That power cable runs from the box to the next building." Danny pointed at the electrical conduit. "If we climb up on the unit and use our holsters, we should be able to zipline to the next building." A metal ladder zigzagged down the side of the neighboring building. "Then we take that down to the alley. The cab is only a block over."

"Your holsters?" Toto looked from Danny to Crowe and back again.

"Yeah, I have one, and he has one. The stitching should be strong enough to hold us."

"You'd just leave us here!" Toto yelled with completely justified outrage, but I knew Crowe would never leave me, and Danny wouldn't suggest anything that put his sister in further danger.

"You'll ride on my back, and Thea can ride with Crowe."

"What about Nick?" I asked, knowing that if he made it out of that stairwell, he'd need a way off the roof, too. Unlike the others, he hadn't put his holster back on after Toto stripped him. Nick would be trapped, and that was as good as a death sentence.

Danny ignored my concerns. "He'll find a way. Nick is harder to kill than a cockroach. He always comes back."

Crowe climbed onto the metal unit, pulling on the thick black cable with his entire body weight. "Seems secure." He unbuckled the holster and looped it over the line. "Get up here, Beautiful. I've got something for you to ride."

"Now is not the time for lame innuendos." I scrambled up the side of the box. Crowe had made this look much easier than it was.

He reached down, lifting me over the edge. "You love my lame innuendos."

I did, but that wasn't the point. Looping my arms around his neck, I hopped up to secure my legs around his waist, holding on like a baby koala. "Are we really doing this?"

Crowe gave my thigh a reassuring squeeze. "Don't scream. We don't need them figuring out where we are."

Before I could answer, he took off at a run, leaping into the air. We soared at an alarming speed, spanning the alley in a blink. With a hard roll, we dropped to the rooftop just before slamming into the opposite electrical unit.

I turned in time to see the other two jumping off the hotel roof. Toto was piggyback on her brother, eyes bugging out with pure alarm. Five feet from the ledge, the wire connecting the electrical units pulled free.

Bang!

An explosion of sparks arced into the air, rocketing the hotel's metal unit into the sky at the same time Danny and Toto seemed to hover over the alley.

My heart leapt into my throat as we ran to the ledge. Danny released the holster, grabbing the wire with his bare hands just as the line snapped taut and swung against the side of the building we were on. Toto's legs came free, dangling behind them as she panicked and gripped Danny's throat.

"Daf—" Danny said with strangled gasps. "Chok— me."

Crowe leaned over the wall, reaching for Danny. There were only inches separating them. "You got a solid grip, Dan?"

Danny nodded his head, as much as Toto's arms allowed.

"Toto, I need you to climb up Danny until you can reach my hand, and then I'll pull you over." Crowe turned to me. "Brace my legs."

I gripped my arms around Crowe's legs while he leaned as far as he dared over the edge.

"Oh, my Oz, this is officially the stupidest thing I've ever done," Toto whimpered, slowly clambering up her brother. All the while, Danny groaned with each jab of her foot and pull of her hand. Toto stretched, fingertips brushing Crowe's outstretched arm.

"That's it, little sister. Hold on." Crowe closed his hand around her forearm and heaved.

"Don't call me little. I'm older than you." Toto's upper body slumped over the brick ledge.

"You're little enough." Crowe grabbed her waistband pulling her up.

We leaned over the edge, looking down at Danny. Sparks showered the ground below him. Without the added weight of Toto, the end whipped around like a snake. He braced his feet against the bricks, walking himself hand over hand up the wall before tumbling over the ledge and onto his stomach.

"Crowe." Danny rolled onto his back, heaving deep breaths and staring at the stars. "This is why you don't make the plans."

Crowe grinned. "You're alive, aren't you?"

—8—
NICK

I leveled my gun, popping off a round into the head of another Wolf, letting his body fall on top of the five men I already dropped. They were forming a nice barrier, slowing the approach of the others. The smoke filtering into the bottom of the stairwell began to dissipate. I could cut my way through the doorway and exit through the lobby.

By my count, I still had three shots remaining. A Wolf climbed over the mound. He was a big *cazzo*,[1] with shoulders the size of boulders and nearly double the size of the others. All I saw was an easier to shoot target. As he crested the pile, I clipped him in the neck, spraying the landing with a thin sheen of crimson.

Two shots left.

Taking cover behind the mountain of dead men, I pulled the mask from the fallen Wolf's face. He gasped for air, mouth opening and closing like a fish on land. A pathetic cry leaked from his lips. It was always the biggest, toughest guys who cried the most. I'd met the reaper enough times that asshole and I were practically on a first-name basis, but I'd never once wept when meeting my end.

"Shh...shh," I hushed while the man scrabbled at my arm. I'd shot him, but he clung to me like I might be able to extend his meaningless life. I pushed my boot into his chest, forcing him back to the ground. He'd chosen this life. You didn't become a Wolf by happenstance. How many times had this man looked into the pleading eyes of another? He would find as much mercy from me as the Wolves had shown their victims—*none*.

I slung the mask over my neck. The boys would take care of Thea, but the only way to ensure that they weren't followed would be to handle the problem at the root. Which meant I wasn't going up those stairs. The only way I'd be leaving was the way I came in.

A stray bullet sank into the concrete over my head. Peering through the legs of the fallen, there were five more ascending from the second flight of steps. Was there a respawn point somewhere in the other room? These guys were endless.

I fired my remaining shots into the leader, dropping him to the ground at the base of the next set of stairs. I tossed the useless gun over the railing, clipping one of the *cazzos* in the head. He stumbled into the man beside him, pitching them both unceremoniously over the railing to the floor two flights below.

With a laugh, I palmed the axe handle. That was some comical, cartoon level shit. The Wolves were supposed to be elite, but these morons were barely a threat. It was absurdly easy to take them down. Em really needed to refine her recruitment standards.

The next Wolf leapt over the pile, issuing a battle cry like the idiot was in some kind of movie. I swung the heavy blade, cleaving into the man's clavicle. His gun arm instantly went limp, dropping his weapon to the ground. It wasn't anything special, but I pocketed the piece, taking every advantage I could.

Spinning the weapon around, the axehead slammed into his temple. The heavy weight of it crushed the delicate bones of his face. The man crumpled to the ground in a twitching and groaning heap.

Diamine,[2] I loved the feel of this thing! Maybe I should start carrying an axe with me everywhere. Axes never ran out of bullets. This one had a particularly vicious point on the back end, which sank easily into the next man's throat, tearing it wide open. *Perfection.*

---

2. Damn

A shot zinged over my shoulder, grazing a thin line over the muscle. Blood dripped from the bisected flower curving over my clavicle. I'd have to redo the entire area to account for the new scar.

Before his feet touched the ground, I cut the axe clean through his neck. It required more force than I had anticipated. The head of the man flopped to the side, the heavy weight tearing free from the remaining tendons and flesh, landing with a thump at my feet.

Kicking the severed head to the side, I picked up his gun and fired it at the third man. This one was smart enough to dip behind the ductwork for cover but not smart enough to realize that the aluminum piping would never stop a bullet. *Idiota.*[3]

Firing two shots through the thin metal, I smiled with satisfaction when I heard the telltale sound of a dead body hitting the ground. That might be my second favorite sound. My favorite being one I refused to acknowledge but could never forget, thanks to Crowe's need for immediate gratification.

I quickly snatched up two reliable-looking guns and pocketed the clips from the others, taking the time to mark how many shots were left in each. Looking down at the axe, I decided to bring it with me. I liked the brutality of swinging the blade into flesh and feeling the resistance give way, seeing the bodies of my enemies cleaved in two. You just didn't get that from a gun.

Carefully, I went down the remaining flight of stairs, only having to take down two more wolves before making it back to the lobby door. The air was barely hazy, but I lifted the wolf mask over my mouth and nose anyway. I didn't need that shit impairing my aim, not when the Wolves had been nice enough to provide me with a mask of my own.

Slowly, I pulled the door open just enough to get a clear view of the room. A dozen people circled a central man.

"He's one man who doesn't matter. We want the girl." He placed his hand over his ear, listening closely to whatever was being relayed to him. The lead

---

3. Idiot

Wolf pointed at the entrance, speaking into the comms device anchored to his shoulder.

Five of the men broke away from the group, making for the shattered front glass, probably headed for the alley or the cab. *Fuck.* I didn't spend all this time defending the stairwell for our crew to get ambushed at the car.

I lined up my shot on the leader first, with two follow up shots aimed for the men on either side of him. I probably wouldn't be able to get off more than three without the rest ducking for cover. So, I needed to make the few clean hits I could get count.

The lead Wolf moved to the door, giving me the perfect clearance to take my shot. As I pulled the trigger, a loud bang shook the building, sounding like the entire roof of the building exploded. The lights of the yellowed sconces flickered out, leaving only the headlights streaming through the windows in beams. The Wolf made a lucky turn towards the sound, forcing my shot to go wide. It zipped past his ear the same moment he made eye contact with me. He dropped to the ground, taking cover and firing back before I could hit the men on his sides.

I should have been present in the moment, focused on the very real danger surrounding me. Instead, the only thing I could think of was Thea, hoping Crowe had done his job and got her out of the building before that explosion. I rolled to the corner of the lobby, using the old mahogany desk as cover. Bullets splintered the wood, and the keystand behind me. Danny wouldn't have to fret about Toto returning. By the end of this fight, there would be nothing left for her to go back to.

The first three were dumb enough to come directly at me, not bothering to take cover at all. They were easy enough to pick off. The remaining four, however, moved in a pincer formation to either side of the desk, with the lead Wolf taking point.

Lights flashed through the window, beams cutting through the still smokey air. I glanced out just in time to see a familiar streak of yellow. A moment of calm washed over me. If I didn't survive the next five minutes, at least my family was safe. I counted my breaths, listening to their boots crunching over debris.

Closing my eyes, I pictured flaming hair and soft features glowing in the flicker of firelight.

If there was no way out of this lobby, then I would shoot until my last bullet and meet my death with her name on my lips. At least this time, when I died, the sacrifice would be worth it.

I readied my muscles, counting down the seconds until I sprang at them.

Tre...

Due...

Un—

A spray of gunfire raked the room, clipping the men to the left of the desk. The remaining two shifted their attention to the door, where Danny stood with his favorite rifle. He cut an ominous silhouette, haloed by the bright headlights of the Wolves vehicles.

While they were still stunned by Danny's miraculous appearance, I stood, clicking several rounds into the two men. The leader toppled, his hand pressed to a wound that was bleeding profusely. The Wolf brand in his neck thumped irregularly as his heart tried in vain to pump.

Danny slowly approached the man. His deep voice was cold and steady, despite the way his pupils vibrated with rage. "I've imagined the day a Wolf was beneath the muzzle of my gun a hundred times. I dreamt of hearing them howl for me." He rammed the toe of his boot into the bullet wound in the man's side, making him cry out.

Danny tipped his head to the side, listening to the sound. "No, that's not quite it." He kicked the man again and grinned when the pitch rose. "Our commune was peaceful. It was sunshine and rainbows, laughter and lollipops. The people there knew only acceptance. They welcomed the Wolves into their homes and were repaid for their kindness with violence."

My brother picked up the Lead Wolf's discarded gun, checking the ammunition. "How convenient; armor-piercing rounds." He clicked the clip in place and fired a test shot into the man's shoulder. It cut through the Kevlar like butter. "My mother was murdered, my sister raped, and our lives thrown to the wind. Brutalized, my family begged for mercy. Today, you will answer for their suffering."

The room was silent, except for the man's fractured breathing. Danny pushed the muzzle into the leg of his quivering prey.

"This is for Daisy." He pulled the trigger, blowing apart the man's kneecap. The Wolf screamed, but they fell on deaf ears. Danny was lost to his memories, the trauma of his past playing across his expression.

"This is for Dahlia." The bullet tore through the man's already ravaged shoulder.

"Please. Please. I've got a family and a new baby girl," the man pleaded, sobs breaking his words into a blubbering and unintelligible mess. "Or, I have money."

Danny pressed down on the man's face, silencing him with his boot.

"You wouldn't hear my sister's cries as you tore her dress from her body and tossed her between you."

"That wasn't me," the Wolf Leader openly wept. "*Please.*"

"She was someone's daughter, too," Danny said, in that eerily calm and detached voice. "This is for Daffodil." My brother didn't flinch from the kick of the rifle or the spray of blood as his bullet cut into the man's stomach.

I moved closer, taking a position beside him.

A single, rare tear dropped from the corner of Danny's eye. "And this is for my mother."

When the bullet slammed into the man's chest, his wails mutated into a wet gurgle. There was a cyclical finality to the sound. Death was what formed the man holding the gun. It drove him, molded him, and in the end, it would be what he delivered to the very people who'd given him his first taste.

The day the Wolves raided his farm, Danny lost his family. In that void, he'd formed a new one. There was nothing we wouldn't do for him, no line we wouldn't cross when it came to saving each other. I knew better than anyone, there was more than one way to rescue a man.

I put my hand on his shoulder. Danny shook from the decades-old rage and pain, the closest I've ever seen him come to broken.

"I loved them," he whispered.

"I know."

"I couldn't save them." Danny looked up at me, silent tears falling from his red eyes.

"That was then. This is now. You don't have to be the savior alone. Not anymore." Without looking away from Danny, I took his rifle and aimed it at the man on the ground. "This one's for you, Dandelion." He deserved to be avenged every bit as much as his sisters did.

I pulled the trigger. "Let's go home, brother."

—9—
THEA

Considering her hotel was now a condemned crime scene, Ginger was remarkably understanding. She insisted on giving Toto a new position. To her twisted logic, Toto's actions proved she could be trusted in a higher position within her organization.

To no one's surprise, Danny was less understanding.

A cute pink convertible pulled up while he was in his fifth rant of the evening. The woman behind the wheel peered over the rim of her large glasses at us. "Hey Totes, ready to go, girl?"

"Shit—" Crowe leaned forward, whispering into my ear "—that's Ginger. I didn't think she'd come herself. She must really see something in Toto."

"You're not going," Danny said, firmly grabbing her arm.

"Let me go, you brute." Toto squirmed, but Danny refused to release her.

"No!" Danny boomed.

It was no wonder Nick's family called him *Leone.*[1] All the man knew how to do was roar. It was a harsh reminder of all the times I'd been on the receiving end of his ire.

Toto kicked his shin, making him scowl and tighten his grip. "Back the fuck off, Dandy. I get a choice now. I'm never letting anyone take that away from me again, and I choose Ginger."

"That's the last time you touch a woman without her permission." Ginger aimed an adorably small pistol at Danny's dick. The pink pearl inlay glittered in the parking lights of the rest area we'd chosen as a meeting site. "Now, kindly release my friend, or you'll be pissing out of a tube for the foreseeable future."

"She's *my sister*," Danny barked, pulling his own gun. "She's not going anywhere."

Ginger flipped her long, glossy ponytail over her shoulder while cocking the gun. "I think you'll find she goes where she wants when she wants, and she will never again have to answer to a man."

"Because answering to a woman is so much better?" Crowe snorted.

"For fuck's sake." I smacked Crowe in the chest, jumping down from the picnic table we were perched on. "You're not helping."

"I mean, except for you, of course. Darling, I'll do whatever you ask me to."

Ignoring Crowe, I stepped between them, centering Danny's raised gun to my chest and Ginger's to my back. "Enough."

"Fuck, Thea! You can't do that." Danny dropped his gun to his side, the entirety of his fury now focused on me. "I could have shot you."

Behind me, Ginger clicked her tongue in appreciation.

I shrugged my shoulder, "You didn't, and look—" I twisted, gesturing at what I knew would be a lowered gun. "Now you can discuss this like adults and less like children squabbling over a toy."

Ginger's smile beamed from behind bubble gum painted lips. "I love a girl who isn't afraid to woman up."

I wrapped my fingers over Danny's gun hand. "This isn't goodbye. You'll see her again."

Danny took a step back. Toto tried to turn, but as she did, he pulled her into a fierce hug. His sister was alarmed for only a second before she was hugging him back.

"I love you." Danny's words were muffled by Toto's shoulder. "I never thought I'd see you again. I would never forgive myself for letting you go if anything happened to you now."

Toto pressed a kiss to his cheek before dropping swiftly into the convertible. "I'll be seeing you soon, Little Brother."

"Wait." Danny put his hand on the door, preventing her from closing it. "Ginger, you got a pen?"

"Yeah, Sugar, I do." She quickly pulled a hot pink permanent marker from her designer handbag.

Danny took Toto's arm, writing a number down its length.

"She probably has paper, too," his sister said, squirming beneath the pen.

When he was done, he capped the marker, tossing it back to Ginger. "Daff, this is my unlisted number. Call me. *Anytime.*"

"Oka—"

"No! Call me every day," Danny corrected. "But also, whenever you need anything, call me. Anytime."

"You said that already," Toto said with a playful smile, pulling her door shut.

"Be good to her, Ginger. She's had enough hardship to last two lifetimes."

"I'm always good to my girls. It's the men of Oz who need to be reminded of where they belong." She shifted the car into reverse and gave a girlish wave of her fingers. "Toodles."

Danny watched the car pull away until the taillights of the convertible were swallowed by the night.

After what felt like eons, we finally made our way down the long wooded drive leading to the YBR compound. I sat up, bouncing a bit in my seat. The early morning fog twisted around the bases of the trees, and the moon still lingered like a ghost in the sky, giving the entire scene a bit of a spooky feel. I loved days like this. The desert sands of the wastes never saw cool, foggy mornings. My childhood was nothing but one large dustbowl.

I wasn't sure what state we'd find the compound in, given that it was under siege the last time we were here. It didn't matter. The place could be taken over by skeletons, and I wouldn't care so long as it meant I didn't need to be in the cramped interior of a car anymore. Two days of nothing but boys was making me feel like I was drowning in testosterone and simmering rage.

For most of the drive, Crowe was busy on his dashboard computer, trying to hack his way into the schematics for Westin's yacht. Danny drove for the better part of both days, leaving me stuck with Nick in the backseat for endless hours.

To no one's surprise, Nick had zero appreciation for car games. He certainly hadn't appreciated my expert portrayal of a squid when I tried to play backseat charades. I'd even turned my lunch wrapper into a respectable tentacle, which really stuck to the side of his face when I tried using it. Take that, Miss Detective Lady and your squid shifter porn! I laughed hard enough tears streamed down my cheeks. Of course, none of my levity reached Captain McSour Pants.

It was fine; I was used to entertaining myself. Who wanted to play Charades when you could play *Count The Mile Markers* instead? It was totally fine. I was still pissed and didn't want his attention anyway. Probably. By the end of the second day, I demanded a front seat. A girl could only suffer through brooding silence for so long.

Crowe sat up from where he'd been sprawled in the back seat, yawning as he stretched his long arms over his head. "Damn, it's good to be home. I can't wait to take a long shower and sleep in a bed." He reached around the seat, wrapping his arms around me. Toying with my hair, he asked, "How's about it, beautiful? Want to join me?"

Large silver walls of what looked like a warehouse came into view. Extricating myself from his tentacle-like grip, I twisted to look at him in the mirror. "In the shower or in your bed?"

"How about we start with both and go from there?" He quickly unbuckled my belt while snaking an arm around my hips and hauling me into the back seat with him.

Suppressing the giggle that wanted to fight its way out, I flailed my arms and legs, nearly kicking Danny in the head as he keyed in the code to the compound gate. A barely audible groan came from the opposite side of the backseat, the first time Nick had been anything but indifferent for the entire drive. He mostly pretended he wasn't there, even though his bulk easily took up half of the space. Nick pushed Crowe onto his side of the car. Thrown off balance, I tumbled between them, landing with my face in Nick's lap and my ass pointing straight up.

"Damn, this got interesting fast," Crowe quipped, at the same time Nick slew him a long string of what I was sure were colorful curses. I pushed myself onto my hands, not wanting to meet his cold, metal grey eyes but being snared by them all the same. After days of being ignored, that single look filled the entire cab with his overwhelming presence.

I licked my suddenly dry lips. Nick's eyes dropped to the sweeping movement of my tongue. A flush of warmth spread over my chest and cheeks, made worse when his hands skimmed over my shoulders to land at my waist. It would take nothing to raise the few inches separating us. One movement and I could be in his lap, feeling the burning press of his lips on mine. I fought the pull of the tension reeling me closer, drawing me to him like a fish on a line.

How had I gone from threatening to kill him to being thirsty for even a shred of his attention?

The high-pitched trill of Danny's phone echoed around the small cab. He immediately jumped, nearly spinning the car off the narrow drive. The sudden swerve threw me fully in Nick's lap. Rather than push me away like he had Crowe, his arms tightened protectively.

The number displayed on the screen said, *Unlisted*. Danny answered the call in a rush, "Daffodil? What's wrong? What happened?"

What responded wasn't a voice; it was music. A classical march that I recognized but couldn't name. It sounded vaguely regal, with a loud fanfare of trumpets.

"What the hell?" Danny said, adjusting the volume.

"That's the former anthem of Oz." Crowe climbed over the front seat, flipping the front dash to reveal a large screen. With a couple of quick keystrokes, a map appeared, pinging from location to location around the globe. With two clicks, Crowe nodded to Danny, "We're tracing."

The music crescendoed with a massive roll of drums. The area surrounding the car glowed with light, followed by a boom so loud I felt it in the center of my chest. My vision blurred against the flare, forcing me to tilt toward Nick to avoid being blinded. His hand cradled my head to his chest, while the other seemed to magically retrieve a gun.

The silver walls of the main building roared with flames, one side of the building torn wide open to show the charred remnants of what had once been their living room.

Over the car speakers, a modulated voice said, "*Did you think you could cross me without consequence?*"

"*Cazzo,*"[2] Nick groaned. A cadence of explosions blew apart the lawn in a long line to the trees.

Danny slammed his hands against the steering wheel. "That'd be the escape tunnel."

I twisted in Nick's grip to look out the back window just as the guard house exploded in flames. Within seconds, every structure of the compound was completely engulfed by flames. When Crowe said they'd rigged the entire place to blow, they'd really rigged it to blow. There wouldn't be a scrap of usable information in there once the flames died down.

"*I don't make idle threats.*" The mechanical voice continued, "*You have two weeks to bring me Westin's emerald, or the next building will explode with you in it.*"

There was a click, and everything in the cab went silent, except for several residual explosions as the fuel tanks in the garage continued to ignite.

"Well, there goes my plan for a shower and bed." Crowe slumped, shutting the screen with a definitive thud.

---

2. Fuck

"You're crying about *a shower*?" Danny shouted, and I was sure at any moment, we would see the steam radiating from his ears.

"Well, I mean, my fish was in the house, too."

Danny swiveled, gripping the seat corners so hard his knuckles turned white. "My *CAR* was in that garage. My vintage, mint condition, one-of-a-kind *CAR*."

I crawled out of Nick's lap. The moment I was clear, Danny slugged him in the shoulder with enough force that the back of his head knocked into the glass window. "This is your fault, you thick-headed, Italian asshole. You owe me a new car."

All three phones buzzed, lighting up with a flashing yellow alert that made my heart lurch into my throat. "What is it?"

How could this possibly get worse?

"Fucking hell." Crowe turned, slugging Nick in his other shoulder. "*Coglione di merda*,[3] Danny's right. This is all your fault. Your stupid plan just put a target on all of our backs."

"What is it?" I repeated, reaching for Nick's phone while he casually ran a hand through his hair.

The screen was split into four sections, each with a picture of our faces and a $1 million price tag.

"Westin just put a price on our heads large enough to pull every semi-decent and truly terrifying hitman into the game."

"A million dollars is a lot of money," I said, wearily handing Nick back his phone. Cold dread trickled down my spine.

"Four million, Princess," Danny corrected, looking like he could tear the steering wheel free of the dashboard. "This hit is a cool million each. This dumb fuck managed to cross The Wizard and Westin with only one bad decision. Now, we've lost our only truly secure location."

"What about the safe houses?" I asked. "We could always go to one of them."

---

3. Fucking idiot

"They don't have the kind of fortification needed to keep back the heat that we'll be under. You don't understand how many monsters live in Oz's underbelly."

Danny grimaced. "I could try calling Alice. Maybe she—"

Crowe shook his head, running a hand through his hair. "Too risky. Chances are she'd see the easy pay day, and pop us all before we'd finished our tea.

"That's what I'd do," Nick agreed. "That *cagna* is probably who The Wizard hired to set the bombs."[4]

Seeming to accentuate his point, another booming explosion rocketed a piece of metal paneling into the air.

"We need somewhere even the Winged Monkeys wouldn't be dumb enough to try infiltrating," Danny said, tapping on the shifter as he thought.

"Ohhhh," Crowe said in a long, drawn-out sigh. He turned in the seat to look at Nick.

"What?" I asked, flipping my gaze between them. The space separating them instantly felt charged, and I was stuck straight in the center of it.

"I know where we could go," Crowe continued.

"No," Nick answered definitively, the blazing light of the inferno outside making the shadows of his stark expression more pronounced.

"Think about it, Nick. It has a fuck ton of defenses. We'd be safe. Thea would be safe."

"From who?" Nick snapped, his accent thick with annoyance. "You don't run from lions to hide in a bed with vipers."

"Where?" I repeated.

"We'd be able to restock weapons, too," Crowe continued. "We can't go after Westin empty-handed. You heard The Wizard, we only have two weeks."

"At what cost, Crowe? What are you willing to pay, because you know he doesn't give kindness for free."

"Whatever the cost, we'll pay it," I said, trying to be reassuring. "It has to be better than sitting in the open, next to the world's largest bonfire."

---

4. That *bitch* is probably who The Wizard hired to set the bombs.

Danny put the car in reverse and slowly backed the car down the drive. "Crowe's right, this is the best option."

Nick looked down at me with more tenderness than I'd ever seen, from anyone. It was wrapped in concern and longing, making my heart twist. His eyes traced over each of my features, tightening the longer his gaze lingered—like it hurt to look at me. Bringing a hand to my cheek, he said, "My father doesn't require payment in money. He's far too sinister for that."

-10-
NICK

Dark clouds rolled over the sky. Heat lightning flickered, making them glow ominously as we approached the Villa. The last time I saw these poppy fields was through half-swollen eyes, more than five years ago—the day I told my father we were out. I'd forsaken my birthright, casting aside all claims to the Morphea empire, and never looked back once.

The only reason he'd allowed Crowe, Danny, and me to walk away that day was because *I'd* paid the price for *his* betrayals. In my father's eyes, giving me my freedom evened the scales. Which meant any aid he granted us would come at a price. The sinking feeling growing in my gut as I watched the lightning spark across the sky told me I couldn't afford it.

"Ooo. The flowers are beautiful," Thea crooned, smooshing her face against the glass, looking at the rows and rows of rainbow-colored poppies that stretched far into the horizon. "Is that the house up there on the hill? It's huge."

I didn't answer her, unable to look at the orange and terracotta buildings nestled at the top of the hill. I hated everything this place stood for. More than that, I hated that it looked so much like my childhood home in Italy. My father twisted every good memory I'd ever had. Even flowers killed violently here.

"The grounds around the Villa are some of the most beautiful in Oz," Crowe said, pulling the hair from her face. In the side mirror, I could clearly see each of her awestruck expressions. I hated that I couldn't look away, almost as much as I hated that anything about this place could make her smile like that.

Thea's hand reached between the seats, smacking my shoulder. "You didn't tell me you grew up somewhere so magical. Look how pretty these flowers are."

"Those flowers almost killed you and Danny," I replied flatly, trying not to think too hard about the panic of that night in the pharmacy. How could she not see that this entire place was danger disguised as beauty? We never should have come here. My father would take one look at her and know exactly what she meant to me. He's been waiting my whole life for this kind of leverage over me. "Thea, you have to mask your reactions while you're here. You can't trust anyone, not even the maids. In the Villa, even the trees are listening."

She rolled her eyes, scoffing under her breath.

"He's not wrong, Beautiful." Crowe wrapped an arm around Thea, tucking her into his side. "Salvatore will seem friendly, but sharks always look like they're smiling before they feast. You have to be smart."

"I grew up *in* the shark tank, Crowe. I know how to handle these people."

He leaned back to look at her clearly. "Darling Thea, I've seen you do some pretty reckless shit with practically no provocation."

"I do not."

Danny barked out a laugh. "You kneed me in the balls while I had an assault rifle in my hands."

"Those were some good times." She smiled effortlessly, seeming to light up the entire cab. I had to use all of my restraint not to smile with her. "I'll give you a sometimes. *Sometimes,* I can be impulsive, but you don't need to worry. I know when to keep my mouth shut and my head down."

I swung quickly, poking Crowe in the shoulder. "And you can't be all over Thea like she rolled in catnip. My father can't know what she means to the two of you."

"Three of us...," Crowe said beneath a terribly faked cough.

I was going to hit him. I would have, too, if staring at the barrel of his gun wasn't still burned into my memory.

"He'll chop her up and dangle her from a stick piece by piece if he thinks it will get the two—"

"Three."

I tightened my gaze on him. "— of you to dance."

Crowe gave a carefree sigh. "It's fine, *Niccolo*. Remember, I grew up here, too."

"Yeah, well, the last time you were here, you were The Scarecrowe." Crowe physically recoiled, finally looking up at the house with appropriate concern. Good. Maybe now he'll start thinking with his brain instead of his dick. "You've changed, *Vincenzo*." I glanced at Thea, before turning back in my seat. "*Siamo cambiati tutti.*"[1]

Danny parked the car in front of a large brick building flanked by green bushes and tall trees that swayed in the breeze. It was warmer here than when we left the YBR headquarters, but this place would always feel cold to me.

Ascending the cobblestone walk, we were greeted by my cousin, Marcello. When I left, he'd been all too happy to take my place at my father's side, proudly ascending to second in line like it had been something he'd earned.

"*Ciao, cugino!*"[2] Pain spiked in the back of my jaw as I ground my teeth. He waved us closer, with a sleazy painted-on smile. I fucking hated this place. He slapped my back in a weak hug, one that I didn't reciprocate. "*Chi non more es rivede.*"[3]

Crowe and Thea moved closer to me. Like a blood-hound, Marcello instantly ignored me and moved straight for her. For the first time since I'd met her, she looked small. Her posture shrank, making her appear innocent and unassuming. Nothing like the vibrant flower I knew she was. She was right. She knew exactly how to play this game.

"What do we have here? *Ma che bel bocconcino.*"[4] Taking her face between his hands, he pressed a kiss to each of her cheeks. She barely reacted, only giving a tight, conciliatory smile and dropping her gaze demurely. His eyes lingered over her body, making my muscles tighten. Crowe and Danny both pushed in

---

1. "We all have."

2. Hello, Cousin!

3. "Who doesn't die, sees each other again."

4. What a nice little treat.

closer, ready to spring the moment Marcello's lingering hands got too fond. He sucked in a long breath through his teeth. "You ever decide you want a taste of real power, you call me."

"You've hardly got enough there for her to taste," Crowe said, pushing his way forward and forcing my cousin's attention away from Thea. He gave a lazy smile, knocking his head back with a laugh. "Am I right, Mello?"

Marcello's shock at the insult instantly faded. "Fuck me, Vincenzo, you still following Nicco around?"

Crowe shrugged a shoulder. "I don't know why you're surprised. You're still *here*, aren't you? You should consider a change of scenery. It might knock loose a bit of that douche in you."

Thea tilted towards me, whispering under her breath, "And you were worried about me?"

I leaned low, so only she could hear me. "Nah, this is typical. Talking shit at each other is how they bond."

Marcello gave a deep laugh, "Fuck, I missed you. I didn't miss that *stronzo*,[5] but it's always fun when you're around. Maybe we crack a few heads before you go, for old times."

"Sorry man, The Scarecrowe is retired."

Marcello shook his head. "Now that's a fucking waste. There are two kinds of killers, murderers and artists. You, *fratello*,[6] could kill a man, and they'd hang it in the E.C. Museum of Fine Art. Never met anyone who could loosen tongues the way you could."

Thea swallowed hard, audibly gulping loud enough that Marcello smiled at her. Was she appalled that she'd let The Scarecrowe fuck her in the rain, or did she just have the good sense to know that she should be?

Danny cleared his throat, rolling his shoulders back to make his form as broad as possible. "Is Sal around? We need to speak with him."

5. asshole

6. brother

"*Ehilà, Leone, come va?*"[7] Marcello nodded his chin in greeting to Danny but didn't wait for an answer before gesturing for us to enter the building. It's not like he actually cared how any of us had fared these past five years. If it wasn't for the fact my father would disinherit him, Marcello would already be plotting to kill the four of us. "He's expecting you. Quite the surprise when the guards at the gate said you were driving up. In a Yellow Brick cab, no less. How the mighty have fallen." Marcello sneered in disgust.

His sight always was as short as his dick.

---

7. Hey, Lion, how's it going?

—11—
THEA

"Let me get this straight." Nick's father scooped a spoonful of tiramisu from a glass cup, his giant hands dwarfing the dessert spoon. He shoved it in his mouth, groaning at the deliciousness before pointing at Nick with it. "You expect me to house you and your crew when all of Ozmandria is looking for you. Marcello showed me the order Westin took out on your crew." He whistled. "A million each. I don't know if I should be proud of my boys or furious."

Nick inherited his grey eyes from his father. They were just as unsettling, but where Nick's were always veiled and impossible to read, his father's seemed unburdened. That in itself told me everything I needed to know about the man. While his face crinkled with joy, I knew that only the truly depraved could eat and laugh like kings while their empire destroyed the lives of thousands.

"Definitely proud, *Zio,*"[1] Crowe interjected. "YBR has done well these past five years. Westin just has a stick up her tight ass about Eastin's unfortunate demise. A deal went sideways, and as always, the self-righteous cunt overreacted."

Sal scoffed, "I never understood what you saw in her. Tits probably, you were barely a man then."

I blinked at Crowe. *What the hell did that mean?* He flashed his attention on me long enough to smirk before giving it back to Nick's father.

Salvatore shifted in his seat, waving a maid to clear the dishes. "Bring the caffé."

I leaned into Nick, saying softly, "More food?"

"Ah, *Carina*."[2] Like hearing the rattle of a snake, the way Sal said *Carina* made my spine straighten. "If you were in a hurry, you could have said something? You have time to fuck my son and his boys, but you don't have time to share a caffè with his father?" The words were harsh, but he was still smiling effortlessly as if we were all sharing a sordid joke.

To my left, Nick protectively leaned so that his body was partially blocking me from view. At the same time, Danny put his hand on my thigh, and beneath the table, Crowe's foot tapped mine. All three men doing their best to remind me that I shouldn't impulsively react to the insult. It was sweet how much they cared, but ultimately unnecessary. These sorts of comments never fazed me. Men like him only ever saw women as tools and never as the craftsmen. Which was their biggest mistake; the kind of thinking that led to entire towers crumbling if they weren't careful.

Nick opened his mouth to say something in my defense, but I cut him off before he could. "Sorry, Mr. Chopper. I'm not used to such extravagance, and the meal was already so plentiful. I'm honored to be given a place at your table." When I was done, I lowered my eyes and folded my hands in my lap, just like the good little girl Em always wished I was.

"I like this one. She knows how to respect her elders." Salvatore sat back and steepled his fingers in contemplation. The maid returned with a tray of espresso cups and cream. "You're Emily Rosen's niece?"

Danny's thumb slowly swiped back and forth against my thigh. I kept my eyes on it and replied, "Yes, sir."

"Her heir?" A cold chill of warning trickled down my spine. Whatever lay at the end of this line of questioning didn't end well.

"Yes, sir," I mumbled, trying my best to shrink into a meek girl whom Sal would see as nothing of value—even if it was already too late for that.

---

2. Sweetheart

Nick's father grunted in affirmation, "The southern wing is vacant at the moment. It's yours. I think it will be nice to have my son...*back*." The word lingered in the room like a bad smell.

Nick stiffened, his overwhelming presence rallying itself for war. "Vacant? What happened to the Rossis? The southern wing was always theirs."

"There was a disagreement." His father took a slow sip of espresso. "Do you want the wing or not?"

A disagreement, like they disagreed with the bullet that passed through their head kind of disagreement?

"We're not staying long. Just until we can deal with Westin." Danny was trying to take the heat away from Nick, diffusing the tension before it could explode, but it wasn't working.

"We'll see. I have a job or two you can help with while you're here." Nick's father turned his sinister smile on me, reminding everyone that I was the bargaining chip on the table. "Do you like my home, *Bellezza*?"[3]

I shifted uncomfortably. His gaze made me feel like I was covered in oil, suffocating slowly beneath its weight. "It's charming."

"A beautiful woman deserves a beautiful home. Don't you agree, Niccolo?" It was more of a statement than a question, the implication clear. He waved around the room. "Did you know that I had this villa imported brick by brick from Italy? It was once a thirteenth-century monastery, consecrated by Pope Innocent IV."

My jaw dropped, imagining what it must have taken to bring over each of the heavy stones surrounding us. Some were as large as whiskey barrels, and the massive wooden beams spanned the entire room.

"Thea isn't staying in Oz long term. We'll only be here for a short time." Nick pushed up from the table. If Sal was shocked by Nick's flippant tone, then he didn't show it. "It's been a long day. I think we'll be turning in for the night.

---

3. Lovely

A domani, papà."[4] He tugged on my arm, forcing me to stand. "Come on, I'll show you the way."

"Stay, Niccolo. Thea, have you ever had limoncello? We make it here. It's the most delicious liqueur you'll ever taste. Sour, yet sweet. I think you'd know something about that."

I looked between Nick and his father. Nick had already pulled open the heavy mahogany door.

Crowe cleared his throat. "*Zio*, thank you for the meal. Maybe tomorrow we can sip some limoncello while we watch the sun set over the hills. You can tell me of all that we've missed." Crowe smoothly, pushed his and Nick's chair in. "Thea, there's nothing like the sunsets in the valley. You absolutely must see it."

Crowe pressed his palm to my lower back, ushering me towards the door.

"That sounds lovely. I look forward to it," I replied, forcing a brightness into my tone that was impossible, given how heavy the room felt.

"Niccolo...," his father drawled, not the least bit concerned by the boys' display of independence.

Nick held the door for me, his voice soft, "Go on. Crowe will show you where to go." He gently nudged me into the hall.

"But—"

"I'll be right behind you." Nick looked past me to his father. The cold indifference forced something in my chest to crack. I didn't know what Salvatore would ask from his son, but I knew I wouldn't like it.

The door closed with an ominous thud. I rested the flat of my palm on the wood, debating on following him. Crowe wrapped his hand around mine, guiding us away from the dining room before I fully processed that my feet were moving. I couldn't shake the feeling that a piece of me went back in that room with Nick.

"What now?" I asked as we wound our way through the halls and down a glass-lined corridor.

---

4. Until tomorrow, father.

Danny answered, "Sal is laying out his asking price. We need safety, guns, and information. None of that is free."

"Especially here," Crowe added. "He'll take a piece of each of us before we can go."

Danny nodded, "We expected this."

Crowe opened a set of French doors. "This way, it's faster." At the center of the home was a massive courtyard, open to the sky, with greenery and benches surrounding a fountain in the center.

"This place is massive." I looked up at the clear night sky. "Who builds a house with a yard in the middle of it?"

"Salvatore likes flashy shows of money, thinks it makes him look powerful," Danny said quietly.

"Gee, I've never seen that before." I rolled my eyes, running my hands through the spray of the fountain to flick water at him. "What does it mean to take a piece of us?"

Crowe opened the opposite door, looking both ways down the hall, then waved us on. "He'll probably ask us to steal something—"

Danny interjected, "Or kill someone."

"—Or both." Crowe finished. Seeing my apprehension, he abandoned the door, returning to my side. "It'll be okay, Thea."

"What about me?" I took a step backwards, nearly falling into the fountain. "He can't expect that I'm going to kill someone."

"Why not? The Wizard certainly had no problem asking you to kill Westin," Danny replied cooly.

That was true.

"More likely," Crowe said, pushing my hair behind my ear and grimacing. "He'll expect you to honey trap someone and for one of us to do the rest."

"Honey trap?"

We were interrupted by shouting, muffled by the glass doors surrounding the courtyard. Nick burst through them. Before I could react, his large hand clamped around my arm dragging me to the opposite door, while still cursing in Italian.

"Slow down." Crowe barred the exit, forcing him to come to a stop. "You know I can't understand you when you speak this fast. What about Sal and a turtle?"

He glared at Crowe like this was all his fault. "Not turtle, *stronzo, tortura* —Torture."[5]

"Fuck." Crowe took a step back, shaking his head. "Who?"

"Tom Aldenari's wife and kids. He wants to send an old-fashioned message, something to remind the other families of their place under his thumb."

"I don't do that anymore," Crowe said quietly, that same shadow I'd seen in the hotel passing through his expression.

"And Thea?" Danny asked.

"She's staying behind—*as collateral.*"

"Fuck that," Crowe said, looking like he was about to charge back into the dining room himself.

"I second that," I said. "Torture turtles aside, I go where you go."

Nick continued, pushing open the door and dragging me down the hall. "According to him, we do this, she stays safe, and we get whatever we need."

"And?" Crowe asked, letting the glass slam closed behind him. "There's always an "*and*" where your father is concerned."

"And..." Nick's grip on my arm tightened. I knew in my gut there was more he wasn't saying in that one word. "I have to resume my position, at his side, whenever he needs me."

"No." Crowe's steps stopped, and I looked over my shoulder. He was furious, clenching and unclenching his fist like he wanted to drive it through the wall.

"I fucking told you this would happen," Nick snapped, unconsciously drawing me to him and wrapping his arm around my waist. "We all knew he'd ask for it. My father never wanted to let us leave. He only conceded before because I died a couple of times to pay off his debts."

---

5. Not turtle, asshole, torture.

"How does one die *a couple* of times?" I asked, pushing against his side to put space between us.

Crowe vehemently shook his head.

Nick stopped, spinning in place to face them both. The muscles along the sides of his neck strained as he tried to restrain his rage. "We don't have a choice, Vin. The chance to turn back was before we made our way down *quella cazzo di strada*."[6] With a roar he swung at the wall, hesitating only a breath from smashing his fist into the stone. He stared at the straining tendons, the lines of his tattoos flexing as he slowly opened his hand. The inked *"never"* shifted along his fingers like an omen. "By the time he's done, all four of us will be so deep in my father's bullshit, the sun will never reach us again."

Crowe faked a smile. "I love how poetic you get when you're pissed."

"Fuck you, how's that for poetry? I fucking hate this place." Nick yanked open a door, leaning in to be sure the room was clear. "Thea is staying with me tonight. The two of you take the room across the hall."

"What?" He had to be out of his damn mind. There was no way I was sleeping with his backstabbing ass, even if this whole raging bull thing was undeniably sexy. "There are literally a dozen bedrooms in this hall!"

"Thea can stay with me," Crowe suggested, eyes dancing between my outrage and Nick's fury.

"No. When I returned, Marcello was bumped from his position as second. He'll be ruthless when he hears of my father's new edict." He pulled me closer, leaning low so that he consumed all of the air between us. "Nobody sleeps alone, and the only place you're sleeping is with me."

Forcing a breath down, I glowered, "Do I get a say in this?"

"No."

---

6. The chance to turn back was before we made our way down that fucking road.

-12-
THEA

Nick pushed me into the room, my heels sliding along the tiled floor. The door clicked shut behind us, leaving only moonlight illuminating the room. It streamed through the large windows, seeming to be swallowed by the shadows in the corners.

The room was surprisingly bare, considering how lush the rest of the villa was. A large bed, two tables, a sitting chair, and a wardrobe. That was it. One bed. No couch, just one very large, very comfortable-looking bed with a crushed velvet comforter that made you want to sink into it.

Fucked, I was so fucked.

"I'm not sleeping with you," I said matter-of-factly.

Nick unbuckled his holster and hung it from the bedpost. "You might want to rethink that. The tiles are imported from Italy. They make the floors extra hard and cold over there."

"Is that supposed to be a joke?"

Nick shrugged, the slightest lift to the corner of his mouth giving him away. With one hand, he pulled his shirt free, and fuck me if the low light didn't make each inch of tatted muscle look that much more defined. The detailed lines of the design twined together, a mix of thorned vines and chains locking shut a broken and empty ribcage. It was masterfully poetic, the rise and fall of his breaths making his abs flex and the flowers blooming along the edges seem to tremble. A dark dusting of hair disappeared beneath his waistband, making me all too aware of the bulge pressing into his jeans...and Nick's hands deftly undoing the buckle of his belt.

"*You* could sleep on the floor," I said, forcing my eyes up. I didn't need a devil on my shoulder, pointing out that I'd been thirsty for him ever since he leaned over that balcony looking like the angel of death. Who needed a devil on their shoulder when one was right in front of them, eyes cataloging every single reaction? *Fuck.*

"Not going to happen." With one hand, the leather slithered through the belt loops of his pants, coming free with a snap. The sound made every one of my muscles tighten. It was so close to the whisper of Eastin's whip, and yet my racing heart didn't have me running for the door; if anything, I was fighting the impulse to move closer.

"Fuck this." I'd be damned if I was going to let this betraying, albeit sinfully gorgeous, asshole force me into bed with him. He'd been noble with the Wolves, and I was relieved when I saw him and Danny emerge from the hotel. That didn't mean I'd forgiven him, and it certainly didn't mean that I was going to spend the night cuddling. "I'm going over to Crowe's. You and Danny can get cozy together instead."

"Thea, you'll be safer with me." As I turned the doorknob, Nick's large hand wrapped around my wrist, enveloping it completely. "Danny and Crowe understand that, but you don't know what it's like here."

"Explain it to me then because from where I'm standing, it looks a lot like I just lost my ability to choose—*again*. You seem to do that a lot." I tugged, and Nick released me without hesitation. I'd been prepared for a fight, but his expression softened. For the first time, he looked vulnerable.

"My father knows."

"Knows what? That your backstabbing got us into this mess."

"That I would tear apart Oz for you, Fiore Mio..." He stepped closer, slowly smoothing his hands up my arms, leaving goosebumps in their wake. "And shred my humanity to ensure you kept yours."

"Okay. Sure," I huffed. "You barely looked at me all night. Fuck, Nick, you've barely looked at me in days. I feel *really* cherished."

"My entire life, my father groomed me to take over. I fought him every step of the way. Before, he didn't have the means to force my hand."

I huffed, pushing my tongue into my cheek and looking anywhere but at him. "What about Danny and Crowe? They seem like prime emotional collateral."

"It's not the same. In my father's eyes, they have a value of their own. He's invested too much to sacrifice them in the name of leverage, but with you..." He looked at the fingers wrapped around my arms, and the NEVER AGAIN inked there. "I don't trust anyone here. *Everyone* has their own agenda. At least if they think *you're mine* they won't dare touch you." When his eyes lifted, the cold grey had a kind of fear in them I hadn't seen before. "Not until he orders it."

I swallowed around the lump in my throat. It was hard to balance everything he'd just said with the claims he'd made in the hotel. His words still stung, like salt buried deep in a wound. Nick was the only man who could make loving someone sound like an insult. Feeling the strength in his hands, standing amidst his gravity, beneath the heavy weight of his gaze, it was overwhelming. I couldn't keep up with the snap between desire and loathing.

"Fine." I pushed past him, my hands sliding over the olive-toned skin of his chest as I did. I refused to acknowledge how they lingered over the empty ribcage longer than they should. "But put your shirt back on. It's too hard to think with all those muscles flying around."

"I don't sleep clothed."

Oh, fucking holy Ozma above. With a slow revolution, I turned back to him. "Come again?"

"Nudity isn't the kind of thing that bothers me. It can be freeing. You should try it."

"I should *try* it?" I looked at the exposed rafters in the ceiling, counting and breathing out slowly as I tried to think of anything but sleeping naked beside an Italian god.

"I barely just agreed to this—" Waving at the decadent wood and fabric of the room, I had to fight back a hysterical bit of laughter. How had this become my reality? "—and now you want me sleeping naked beside you?" Saying it out loud didn't help. Hurt feelings aside, the man was fine and the idea was more than tempting.

For the first time, Nick smiled at me, really smiled. He was beautiful, like something that should have been etched in marble or cast in bronze with tiny little cupids shooting arrows.

"Do you see any other options?" He popped the button of his pants. "Unless, of course, you *want* to stay in filthy, three-day-old clothing that smells faintly of gunpowder."

Before my treacherous eyes could sucker me into watching him strip more than he already had, I moved to the wardrobe. There had to be something, a robe or the forgotten collection of whomever Salvatore had disposed of after their disagreement. Anything.

Empty hangers swung along the rod, just as the definite sound of his pants slapped against the tile floor. My hands gripped the doors, biting into the wood. I could almost feel the glide of Nick's body notching against mine, my curves pressing into his harsh angles of muscle and bone.

Shit, Thea. Get it together.

"I'm going to wash up. Do not leave this room. Thea, *guardami*. Look at me."[1] There were several heartbeats where I was certain I didn't know how to breathe. "Thea," he repeated with a harsher command to his voice.

Slowly, I turned. My eyes stayed trained on the tiling. It was beautiful tile, a soft cream color with a tessellating blue pattern that didn't at all make me think of what it would be like to kneel on it.

"Thea." The stern timbre of his voice made my eyes snap up to his. *Fucking, traitorous eyes*. "Don't leave this room. Don't open the door. Not for the maid or for Crowe looking for a quick midnight fuck. Do you understand?"

Quick midnight fucks. There was nothing quick about the scene playing out in my mind, especially now that he'd mentioned Crowe. The universe was seriously testing my willpower right now.

---

1. Look at me.

Nodding, I bit down on my lower lip, and my eyes slipped. I couldn't fucking help it.

It was only for a second, and yep, this man deserved to be cast in bronze. Nick had a sculpted physique straight out of the pages of a history book, rolling abdominal muscles, tattoos adorning every inch of his body, and there was just enough light that the gleam of metal piercings ensnared my vision.

I licked my lips. What had begun as an innocent slip of my eyes turned into outright staring. I was most definitely gawking at what might be the most beautiful cock I'd ever seen, fucking perfection in flesh, ink, and metal.

Vines of tattooed nightshade curved over his pubic bone, the purple flowers snaking artfully down the length of his shaft. Several bars studded the underside of his cock. The second to last bar was thicker than the others, with a bigger ball framing either side of the crown, and a matching Prince Albert topping the ladder. *Fuck me.* No, really, fuck me.

His hand entered my field of vision, snapping. "Thea."

I blinked, my palm slapping over my face in mortification.

"Sorry. I…" I didn't even know how to finish that sentence. Even shut, the vision of his dick was burned in the back of my eyelids. I wasn't even trying to think about it, and already all I was imagining was how those bars would feel sliding along—

"Get into the bed. It's been a long day. I'll be back in a minute. Stay here."

"Right. Wait in bed. Don't leave room. Got it." Keeping my eyes closed, I gave a mock salute. I'd just be over here, waiting in bed for this demon-born adonis to return. *Fucking naked.*

"Good girl."

Kill. Me. Now.

My throat buzzed with static. Even without opening my eyes, I knew he stood right in front of me. The tiny hairs along the top of my spine lifted in anticipation of the touch that hovered over them. I leaned into it, ready for him to grab my neck and pull my lips to his. The ache for it pulsed through me like a second heartbeat. I couldn't breathe beneath the tension coiling low in my stomach.

"*Sei così bella.*"[2] His sinful voice drifted over my skin, lips brushing the shell of my ear.

Nick lingered for several long seconds before he retreated with one measured pace after another. It was only after I heard the door of the ensuite bathroom click shut that I dared open my eyes again.

I let out the breath I was holding in a long exhale.

What the hell was wrong with me? Three days ago, I was wrath of the gods, knife to the throat angry. So, why was I certain if he so much as breathed in my direction, I would drop to my knees? All it would take was Nick brushing against me in that bed, and it would be over. My willpower would crumble, and the rest of the night would be spent testing the construction quality of that bed frame. It looked old...sturdy.

Hate fucking was a thing, right?

Maybe it would be good for us to knock out an orgasm or two, or ten.

---

2. You look so beautiful like this.

-13-
NICK

I'd punished myself before, but this had just taken things to an entirely new level. Water crashed over my head in an icy torrent. The way she'd looked at me, biting her lip so that blood rushed to the surface, turning them the same rosy hue of her nipples.

Fuck.

My hand gripped my cock at the base, giving it a long slow tug and imagining what it would feel like to push the head past those lips. Fucking hell, I was an idiot. How had I gone from assuring she'd be out of my life for good to commanding her into my bed...naked?

I knew how. It was my father's smug grin when he told me just how many ways he could defile a woman before killing her or which of those ways would still allow her to produce an heir if he decided to be merciful. Of course, forcing me to assume the role I'd been groomed for would also require I create spawn of my own to inherit this debauched empire.

That had been his price. In order to give us what we needed to take out Westin, I had to reclaim my place and ensure his legacy lives on in a whole pack of Chopper heirs. What would he do when he discovered Thea was incapable of having children? It was enough to shake me.

Unlike Orin's threats in the construction yard, I'd seen my father dismantle more than one body. Imagining Thea as one of the ghostly women walking from his room had fractured something in me. Like an icepick straight to the heart, it cleaved me open. Not only would he make good on his promise, I knew that when he did, I would be forced to watch. The irony was, this was exactly why I tried to amputate her from our lives in the first place.

Fate really did have a fucking twisted sense of humor.

I killed the water. Standing here, stroking my cock, was only prolonging my torture, and it wasn't even remotely gratifying. I should have let her stay with Crowe. He'd die before letting anything happen to her. No, my father had shaken me so completely that the idea of Thea being anywhere but in sight made my palms itch...and what a sight she would be.

Unlike last time, I wouldn't be watching her through glass. She would be right there, waiting for me. Alone. Mine.

I was so fucked.

Wrapping a towel around my waist, I stepped out of the bathroom, hissing when I stepped barefoot onto the bedroom tile. I hadn't been kidding when I said Italian tile was cold, but blood cleanup was so much more time-consuming with area carpets. I'd call for a change of clothes to be brought, maybe a pair of slippers. The laundress would have something suitable. The sleeping naked thing had mostly been teasing to see what she'd do. Mostly.

I should have known better than to present Thea with a challenge.

The warm light of the bathroom mixed with the silvery moonlight streaming through the window, highlighting every dip and curve of the bedding from where she lay on her side. The velvet comforter was under her chin, but from my view, the fabric sagged enough to expose the long line of her spine. Red stripes crisscrossed the surface from where her scars were barely healed.

Some people might have been repulsed by the marred skin, but I only saw the way she'd fought crying that night when I patched her up. There was strength within those marks, and I wanted to trace my tongue along each and every one of them. I bet they'd be terribly sensitive. I could almost hear her broken breaths now. The fact that she could steadily stare down a gun, but trembled when I touched her, was a stroke to the dick like no other.

Thea rolled towards me, tucking the sheet around her like it could somehow protect her from my gaze. "I believe it's customary to actually lay in the bed, not merely stand beside it like you've been possessed."

I ran my hand along the towel. Crowe would have something charming to say, but all I could think was that only a sheet and a towel separated me from this beautiful flower. If I got in the bed, then it would be my willpower alone keeping us apart, and that was feeling very thin at the moment.

"Fine, stand there," she snapped with annoyance. "Ignore me. *Again.*"

Fuck, I still hadn't said anything and was looming over her like a *stronzetto.*[1] I dropped the towel because if she'd taken my challenge, I couldn't very well back out of it now. Watching her eyes as they slowly traced over me, I felt every single inch they descended. Thea licked her lips—beautiful, full, rosy lips glistening in the moonlight.

"Enjoying the view, Fiore Mio?" My voice was uncharacteristically low, the accent thick as it rolled over each syllable.

Her eyes snapped up, like my words had tugged on an invisible leash. "No."

"You're a beautiful liar."

As I slid into the bed, I couldn't help but notice the way the mattress and blanket were already warm. It was weirdly satisfying, making my heart taunt me with every thump. Seconds ticked by where all I could do was look at her, the way her hair curled along her temple. In the low light, her hazel eyes looked black and rimmed with silver. As they gazed steadily back at me, I couldn't help but think they were the most stunning thing I'd ever seen.

"I hate you," she whispered, too low to feel genuine.

"I hate you, too, Fiore Mio." I brushed my thumb over her cheekbone. The tightness at the corners of her eyes and their glassy sheen made her look like she might cry.

"Good," she whispered. "So long as that's clear."

Like *anything* about this was clear. My emotions were top-tier confusing. She had invaded my blood, coursing like poison through my veins with each pump of her heart. I didn't know how to free myself from it. I hated that I didn't want to. From the twist of her cherubic features, she felt exactly the same way.

---

1. little shit.

111

Thea tucked a hand beneath her cheek, looking so damn innocent that an ache pushed at the center of my chest. "What does that mean? Fiore Mio? Sometimes you say it with such...sadness."

Images of Thea in Gorba's construction yard flickered through my mind: the raging fire lighting up the confidence in her features, her dark hair haloing her face in a red blaze.

"Did you know that in Italy, the poppies are red?"

Her head tilted in confusion, pressing into the pillow and exposing the smooth contours of her neck. The softest shadow of her fading bruises still lingered, drawing my eyes like an invitation. I wanted to know what her pulse felt like against my lips. Would it be raging or steady like a war drum?

"Here, they grow in a rainbow like they can't make up their mind, but in late spring, the Italian hills are carpeted in deep red. I haven't seen a real poppy since I was a child. When I close my eyes and think of home, they're what I see."

"Why are you telling me this?"

How was she doing this to me? Being near Thea unlocked something, the chains of regret falling away. "It means 'my flower.'"

She pulled back. "I'm not fragile or something pretty to sit on a mantle. I'm *not* a flower."

I gathered the hair spilling down her back, twisting it gently around my hand. "I never said you were." With a tug, I drew her forward, close enough that I could feel her heat through the sheet tucked around her.

With each quickening breath, she opened like the flower I'd named her.

"Your hair glows red like poppies, and when I close my eyes, I no longer see fields of flowers; I see you." Pulling down on the strands, her lips lifted to mine. "I hate how much I love it."

Thea's lips parted and her chest rose with a held breath. Tension built in her muscles, like she was preparing for a fight even as she arched into me.

"I hate that all I can think about is you, the way your skin feels and your hair smells." I pulled harder, exposing her neck. I dragged my nose along her jaw, drawing her into me like a drug. When my lips met her throat, she gasped.

"Your voice echoes in my head, tormenting me with how perfectly breathless you are whenever I'm near."

Thea's free hand gripped my shoulder, the bite of her nails cutting into the muscle, pulling me closer. Her leg pressed against mine, dragging the soft cotton of the sheet between us. Rather than resist it, I pushed her flat, using my grip on her hair to anchor her into position. As we rotated, the hand tucked beneath her cheek sprang free. I pinned it to the mattress before she could use it against me. Thea's legs dutifully framed my hips, falling into position like she'd been ready for this since the moment I told her to lay in the bed.

"Nick." The breathy exhale of my name drifted over my cheek. I don't think I'd ever heard anything sound so damn good.

"I hate that every time I stroke my dick—" I surged forward, rocking my hips into hers with the full weight of my body, "I do it imagining what it would feel like to sink into you." The sheet coasted between us, moving with each thrust as I drove the hard length of my cock against her.

She pushed back, arching her spine and raising her chest to me in offering. I pulled harder on her hair, using it to raise her further. The upper swell of her breasts pushed above the edge of the sheet. I lowered my mouth, drawing my tongue over the newly exposed flesh. This time, she audibly whimpered, using what muscle she had to fight against me for control—only to learn that my weight was more than she could move.

"Tell me you hate it, too." I closed my mouth over where the hardened peak of her nipple fought against the constraints of the sheet. "Tell me you loathe how badly you want my mouth on you."

"I hate—" she panted, her legs winding behind mine and tangling the sheet between us further. "—that fucking you would break me, and I hate that I want to beg you to do it."

"You could never break, Thea." I ground down harder. "But I would bend you right to the edge of shattering." The piercings rolled along my shaft, already feeling a hundred times better than when it had been my hand gripping them. I intentionally drew them over her clit, causing her to cry out. How she would scream when I drove into her, that slick heat swallowing me down and clinging to each rung as I pulled back and did it again. "I would push you past your limits until you learned what it means to truly lose yourself."

This wasn't enough. The thought played on repeat like a curse. The more I allowed myself to take from her, the more I wanted.

"Fuck me." Her hips tilted, rocking in counter motion to my thrusts. "Now. I want this. I want you."

"No."

"Please." With a broken exhale, Thea futilely pulled against the grip I had on her hair, raising her chest as she attempted to arch. *"Nick, please."*

This would end me. Once I knew what it was to be inside her, I'd never be able to let her go, and I had to, before this world destroyed everything I loved about her.

The friction of our movements shifted and pulled against the fabric. Her sighs of frustration melted into moans. It would take nothing to drive her to release, to take this one thing and claim it as my own. If I was going to be plagued by memories of her cries, then at least they would be the ones I drew from her.

Moving my mouth to her other breast, I bit down, hard enough that she screamed. The hand beneath mine strained against where it was pinned. Bowing as much as my grip could allow, she pushed, every muscle tightening as she fought the inevitable.

"I crave the way your body responds to me." Quickening the drive of our hips, I lifted my lips to her ear. "Come for me, Thea. Let me hear those intoxicating cries." Lowering my mouth over her pulse, I felt her heart rate ratchet up until all of that coiled tension exploded in a devastating display that would haunt me for the rest of my days. "Good girl. Bravissima."[2]

Her heaving breaths slowed as she came down from the high. I released her hair, massaging her scalp to ease the pain of my grip. She blinked up at me like she couldn't comprehend what happened.

---

2. Very well done.

This was an out-of-control freight train barreling over a blown-out bridge. We were in free fall, the crash inescapable, and I was helpless to stop it.

Against her temple, I whispered, "I hate you, Fiore Mio."

She took my face between her hands, lowering my lips to hers. "I hate you, too."

With the last word still lingering between our lips, she kissed me. It didn't taste like the wrathful kiss of enemies, filled with all the fire that came from surrendering to your hate. Her mouth moved against mine tenderly, feeling more intimate than anything that had transpired this evening. Slowly, I sank into the feeling. Warmth spread out from the center of my chest, blanketing my entire body in a tingling sensation that felt like life returning to numb limbs.

I curled Thea against me, enveloping her small frame until we settled perfectly together. A part of me that I never thought would return thrummed happily against her back.

-14-
THEA

C rowe lifted the layers of a massive vellum blueprint up and down, comparing ventilation shafts from one deck to another.

"She has a filtration system at every single juncture. Every. Single. One. Fuck, I knew the woman was paranoid, but talk about not taking any chances."

Danny walked over to the yellow notepad and crossed off "gas" from a list that was starting to get very short.

"Not only that, but it means we won't be able to use the ventilation network to gain access between decks either," Nick added from the other side of the room. He had what looked like a hundred little bits of machinery all laid out while he slowly assembled something that would allow us to access the ship from underwater.

I drew a big X over my stick figure drawing of Westin in a fog bubble. This was how I was keeping myself sane. I made tiny storyboards out of stick people for every scenario the boys tried to create. They weren't beautiful, but they were entertaining. My favorite was when I dropped a piano on her. Nick hadn't thought it was funny. Apparently, bringing a baby grand piano with us on a mission aboard a yacht was impractical. There was also this hilarious one where she melted in a giant puddle of water, but again, the man had zero sense of humor.

I balled up the paper and tossed it at Crowe. It bounced off his forehead, perfectly on center. Jumping to my feet, I cheered, "Ten points to Thea!"

Crowe slowly lifted his gaze to me. "Just remember you started this when I decide to start playing games of my own."

Crossing my arm over my chest, I stretched. "That's hardly a reason for me to stop. I like your games."

"I know you do." Crowe pushed back from the table, the blueprints fluttering closed as he released them.

A subtle knock rapped against the door, and it opened without waiting for any of us to answer. Marcello pushed through the doorway, walking straight to me and beaming a wide smile that made my blood turn to ice.

"*Porca miseria. Sei così dolce che mi è venuto il mal di denti.*"[1] Marcello twisted a lock of my hair around his finger, rubbing it between his thumb and forefinger with enough tug to pull. "I wouldn't mind a taste."

Nick stopped tightening the gear he was working on, pinning his cousin with a glare. "She's not as sweet as she looks."

I twisted, slapping his hand so that it wasn't near me. "If I had wanted your hands on me, then you would know. I'm not known for being subtle."

"That's true," Crowe chuckled quietly.

Dismissing my warning, Marcello reached forward again.

I side-stepped him. "Until then, your sleazy ass can back the fuck off." Shit. So much for watching my mouth.

Danny took several steps forward, moving close enough to intervene if necessary. "Was there a reason for your visit, Marcello?"

"I can think of a few reasons to visit." He licked his lips, eyes dropping to my chest and back up.

Bile rose in my throat. I grabbed Nick's discarded hoodie, wrapping it around myself to hide from his lecherous eyes as much as I could.

"You should really let me give you a tour of the grounds. My wing of the villa is substantially nicer than where you've been sleeping. Unfortunately..." His slimy gaze snapped up to my eyes while he stroked the length of my neck with a single finger. "There's no time for detours."

Resisting the urge to break his hand, I took a half step back. "Never touch me without permission again. You won't like the consequences."

---

1. Damn, you're so sweet my teeth ache.

"Feisty." Marcello closed the space I'd created, laughing at my display of aggression. "You're being summoned, *Fragolina*.[2] Sal would like a word with you."

Nick abandoned the machine he was assembling, rising so abruptly that several pieces clattered to the floor. "The hell he fucking does." Grabbing my shoulder, he pulled me roughly behind him. I stumbled over my feet, falling into the hard chest of Crowe.

"Not you, Nicco. Just her," Marcello said, tipping sideways to peer at me from around Nick's bulk. "There's some *business* they need to discuss."

The way his cousin snickered as he said business sent chills skittering down my spine.

"Thea isn't going anywhere near Sal." Just as quickly, Crowe handed me off to Danny. "I've lived here my whole life, Mello. I know the kind of business the women get pulled into."

Marcello tsked at him, saying something low that made Nick and Crowe bristle. I guess we were all breaking the no displays of emotion rule. The three of them argued loudly in Italian. Even Crowe, whose command of the language was better than he let on. Hearing them both speak with such ferocity, syllables rolling faster than I could follow, was one hell of spectacle. No one had ever fought for me as viciously as they were now. It made my blood feel hot and a flush climbed up my neck.

Raising his hands in surrender, Marcello stepped back and whistled at the possessive display. "So, how does this work with the three of you? Does she fuck you all at once, or do you wait in line for your turn to ride?"

The insult had barely left his mouth when Nick's fist slammed into it. "*Levati dai coglioni!*[3] Before I break more than your face. If my father wants to talk to her so badly, then he can come here and do it himself. Until then, Thea doesn't go anywhere near him, or you."

---

2. Little Strawberry

3. Get the fuck out!

"You really don't want me to deliver that message." Marcello pulled a handkerchief from his pocket, dabbing his split lip. "This one is so pretty looking. It'd be a shame for her face to become the canvas for a message of his own." His attention turned to Crowe. "You know how much Sal enjoys setting reminders you have to look at daily."

Crowe's bright blue eyes darkened, looking as hard as glacial ice, the cut of his jaw hardening in a way that would be terrifying if I didn't know the softness he was capable of. "Marcello, I'm going to speak slowly so that I know your dumb-shit brain understands me."

The young mafioso lifted his chin, rolling back his shoulders to seem taller, but the hard way he swallowed and the bead of sweat pooling along his temple betrayed him.

"I'm holding *you* personally responsible for Thea's wellbeing..." Crowe tipped his head. The unhinged quality and even tone of his deep voice were enough to make even me prickle with fear. Crowe was a scary fucker when he wanted to be. "You. Not them. Not Sal. You, *fratello*. If one of your men so much as looks at Thea crookedly, I will pluck out that dishwater eye and feed it to the fish in the pond." Crowe pushed into Marcello's space until the man stumbled against the wall. "If they touch her, then I will remove your fingers one bone at a time. The hand has a lot of bones in it, Mello. You don't want to know what having them pulled apart feels like."

Marcello's eyes flicked nervously to me. I placed my hands on my hips, shoring up my stance. Crowe might be terrifying, but he was *mine,* and it was about time Marcello learned that behind this woman were three men who would not suffer some insignificant prick's threats.

"Don't look at her." Crowe slammed his palm against the wall beside Marcello's head, making him jump. "You look at me when I'm speaking to you. *You* don't deserve to look at *her*. Now nod your head and tell me you understand."

Flicking his eyes back to Crowe, he mumbled, "But Sal—"

"I don't care what Sal says. The voice of god could deliver a divine edict for her death, and I would still hunt you down in the night. I guarantee that when I do, you'll beg for a death that will never come. Is *that* a clear enough message for you?" Crowe lightly slapped his cheek twice. "Now be a good dog and run along back to your master."

Marcello shoved Crowe, venom returning to his gaze. "Watch your fucking back, Vincenzo. It won't always be Sal on top. The three of you are only untouchable because Sal's precious heir is in your ranks."

Danny cocked his head to the side. "That sounds an awful lot like a threat."

"It's not a threat, Leone." Marcello straightened his jacket and tugged on the cuffs of his sleeves. "Just some advice. Tides are changing. The old man's reign is coming to an end—" His gaze shifted back to me, the intent behind his tone unmistakable. "—and it wouldn't hurt for you to spread a bit of that wealth for the next man on the throne, because it won't be Niccolo."

Shaking off Danny's hands from my shoulders, I strode towards the man and ran my fingertips along the satin lining of his lapel. Marcello's eyes sparkled like he was winning a prize. Moron.

"Keep fucking me with your eyes like that, and Crowe won't have to threaten you with plucking them out. I'll do it for him, only I'm not as gentle as he is."

Danny huffed a laugh under his breath.

Marcello's eyes dipped to my lips. "It's a shame so many people want you dead. You'd make a brilliant queen."

Marcello wanted to throw his machismo around and play at being intimidating? Then he could learn what happened to those who played with me. My knee collided with his groin, causing Marcello to buckle forward into my chest with a wordless wheeze. I stroked my fingers through his dark hair, seizing a fistful of the oily strands.

"I'm already a queen. That's *why* they want me dead."

I released Marcello, dropping him to his knees.

"Fuck me, I love when you go savage, Pretty Girl." Crowe palmed the back of my neck, drawing my mouth to his for a sinfully deep kiss, the kind that rocked me to the edge of ecstasy and made my body ache.

From his position on the ground, Nick's cousin watched us intently, hands still firmly cupping his insignificant dick.

"You're going to regret that, Fragolina." He climbed to his feet. "The next time, it will be you on your knees. I could have been good to you, could have given you everything you asked for. Turns out the only thing you ask for is punishment."

Crowe ran a thumb over my cheek, staring into the depths of my eyes with none of the ferocity that he'd just shown Marcello. "I suggest you leave, Mello—while you can still walk from this room." The tenor of his unusually deep voice vibrated the air around us. I felt its pulse like a separate heartbeat.

The door slammed, signaling Marcello's exit.

"That's a problem." Danny pointed at the closed door.

"I told you he would be." Nick moved closer, tipping my chin up to him with a single finger. "Are you okay?"

I nodded. "I've already forgotten it. Men like him don't even register for me. He's not worth the mental space."

"We should kill him," Crowe said simply. "Sal, too. We should just take the lot of them out. One night. One hit and be done with it before your pigheaded cousin makes a move of his own."

"Money says Marcello is already planning to take all of us out, along with Sal," Danny added.

Nick was quiet as the eyes in the room settled on him. He gave a tiny dip of his head in affirmation. "When we leave to head West, we can leave the bones of this place behind us."

"When is that?" I picked up the blueprints from where they'd slid off the desk.

Danny handed a piece of the machinery to Nick. "Tomorrow, maybe the day after. I have an idea that might work."

-15-
THEA

N ick placed his contraption into the case sitting on the floor, snapping the latches shut. "We need to inspect the scuba gear to see what needs to be replaced."

"Thea will need training on the equipment, too," Danny added.

"I volunteer." Crowe's large hands circled my waist, pulling me into him. "Thea in a bathing suit at the bottom of a pool sounds like my kind of lesson. How about we start now with breath control?"

I slapped at his hands, but the more I tried to wiggle away, the firmer his grip became. It was like he was made of Velcro.

My stomach growled loudly. We'd been planning all night, only breaking for sandwiches once—nearly six hours ago. Danny's last plan finally gave us something solid to work with. It wasn't without considerable risks, but I was almost feeling hopeful. Outside, the horizon was already starting to lighten, turning the clouds a pale pink against the inky purple sky. The first rays of light broke free, making the rows of poppies stretching over the hills glimmer with vibrant color.

"Wow." I half dragged Crowe to the window, throwing the curtains wide to get a better view of the vista. "It's so beautiful, like thousands of rainbows."

"Killer nightmare flowers, Darling Thea." Crowe turned my face from the mesmerizing display. "Trust me, none of us want you to travel over that rainbow again."

The rumbling of my stomach grew to an embarrassing volume.

"You're starving." Nick pulled the drapes closed.

"How nice of you to care again." I tried to be snarky, but the fact that my stomach wouldn't shut up took away a bit of my authority.

"I never stopped, Fiore Mio." Nick dragged his fingers through my auburn waves, glowing red in the sliver of still visible morning light. "My problem was never a lack of caring."

Crowe cleared his throat, dispelling the charge forming beneath Nick's heady gaze. "I'm sure there's something in the kitchen."

"I'll take you," Nick said, quickly cutting Crowe off before he could offer. He looked down at his watch, eyebrows raised in surprise at how long we'd been at it. "5 AM seems too early for bothering the staff."

"Smooth." Crowe rolled his eyes at Nick, then pulled me in for a soft peck on the side of my temple. "Save me something. While the house is still asleep, I'm going to snoop around and see if I can't get a feel for what Marcello is up to. "

"I'm coming with you. If you end up killing him, I want to be there for it." Danny placed both hands on my shoulders, turning me to face him. "Stay with Nick. I know his ass is moody, but don't go anywhere without him."

"Awwww, Kitten, don't worry."

Crowe snickered, *"Kitten."*

I air-blew them a kiss, twiddling my fingers goodbye. "I'll keep him safe. Have fun spying. Try not to get shot in anywhere that counts."

The end of the dark hallway was painted with warm light, spilling from the open kitchen door, the stillness of the house disrupted by the soft clinking of glass from within.

"I thought you said it was too early for the kitchen staff," I remarked, puzzled by the obvious person in the room.

"It is." Nick pulled the gun from his holster, aiming it at the partially open kitchen door.

"A bit overkill, don't you think?" I hissed under my breath. "It's probably just someone else working the night shift looking for an early breakfast."

"Have you met you?" Nick slid me a side-eye. "I think your track record speaks for itself." With one hand, he pushed me behind him.

I opened my mouth to protest, then shut it again. "Fair enough."

Nick entered the kitchen on silent steps. A tiny, elderly woman stood at the sink, dancing in place while scrubbing a blue glass jar. Stacked along the counter were dozens of other jars in various sizes. She softly sang along to the song playing from the quiet radio, while swishing her hips.

Nick sighed, resetting the safety and lowering his gun.

"Who is it?" I whispered, pulling on Nick's arm to see around him.

The old woman, noticing our movement, screamed and brandished the frying pan from the stove. Leftover bits of roasted garlic and egg went flying through the air.

"*Mannaggia santissima, Gesù bambino! Ma porca miseria, mi hai fatto venire un cazzo di colpo! Come cazzo ti è venuto in mente!*"[1] Sucking down a breath, she dropped the frying pan. "Niccolo!"

"*Ciao, Nonna.*"[2]

Wiping her hands on her apron, she grabbed at his cheeks. Even pulling him down to her, she still needed to go on her tiptoes to give him a kiss on the forehead. Her salt-white hair was pulled into a tight bun at her nape and slate-grey eyes crinkled behind glasses that were too large for her petite frame. I could see why Nick had spoken so fondly of the woman. She radiated love in a place that felt so unforgiving.

Releasing him, she smacked the back of his head. "*Ciao, Nonna? E me lo dici così? Sono passati cinque anni, Nicco. Cinque! Ciao, nonna un cavolo!*"[3] She whacked him again and immediately pulled him down to kiss the spot. "*Perchè non sei venuto prima a salutare nonna tua?*"[4]

"Nonna, please." Nick looked panicked in a way I'd never seen. The man was as cool as ice when an entire pack of Wolves were hunting us down, but one little granny had him completely undone. It was adorable. I had to cover my mouth to hide my giggle.

"Don't please me, you ungrateful child," Nonna snapped in heavily accented, yet perfect English.

Nick blinked, stunned into silence for several long seconds. "When did you learn English?"

"I'm not so old that I can't learn something new. You've been gone for five years, Nicco. Five. That's a long time to leave your Nonna Lucia alone in this house with only gangsters for company. Who is this beautiful girl—" She

---

1. Holy spirits, baby jesus! Fucking hell, you gave me a fucking fright! What the fuck were you thinking!"

2. Hey, Grandma.

3. Ciao, Nonna? And you say it just like that? It's been five years, Nicco. Five! Ciao, nonna my arse!

4. Why haven't you come sooner to say hi to your nonna?

lowered her frames to look over her glasses at me. "—that you're bringing to the kitchens at *five in the morning*?"

I opened my mouth to answer, but Nick cut me off. "You're avoiding my question."

"Rosalina taught me."

"The maid's daughter?"

"Well, someone had to. You and Vincenzo left, and all I knew how to say in English were a few dirty words." The tiny woman pushed past Nick, moving him aside like laundry on a line. "Are you hungry, sweet girl?" Her knobbly finger pinched the side of my arm with more force than I ever imagined a frail woman like her was capable of. "You look like you haven't eaten in a year." She pulled down two mugs from a cabinet and thrust them into Nick's hands. "There's espresso on the stove."

"I bet a smart thing like you loves her caffé like her men, strong."

"Nonna," Nick grumbled.

The old woman waved him off, ushering me into a kitchen chair. I stumbled over my feet, landing on the seat with a thump. "I know because so did I when I was your age." She gave me a cheeky wink. "Where do you think Niccolo inherited all those muscles from? His Nonno looked like a Roman god."

I glanced with amusement over my shoulder at a shell-shocked Nick.

"When Nicco was a babe, I used to put a drop of espresso in his milk and tell him he was having a cappuccino. The boy has always loved his caffé." I smiled at the image of a tiny Nick sitting at the table, kicking his legs and sipping his fake cappuccino.

"Would you like biscotti, or there are some cornetti in the cabinet set aside for this morning?" She radiated warmth like a halo of love circled her. I could spend days in this woman's company and never tire of the way she made you feel instantly loved.

"Cornetti?"

"It's like a croissant." Nick set my coffee in front of me, its curl of steam warming the air. There was a tiny splash of milk in it, lightening it to the perfect shade. I took a slow sip and moaned. The man seriously knew his coffee.

Making a pleased hum, she slid a plate with pastries and a small jar of jam in front of me. Even though I was sitting, we were almost eye level. How could a woman so tiny be related to a giant like Nick?

"Thank you, Mrs. Chopper."

"Pfft." Her exasperated exhale blew back the hair hanging over my brow. "It's Ciopriani. My son, *quell'idiota*, changed the name to *Chopper*."[5] She made a disgusted sound in the back of her throat. "His papa is rolling in his grave. Fifty generations of Cioprianis." She shook her hands in the air. "Did you know that he's directly related to Andrea Ciopriani, the poet? The man wrote epics, and Salvatore changed it like it meant nothing." She rattled off another long string of curses in Italian, having obviously held in her outrage for a long time, or maybe Nonna Lucia always went through life with her passion set to high.

"Nonna, *calma*, you'll give yourself a stroke going on like that."[6]

Nodding in agreement, Lucia took a long, slow breath before cupping my cheek with cool fingers. "You call me Nonna Lucia like everyone else."

"Okay. I've never had a Nonna before." My heart squeezed from the way she smiled so lovingly at me. "My name is Thea."

"Thea." Her gaze flicked to Nick, who still looked like he was staring at ghosts. "*Un nome così bello per una ragazza altrettanto bella. I vostri bambini saranno degli angioletti.*"[7]

Nick choked on his coffee, the olive tone of his skin draining completely away.

I blinked rapidly. What had she just said to him? "What's *bambini*?"

"It's nothing. Just an old woman's foolish hopes," Nick snapped.

"Bah...*I figli sono pezzi di cuore*. You'll see."[8]

---

5. My son, that idiot, changed the name to Chopper.

6. calm down

7. A beautiful name for a girl that's just as beautiful. Your babies are going to be little angels.

8. Children are pieces of your heart

Nick rubbed at his temples, squinting like he had a headache and muttering something too quiet to understand.

"Well, Nonna Lucia, I think your English is fantastic."

"Eh. It's passable. None of the boys seem to realize that I understand them. Or they didn't care enough to pay attention, but these old ears hear everything: Marcello's late-night phone calls with the west coast and Sal's plans to expand to a second set of fields in the South. Foolish, if you ask me. It's too warm down there, but nobody ever thinks to ask me anything. "

Nick drained the soapy water in the sink. "Nonna, why are you in the kitchen at 5 AM? Even earlier, from the looks of it." He gestured at the mismatched pile of jars. "You've already opened every window on the floor and washed dozens of dishes. There are staff to do that sort of thing."

"The kitchen staff aren't working today. *E poi lo sai che questa è la MIA cucina.*" [9] Nick frowned at her, not that it stopped Nonna. "Aww, *Topolino*, how quickly you forget. *Oggi devo fare la salsa!* It's Salsa Day." [10]

"Salsa Day?" I asked around a mouthful of biscotti. "What's that?"

Nick turned back. "It's a big day where we make all of the sauce for the rest of the year."

I popped up, looking at the massive stack of crates in the corner, realizing they were hundreds of tomatoes. "That sounds like fun. I've never made sauce."

"Thea," Nick warned, but I shooed him off. Sure, we'd already pulled an all-nighter, and everyone in Ozmandria wanted me dead, but how often did I get the chance to make sauce with my very own Nonna?

The old woman's wrinkled face brightened. "Since this big hunk of space left, no one has been here to help me. The rest of the family is too busy to care,

---

9. And you know that this is MY kitchen afterall.

10. Aww, Little Mouse, how quickly you forget. I have to make tomato sauce today.

but not too busy to eat my food, mind you. *E se non la faccio io la salsa non la fa nessuno.*[11]

"Nobody wants to make sauce because all of this..." Nick swept his arms around the room. "Isn't necessary anymore. You can buy a hundred different kinds of sauce in store."

Nonna took a step back, reaching behind her for a large wooden spoon and brandishing it like a sword. "Niccolo Ciopriani, tell me you are not buying factory salsa. You have no idea what they put in there. It's all chemicals that give you heartburn." She poked at the center of his chest. "My ingredients are all fresh, *è tutto fresco.*[12] The only thing my salsa gives you is a full belly."

The old woman shook her head, turning to walk away when I took both her hands in mine. "Nonna, I would love to help you make the salsa."

"*Angioletto,*[13] you can start by washing the tomatoes. Nicco, you go get the press from the shed." She leaned in like she was sharing a secret with me. "Niccolo is the only one that my Giorgio trusted with the press. He used to say that only he knew how to work it properly. The other boys always tried to force the tomatoes through, never stopping to clear the skins. Not my Niccolo. He knows how to handle something precious and has the patience to see it done correctly."

Nick's eyes met mine over the head of Nonna Lucia. I'd have given anything to read his mind as his expression softened to something nearly unrecognizable. For the first time, I truly saw the man he had wished to be: someone who lovingly cared for his Nonna and cooked recipes passed on for generations—a man who wasn't hardened by the world he'd been forced into.

---

11. And if I don't make salsa no one will!

12. It's all fresh.

13. Little angel,

-16-
CROWE

The house was quiet as Danny and I made our way into the Northern Wing of the villa. With each step, Marcello's words simmered in my mind. The way he'd looked at Thea, it made my blood boil. Just the idea of him touching her made me want to slice off his hands and shove them down his throat. The only thing that kept me from slaying him where he stood was Thea. I didn't want to be that man when I was with her.

That wasn't stopping me now. If my knife just so happened to slip and slice something off that he'd miss—like his head—well, accidents happen every day.

Pausing outside his apartment door, I listened for signs of life. We'd heard Marcello and his boys drinking in the courtyard well into the late hours of the night. I was betting that Marcello would be sleeping off his hangover. He was so overconfident that he believed he was safe while sequestered in his room. Moron.

"Fifty bucks says you can't get it unlocked in under a minute." Danny flipped open his wallet, pulling out a crispy fifty dollar bill and waving it in my face.

"30 seconds, double or nothing."

"I'll take that bet. It's been five years. Nothing says those locks are the same ones."

"Doesn't matter. I haven't met a lock I couldn't crack," I said, pulling out a small pick set.

I could tell just by looking that these locks hadn't been updated while we were away. A decade ago, a member of the cleaning crew decided to relieve Sal of half a million dollars worth of art and silver. After Sal made me track the culprit down and teach them not to touch things that didn't belong to them, I spent a month modifying each room with an electronic locking system. When I was done, the villa was considerably more secure than before, unless, of course, you'd designed the system and built it in a way to access any lock of your choosing.

"Go." Danny pressed the start button on his stopwatch app. Red numbers spiraled on a counter, counting the milliseconds.

Quickly, I used a small screwdriver to open the side panel of the lock and pulled out an electronic decoder roughly the size of a credit card. I inserted two thin wires protruding from the card into a small jack at the bottom corner of the panel.

Danny leaned in, purposely hovering over me. "Ten seconds."

"You know, you don't always have to be an arrogant prick. There are other personality settings."

The display flashed red, blinking quickly.

"I'm only an arrogant prick because I'm always right."

With a small beep, the light switched to green, and the tumblers within the casing turned. In a near-silent pop, the door swung toward us. The time on Danny's stopwatch read 28.77 seconds.

I held out my hand. "Pay up, *Leone*." I snickered at the overdramatic roll of his eyes.

"You cheated."

"That's a loser's claim." I folded my kit, popping him in the forehead with it before slipping the tools into my back pocket. "Pay. Up."

Soundlessly, he shoved the bills into my chest and entered the room. Marcello lay face down on his sofa, drool pooling beneath his open mouth. He reeked of vodka. It oozed from his pores like a garbage heap being vented. How the hell did this idiot ever think that he could replace Salvatore? Nick's father was like a cyclone, a terrifying force of nature capable of pure devastation. Marcello was more like the trash that tumbled aimlessly in the wind.

Using the tip of my shoe, I pushed his slack jaw closed. Marcello snored, the sound catching in the back of his throat like a warthog. "Ugh, he drooled on my sneaker."

"Did it make you want to skin him alive when he touched Thea?" Danny's voice was cold and layered with disgust.

"And then some." I pulled a set of zip ties from my pocket, pulling his hands behind his back and looping them easily around his wrists. Then I did the same to his ankles, trying my best not to inhale the stench of his day-old socks. Pulling on his uncooperative legs, I secured the two of them together, leaving the warthog hog-tied. I smirked at the unintended pun. Marcello snorted again, mouth falling back open. A truly brilliant idea came to me.

Sauntering into his kitchenette, I snatched an apple from a basket on the counter. I shoved it into his mouth, doing my best to wedge it between his teeth.

"Perfetto."[1]

"That's actually hilarious."

With Marcello still unconscious and secured, I took some time to poke around the room. Danny was already thumbing through a stack of papers on the corner of his desk, but it was the flash of his abandoned phone on the floor that caught my attention.

A green icon flashed across the screen, the incoming caller identified as "Bitch Witch #2".

"Interesting."

"Answer it." Danny sat the phone on the coffee table between us.

With a last look at the unconscious man, I flicked the call open. "*Pronto.*"[2]

"*It's been arranged. The deposit has been transferred; you'll get the rest after fulfillment.*" I'd know that cold indifference anywhere. A chill snaked its way down my spine. I can't believe I'd ever found anything about that psycho arousing. It took everything in me to not immediately hang up the phone. "*And Marcello, if she arrives lacking a pulse, I will be very displeased.*"

---

1. Perfect.

2. Hello.

Danny's eyes were blazing with the same fury I felt boiling within me. His gaze bore into the side of Marcello's head like he could blow it apart with his vision alone.

Faking my best Italian accent, I said, "What about these other *stronzi?*"[3]

Westin sighed like she was bored. *"Vincent is afraid of fire. Maybe try adding some gasoline to the mix."* Fucking sadistic bitch. It was one time, and I was rightfully afraid. We were trapped in the back office of a warehouse while the building was burning down on top of us. The maniac laughed through the entire experience and then had the nerve to call me pussy for not wanting to fuck her while we burned alive. Apparently, wanting to survive made me a coward. *"I really can't be bothered to care. Just make sure they don't make it to tomorrow. I don't want to deal with the stupid one's idea of a rescue mission."*

Danny's hands flexed. I knew the fact that Westin could never remember his name ate at him.

"Certo. Just make sure I get my money."[4] I was about to add something ignorant to really seal the Marcello persona, but Westin had already hung up the call.

Murderous rage was flashing across Danny's features. His veins pulsed with it, making his skin turn scarlet. If it wasn't for the silencer he was spinning, I'd say he looked ready to chop Marcello into tiny pieces.

"Wait." I lowered his arm. "We need to know what plans he's already put in motion." Danny raised his gun, seeming to lose his ability to think logically. "Where the fuck is your head, man? Aren't you supposed to be the strategizing one? Interrogate, then kill." I flicked the side of Marcello's face. "Besides, I'm an artist, remember?" I laughed, remembering the way Mello boasted about my skills. He had no fucking idea, but he was about to receive an intimate demonstration of what happened to those who dared touch what was mine. "Now, I just need to find the right *brush.*"

---

3. What about these other assholes?

4. Of course. Just make sure I get my money.

I pulled a paring knife from the butcher block in the kitchen, giving it a gleeful flip as I made my way back into the living room.

"What, you couldn't find a smaller knife?" Danny dragged a chair over, spinning it around to sit backwards in it. The twat looked like an absurd cross between a gangster and a cowboy.

"I like the feel of this one. It's got a little hook on the hilt, better for carving. Besides, it's not the size of the knife that matters—"

"It's how you use it?" Danny shook his head, casually pointing his pistol at Mello. "Fuck, your jokes are lame. How is it that you keep getting Thea to ride your dick?"

"Because she loves my cock. I can't help it that I'm playing with a stacked deck." Danny scowled, redirecting the gun towards me. With a laugh, I added, "Hey, don't get bitter just because she's decided she doesn't want to play with yours anymore."

He scrubbed his face with his free hand. "I don't fucking know what's going on there. Half the time, it feels like my heart is beating outside of my chest and completely disconnected from my brain."

For someone so smart, Danny really was oblivious sometimes. "Or try this on for size; stop being a coward and talk to the girl."

"Ugh. It would be so much easier if she would just let me fuck her into forgiveness. Orgasms are a completely credible form of currency in my book."

"That wouldn't really be an incentive to behave. What exactly did you do that has her icing you out?"

"Before the bomb in the bank, I may have insinuated that she was a whore and only good for an easy fuck."

My strike was instinctual, pummeling his stomach before I'd fully registered the attack. Danny toppled to the side, bringing the chair with him.

"Fuck, Crowe." He climbed to his feet, righting the chair before slumping into it with a dramatic sigh. "That wasn't necessary, she's already punishing me plenty."

"You're an unbelievable cunt."

Prickish comments were second nature for him. Sometimes it was like someone left Danny's factory setting switched to asshole. It was infuriating. I'd say he didn't know better, but he absolutely did.

"That's not all." My brother looked at the ceiling, his face tightening like admitting he fucked up was causing him actual pain. I don't think I'd ever seen him look so remorseful. "The worst of it was that it was right after I'd railed her in the vault. I could still smell Thea all over me the entire time you were fucking her against the glass. I know you thought you were punishing Nick with that display, but her eyes were on me just the same."

"The fuck were you thinking?"

Danny twisted, anticipating the next punch with plenty of time to save his kidneys. "I fucking wasn't," he groaned, dropping his head to the back of the chair. "I was hurt and angry. The wizard had just shown us Didi's autopsy report, and Thea made the mistake of standing in the path of my rage."

"That doesn't give you the right," I spat at him. Between Nick's shit and Danny's, I was spending half my time playing referee. For people who loved our girl, they sure had a shit way of showing it. "Besides, I know for a fact the idea of sharing her actually turns you on."

"It fucking does." Danny scuffed his feet idly against the carpet. This might be the first time in our long friendship I'd seen him look genuinely remorseful.

"Fix it. Because if your pigheadedness ruins my chances for a Thea Eiffel Tower, I'm going to beat your stubborn ass to within an inch of your life and back." I took a second to let the ménage fantasy really take root. Thea'd take two dicks so well. Shit, maybe even three. I wonder if Nick could be convinced to play with others for a change. Oz damn, the idea was hot. Just thinking about it was making me hard.

"Eiffel Tower, really?" Danny rolled his eyes; except I could see him rolling the idea over in head the same way I was.

Marcello coughed against the apple juice gagging him, and my dick instantly deflated. His eyes flew open, a bit glassy at first as he tried to make sense of the position he'd just found himself in. Angry, muffled gagging came from him as he writhed against his binds, sounding more and more like a pig by the second.

Cracking my knuckles, I said, "Let's get this over with. I want to see our girl come at least twice before dinner."

—17—
CROWE

I wiped the back of my knife against my pants. There would be no saving these. Blood stains coated the better part of my legs and chest. It wouldn't have been so bad if Marcello hadn't been flailing around so much. He'd grown up here, same as the rest of us. You'd think he'd be able to take a bit of light torture better than this.

His bleached hair hung limply in his eyes, and blood-tinged sweat dripped from the tip of his nose.

"I'm getting bored," Danny huffed. The obnoxiously loud crinkling of a bag of chips filled the room as he eased into a nearby armchair.

I gripped Marcello's hair, craning his head back so he could see me clearly. "Give me—"

Danny crunched on a mouthful of chips, drowning out what I was saying with the world's loudest chewing.

Slowly, I turned my head to look at him. "Do you mind?"

"Fuck off. I'm hungry. It's been hours, Crowe. Hate to say it, but you've lost your touch."

I loathed that he was right. This was taking far too long. "Something useful, Mello, or I'll be forced to start living up to Danny's expectations. Trust me, literally no one wants that. So, if you don't want me to get more creative, then give me something I can use."

"More creative than playing hangman on his forehead?"

I smirked. That had been fun purely for fun. "If he had just started by guessing some vowels, he could have saved himself some agony." DICKHEAD had so many vowels in it. "Everyone knows you start with the vowels." Of

143

course, I would have carved him up for how he'd touched Thea, anyway. Her flinch was burned into my mind — right next to that fat asshole pinning her to the sidewalk outside of the bank, and I'd put a bullet in his brain.

"Fine. Fine." Marcello let out a conciliatory whimper. "I'll tell you."

"Fucking, finally." I side-eyed Danny. He licked the cheese dust from his fingers, leaving the middle one extended. Prick.

"Start with your deal with Westin. What did you promise the bitch?"

"And be specific," Danny added, finally abandoning his snack.

"It doesn't matter. It's too late."

"Too late for what, Fuckwit?" I flicked him in the center of his bloody forehead. "What did you do?"

"She promised me the Villa in exchange for your girl. A team is already on their way. You can't stop it now."

Danny looked to the hallway door like he'd somehow developed X-ray vision and could see Thea through it.

"She's with Nick. She'll be fine," I said, assuring myself as much as him.

Marcello shook his head. "Not likely. Can you untie me now? My arms are fucking killing me."

Danny loosed a punch into Marcello's cheek, sending a spray of spit in my direction. I recoiled. It was bad enough I was covered in his blood; I didn't need his spit, too.

"You traded Thea to Westin and you really think we're just going to let you go?"

"Yes, because I'm going to get the two of you out of here before everyone else ends up dead. Westin's goons are going to level this place. There's no saving your girl or Nick, but I can still save your life." He shifted his attention to me. "Both of you."

"There is no life without her," I intoned.

A muffled *whomp-whomp-whomp* vibrated the glass in the window frames. Outside, a large black helicopter landed in the middle of the poppy field, sending a cyclone of rainbow petals into the air.

"That's our ride." Marcello wiggled, the panic from earlier evaporating. "Cut me loose. Hurry."

The stupid moron still thought he was walking out of this room. I pulled the gun from my waistband and pressed it to the middle of Marcello's scarred forehead. A second, unfamiliar sound added to the chaos rattling outside the doors.

Over the flower fields, a swarm of something black hovered. Slowly, the mass crept closer, blotting out the blue sky.

"What the fuck is that?" I flicked the safety off, pressing harder into his skull. "Talk quickly."

"That's why we need to leave right now." Marcello wiggled again. "You know how Monkeys like their gadgets. I, personally, don't want to be here when that swarm arrives."

"How were you going to deliver Thea?"

"There was no handing her over specifically. I just had to shut off the border security and pull the guards from the outer gates."

"That explains why whatever that is flying towards us isn't being shot down." The swarm swooped in the sky, reminding me of the murmuration of birds that sometimes migrated overhead. Thousands of tiny robots flew as one.

"We have to get out of here." Marcello started wriggling on his sofa like he'd somehow free himself. What made him think he'd work free of the ties now, if he hadn't been able to free himself when I was carving apart his face? The buzzing grew louder, making it hard to think. "There's a kill order on everyone in the main building. When the dust settles, I'll be in charge. I can set the two of you up real nice. I always liked you, Vincenzo. You could do well under me."

"You're such a dumbass, Marcello. You always have been." Before he could protest, I pulled the trigger. Blood and brain matter sprayed the sofa, misting my face.

Danny was already moving for the door. "We need to get Thea on that helicopter before the swarm gets here. What do you think those are?"

"Drones. Small ones. What they're loaded with, who knows? Explosives, Gas, Bullets. Could be anything. Shit, knowing Orin, it might be nanotech."

Not bothering to close the door behind us, we ran towards our wing. Hopefully we'd get to their room and Nick would still be with Thea. All we needed was a small bit of luck to be on our side.

"Where are you two going in such a hurry?"

We spun. The commanding tones of Salvatore's voice bounced off the tile. "I'm so disappointed, Vincenzo. To think you could betray me like this, after all I've given you." Four of his personal security flanked him. No doubt, they ran to his side the moment they realized something was happening. "I raised you like a son. Supported and trained you, all in honor of the love I bore for your sister."

"You killed my sister." I spat the words at him. The venom of years of repressed anger bleeding into my vision.

Sal's olive skin reddened. Just like Nick, the veins at his neck bulged as his expression darkened. The only people I'd seen at the receiving end of that stare died terrible deaths. I didn't care. I'd kept my mouth shut my entire life, jumped through every hoop, did whatever I could to try to gain his approval. What did it get me? Fucking nothing. The only thing Sal ever gave me were disapproving glares.

"You *never* loved her," I continued. "You loved her submission, keeping your good little girl in exchange for the drugs you shoved down her throat along with your cock. She knelt at your feet right up until the day those drugs killed her."

"That's enough."

With measured steps, I strode back towards the man I once wished would love me as a son. The security on either side of him leveled their guns on us. I knew they'd never shoot unless their boss commanded it. "You only kept me because Nonna demanded it, and you trained me because you needed a bird of prey at your disposal. I was young and dumb enough to think I wanted your pride. Love was never a factor."

Danny's raised gun flashed in my periphery. That was love. My brother stood by my side, backing my choice to advance rather than fleeing, despite knowing that it would likely lead to our deaths. Sal's eyes didn't so much as flash in his direction, completely confident that he was in no danger.

"You say you loved me like a son?" My body vibrated with rage. "I've seen the love you showed your *actual* son. Tell me Sal, how long did it take you to decide he was a worthy sacrifice for your betrayals? Did you decide to abandon him to Eastin's machinations that same day, or did you at least sleep on it for a night?"

"*Quando parli con me, devi farlo con rispetto!*"[1]

"Respect?" I could barely choke out the word. "Do you know what she did to him, the way she shattered every piece right down to the marrow? When we found him, Niccolo was a twisted mess of broken bones and mutilated flesh. All that remained of his soul was shadows. *Te n'è fregato qualcosa*, or did you breathe a sigh of relief for slipping the noose?"[2]

Malice flashed in his eyes, making them look nearly black. Salvatore extended his hand to the side, snapping at the man to his right. The closest goon placed his pistol in Sal's palm. The asshole couldn't even be bothered to carry his own weapon.

I stood my ground. "The only thing you love is yourself."

The stained-glass window at the end of the corridor rained to the ground in a shower of jewel-toned light. The tinkling of broken glass momentarily confused me, sounding so juxtaposed against the tension in the corridor. The four security guards slumped to the ground, their guns sliding in every direction.

Eyes wide with shock, Sal's hand went to his chest. A stain, bright and red as a flower spread across the front of his white shirt. It took too long for me to piece together what was happening. Danny grabbed my arm, pulling me to the ground only seconds before more silent bullets clipped the wall where we'd been standing.

Nick's father fell to his knees, a long trickle of blood dripping from the corner of his mouth. Just before he toppled forward, the focus dimmed in his eyes—dead before he hit the ground.

---

1. You will speak to me with respect!

2. Did you care, or did you breath a sigh of relief for slipping the noose

A flying bug hovered where the great Salvatore Ciopriani had just been standing. It looked like an oversized bee, with two segments gleaming in the light like they were made from molten black-gold. On either side there were two wings quietly humming and keeping the drone aloft. Instead of legs, however, there were four finger long barrels. No doubt, this was where the flying bullets had fired from.

The insect clicked, a red light blinking ominously where its eyes should be. The guns swiveled in a circle, aiming directly where Danny was spread on the ground. He rolled, hissing in pain when one of the bullets grazed his arm. Not slowing to realize how stupid this was, I sprang up, sprinting down the corridor towards the thing. I swerved left, snatching a lamp from the side table. More bullets peppered the wall behind me in a long stream.

Lifting the lamp, I swung it like a baseball bat. The light bulb in the lamp shattered, sending glittery glass dust into the air and the flying bug slammed into the wall. It twitched. One wing was broken, thumping against the ground in an attempt to rise. A single gun barrel rotated to face me. I swiveled the lamp in my palm, bringing the base down hard on the contraption with a satisfying crunch.

I picked up the insect. It was slightly smaller than the palm of my hand. Turning it over, the telltale WM logo gleamed back at me.

Fucking Marcello.

Fucking Orin Barret.

Pocketing the bug, I snatched two of the abandoned guns. Outside, the buzzing crescendoed as the swarm descended on the house.

I gave one last, long look at Sal. His death was too quick. "We need to find Thea and Nick. Now."

-18-
THEA

R ed sauce streaked Nick's arms, soaking his black shirt and making the fabric of his rolled-up sleeves cling to his biceps. He pushed away the hair hanging in his eyes, getting the paste in the strands and streaking it across his forehead. Grumbling something under his breath in Italian, he poked at the skins jammed in the spout. The small metal spoon looked like a child's toy in his massive hands.

"Of course, Crowe couldn't have come down, too. No, he had to go spy on stupid scheming Marcello. What are you doing on the phone with the west coast, Marcello? Not helping Nonna with the salsa, that's what." His hand slipped. A massive skin sprang loose, slapping him in the face with a wet-sounding *thwack*. "*Ma porca puttana!*"[1]

I scooped a big ladle full of the pressed tomatoes into a jar, watching in fascination as Nick seemed to be losing his mind.

"*No, Nicco, you run the press.*" His Nonna impression was impressively accurate. Even in his semi-reclined position; he perfectly mimicked her adorable head tilt. "Sure, make the man with the biggest hands clean a pipe with the world's tiniest spoon."

I snorted a laugh.

Nick flicked a handful of tomato slop into the bucket, his cold glare pinning me in place. "Something funny, Fiore Mio?"

"Nope." I bit my lip, failing miserably at hiding my laughter. In my distraction, my next spoonful missed the jar, half pouring over the rim and down my

151

arm while the other half somehow managed to splash up at my face. The heat of the liquid made me hiss, sucking in a breath through my teeth. It was tart, nothing like the sweet and savory sauces Nick usually made.

His cool metal exterior cracked with laughter. "The salsa is supposed to go in the jar, not in your lap."

I sucked on my burned knuckles, biting back an embarrassed laugh. "Who knew boiling tomatoes were so hot?"

Loud yelling, mixed with the prerecorded laugh track of a telenovela, filtered through the door to the connecting rooms. Nonna left us nearly an hour ago, proclaiming that her shows came on at ten, and she never missed them. Apparently, finding out how Maria would tell Federico about her secret love baby took precedence over anything else.

"She's not even in the next room." Nick's features lightened with amusement, turning to look at the kitchen door. "Her lounge is two rooms over. That's just how loud she has the television." Nick climbed to his knees, crawling the few feet to where I was perched on a tiny wooden stool. "How have you managed to get more salsa on you than in the jars?"

"I don't know. Beginner's luck?" I pulled at my soaked shirt. The white fabric was stained red in so many places that I looked like a murder victim from one of those true crime documentaries. "What's your excuse?" I ran my fingers through his tomato paste-matted hair.

Nick's eyes closed, humming a low, pleased sound like you might make when tasting rich chocolate. With a deep breath, he sat back on his heels. "You're doing it wrong."

"How can you ladle wrong?"

"I'm as surprised as you are. The spoon is larger than the jar, so you have to hold it higher and angle it so the salsa runs in a thin stream. Otherwise, the entire spoonful empties at once and goes everywhere."

"Here, let me show you." He leaned forward, resting one hand on the bucket for stability and reaching with the other. There was a loud crack echoing over the tiled interior. Time seemed to slow, my heart stopping as everything was upended. The side of the bucket broke apart, throwing Nick's entire body weight onto me. Gallons of steaming, hot liquid flooded over us.

I shrieked, scrambling to escape the deluge. The stool tipped, sending us into the massive puddle of cooling liquid. Nick's foot slammed into the leg of the table, toppling the small stockpile of completed bottles to the ground.

Nick seemed completely unfazed by the heat; instead stark concern had him tearing at my soaked shirt. "We have to get this off before you burn."

Knees bracketing my hips, he tore at the hem of my shirt, pulling it in pieces over my head. His hands quickly roamed over my chest, inspecting my skin for signs of a burn, and smoothing away the sauce. "It's impossible to tell what's burned and what's stained. Everything is pink."

The way I could feel my entire body flushing from the slick slide of his hands and his thighs pushing me into the ground probably wasn't helping either. The left side of his shirt was dripping wet. He'd taken the brunt of the sauce, and yet his focus was solely on me.

"What about you? You're wearing more of it than I am." I grabbed at the buttons of his shirt, pulling them apart. Beneath the saturated fabric, his skin was rosy and warm to the touch, but didn't seem harmed at all.

"You don't have to worry about me, Fiore Mio. Half of those nerve receptors don't work anymore."

I paused with his shirt half pulled down, pinning his arms in place. "What kind of wounds cause permanent nerve damage?"

"The kind you never really come back from."

The raised surfaces of dozens of fine scars raked his side, the web of lines hidden beneath layers of beautiful ink. Nick's shaky exhale blew over my damp skin as my hands mapped the forgotten wounds, making the shiver coursing over me match the way he trembled beneath my fingertips.

Crowe's words echoed back to me, reminding me that Nick had endured unthinkable torment. Someone had tortured him, the same woman who would have destroyed me. An ache in my chest squeezed my ribs, my heart thumping hard enough to make me light-headed.

Swallowing hard, I yanked at the dripping fabric. "That doesn't mean you're not burning."

The shirt came free, pulling Nick's entire body flush with mine. His hands on my stomach flexed hard enough I knew I'd be explaining bruises to Crowe in the morning.

"Fiore Mio..." his voice whispered over my lips, overwhelming all of my senses to the point that I had to close my eyes to remember how to breathe.

"*Mi ricordi cosa significa sentirsi vivo.*"[2] He inhaled slowly, his hand skating over my chest and circling my throat. Rather than squeezing in command like Danny would or cutting off my air with a loss of control like Crowe had, Nick's fingers stroked at my pulse reverently. The steel of his eyes smoldered with more emotion than I realized he was capable of. "I crave the way your pulse races beneath my touch. My heart beats wildly every time you touch me, *come il fragore delle onde che si infrangono sulla riva.*"[3]

I burned to know what he was too enamored to say in English. While at the same time, I loved the timbre of his hushed Italian. The roll of each syllable resonated in the air, making me feel hot all over. I could drift away into eternity so long as I was lulled by his voice.

"I can't escape you, Fiore Mio, no matter how hard I try. I'm hooked without ever having more than a taste." His gaze dropped to my lips. "*Sei la scintilla che ha messo a FUOCO la mia anima.*"[4]

Internally, I was screaming for him to kiss me. He was so close, yet the distance between us felt like miles. My heart ached, his hateful words still ringing in my ears, but I also needed this man right now more than I needed air. The conflict ricocheting through my chest left me frozen in the same way he didn't seem to be breathing.

---

2. You remind me what it is to be alive.

3. Like the roar of waves crashing on the shore.

4. You are the spark that ignited my soul.

"What is it you want from me, Nick?" I whimpered the question, unable to withstand the limbo between love and hate.

Finally exhaling the breath he was holding, his forehead dropped to my chest. "*Tutto e nulla.*"[5] Dropping his lips over my heart, he added, "I want to take from you until there is nothing left to give, and then keep taking."

Slowly, the warm, flat of his tongue dragged over my collarbone. My body bowed against the weight pressing me down. His fingers hooked into the strap of my bra, yanking hard enough the seam of the cup tore apart.

His grey eyes flashed. It was like watching lightning on the horizon and knowing the crash of thunder would follow. "Thea—" The way he said my name held all the power of that storm. What was left of the delicate lace bra shredded in his hands like it was made of cobwebs. "I want to shatter you into pieces so small there's no telling where you end."

His mouth closed over my breast with a shared groan, the lines of tension in his muscles ebbing away. I surrendered to the inevitability of this moment. My hands dropped, palming the erection pushing into my stomach. Through the soft linen of his pants, each hard ridge of his piercings rolled against the heel of my hand, causing him to rake his teeth against my nipple. Knowing that Nick would have nothing beneath made my mouth go dry, my fingers trembling with anticipation so badly that I fumbled with the simple ties of his slacks.

"Not yet." Gently, Nick circled my wrists, pinning them to either side of my head. His long arms effortlessly held me in place while lowering to trail small bites down my stomach. His teeth pulled at my sleep shorts, tugging the fabric with surprising ease over my hips.

Releasing my wrists, he said, "Keep them there."

The serious demand in his gaze cemented me in place, despite the way I was aching to kiss every scar and learn every mark. I wanted to know how those piercings would feel against my hand, sliding along my tongue, and driving into my core.

"Nick, please."

---

5. Everything and nothing.

His fingers lovingly stroked over my raging pulse. "No, Fiore Mio. You wanted my attention. Now, you will take what I give you until I've had my fill."

-19-
NICK

Her heart fluttered against my fingertips like a hummingbird's wings. I didn't deserve to be taking anything from her, but logic had fled the moment her hands skimmed the bare flesh of my side.

It'd been years since I'd let anyone touch me. After my extended stay in Eastin's basement, I tried to reclaim what was stolen from me. Cold turkey, I picked up a girl in a West Emerald City bar. She was pretty enough, more importantly, she didn't care that my skin looked like someone had taken a potato peeler to it. It didn't matter. When she pressed her hands to my bare chest, I felt like vomiting.

Slowly, I reclaimed control. One tattoo at a time, like a snake shedding its skin, I transformed. I pushed myself, casting aside all my weaknesses and rebuilding my atrophied muscles until I once again felt strong. Broken and reassembled, there was nothing left of the man who went into that basement.

But I was never able to let them touch me. Touching was too intimate, too personal, and I didn't want either. I let the part of myself that craved affection wither away in my darkened cell. I gave it to the shadows and bid that vulnerability good riddance.

Then, Trouble came waltzing into our lives.

Day after day, Thea broke down my resolve with small touches of tenderness. I couldn't deny her. It was unbearable, and all I could think of was—*more*.

I pulled her shorts free, tossing them onto the counter. I wanted more of everything, but mostly, I needed the way she made me feel like coming back to life. When we were together, I felt like the man I used to be, and not this machine I'd allowed myself to become.

Running my hand over the goosebumps pebbling her pink skin, Thea arched into my touch. Her eyes pleaded for what she wouldn't allow her lips to ask for. Gripping her thighs, I spread them wide enough to accommodate my shoulders. The muscles of her abdomen flexed as she fought the impulse to squirm.

"Always so impatient," I chided, blowing against her flushed skin. Her stomach sucked in, and her legs tightened against my shoulders like she couldn't decide if she wanted to retreat or hold on. "The best things in life require time."

I'd imagined this countless times: what she would feel like, how she would sound as I pressed into that wet heat, letting her grip me as our bodies rocked together, the cut of her nails against my skin as I made her scream. My fantasies were agonizingly accurate since Crowe had forced us to listen to her coming in his lap mere feet away. As I drew a single finger through the beckoning arousal, Thea threw her head back, biting down on her sweet lips to avoid making a sound.

"So wet for me." I'd barely touched her, and already her body was crying out.

I sank my finger into her, sliding with ease and curling back as each of her muscles fought to keep me in place.

Pushing onto her elbows, she panted, "Nick. I swear if all you're going to do is tease me, then I'm going to scream."

Impatient.

I chuckled, forcing a second finger into her. "No, you won't, Fiore Mio." With my free hand, I pushed her flat while lazily pumping with the other. "You're going to lay there, and the only screams you make will be the silent ones I draw from you." Grinning, I circling her clit with my thumb for emphasis.

Her mouth parted like she couldn't remember what to do. Thea was mine and was always meant to be mine. Fighting it was only tormenting us both.

"We don't need your siren cries luring anyone in here. Right now, your pleasure belongs to me alone." I slid a third finger along the other, rotating and pulling against her inner walls until her expression broke with surrender. She didn't make a sound, holding her breath against the rolling pleasure. "Good girl, but I think we can do better than that."

Thea trembled violently with the effort of holding back, and I loved it.

I loved how her already pink and stained skin flushed scarlet, the way her fingers flexed against the wet tile, and her pelvis warred against my palm to quicken the pace. All for me. Mine.

"*Sei così bella.*"[1]

She closed her eyes, rocking up with her hips in a barely audible whimper. I smoothed my free hand over her breast, feeling the malleable way she bent into each stroke. A parade of possibilities reeled through my mind, imagining all the beautiful ways she could be trussed up. I would teach her the true meaning of want.

Tossing her knee over my shoulder, I drew my nose along the seam of her legs, forcing the quake of her body to intensify. I could almost taste the tangy sweetness, the floral perfume of her arousal begging me to drink deep from her. "You're going to come for me, Fiore Mio, while I tongue this sweet cunt into ecstasy. Then we're going back to our room, and I'm going to do it again. *E ancora, e ancora.*"[2]

Thea mumbled something unintelligible, caught somewhere between speaking and moaning. This undone version of my troublesome flower made me want to devour her. I loved it.

Closing my mouth around her clit, I sucked hard enough I knew it edged on pain. The barest whisper of a cry escaped her, but she locked it down the second it formed. I smiled at the challenge, glancing up at the clock. We had at least another thirty minutes before Nonna returned. How hard could I push her before she forgot who and where she was?

Raking my fingers back, I stroked with slow precision against the spot that I knew was responsible for the way her legs were shaking. Drawing her deliciously swollen clit between my teeth, a breathy stream of curses pushed past her defenses. Thea was almost there. Riding my face, her legs pressed hard against

---

1. You are so beautiful.

2. and again and again.

the shoulders keeping them spread wide, like she could somehow control when and how she detonated. Next time, I would strap her like this, let myself truly have free rein without having to spend half my energy restraining her.

Gazing up at Thea from between her thighs, I clamped my hand over her mouth. Thanks to my brothers, I knew exactly how loud this little ball of trouble could be. Any minute, the entire house would know exactly what was happening here. Her eyes went wide, thin circles of sea green eclipsed by black pupils. Sweat clung to her chest and brow, glistening like diamonds in the morning sun. Despite the way she fought against my hold, I easily kept her in place, feasting until she shattered in a way I'd only dreamt of.

She was perfection.

"*Splendida.*"[3]

I lowered my hand from her lips, resting it over her racing heart. Its quickened beat flushed her cheeks with a rosy hue, splashing down her neck all the way to her still-heaving breasts. *Miseriaccia*,[4] I loved the feel of it, knowing that I'd made her bloom so marvelously. Every moan, every fractured breath, they were all mine.

Climbing up her body, I lifted her lips to mine with a swift pull. There was no time to adjust or think. I wanted to consume her, swallow her down until there was nothing left.

Ignoring my earlier command, Thea raked her nails down my back, leaving a trail of shivers unlike anything I'd felt in a long time. The bliss was so intense it burned. I groaned her name into her mouth. Nothing felt like her hands on me, not the slice of a knife or the pierce of a needle.

I needed more; that word cycled on repeat. More. More. More. A cadence that kept time with my pounding heart. The obsession with how she felt beneath me rose to a crescendo until I was certain I would explode if I wasn't inside her.

---

3. Wonderful.

4. Bloody hell,

Not pausing to consider where we were or the ramifications to my soul if I fucked her here, in the middle of the kitchen, surrounded by gallons of salsa. I pushed my pants down as Thea's legs wrapped around my hips, inviting me in. The head of my cock settled against her entrance, the wetness coating my length as she eagerly rocked. Fighting the need to slam into her, I slowly thrust forward. My soul left my body, shredding into ribbons as each rung of my ladder sank into her unrelenting heat.

Every prayer I'd ever heard fell from my lips, followed by an equally long string of Italian curses. Her body clutched around me, tightening into a blissful vice. Thea's nails cut deep, her heels pressing into my ass as she rolled her muscles upward in a demand to continue, but I couldn't. I was paralyzed, lost in her. Like falling into quicksand, I was sure I would never emerge again.

"Please," she whispered, fighting against my weight pinning her to the floor. It pulled at the piercings studding my shaft, rolling the bars and making a bolt of lightning streak down my spine. Not moving was almost as much torture as refusing to touch her had been. It amplified every sensation.

"Danny was right. You do beg *so prettily*."

Threading her fingers into my hair, she tugged until my vision lifted from her lips to her sea-green eyes. "Nick, Angel, fuck me."

I blinked, looking down at her. "Did you just call me Angel?" I certainly wasn't imagining doing anything angelic to her right now.

"I've always thought of you as my dark angel of death. All you need is the scythe. I want to feel what it is to be at your mercy. Put me beneath your blade and take all you can."

I bent to kiss her pulse, drawing almost completely back. "This spot right here." My lips grazed the fluttering beneath her skin that had tormented me for weeks. I was rewarded with a whimpered exhale. Her entire body shook with anticipation. "I think it's my favorite. You've always responded beautifully when I'm near, but watching your pulse race is my favorite."

"Nick, I—" Her voice caught as I slammed home. "Fuck." I repeated the action, harder this time. "Those piercings are fucking magical."

"Not as magical as the way you take them." Hiking her leg up so I could press deeper, I drove hard enough to rattle the empty bottles on the table. Several tipped, rolling over the edge and plummeting to the ground. Glass exploded around us like fireworks as we collided over and over again.

Using my body to shield her from the broken glass, I pushed myself upright. With her leg still hoisted over my arm, Thea spread wide, giving me a vantage point like none other. "No. I was wrong."

"Wrong?"

"This..." My thumb rolled over her clit, making her muscles clench. My fingers pressed against her abdomen, feeling the glide of my cock as I thrust into her. The studded length disappeared, her pussy greedily claiming every inch. Thea arched into my touch. "This is my favorite."

With every change in position, her expression became more euphoric until she was nearly purring. I'd driven cars that weren't as responsive. It was fucking addicting. It made me want to explore every position my twisted mind could imagine if only to watch how beautifully her body obeyed.

"Next time, it'll be your ass, and I won't stop pounding you until your screams turn your voice ragged." On a barely restrained moan, she flexed around me, growing impossibly tighter. The heat of her body seared me at every point of contact. "You like the sound of that, don't you, Trouble? *Vediamo se riuscirai a camminare quando avrò finito con te.*"[5]

Thea's expression tightened, hovering on the verge of release. Her hands rested on my stomach like brands. I wanted to be branded, marked by her, so that the entire world knew I was hers.

I barely managed to clamp my hand over her mouth before she was detonating around me. All that heat and pressure was like standing at the center of a star while it went supernova. As much as I wanted to draw it out and send her back into another climax, it was too much. I'd been denying myself for so long that there was no holding back now. With two more punishing thrusts, I came hard enough my spine felt like it was splitting in two. Heat speared through my

---

5. We'll see if you'll be able to walk once I'm done with you.

body, lancing from the soles of my feet to the tips of the fingers pressing into her cheeks.

Not wanting to relinquish an ounce of what she'd given me, I sank down, shifting my grip to cradle her face. I drew her into me, savoring the taste and feel of her sated body beneath mine.

It was as close to a perfect moment as I'd ever known.

Thea always moved with me, folding into my embrace like she was always destined to be there. Maybe she was what I'd been chasing all these years, thinking the shadows would cloak me when all I needed was to bathe in her light.

It was time I did just that.

Taking a deep breath against her lips, I rolled us so that I was on my back. A tinge of something sharp scraped against my shoulder, the burn feeling oddly appropriate for all I was about to confess.

—20—
NICK

T hea tried to sit up, but I flattened my hand on her back in a silent command to stay still.

"When I was eighteen, a girl arrived in Oz from back home. She showed up on my father's doorstep in the middle of the night." I closed my eyes, remembering perfectly the way the rain poured through the lights on the walk, plastering her raven hair to her cheeks—how it was impossible to discern the tears from the rain. I'd never dared to care for anyone other than Crowe and Nonna, but she was so fragile, like a china doll.

I hadn't allowed myself to think of her in years.

"When my father left Italy, he crossed a lot of people. He didn't just burn bridges. He razed villages."

Thea's hands traced the lines of the tattoo stretching across my right pec. It was the branches of an olive tree, but not a full one with green leaves. This branch was gnarled and burnt to charcoal.

"Caterina..." Her name caught in my throat. How long had it been since I'd said it? It hurt more than I was prepared for. "She ran away after she'd been assaulted by her betrothed, the future heir to what my father left behind. Enzo DiMedia was an asshole who thought all she needed to assume her position was to be shown what it would be."

Thea's body went tight, meeting my eyes with a roll. "That after he'd forced himself upon her, she'd accept her situation for what it was. I know the type."

I dipped my chin to her brow, using the palm on the back of her head to redirect her to my shoulder. This confession was hard enough without adding the weight of her gaze to it. There was an honesty in her eyes that was raw, and it stripped me to the bone.

After staring for several long moments at the heavy ceiling rafters and centuries-old stones, I continued, "My father didn't trust her, but in a rare show of defiance, I refused to let him shoot her. So, he gave Cat to me, said that he always knew I'd never do better than another man's trash—that at least this way he'd get a grandson who might one day live up to the Ciopriani legacy. To him, saving Caterina was just another in a long line of disappointments, and Cat, she went from being promised to one heir, to being in debt to another."

I could feel the muscles of Thea's neck flex as she swallowed. She was being uncharacteristically quiet.

"Despite the circumstances, over the next year, we grew closer than I've ever allowed myself to get to a person."

"You loved her." It wasn't a question, more of an affirmation.

"I think, I thought that I loved her. I know now she never loved me. She was looking for something she could take as her own, and I was stupid enough to give it to her." I sank my fingers into the hair at Thea's nape, watching the strands grow bright red in the light streaming through the window. Seeing them match the sauce staining my fingers was oddly comforting. "When Enzo discovered that Cat had left him for the son of the man that had ruined his father, he gathered the old families, and they hired Eastin Witcher to even the scales."

Thea involuntarily recoiled at the sound of that witch's name, only held in place by the wrap of my arms. I understood the impulse. It was the same reaction that made my hand curl into a fist along her scarred spine.

"Eastin offered Caterina the autonomy she craved in exchange for me. She set Cat up in her territory, carving out a tiny kingdom where she didn't have to be under anyone's control ever again. I followed her blindly right into Eastin's trap, and she never showed an ounce of remorse. Eastin placed the hammer in her hands. I think more than any of the physical pain she inflicted on me, what Eastin delighted in most was corrupting someone who looked so sweet."

"When you say hammer?" Thea pushed against my chest, leaning up on her elbows to peer down at me.

I closed my eyes, unable to forget the way Cat's gleamed with power as she dropped the mallet.

"Caterina broke my heart and my leg with a single swipe."

Thea's face twisted into one of abject horror, but now that I was telling it, I couldn't stop.

"They took turns. Breaking each bone, one at a time. The louder I screamed, the harder they went. It took 37 surgeries to set my skeleton back into the semblance of a man. Several bones were shattered so completely that titanium implants are all that hold them together, a few of the joints had to be entirely replaced." I tried to laugh it off but couldn't bring myself to do more than huff. "I'm more metal than flesh."

I flexed my hand, feeling the weight of the pins holding the bones in place. Thea's eyes fell on the tattoo inked over my fingers. Her lips mouthed their message. *Never Again*. But I knew in my soul that those words were a lie because I'd follow this woman into the fires of hell.

"The day I went missing, Enzo sent my father a letter. He made sure that Salvatore Ciopriani understood that all of my suffering on the way to a very long death was by his own hand...maybe not directly, but by his action. My pain was the price demanded by the old families in retribution for my father's betrayal."

A tremor vibrated within Thea; it was slight, but I recognized the barely controlled rage. Now she knew why I didn't trust the man who raised me.

"Over the months of my captivity, she'd send videos to my father. I know because she'd always make me say hello, even when she wired my jaw shut so I couldn't scream."

Thea's hand sprang up to cover her reaction, but she was unable to hide the way her eyes sparkled with the tears building in them. I cupped her cheek. There was a macabre beauty to her shock.

"He assessed that I was an acceptable loss in exchange for the kingdom he'd created for himself."

"Why can't we kill him?" Thea pushed away a tear at the corner of her eye with the heel of her hand. Blood rushed to her cheeks, making her eyes look greener. I traced the lines of her face, wishing that I could remove the hardness in them. I didn't deserve her rage.

I blew out a hard breath. "I've been asking myself that question since we arrived." Despite all he'd done to me over the years, I'd never truly considered patricide until I'd seen how he'd looked at Thea.

"Danny and Crowe eventually figured out a way to free me. When I was well enough to stand before my father, I told him I was out. We were out. On that day, I vowed that I would never again trust or love another." I tipped her chin up, my lips ghosting over hers. "Until you."

The truth of my statement grew, and with it, I pulled her into me, kissing her like she was the beginning and end of everything. A new person formed beneath her with each press of our lips until, more than any metal pin, it felt like the only thing holding me together was her.

Thea pulled away with a long exhale. Her hands coasted down my arms, slowing along each curve like she was memorizing the map of scars. Drawing one finger through the sauce streaking my chest, she drew a heart over where the organ beneath thumped, happily sated. The tingling sensation of her fingers swelled, spreading out from the center and enveloping me in a blanket of warmth.

She swiped her hand through the tomato massacre on the ground, wiggling her fingers with a tiny hello. Salsa gleamed on their surface. It made my heart skip with a weird pang of possession. Her lower lip pinned mischievously between her teeth, Thea slapped her handprint directly over the drawn heart.

"Just so there's no confusion, this is me officially calling dibs. You're mine, Angel."

If it wasn't for the slow rhythm beating in my chest, I'd have thought I was having a heart attack. I took her hand, placing a kiss in the center of her palm. She blinked, a crooked smile breaking across her face and setting her features alight. A riot of emotion all quieted with that smile, focusing themselves into one devastating thought. I loved this girl.

"What about the others?"

Thea looked down, tracing tiny patterns in the paste coating the ground. "They're mine too. You're *all* mine." When her eyes lifted again, I knew I could never deny her. She could ask for the entire world right now, and I'd be figuring out how to gift-wrap it. "I can't explain it. But I think being loaded on that truck might be the best thing that ever happened to me."

Panic and worry, unlike any I'd known, caught back up to me. My father's warnings were still too fresh in my mind, eclipsed only by images of her beautiful face flashing on the screen with a price attached. Thea was a prize that so many wanted. We were in The Villa, under the same roof as the most cutthroat and opportunistic members in Oz's underworld. The only thing keeping her safe was the thin promise of a corrupt old man. How long could that really last? Thea was worth more than most men saw in a lifetime, and I'd brought her straight into the viper's den...and then stopped to fuck her on the kitchen floor.

It was reckless and impulsive, two things I never was. Crowe, maybe. He was the spontaneous one. He'd follow his dick into a vat of acid, declaring he'd discovered a new kink. But not me. I was methodical, reserved, calculated. I picked a thing I wanted to destroy and applied pressure until it shattered. Maybe that was what I'd been doing all along. It just turned out that it wasn't her that shattered, but me.

I scanned the room, spotting the cameras in the corner. Fuck, we'd probably just given the security team a solid show. Now, I'd need to track them all down and erase the feeds.

Following my gaze around the room, Thea laughed, "The kitchen is wrecked."

I pulled her to her feet, carefully avoiding the strewn bits of broken jars. Tomato puree and juice covered nearly every surface. Somehow even the ones we'd never touched were spattered with streaks of red, transforming the warm kitchen into a murder scene. There was no saving the salsa. I could already feel the sting of Nonna's spoon. She'd beat me black and blue for ruining it, but fuck, it had been worth it. I'd take a hundred beatings for her. On cue, Nonna's angry shouts carried over the sound of the T.V..

"We need to get out of here."

"What about the mess? We can't leave this for Nonna to deal with."

"Did you want her to see you like this? Thea, you don't even have underwear on."

"And whose fault is that?" Hands on her beautifully naked hips, she cocked her head at me expectantly. Her stance pushed her chest up, causing her nipples to rake against me. "Fucking hell, Trouble. Keep thrusting your tits in my face, and the only thing anyone is going to see is your body spread on that counter while I fuck them."

Thea's indignant expression flickered, her jaw dropping open and her bottom lip drawing me to her like a damn beacon. I gripped her chin and gently closed her mouth, letting my thumb linger on that all too enticing pout.

I snatched my shirt from the ground, draping the sauce-stained fabric around her shoulders before my apparently missing restraint completely vaporized. "I'll send the cleaning staff up to deal with the mess. Nonna will be madder than a hornet, but I'll figure out a way to make it up to her."

Thea slipped her arms into the sleeves, giving them an adorable flap. I'd thoroughly destroyed hers, and there was no saving the shorts either. Luckily, my shirt was practically a dress on her, hitting just below her upper thighs. Fuck, even filthy, seeing her in my shirt was a sight. I ran a hand down her arm, feeling her petite frame beneath the familiar cotton. Crowe was on to something dressing her all those days in his clothing. Maybe once she was clean again, I'd throw her back in another one. It tugged on some primal part of me that liked staking a claim on her.

Thea wrapped her arms around my middle, going up on tiptoes to press a soft kiss to my lips. I folded my arms around her. She was so small. Thea's presence always seemed larger than life, but in moments like these, I was reminded of how flower like she really was—It was terrifying, knowing just how many people wanted to crush her.

Tightening my grip, I whispered into her ear. "Let's go back to our room and clean up. Then I want to fuck you nice and slow against the shower wall."

Thea shivered, her smile stretching from where her lips were pressed to my chest. A dull buzzing sound filtered through the sounds of Nonna's television and the radio strumming Italian melodies on the counter.

"Do you hear that?" Thea tilted her head to the side. "It sounds like bees? Thousands of bees."

-21-
NICK

Slowly, the colors of the flower fields were blotted out as hundreds of flying drones hovered outside of the Villa. The whirring of blades drowned the noises of alarm.

Thea slowly took two steps back, her voice quivering with trepidation, "Nick, tell me those are some kind of weird harvesting robot bug."

In eerie unison, all of the drones rotated. Their shimmering liquid black surfaces catching the midday sun.

"Nick?"

Tiny barrels mounted to the underside of each bug rotated until every single one pointed at the row of windows we were currently watching from.

I threw Thea to the ground, plaster exploding around us. I wrapped my arms around us, covering as much of her body with mine as I could. Shards of wood sliced from the sills and chunks of masonry rained down on us, pelting my back.

"Are you okay? Are you hurt?" I pushed the hair from her face, inspecting her for signs of pain.

A room over, an explosion rocked the walls, making their plaster and tile surfaces sway. A second and third immediately followed, each sounding closer than the last.

"What the fuck was that?" Thea pushed off the ground, looking in the direction of noise—towards where we both knew Nonna was watching her Telenovelas.

Time slowed, the details of the room coming into hyper-focus. Dust drifted through the sunlight streaming through the hundreds of tiny holes peppering the outer wall. It landed on her lashes like snow. A small blinking ball arced through the window, landing on the counter beside the small radio. The heavy tones of a rock song strummed, the energy of the music fitting perfectly with the chaos erupting around us.

Only one word managed to slip past my lips before time sped back up, "Bomb."

I pushed her under the heavy wooden table, hoping that it would shield the worst of the blast. Sliding in beside her, light and a flare of heat flooded the room. The concussive force shook my vision at the edges. Blistering pain burned across the exposed flesh of my back. I didn't care that I'd taken the brunt of the explosion because Thea was still breathing beside me.

Beams from the ceiling and tiles piled on top of the table, blocking out our view of the kitchen and the chaos raining down.

Clearing the dust from my eyes, I ran my hands down Thea, inspecting her from head to toe and back up again. There were no wounds other than a few small scratches. She blinked at me in confusion, mouthing words I couldn't hear over the ringing filling my ears. I gripped her cheeks, pulling her lips to mine before cradling her to my chest.

A fine tremor shook beneath her skin from the adrenaline flooding her system, her eyes bright with concern. Through the cracks in the rubble, the warm light of a fire flickered, casting deep shadows over the contours of her face.

Fire. Had the explosion broken the gas line? How long did we have before we were blown apart? I had to get Thea out of here.

A thick wooden beam appeared to be supporting the majority of the wreckage. Using my feet to leverage against the ground, I pushed against it. Thea prodded the bigger pieces pinned beside. Stones tumbled into the space, sending a fresh wave of dust clogging the air. Thea coughed, waving her hand in front of her. I pushed again, and something shifted overhead, landing above us with a loud thud. The wood of the table groaned in protest.

Like hearing underwater, Thea yelled, "Stop! Stop!" I froze, following the finger pointed above us. A crack snaked down the wooden plank of the table, splitting at the seams like the hand of god was tearing the wood apart.

Thea reached up, gently poking at the jagged points of wood that jutted straight at us like spikes in a pit.

"*Cazzo!*" Blood rushed in my veins, the anger and frustration boiling over. The look of desperation on Thea's face as she realized we were trapped in this confined space wasn't helping.

I cupped the back of her neck, bringing her forehead to mine. "Just breathe, Fiore Mio. I'll get us out of here."

She nodded, but I could feel her trembling like a scared rabbit. It fucking gutted me. The peppered sound of machine guns rattled in the distance, becoming louder and louder as my hearing returned.

Thea pulled away, shifting abruptly at the space against the ground where her gaze had just been focused. Her voice was still muffled at first, but towards the end I could make out the words, "—might work."

I pulled at my ear, trying to will the rest of my hearing to return. "What might work?" I tried to keep my voice low, but with my hearing shot, it was impossible to know. The last thing we needed was for the wrong people to realize we were pinned under here.

Thea dropped to her belly, sticking her tongue between her teeth while she scooped away the smaller debris. Light and fresh air streamed around a large stone. Of course, my father couldn't have just built a normal pre-fabbed home made from pine and sheetrock. No, this one had to be made from old ass masonry and hardwood beams. Five hundred years of rubble pinned us in place while we sat here surrounded by the rattle of machine guns and the flicker of a fire, which may or may not ignite the gas lines.

"This stone doesn't feel like it's supporting anything. If we shift it towards us, I might be able to shimmy around it. Then I can find something to leverage the bigger debris to the side, and you can get out, or maybe I can find the guys to help."

"No." There was no fucking way I was sending her out there alone. Anything could be waiting beyond these walls.

"What do you mean, no?" She pushed against my shoulders, sending my back into the beam. I hissed when the blistered flesh of my back rubbed against the wood. Not caring at my cringe of pain, she continued, "We don't exactly have a menu of options to choose from. Furthermore, you don't—"

Boots crunched nearby, a small sprinkle of dust drifting down with the vibration. I gripped Thea tightly, plastering her body to mine and wrapping a hand around her mouth, silencing her. She wiggled, reflexively fighting me without waiting to find out why I was muting her.

A voice from the speaker box of a walkie-talkie crackled, *"Last report had her in the kitchen. She's there somewhere. Do I need to come down there and find her for you? If the Rosen girl is still alive, she couldn't have gone far."*

Thea's heartbeat thundered beneath my forearm, making me all too aware of what I held in my arms. The exchange of gunfire echoed outside, creating the terrifying symphony of a war zone. I couldn't help but wonder if that was the sound of my brothers making their way here, but then, they'd have no idea we were here, unlike our new friends who knew exactly where to find Thea.

The light streaming into our tiny sanctuary blocked out, casting us in near darkness. The deep voice of the man said, "Roger that, you arrogant prick." He moved around the space, pushing aside timbers and stones as he went. He tapped on the tile, barely feet from us. "Knock-knock. I know you're in here, little bird."

The smooth way he called to her tugged on all of my instincts. If I was in the room, I'd have already stabbed this fucker in the throat. Worse, I was pretty sure I recognized the voice, and I really hoped that I was wrong. If King Avian was coming for Thea, then we had much bigger problems than being pinned beneath a table.

My hand pressed harder against Thea's mouth like I could somehow hide her through sheer will alone. Somewhere in the distance a woman screamed, her cries for mercy instantly silenced with the bang of a gun. *Fuck. Fuck. Fuck.*

"I have a pretty cage to put you in." The tinny sound of metal crashed against a wall, causing Thea to flinch. I guessed it was the old tomato press being tossed aside, meaning the man wasn't more than a few feet from where we hid.

"Just after we hear how prettily you can sing." A hand curled around the edges of the beam concealing us, a silver signet ring showing a crow with an arrow in its heart glinted in the firelight. He tugged on the heavy wood with a grunt. Above us, the table cracked further, bowing down in the center.

The loud thump of several pairs of boots moved into the space. "Yo, King. You find her?"

We were fucked!

The ringed fingers retreated. King took several steps away, clapping the dust from his hands. "Nah, there's nothing here. Barret must have his intel wrong."

"What about all that blood?" One of the men scrambled over the wreckage, presumably climbing over the outer wall.

"It's not blood." King kicked a broken jar as he walked, glass crunching beneath his feet. "It's sauce. Look at all these broken bottles. The Stingers must have strafed them in the initial attack."

"What'd you find that way?" King grunted as he climbed over the wall, the sounds of their discussion moving further away. The tension in my body relaxed with every step they took.

"No one, just the old woman."

Old woman...My heart lurched into the back of my throat. Nonna. I felt like I couldn't breathe, choking on the memory of the cloud of smoke rolling through the doorway to her apartment as a succession of explosions rocked the walls. She wouldn't have heard the sounds of the coming attack. Watching her shows, she'd have been in her rocker yelling at the T.V., not ducking for cover. My heart felt like it was bleeding out.

"Alive?" King asked, saying the question burning in my mind.

"Mostly. We questioned her, but the old bird only spoke that stupid language. She didn't have any clue what was going on."

When finally, I couldn't hear their conversation, I eased my grip on Thea. She looked up at me with wide, terrified eyes.

179

"Nonna, we have to get to her." She dropped to the ground, and I pulled her back. "What if she's dying? I'm crawling out of here, Nick. You can't stop me."

"Like hell I can't," I hissed at her. "They won't be the only search team, Thea. I'm not sending you out there without me."

I threw my shoulder into the beam with as much force as I could muster. The table dipped lower, groaning in protest. I did it again, sure that if I just pushed hard enough, the thing would give way, and we could escape together.

The smooth palm of her hand rounded along my bicep, the oversized sleeve of my shirt bunching at her elbow. I followed the line of that connection, up the slope of her neck to meet with remarkable confidence.

Thea climbed into my lap, pulling my mouth to hers. The brush of her lips was brief, but the emotion pouring into me felt like a tidal wave. I couldn't lose her.

"I can do this, Angel. You have to trust me."

Two months ago, I was sure that my heart was gone, torn from me as so many parts had been over the years. I realized now that it was never gone. It had been safeguarded all this time by her, just waiting for the moment when it found its way back to me.

I lowered my head to her shoulder, circling my arms around her waist as tightly as I could. Beneath the ash and tomatoes, her uniquely feminine scent was there. I didn't think I could live without smelling this every day. "Be quick."

"I'll be right back."

I pressed a kiss to her temple, hoping that this moment wouldn't haunt me for the rest of my life.

She pulled on the stone, shifting it back and forth until the hole widened enough for her to fit. We listened for several long minutes. The noise beyond the house had lessened, and the immediate area fell silent.

"Go now. Before I change my mind."

With a quick kiss, she dropped to the ground, shimming her torso into the tight space. She barely fit, made tighter by her rapid panting. I knew she hated small spaces, and being pinned like this was probably her worst nightmare.

Thea rotated, bending her waist around the stone and clawing at the ground to pull herself free. Her hips snagged on the edge of a diagonal bar that was wedged between the beam and another jumble of stones. The rubble shifted beneath the bar, and all at once the entire structure shifted. The beam descended, cracking the table in two with a loud thud. I forced my shoulder beneath the beam, gritting my teeth against the weight. "Go Thea. Now."

She scrabbled, slipping her feet free just as the heavy wood and everything crashed to the ground.

Pain tore up my side. I pushed at the stones that settled against my cheeks. Thea stood over me. Free. I sighed with relief. She wasn't hurt.

"Nick." A sob tore from her throat. She dropped to her knees.

"That could have gone better," I mumbled, choking on the dust floating in the air. I looked over my shoulder at where the beam lay on the ground. "At least we're out now."

Her hands fought the remnants of the table pinning me to the ground, throwing them aside. Blood dripped from a jagged point of wood. I blinked at it, taking several long seconds to comprehend what I was seeing.

A spear of wood pierced through my abdomen, coming out the other side. As if my brain hadn't registered that something was wrong until I saw it, pain lanced down my limbs, rolling in waves of lava from the center of the wound. "That's concerning."

I tried to move, but my leg was pinned beneath another chunk of masonry. I wiggled my toes, breathing a sigh when they responded, and the pain along my ankle was only minimal. At least it wasn't broken. The blood pooling beneath me, on the other hand...That was a lot of blood.

"Concerning! Concerning?" Thea slapped my shoulder, and I groaned. "You look like a human kabob."

"Thea, look at me." Supporting myself as best I could, I pulled her down. The new position hurt like a bitch, but I breathed through it. "You have to go."

"Nick, you're going to bleed out. I can't just...there has to be something..." She spun, looking for anything to staunch the blood.

"Stay low and in the shadows," I continued. "Find Crowe or Danny, and then get as far away from here as you can."

"I'm not—" she shrieked, then realizing her mistake, slapped her hands over her mouth. "I'm not fucking leaving you."

"Thea, look at me. I'm not going anywhere."

"No." Tears streamed down her face. She shook her head vehemently. "No. I won't."

"There are too many people looking for you. There's too high of a risk. I'm not going to...*fuck*...You have to leave, Fiore Mio."

"No. No. No." The fight left her as she whispered it over and over. "I can't. I love you. I can't leave you here to die."

"I wish I deserved your love." I breathed her in one last time. "Please, Thea." I lifted my hand to her cheeks, smearing blood across her skin. My fingers tingled with the blood loss, and a wave of chills snaked down my limbs. Oddly, the pain didn't even feel that bad anymore, dulling to a warm burn.

Thea pressed her lips to mine, the salt of her tears mixing with the copper of blood.

"*Ti amo, Fiore Mio.*" [1] Her beautiful face swam in my vision. "I love you." The tears streaming down her cheeks were the last thing I saw before the world spun into black.

---

1. I love you.

-22-
CROWE

The husk of what was once Ciopriani Villa spewed black smoke, blotting out the blue sky. Danny held my arms, keeping me from running straight into the carnage. I knew in my gut that Thea was in that building. I couldn't get the image of her broken body out of my head...or pinned beneath rubble and burning alive...or gunned down by a fleet of bees. What I wouldn't give to wrap my hands around an EMP bomb right about now.

Our movement was slow, needing to cut through hoards of drones to make it to the other side of the Villa. My heart plummeted to the ground when there was zero sign of Nick or Thea in the south wing. In fact, it hadn't looked like they'd ever returned. Their room was still pristinely clean, not at all like Cyclone Thea had been there. I half expected to arrive at their room and see the two of them wrapped around each other. Despite the feigned indifference, I'd heard the telltale sound of Thea's cries the night before. I'd recognize them anywhere. I knew it was only a matter of time before the two of them worked through their respective damage.

If they hadn't made it back here, then the only other option was the main building. Hours had passed since Nick took Thea for breakfast. I didn't know what could have kept them there for all this time, but it couldn't have been good.

We took the long way around the buildings, carefully approaching the main building from the fields and getting a front-row seat to it being blown to pieces. Fire raged in multiple areas of the building, while others looked completely demolished. Having done their damage, the fleet of drones took to the sky, buzzing towards the horizon. In their place, a small army crept silently over the grounds.

"Because killer robot bees weren't bad enough," Danny muttered.

The men were clad in black from head to toe and highly armed. There was nothing amateur about this team. Each held a semi-automatic rifle, with dual pistols on their hips, and a utility strap crossed their torsos with what looked like a candy store's worth of treats and surprises.

Danny zoomed in his scope and groaned. "Precision grenades, tasers, and...fuck me, are those Tranqs?"

"They aren't lollipops." I rubbed at my neck, where I could still feel the dart piercing it. Tranqs meant this was the retrieval team. Fucking Marcello. If I could, I would shoot him again.

"Oz damn it all to hell. How many different ways can we be fucked in one day?" Danny handed me the scope, slapping it into my chest with more force than necessary. "Since when do the Monkeys and the Crows work together? This seriously couldn't get worse."

I peered through the lens, adjusting the dial until they came clearly into view. "It gets worse."

"How can it possibly get worse?"

"See that blue light on the side of the rifle. They're using an electronic trigger, probably with a target-tracking system too. They wouldn't even need to seriously aim, and every single shot would be a bullseye." It was new tech, that I'd only read about. With the advent of AI, came the bright idea to put it in a targeting system. Official military channels had ruled it out as being too risky, but here, among the dregs of society, they had no qualms about handing over targeting to a computer.

Like watching birds in flight, the teams split off in well-coordinated patterns. Leading the flock was a man with a cropped mohawk of black curls. He was built like an ox, probably needing to special order that Kevlar. A large blackbird with an arrow lodged in its heart was sewn into his sleeve. The Dead Crows.

"King-fucking-Avian." Even saying his name felt wrong.

"Fuck off, he did not come out for this." Danny held out his hand, and I dropped the scope back into his palm. "I thought he retired after that hospital job in the Southern Quadrant last year. They still haven't found Sorren Singrala."

I nodded, feeling a chill creep down my spine. Sorren Singrala was the former, and now missing, leader of the Southern Quadrant. The running story was that Sorren left on a tour outside of Oz, but there had been lots of speculation that King's team had been the ones responsible for the demolition of the hospital where Sorren received her dialysis treatments. Of course, they'd never been able to corroborate any of it.

King redefined special ops. He and his team were more than elite. If you wanted to topple an empire, these were the guys you called in to be your triggermen. We'd crossed paths a few times, always when we were going after the same prize. He'd bested me *every* time. King's idea of playing in the game was to clear the board; total annihilation of his enemies. The only reason I'd walked away from our fights was because I was never his target. If he was after Thea...

I couldn't even finish that thought.

Within minutes, a woman and a man were dragged outdoors. I recognized the man, Sal's youngest brother. He was bargaining his entire fortune while the woman kneeled praying to a god that was not listening. Sinners like us didn't get saved. If Ozma had ever been watching, she'd turned away from this place long ago.

The soldier standing beside King drew his pistol and walked around the back of the woman. With a gun to the back of her head, he didn't hesitate to pull the trigger. Methodically, he moved to the man and repeated the action. We watched as two more members were dragged and executed with zero remorse.

"I swear he just mouthed, 'It's not her.'" Danny pocketed his scope and checked the rounds in the pistol he'd taken from Sal's goons.

"If I don't make it through tonight, then I'm chasing Marcello down in hell and tearing him to pieces. I killed him too quickly. Fucking Dead Crows *and*

Monkeys. You know, I still owe that bird mother-fucker for shooting me in the leg...and the knife in my shoulder."

"Stop whining. We need to find Thea before he does."

We needed to do a lot more than that, and if one stupid merc happened to take a bullet in the face while we were at it, well, then who was I to complain?

"Let's go. We can swing around the other side and come up behind them."

The door to the small apartment opened on rusty hinges, smoke billowing in a steady stream through the blown-out windows. Somewhere further inside, a television was still playing, the prerecorded laugh track feeling surreal among the broken walls and missing roof. Danny stepped through the doorway, clearing the room before taking up a position to clear the next.

Stone and tile crunched beneath my steps no matter how lightly I tried to tread. In the next room, the television was on its side, the screen flickering and cracked in a spiderweb. Only the sound seemed to be intact, the quick Italian staccato relaying the drama of a telenovela.

I spun, looking at the walls. Several yellowed pictures showing a young couple were framed along with several more children, the last of me and Nick when we weren't much older than 10. Fucking hell. We entered through Nonna Lucia's apartment. She was the only person who still truly cared about family in this god-forsaken place. They must have moved her from the Eastern Wing, where Salvatore lived, to this small apartment attached to the kitchen. Shit, she'd probably requested being closer to the main kitchen.

Was she here? Please, Ozma if you were ever listening, make the old woman be at the market. How could Marcello have let this happen? She was his grandmother, too. Everyone loved Nonna. Surely, he'd have sent her away. Or maybe he would have...except he'd spent the morning under my knife.

Dread sank deep, landing in my gut.

There was a soft moan coming from the enclosed portico. We followed the sound. Bloody handprints stained the door jamb like whoever had come this way had struggled to keep themselves upright.

Danny pulled the door open. The body on the ground was like having a knife thrust straight into my chest and twisted. Collapsed in the middle of the sunroom was Nonna Lucia, her body looking frailer than ever. She was so tiny, the massive pool of blood making her look like a haloed saint. I tucked the gun back in my waistband and dropped to my knees beside her, the fabric of my jeans instantly soaking through.

The blood was warm, giving me a tiny bit of hope. She'd only just fallen, her injuries recent enough that the blood hadn't cooled yet. I rolled her gently onto her back. Nonna moaned again, her eyelids fluttering open.

When she spoke, her teeth were stained red, her voice sputtering small drops of blood onto her cheeks. "Vincenzo." She smiled with recognition, lifting a crimson hand to my cheek as she'd done so many times during my youth. "*Mi sei mancato, amore di nonna.*"[1]

"Ciao, Nonna." I blinked back the tears clouding my eyes.

A large gash tore apart her stomach, another bruising her brow, and an unmistakable gunshot wound pierced her chest. Black blood stained her blue flower-printed dress. Hot rage replaced my tears. King, or one of his fucking flock, had done this to her. They'd shot a defenseless and wounded old woman, then left her for dead.

King would suffer for this.

I pressed my hand to the wound, but she had more holes in her than a cheese grater. I should have come to her sooner, but I was so preoccupied with figuring

---

1. I missed you, my love.

out a way to get to Westin that I hadn't even made the attempt. The sourness of regret coated my tongue like the ash floating in the air.

"It's okay, Topolino." She tapped a weak hand over mine. This tiny woman was the first person to ever love me, truly and with no conditions. I knew she was the only reason Salvatore hadn't sent me to a workhouse. Never mind what he said about my sister. I'd never forget the day Nonna put Sal in his place, demanding that he take me in.

Danny knelt on one knee beside me, reminding me that I had the fraternity that he, Nick, and I forged. He reached forward, wrapping her other hand in his. Nonna loved with her whole heart, bringing everyone in like they were family, Danny included. She would love Thea. Fuck, she'd probably insist Nick marry her and begin planning the nursery the second they met.

There were several loud bangs as the adjoining door was forced open. A broken lamp tipped sideways from where it was precariously balanced, landing on the flooring with a loud crash.

We pulled our guns, ready to take out whichever of King's men had decided to return and finish the job they'd started. Then, all at once, my heart came tumbling through the doorway, looking like a phantom in the night despite the daylight streaming through the dust.

Danny was already moving, pulling her into a tight embrace before I could process everything I was seeing. She was coated in red from top to bottom. The large black shirt wrapped around her looked nearly gray from all the dirt clinging to it. She coughed against the cloud pluming up from where the lamp landed.

"Go," Nonna said, giving me a gentle tap on the shoulder. I looked between Lucia and Thea. "Go to her. Leave an old woman to die in peace." She tried to laugh, as though the idea of dying was the funniest thought she'd had all day.

I didn't have to choose. The second Thea saw Nonna Lucia, she dropped to the ground beside us. "No. No. No. No. Not you, too." Fresh tears spilled down the tracks already drawn across her cheeks. Streaks of pale skin were cleaned of the dirt and blood coating her skin like she'd been crying long before pushing through that doorway. Thea was covered in blood, and yet she didn't look injured at all. Her knees were stained darker than the rest of her legs...from kneeling in blood. It dripped from her shirt, and a dark handprint was visible against her neck.

My stomach bottomed out, looking from her to the doorway she'd just pushed through.

"Thea Darling, where's Nick?"

Her hazel eyes lifted to mine; they were bloodshot and puffy, making them look electric. She shook her head, trying several times to speak. Even wrapped in Danny's arms, her whole body was trembling. "He... there was a bomb, the ceiling fell, and he saved me... He... Crowe...I tried, but it was too heavy, and there was so much blood."

"Fuck." I rose to my feet, looking between the doorway, the love of my life, and the tattered remains of my family. How did you pick who to save when everyone needed saving? My heart beat so hard that tiny flecks of light peppered my vision.

"Is he dead?" Danny asked. The lines of his jaw hardened with dread.

"Yes. Maybe. *I don't know.*" Her voice shook. "He went limp, and I ran for help."

I was vaguely aware that they were talking. I could hear them but couldn't take in what they were saying.

"Crowe." Danny gripped my shoulders, giving them a little shake. "Crowe," he repeated louder and firmer until my vision came back in focus. "He still might be alive."

I nodded. "Take Thea to that helicopter. If I'm not there in five minutes, you get the fuck out of here."

"I'm coming with you." Thea was already heading back to where she came from.

I snatched her arm, swinging her back into Danny's waiting grip. "No, you're getting the fuck out of here. This entire attack was done with the intention of kidnapping you. I'm not about to let them win by sitting around waiting for those Dead Crows to swoop in and snatch you up."

"Fuck them. I'm not leaving without Nick," she barked, her grief transforming quickly to rage.

"You're not listening." I caressed her cheek, using her tears to wipe away the blood staining them. "You're going with Danny because if anything happened to you, the world wouldn't survive my wrath. Do you understand? There is no corner of this planet that I wouldn't burn, so you're getting on that helicopter."

Thea nodded, staring at the doorway. "Okay." Her voice was soft and defeated. Going onto her tiptoes, she pressed a kiss to my lips. I could taste the tears coating them. "Save him."

"Nick is too stubborn to die." I bent over Nonna one last time, unable to leave without saying goodbye. She gave me a slow blink, wrapping her tiny fingers around my hand.

"*Grazie per avermi accolto nella tua famiglia.*"[2] I took a deep breath, swallowing down the heartbreak that I wasn't prepared to face. "Thank you for loving me when no one else would."

"You were easy to love." Her lips tipped up, and her eyes closed in a gentle expression of peace, despite the extreme pain she must have been in. Nonna Lucia's hand went limp in mine, slipping from where I held it and falling to the ground with a slow exhale.

"Nonna?" Thea whispered. "Nonna?" More tears flowed from my girl's hauntingly sad eyes. Fuck, I could go the rest of my life without seeing her ever shed another tear.

I reached up to Nonna's pulse, pressing my fingertips into her surprisingly cold skin. There wasn't the slightest flutter.

Fuck this day.

Fuck Marcello and his pointless scheming.

Fuck Westin and her need for power.

Orin. King. Sal.

---

2. Thank you for making me a part of your family.

Fuck them all. My vision bled red, vibrating with a rage that shook down to my marrow. I would bathe in their blood and dine on their screams. This day would not end until I'd soaked the ground crimson.

"Crowe." Thea's sweet voice echoed around me. Her soft touch against my heart was the only thing tethering me to this world. I wrapped my fingers into hers, letting her bring me back. She blinked up at me, tears falling from the corners of her sea-green eyes. She looked so sad, and still the most beautiful thing I'd ever seen.

"We've gotta go," Danny said, breaking the suffocating silence. Outside, the gunfire had ceased. There were no shouts or screams of agony, only the creaking of charred wood.

The only sound in the Villa was the sound of death. Quiet and Heavy, the air was thick with it.

Still looking at the steady pools of Thea's eyes, I vowed, "I swear to fucking Oz, Danny. You keep her safe."

"I've got her. You worry about Nick."

— 23 —
CROWE

T he kitchen didn't exist anymore. I stood in the threshold, covering my mouth and nose from the smoke and floating debris. A fire raged in the corner, eating away at a beam and what used to be a painting on the wall. I eyed the stove wearily to see how intact the gas line was.

How had Thea survived the destruction of this room? It was astounding. She was astounding.

The ceiling was gone in all but the corners, allowing the bright midday sun to beat down. The pile of rubble was coated in streaks of red like it had been painted even before the room caved in.

When my foot crunched down on a shattered jar of Nonna's salsa, I realized why Nick and Thea had never returned to our wing. Knowing they'd been making sauce when Orin attacked made the fresh ache of Nonna's death flare in my chest.

I couldn't lose them both in the same day. Nick was here, pinned beneath something. I would find him and save him. I wouldn't let myself consider an alternative.

A bloody handprint wrapped around the tumbled stones. I placed my hand over it, feeling the warmth of Thea's presence in the tiny print. She was so small, but far from delicate. Seeing her print formed from blood was oddly fitting. A bright red stain gleamed further in the room. I followed the trail, tracking Thea's route through the room.

Then I saw it: a pool of blood seeping under the edge of a broken table. I clambered over a massive beam, rounding the mound with a sloppy level of speed.

"Fuck, Nick!" A hard lump lodged itself in my throat.

He didn't respond. I couldn't be sure he was breathing. There was an eerie level of stillness to him that made my heart gallop and pushed the air from my lungs. A spear of wood was jutting through his side, and a massive chunk of masonry pinned his leg in place. There was evidence everywhere of Thea trying to help him. Blood and sauce were spread in slick marks along every surface, a depression in the pool beneath Nick showing where she'd knelt beside him.

Lifting his arm gently, I pressed my fingertips against his wrist and held my breath for several long seconds. A faint beat pulsed beneath the skin.

Alive.

I exhaled, pushing back the hair that had fallen in my eyes. First thing I had to do was get him out from under the debris. The stone on his leg was too large to move on my own. I could see where Thea had fought to free him from it, but this would have been impossible for someone so small. I grabbed a bar from the ground, feeling the solidity of the metal in my palm. Wedging it under the stone, I was able to lean the bar against the broken half of the table.

With a roar of frustration and pent-up emotion, I pushed, levering the bar down. It moved, but only slightly. I did it again, screaming at the universe to provide us with just one break. The heavy brick rolled, releasing Nick's leg.

First challenge fixed.

I pushed aside the panic, digging into that deep, cold void that I usually stayed far away from. Nick has come back from the dead more times than I could count. I just needed him to hold on until I could get him to the triage room on the other side of the building. It had everything we needed.

I pulled out my phone, dialing a number I hadn't dialed in years.

"Please be alive," I prayed.

Flashes of the family being executed on the lawn reeled through my mind. Were any of them left? Sitting the phone on the beam beside my feet, I listened to it ring while feeling for where the spear had entered Nick's back.

The ringing clicked off, and I dialed it again, shouting at the speaker, "Pick up, you stupid bitch. I don't care if you're dead. Pick up."

Like she'd heard me from the grave, the call answered. "*Pronto.*"

"How far are you from Ciopriani Villa?" I heaved a dishcloth from inside a broken drawer, the fabric whipping me in the face when it came free.

"*Vincenzo?*"

"Answer the fucking question, Gabby!" I snapped, dropping to the ground and pressing the rag to a stream of blood flowing from his side.

"*I should hang up on you for the way you left me in—*"

"Oz damn it, woman!"

"*Va bene. Va bene, ho capito.*[1] *Fuck, you're a needy asshole. I'm in town, maybe fifteen-twenty minutes away. Why?*"

"Nick is dying. I need you here now."

"*Dying? Gah, you're always so dramatic. Niccolo can't die. The devil doesn't want him; he just keeps sending him back.*" She would know. After all, it was her scalpel that saved his life after we pulled him from Eastin's clutches. Gabriella Ciopriani was the reason Nick could walk or fire a gun. Without his aunt, he never would have survived.

Through the line, there was the sound of a door closing and the jingle of keys. Some tension eased from my shoulders, knowing she was already on her way here. She may hate me for that time I talked her into sucking me off, then, like the prick I am, left her at a bar filled with fuckboy jocks, but she cared for Nick in her own way—or at the very least, she felt responsible for him.

"*Explain to me how my nephew ended up dying on the floor of Ciopriani Villa. I thought you two were out after that shit with Eastin. Vaffanculo!*"[2] Tires screeched and a car horn blared through the phone's speaker. Gabriella shouted a litany of Italian curses, before continuing her thought like she'd never stopped. "*Did you know she's dead? I saw it on the news. Someone finally had the balls to beat her face in. They had to use dental records to confirm her identity.*"

"Yeah. I heard." I smiled at the memory and picked up the phone. "Listen, Gabs. We're in the kitchen. There may be some heat here when you arrive. The

---

1. Fine. Fine, I understand.

2. Fuck off.

Dead Crows and Winged Monkeys both came down on the Villa this morning. Sal is dead, and most of the family." I couldn't bring myself to tell her about Nonna Lucia.

Gabby was married to Sal's youngest brother, not willingly. She was sold into the marriage as so many women in this family were. At the time, she was barely legal to fuck, much less marry. There would be no tears when I told her that I watched her sniveling husband take a bullet to the brain.

After graduating top of her class from Oz U., Gabriella was sent into a surgical program and taught how to save lives—all so that Salvatore didn't have to answer inconvenient questions when someone had an unfortunate bullet lodged in their gut or multiple fractured bones.

"Seriously? Someone popped Sal? Who do I send the Thank You card to?"

I snorted a laugh. "I don't think this a tha—"

There was a scrape behind me that I registered too slowly. I turned towards the sound—straight into a fist, the silver signet ring making contact with the bridge of my nose with a crunch.

The phone clattered to the floor, sliding beneath the stones. Gabby's faraway voice called my name as I stumbled back. A long familiar pain flowed in waves, the pressure in my eye feeling like it might burst. The faint tang of blood hit the back of my throat. Fuck, how long had it been since I'd taken a cheap shot like this?

King's dark eyes glittered, ready for the fight. He lifted his fists in wait. "Come on, Scarecrowe. It's been a while since I got to kick your ass."

I spit a mouthful of blood onto the ground. "It's just like you to hit a man while his back is turned. You'd never win in a fair fight."

"There's no such thing as a fair fight. There's only winners and losers. How's the knee, by the way?"

I truly hated this man. His stupid mohawk and the dying crow emblazoned on his sleeve. Everything about him was smug, like he knew he was an unstoppable force, and that gave him permission to be a prick.

"It still hurts whenever it rains." I wiped the blood pouring from my nose with my sleeve. Rolling my shoulders, I lifted my arms into a blocking position. "Come closer, and you can find out for yourself." Smiling at the zing of adrenaline hitting my system, I swept low with my leg. I expected him to avoid it. I'd made the move obvious on purpose; the sweep and spinning back kick were all a distraction to allow me to pull the pistol from my waistband.

King was almost too slow. He blocked my hand just as I pulled the trigger, sending my shot wide. The bullet lodged in the tile floor, only feet from where Nick lay dying.

"Careful, I don't think poor Niccolo would survive *another* wound. Shame about the building falling on him when it did."

"You're a dead man, Avian."

"Where's that girl of yours? I heard she's a real stunner; likes to fight, too." King's heavy right hook swung at my head. I dodged, rounding back to connect with his ribs. He barely noticed my strike. "Sounds like just my type. I appreciate you breaking her in for me. Though, from what I've heard, you all took a turn."

The whirring of helicopter rotors fired up. I prayed to whichever dark god was listening that she was on that bird.

King swung at my center. He was a big fucker. His reach was long, and the force behind his movements was powerful. He spun with surprising speed, landing a sidekick straight into the center of my chest. The air knocked out of my lungs, and I tumbled backwards over the broken table.

"Oz damn," I wheezed. Blood streamed down my arm from where the jagged pieces gouged out my bicep. "That was a good fucking hit."

"I know it was." Arrogant prick.

"You made a mistake, though." I popped up, aiming my gun straight for him. All that muscle didn't mean shit to a bullet. They weren't picky about whose flesh they tore through. I aimed for the center of that smug fuck's face. "You never should have given me distance."

My finger descended on the trigger, nearly firing my weapon, when burning heat tore me apart from the inside out. Every muscle in my body contracted at once, the pistol tumbling from my suddenly slack grip. Pain lanced through me, and I dropped to the ground like a forgotten ragdoll.

"No, I don't think I did." King slowly approached; the bright yellow stun gun still gripped in his hand.

Seconds bled into an eternity. Just when I thought I was actually dying, the current flooding my body ceased.

"You fucking cheated." My voice was tight, the air not entirely filling my lungs. My cheek and mouth smooshed into the ground. Bits of gravel and glass fragments stuck to my lips, a long string of drool leaking from the corner of my mouth.

"Did I? You were going to shoot me, Vincent, so I feel like this is pretty fucking fair."

I definitely was, and I would do so much worse than shooting him in the face—If I could just manage to get my extremities to respond. Fucking tasers sucked. I'd never been tased before, and honestly, I'd rather take the bullet.

"I might even let you live," King chuckled. "How's that for fair?"

I tried to lift my hands, but nothing in my body was working. A feeble sense of helplessness washed over me. I couldn't even lift my middle finger.

"Don't know about him." I watched the soles of his boots move across the floor and kick Nick hard in his ribs. Nick didn't move, but the gush of blood shifted to a dark, almost black color. "He might already be dead. I've never seen the young Chopper heir look *so pale.*"

"Fuck you."

King crouched low, grabbing my top knot to wrench my head back. "Sorry, what was that? You'll have to speak up."

"I said, fu—"

King's feral smile beamed at me while he waved the sparking taser like a conductor before a symphony, my agonized wail his music. The flare of electricity was bright, like a small explosion of energy. The echo of that light danced across my vision.

When the pain finally stopped, I wasn't entirely certain that I could breathe. It required all of my focus to force my lungs to expand.

"Oh look, there's my little bird. Right on time."

My heart lodged in my throat. I tried with all of my might to look up, but my fucking body wouldn't do anything but twitch uncontrollably.

"Damn, she really is beautiful. Tits of a goddess, that one. No wonder you three are so twisted over her." King gripped the collar of my shirt, contorting my spine until I had a clear view of Danny and Thea on the far side of the Villa. "Think she's got room for one more? I bet she feels like heaven."

"You touch her, and I'l—" King dropped me, sending a fresh current of electricity burning down my spine.

"Oh, I am going to touch, and lick, and fuck her. Then, when I'm done, I'm going to kill her." I could barely hear him over the shrieking in my ears. Actually, that might have been me making those sounds. "Maybe I'll kill her while I fuck her. Do you think she'd like that?"

The pain of the gun stopped. Before I could catch my breath, he grabbed a handful of my hair, heaving me towards the blown open wall. My body raked over the debris on the floor, glass carving into my arms and shards of metal from the counters tearing open my pants and shredding my legs. It felt like my insides were spilling out, stretching me too thin.

He propped me against the wall. My head lolled lifelessly to the side. I wanted to tear him apart, but the best I could do was mumble at him. "I'm going to kill you, King. You will die slowly, and I'm going to let her help."

"Promises. Promises." Gripping my chin, he angled my head so that I could watch the scene clearly. My eyes focused over his shoulder on the auburn hair streaming in the wind. "Now sit here and try not to die before I've claimed my prize."

He lifted the taser into my view. Those large ring-clad fingers flicked off the safety timer, the dead crow on the signet mocking me. That timer was the only thing keeping the gun from shutting off after five seconds of agony. As he dialed up the current, King's grin grew in tandem with the climbing numbers until the gun had maxed out at its highest level.

"Keep an eye on the shadows, King, because The Scarecrowe will come for you."

King laid the taser on the ground just out of reach of my useless hands. "I don't think so, Vincent. See, you're going to lay here with 50,000 volts of electricity funneling through your body until either the battery or your heart gives out. Nick has probably already bled out, and Danny... well, you can watch what I have planned for him. Your girl, regrettably, has a price on her head. But if you think I'm handing her over without getting a taste for myself, you're *dead* wrong." King laughed at his joke. It was a maniacal-sounding thing. "Nobody is coming for you, Scarecrowe...and the only one coming for her is me." He wedged a rock onto the trigger, keeping it depressed.

My entire body jolted, the new amperage feeling like I was being torn apart at the cellular level. The pain strafing my heart was nothing compared to the scene that played out before my eyes and was powerless to stop.

– 24 –
DANNY

he blades of the helicopter slowly spun. The rows of poppies flattened under the onslaught of sudden wind. If a start-up sequence had already been initiated, then we were almost too late. I scanned the area, looking for who was getting on this bird, but there was no one.

"Come on. That's our ride." I took Thea's hand, dragging her behind me. We stuck to the hedges running along the side of the building. That was the best I could manage, given the lack of shadow or cover. It was brazen to do something like this in the middle of the day. These kinds of onslaughts were usually a night raid. Out here, in the open daylight, everything felt so much more raw than under the cover of darkness.

"Can you fly a helicopter?" she said, having to nearly run to keep up with my steps.

"No, but I don't need to know how to fly. The pilot does, and I have a scary gun." I waved my pistol at her, earning me a rare smile. Fuck, she was beautiful, even coated in blood and who knew what else. I had to remember how to breathe whenever I looked at her. If I wasn't careful, that beauty would strike me down.

We sprinted across the field, nearly making it when a man appeared in the doorway of the helicopter, his dark silhouette ominously blocking our only escape route.

Wind tossed the auburn locks of Thea's hair, the sound of the blades already deafening. She was wild and brave, lifting her chin to the man in challenge. The man leveled a tranq gun at us, a dark smile twisting his features.

I pushed Thea behind me, trying my best to keep her blocked from this man's line of sight. Not that it would matter; that gun could take down a rhino. Once I was down, there'd be nothing between them and her. I aimed my gun at him, shifting my aim to accommodate for the air spiraling around us.

I didn't hesitate, firing three quick shots. In movies, people were always waiting to hear what the villain has to say, when they could just shoot the fucker. I was never that stupid. Two of my hollow points sank into the hull of the helicopter, the third taking out the man's knee. He dropped to the ground, screams swallowed by the whirr of rotors. His tranq gun tumbled out of the doorway, landing only feet from where we were standing.

Just as I was reaching for her to follow me, Thea shrieked in my ear. It was a blood-curdling cry of surprise and pain. Her legs instantly gave out, sending her entire weight falling onto my arm.

"Danny—" The slurred end of my name cut off.

I spun to see her eyes rolling into the back of her head. Her body slumped to the ground at my feet. At the same time, the sharp pierce of a needle sunk into my neck, the plunger already dumping a drug into my system.

A thick arm banded around my throat, closing off my air supply. I swung my elbow back, but my limbs were already sluggish, and the hit had zero strength behind it. A cold tingle spread over my body, like jumping into an ice bath. I dropped my eyes to the unconscious Thea at my feet. Panic and fear swirled with a rage I couldn't express.

Against my ear, he said, "Don't worry. I promise to take good care of my new little bird."

The attacker dropped his arm. The world tipped sideways, slamming my cheek into the flattened flower bed. King stepped over me, bending down to brush the hair from Thea's face. I stared helplessly at the smattering of freckles painting her face, blood and ash streaking the rounded curves of her cheeks. His thumb traced her delicate features with almost reverent delicacy.

I fruitlessly reached for the bastard, but all that happened was some pathetic moaning and a small twitch of my fingers. When this drug finally released me,

I was going to track him down and tear him limb from limb. They'd be finding scattered bits of crow across all of Oz.

Alternating spots of black and white blurred my vision, and the last thing I saw was King throwing Thea over his shoulder and walking toward the helicopter.

Blinding light pierced through the darkness of my mind, pulling me back into consciousness. I rolled my dry tongue in my mouth, overwhelmed by the taste of charcoal and pennies. My stomach flipped with a dizzy kind of uneasy.

What the fuck happened?

Something cold and hard pushed into my cheek, rotating my head from side to side.

I lifted my hand to block the light from my eyes, but my arm didn't respond. Instead, a sharp pain tugged at my wrist, radiating up to my shoulder.

Slowly, the shifting world around me came back into focus. I was slumped in a ball on my stomach, leaving me with a limited view of my surroundings. Everything was white. The ground, the floor, the ceiling. Shining white tiles extended in every direction. The industrial light fixtures above me reflected off of their surfaces, making it impossibly hard to keep my eyes open.

A dark shadow shifted over me, the sharp point of something thin pushing into my jaw.

"Wake up, you worthless sack of man flesh."

"What?"

I pushed with my chin, flexing my stomach to get my knees beneath me. My legs flopped in an uncoordinated mess. Twice, I tipped sideways, falling with a crunching thud and sending a fresh wave of pain into my sore shoulders. The chain linking me to the floor was barely long enough to allow me to kneel. It pulled at my wrists, causing the metal cuffs to cut into my tender flesh.

I swayed, closing my eyes against the wave of dizziness that threatened to topple me back to the floor. The room was gently shifting from side to side...or my equilibrium was fucked up enough that the room was moving.

How long had I been out for? It felt like I'd been in this position for days. Everything hurt.

I curled into myself, pressing my forehead into my knees in a futile attempt to alleviate the pressure behind my eyes. The dull hum of a fan droned in the background. The thumping whomp-whomp-whomp of the blades pulsed in time with my temples.

How did I even get here?...wherever here was. My memory was as blank as this room.

The shining point of a silver set of heels pushed into my chin, the heel pressing down on my Adam's apple and causing me to cough.

"How's my little cocktail of drugs treating you? Does it feel like a marching band in your skull?"

I huffed a laugh, finally meeting the gaze of my captor. This bitch had no idea. It felt like my brain had been put in a blender.

She had a surface-level beauty. The kind that seemed pretty at first, but the longer you looked, you realized that her features were too sharp to be alluring.

"Where am I?"

"Give it a few minutes. It'll come back to you. I was wondering why you weren't screaming about the girl."

"Girl?"

Have you ever been chained to a wall?

Eyes, the color of a stormy-sea popped into my mind. The small divot between them creasing the otherwise delicate landscape of her face. My heart ached with a memory I couldn't quite grasp.

"Ah, see, you're already starting to remember. That's good, because I have some questions for you."

I blinked away the vision of the girl, instead settling my eyes on the emerald dangling between the woman's breasts.

"Are you wearing a swimsuit...and heels?"

The sharp point of her foot slammed into the underside of my jaw. Along the heel of her pump was a jagged bit of silver, like the serrated edge of a knife. It scraped my neck, leaving a trail of blood welling in its wake. The black chiffon robe fluttered around her, doing little to cover the obscenely small bikini.

"What's the point of wearing a bikini when I can still see your nipples?"

A second hit knocked me back to the floor. My jaw hit the ground, making me take a bite out of my tongue. The bitter tang of blood flooded my mouth. This time, it was easier to get back to my knees. I'd have met this cunt eye to eye, but the chain kept me forced into this absurd submission.

You've never knelt at the feet of someone you despised and pretended you liked the view.

Memories slammed into me with a tidal wave of images. I shook my head, fighting the onslaught. A bath. A bank vault. A woman screaming. A soft form curled in my arms. Ciopriani Villa exploding with my girl inside. Thea. Fuck. Thea. So many images of her, finally settling on the image of King-fuck-ing-Avian carrying her away from me.

My tormentor smirked down at me, looking like she'd already won. "So here's how this is going to go—"

I spat, landing a large, bloody glob on the top of her shiny shoes. Seriously, only a cunt like Westin wore patent leather stilettos and a bikini to interrogate someone.

Westin made a curdled sound of disgust in the back of her throat. Without looking at the door or saying a command, a man scurried in, wiping the offense away.

"Do they wipe your ass for you too?"

"Mind your tongue, or I'll put it to better use."

"As tempting as that sounds, I've never really had a taste for rancid bitch."

I heard the crack of her hand on my face before I fully registered the sting. "Get this through your insignificant brain—" She gripped my jaw in one hand, her manicured talons cutting into the throbbing skin. "You no longer matter. No one knows you're here, and everyone who cared that you were alive is dead. You belong to me now, pet. So you will listen and do as I say, or I'll put you down."

Oh. This bitch was definitely going to die.

She released my face with a push, causing me to nearly tip over...again. With a snap, the wall of my cell slid to the side, revealing a large screen. It flickered to life, bathing the room in blue light.

The moment I saw her, my heart stopped beating. I moved as close to the screen as the chain would allow. "Thea."

"Isn't she lovely?"

Thea was pressing the heels of her hands into her eyes, sitting on the edge of a bed and reeling from the same effects that were pounding in my temples. As I watched her, I was sure I could hear her heart pounding in my ears. The need to get to her burned through me like gasoline. The cuffs cut into my wrists as I thrashed frantically to get free.

"You fucking bitch. Let her go."

"Manners, pet." Westin backhanded me with truly unexpected force, clocking against my temple hard enough to make my vision swim. Despite the dizziness, my eyes never left the screen.

"Please, let her go, you fucking bitch," I growled through gritted teeth. For good measure, I plastered on the fakest smile I could muster.

"A day will come when you regret your insolence."

Unlike the last time I saw her, Thea was clean and in a white nightgown. It clung to her curves, thin enough to see the dark outline of her nipples. She must be freezing. I studied each feature, cataloging the details, but none were as alarming as the bracelet strapped to her wrist. A tiny red dot winked on and off.

It was too big to be a locator; it could only be a failsafe. Should Thea try to escape, Westin wouldn't need to know where she was, not when all she had to do was trigger the device on her wrist. Poison, electrical shock, explosives. It didn't matter what was in that band; they all ended with my girl dead on the ground.

"You're going to answer my questions. All of them." Westin rotated the phone in her hand, showing me a red button. I looked from the console to the screen at the blinking red dot. "And then, you won't have to watch what happens next."

"Don't hurt her."

"Who said anything about *hurting* her?"

Thea lifted her head, eyes trained on a dark figure entering the room.

"It took a few doses to get the desired effect, but King has more than proven his worth. "

"Doses of what?" The weight of Thea slumping against me echoed through my senses. I rubbed my palms together, trying to erase the feel of her soft skin slipping from my grip.

"Just something Orin whipped up, a special cocktail of benzodiazepine, beta-blockers, and a few hallucinogenics to keep things interesting." She cackled and pet the side of my head, trailing her nails down my neck. I arched away from her acidic touch. "Of course, there was the chance the mix could have killed her...but turns out that little thing has a unique will to live."

Thea rose from the cot, moving towards King Avian. Panic and anxiety stretched over me, growing with each step she took towards that monster... He would snap her in two without even trying, and I was powerless to look away.

He reached out, tenderly cupping her cheek. I blinked in surprise, feeling my heart in my throat. I expected her to recoil, but instead, she tilted into the touch. Her expression brightened in a way it never had when I entered a room. She looked fucking hopeful. He opened his arms and folded her into his embrace like they were lovers.

I couldn't breathe.

"The thing about this little drug of mine is that it has a rather spectacular side effect—memory loss. It can leave one rather disoriented and confused."

King's hand drifted up her side, coasting along her curves until it reached her chin. A low-pitched roar was building in my chest, barely caged beneath my ribs.

"Luckily, I have just the person to set her straight. All he has to do is remind her, and there are so many blanks in her memory just waiting to be rewritten."

He tipped Thea's chin to look up at him. Her full lips tilted into a smile, and everything within me shattered. I felt like a volcano with fissures cracking along the surface, ready to rain down magma on everything surrounding me.

"Dorothy doesn't remember any of you. As far as she knows, King is her protector, her lover, and everything else is white noise. She will walk us right into the Emerald City bank and place Eastin's necklace in the palm of my hand."

King's large hand circled her jaw, lifting her to his lips. Thea parted her mouth, welcoming him to drink deep.

"How rude of me. I forgot there was sound." Westin clicked a button.

His hands sunk to her ass, sliding beneath her gown and grabbing a rough handful of peachy skin. Thea let out a breathy moan as he lifted her into the air, her legs circling his waist like it was the most natural motion in the world.

"No!" I roared the word, the exclamation thrumming through every single muscle. Blood trickled down my wrists from where I strained against my cuffs, but I didn't feel the pain. I couldn't feel anything beyond my chest tearing open.

"*I missed you, little bird.*" King's words were muffled, speaking directly into her mouth and drawing her lower lip between his teeth.

"*I missed you, too.*"

Erased? All three of us, erased like we'd never existed. It wasn't possible. This emotion was too big, too consuming...too devastating.

Thea kicked her head back, exposing her throat to him. The crow signet ring pressed into her flesh, shining like a laser straight at my heart.

"And if it doesn't work, then there's always the traditional means of coercion. Why else would we bring you along?"

Swallowing a tangible pang of despair, I hissed, "This is wicked, even for you."

—25—
CROWE

A tiny dot blinked on the map displaying over the cab's console. Beside me the receiver from one of the insect drones was plugged into my computer. It would lead me straight to the asshole who'd taken everything.

My hands flexed on the steering wheel, looking uneasily in the rearview mirror. The cab was empty. Too empty.

I kept expecting to see her snuggled in the back against Nick, who'd be doing his best to pretend he didn't love it. Or Danny, bitching beside me about how she was too comfortable in his cab like she hadn't been designed to fit perfectly into our lives.

Instead, everything was empty.

It felt like I'd been hollowed out and wouldn't be right until I got them back. It was all I could focus on. Find them. Save them. Kill the people responsible.

The scrolling text at the bottom of the screen read: ETA 5 minutes.

Because if I didn't, then like a revolving door, all I saw was her lifeless body being hauled onto a helicopter, Nick's bloodless face, and that bird disappearing into the sky while everyone on the ground lay dying.

A call flashed on the screen, momentarily blacking out my map, Gabby. I pressed the red button, sending her to voicemail. I was grateful that she'd kicked the stun gun away, but I didn't need another lecture about the long-term effects of electrical shock. I simply refused to acknowledge the weakness in my grip or the involuntary muscle twitch in my right ass cheek.

It would go away, just like the heartache...eventually.

The answer to finding her was lying in pieces beside me. Gabby walked in on me cussing out the tiny electrical beast more than once. During those first couple of days, my fine motor skills were non-existent. Spinning the micro-screw-drivers needed for circuitry of this size proved...challenging. What should have taken fifteen minutes took me two excruciating days and an additional three to decode the mapping software.

Five days.

Five days of King Avian doing whatever he wanted to my girl because I couldn't work fast enough. It was torture. Those screams from my dreams came back in full force, bleeding into my waking hours. Like a song stuck in your head, all I could hear was her raspy voice screaming for mercy. The only comfort I had was knowing that Danny was with her and that he'd do what he could to keep her safe.

I ignored the voice in my head that said he was in just as much danger as her.

The screen flashed green, announcing my arrival. The dot on the map finally appeared before me. It looked like a regular suburban home. There was even an SUV with a *Proud Parent of a DES Honor Roll Wildcat* bumper sticker sitting in the driveway and an abandoned mountain bike in the front yard.

I switched over to my laptop, scrolling through the relay feed. This was definitely where the drones were being controlled from. I didn't know what I'd do if it turned out to be some snot-nosed teen drinking Mountain Dew in his mom's basement. After all, I'd been thirteen when I hacked the Treasury. Commanding a few drones was child's play.

Parking the cab a block over, I walked through the dark neighborhood. It was 3 A.M., the perfect time for this sort of thing. I'd always had the best luck at 3. Even the night owls and party boys called it quits by now. A small suburban street like this was as quiet as a graveyard.

Gripping the edge of the wooden privacy fence, I hauled myself over the barrier. My hamstrings protested the impact, but I kept moving. There were large sliding-glass doors in the back that looked in on the kitchen. Someone had left on the light over the stove, and a coffee maker on the counter blinked, ready to brew the morning's pot. A purse hung on the corner of a chair, and a half-eaten bag of chips sat on the center island. The backdoor going down to the basement had an average lock with a simple keypad for access, the numbers worn and smudged with dirt.

I did a small turn around the backyard, taking inventory of the scene: A grill, a hose curled on a hook attached to the wall, a shed for tools closed with a stick in the latch, a small abandoned Captain OzMan toy sitting on the table. I picked up the figure, turning it over in my hands.

What the hell was going on? It was hardly what you'd expect a high-level mercenary with infinite access to technology to be working out of. There was a fucking *This home is protected by OzDT Home Security* tag in the window. What reputable agency used civilians for security?

A small flicker in my peripheral caught my attention. At first, I thought it was one of the floating lights that appeared in my vision occasionally, a lingering gift from my friend Mr. Stun Gun. A faint blue light was glowing around the edges of the number pad. Beyond the dark windows of the door, I couldn't see anything, but that didn't mean there was nothing inside. I thumbed at the seams of the lock, feeling the front plate loosen like it hadn't been properly latched. Flicking it up, the small panel revealed a thumbprint scanner.

Motherfucker.

Oh, he was good. I looked down at the Captain OzMan and laughed. He almost had me fooled.

I quickly pulled my kit, disabling the lock and the alarm in under a minute. *Take that, Danny.*

The door silently swung in. From the inside, I noted the blackout film coating the windows. I descended down a long staircase, with only a small line of lights along the ground to lead my way. Eventually, a series of rooms branched off of the hallway. Bedrooms with military-style bunks. They were all empty except for one bed that was mussed from a night of sleep. Further down, I passed through a kitchen with an old pizza box on the table, and a half-drunk can of soda. But what was guiding me was the blue glow of screens bleeding under a cracked door on the far side of the room.

I carefully opened the door. Rows of monitors covered one side, and a wall of guns lined the other. This definitely wasn't Winged Monkey headquarters, but for a safe house, it was packing some serious hardware. I was almost jealous.

Pictures of the four of us were pinned to the wall with statistics and facts listed beneath each photo. A man was sitting at the desk, flipping through the security feeds of EC Central Bank, specifically the lower vault area.

The screens on the left showed a live feed of the hallway. On the right, they showed a series of recordings from the day of the bank attack. I recognized the same feed I'd tapped and watched from the cab. Thea, Danny, and Nick left the vault, heading for the elevator. Danny looked like he was ready to destroy the world, and Thea looked like she was ready to destroy him. The man sitting before the screen clicked on a smaller display, enlarging a video of Danny aggressively fucking Thea against a table in the vault.

My brows rose into my hairline. So much for there being no cameras in the vaults. Apparently, Orin had found one that I'd missed. Probably for the best because this definitely would have been a distraction.

Danny's hand cracked over the globe of her ass, leaving a bright red imprint behind. I paused my stalking, momentarily struck by the pure erotic bliss on my girl's face. Say what you will about how they challenged one another, they both obviously got off on the fight.

Fuck, I missed her. I missed them.

The sound of slapping flesh broke me from my reverie. "That's right, take it all, you whore."

Danny grabbed Thea's hair, arching her back while he railed into her. When he said he'd fucked her in the bank, I hadn't fully realized how rough he'd been. The dick marked her, then called her a slut for wanting more. Mentally, I made a note to punch Danny again...and also to track down the video for later perusal.

Silently approaching the man, I pressed the muzzle of my gun to the back of his head. "Call my girl a whore again, and I'll cut your tongue out."

Orin released his dick, slowly spinning the chair to face me. "I was wondering when you'd show up. It was sloppy, not killing you. I told King not to leave anything to chance. Honestly, I'm disappointed it took you as long as it did."

"Well, I'm disappointed that your only line of defense was a simple alarm system and a 2016 Suburban. The housewife schtick was pretty convincing, I'll give you that."

His shoulders shook with a laugh. "You really think that's my only line of defense?"

"I caught you with your pants down, literally. So, unless you're about to accost me with your dick, then yeah, you look pretty fucked right now." I tossed a pair of cuffs down to him. "Put them on."

Orin held them up, letting the circlet dangle from one finger. "These aren't really my kink."

"Put them on, or I will break your arms and put them on myself."

"Another tactless brute. You and King have more in common than I think you'd like to admit." The bastard sighed. "There's no art to this game anymore."

I cocked my arm back, ready to smack him with the butt of my gun.

Orin held up a single finger, pausing me. "I wouldn't do that if I was you."

I was being baited. I knew it. Barret was the king of mind-fuckery. He probably had jack all in terms of fail safes and was counting on his arrogance to protect him. None of that stopped me from asking, "Why?"

Orin lifted his chin, pointing at the row of monitors. "Hit F5 and switch to the alpha feeds."

Keeping my gun trained on him, I leaned over the keyboard and hit the button.

"I can't wait to see your face when you realize." Realize what? Images of Thea broken in a dozen different ways flickered through my mind.

The feeds switched from the bank to a series of rooms that I instantly recognized, but only one monitor mattered. In the center of the mass of screens was Thea. She was lying naked in bed, curled on her side with one hand tucked beneath her cheek. My heart sped up, and I moved closer, trying to take in all of the details.

Oz damn, she was beautiful. I took what felt like my first breath in days. She looked good, so much better than I'd feared. Healthy. No scratches or bruising.

She was okay. Fuck. I gripped the side of the desk, trying to push down the tremor shivering along my spine.

She was okay.

"See that pretty bit of jewelry she has blinking on her wrist?" Orin lifted his phone, showing me a screen with a large red button. "One press of this and 3mg of Morphan will be instantly injected into her system. It's quite lethal at that dosage and a terrible way to go. Oh, I'm sorry. I forgot. You'd know all about that, wouldn't you? What was her name, Vanessa?"

I cocked the gun pointed at him.

Orin rolled his eyes and gestured at the bank of computers. "You can have everything in here. My files are really very comprehensive. Use them, burn them. Whatever. I don't give a fuck about Westin. Kill the bitch. Do your whole terrifying Scarecrowe thing on her. I was already working on a plan to take her out anyway. You'd be doing me a favor, really." I scanned the wealth of information sitting plainly on the desk, wondering what else I'd find hidden in the computers. "But you're going to let me walk out of here because if I don't key in the safety code every 12 hours, then your girl gets to relive the best bite of pie she's ever had...and guess who won't be there to save her this time?"

The smug as fuck bastard sat back, kicking his feet up and shaking the screen in the air like it was check and mate all in one move. I didn't hesitate, shifting my aim from his head to his hand. The bullet cut cleanly through his palm, sending the phone flying into the air before he'd even been able to twitch.

I slid to the ground, snatching the device before it crashed on the cement floor.

"You shot my hand!" Orin's voice raised two whole octaves, sounding hysterical. "You've killed her."

"I haven't killed anyone, you overdramatic prima donna. You think I can't hack your disarming codes? Please."

Orin spit, clutching his wounded hand to his chest like a baby. "You can't hack my biometrics, moron. I never leave anything to chance. You'll never get in that phone. Your girl is as good as dead."

I looked from the phone's scanner to Orin. A familiar hum built in my spine, something I hadn't felt in a long time. "Then I'll just have to take them with me."

The blood leeched from his face. "What?"

"What are they, thumb-print and iris? Or is there facial recognition as well?" I pulled out the tin snips that I'd shoved in my back pocket. It was amazing how often these came in handy. The gleam of my expression must have changed, but all I felt was calm. "Maybe I should take all three to be safe."

"Don't touch me." All of Orin's bravado fell away. He tried scrambling backwards, making his desk chair roll into the wall with our faces on them. The taped pages fluttered above his head.

I looked up at the picture of Thea, a security cam photo from The Farm. Even with the distress of that hell coating her, she was still breathtaking. "Don't worry, beautiful. I'm coming for you."

"Don't. I'm warning you—"

Shoving my knee into Orin's stomach, his words choked out with a gasp. My shoulder notched under his throat, pinning him in place while I gripped his hand. Movies always made severing digits seem so easy, but it really took quite a bit of pressure to cut off a finger. Unless, of course, you knew where to cut, then they popped right off. I had Gabby to thank for that particular bit of knowledge.

Orin screamed at first, but not the fear-drenched squeals that he made when I took out his eye next. He attempted to fight back, clawing with his mutilated hand at my back and kicking his feet on the ground like a toddler throwing a tantrum. This was the problem with being a thug with hired muscle. Orin didn't know how to get his hands dirty anymore. He'd grown soft, like the eyeball sitting in my palm.

I pulled out a baggie from my jacket and dumped the contents, replacing them with bits of asshole. Pocketing the bag and Orin's phone, I assessed what was left of him, debating on how exactly I wanted to dispose of this prick. Blood oozed down his cheek from the empty cavity while his other eye watched the screens behind me aimlessly and smiled.

"Shhh, baby. You're dreaming."

I spun towards the screens and the deep voice that had just whispered over the speakers. A large hand flexed against Thea's stomach, moving so that his arm draped possessively around her waist, pulling her backwards.

"What the fuck?"

Orin's whimpers turned to chuckling. I didn't look, pulling the trigger and not caring what part of his body the bullet hit, only that it caused him pain. The chuckling stopped, replaced instead by a choked wheeze, "Weren't expecting that, were you?"

I grabbed the mouse, making the camera zoom in on a silver signet ring pressed into the soft flesh of her belly. "What in the name of Ozma is she doing in bed with King Avian?"

Orin's damaged hands clutched his stomach, smirking in victory despite the blood leaking from the corner of his mouth. "I assume she's sleeping off what I can assure you was a very entertaining night."

I fired another bullet into his knee. "She *is not* fucking the Dead Crow asshole. So start talking."

"Look at her, Vincent. Does that look like a woman who is being traumatized? Does it look like she's been forced into being the little spoon against her will?" He laughed, causing a cough to splatter blood across the unstained part of his shirt. "Trust me, the only screaming she's been doing isn't the kind that comes at the end of a blade. Although, from what I've seen, she can swallow a sword like a champ."

"Fuck you, Barret."

"Haha. Why when she's been fucking around enough for both of us?"

There was something particularly satisfying in the way he squealed when my next bullet pierced through his floppy excuse for a dick. Satisfying, but impulsive. Hopefully, he wouldn't bleed out too quickly.

"Shhh. Baby, I'm here."

King's hand pushed between her thighs, causing the sleeping Thea to arch backwards. His heavy leg wrapped around hers, spreading her wide enough that he was able to push a long middle finger into her. She moaned, eyelids fluttering as her body fought the pull of sleep.

Blood pumped thickly against my temples, making the color bleed from my vision. My hand tightened on the grip of the gun, my other forming a fist that hurt along every joint.

He rutted against her ass, making their bodies rock in time with the movement of his hand. *"That's right, little bird. Give it to me."*

Thea moaned, a single sound which could have been anything but made my heart crack. *"rOhhh."* Was that my name on her lips as King forced a second finger into her? Was she dreaming of me?

Orin let out a wheeze. I looked over my shoulder at him. "Don't pass out on me, Barret." I smacked his face until focus came back into his eyes. "We aren't done here."

"King. King. King," he repeated his name with each thrust like it could somehow force her to say it.

"You did something to her." I pressed the muzzle of my gun into the bullet wound on his knee. "You drugged her or forced her into that bed." Orin screamed. I closed my eyes and let that sound sate the rage eating away at me. How many times had he watched King rape her?

Thea cried out, a sound so pure, so wonderful that I would know it anywhere.

"That's my good little bird."

That fucker had made her come, and she never woke. Her eyes never opened, even with the rush of endorphins that came after orgasming. She looked just as peaceful as ever.

Drugged.

She had to be. Had to. The alternative was too awful to imagine.

"Orin, I'm going to kill you. I promised you that back at Gorba's yard." The leader of the Winged Monkeys cried, bloody hands cradling his mutilated dick. It was pathetic. How many times had this man tortured someone, executed them? He could at least die with a bit of dignity. "I want to flay your body one terrible piece at a time, but I'm in a bit of a hurry here. So, I'll make you a deal.

Tell me everything I need to know, and I'll let you bleed out with your skin intact."

Orin lifted his chin, glaring with one dark eye. "There's nothing to tell. You were played, Vincent. Accept it. She's sleeping naked in bed with him, taking it nightly like the good little whore she was raised to be."

My next bullet grazed his ear, the spasm in my hand forcing my aim wide.

"Fucking electric shock." King was a deadman. I tried again, using both hands to steady the gun.

"Wai—" A satisfying spray of brain matter painted the wall of photos behind Orin. One long drip ran from Thea's eye like she was crying bloody tears.

My heart pounded in my ears, accompanied by a high-pitched whine and the sleepy sounds of contentment whispering from my girl.

I was going to murder King Avian, and then I was coming for Westin Witcher.

-26-
THEA

Crowe. Danny. Nick. Crowe. Danny. Nick.

I recited my mental mantra, deliberately noting the things about each that make them stand out. Crowe's piercing blue eyes, the golden hue of his hair, and a smile that makes you feel like you're lying in the sun. Danny's eyes are green like moss when he's happy and sharp like emeralds when he's angry. Nick's are a cool gray, like polished tin. There's a slight dimple to the side of his cheek when he truly smiles, and I'm sure I'm the only one who knows it's there.

The faces of each of my boys flickered into focus as clearly as if they were standing before me. If I was less sane, I'd think I could reach out and touch them...but I know it's the drugs. After each time, it gets harder to keep the line of reality clear. So, I etch their images into my memory and refuse to let them go.

"Good morning, little bird."

Knock-knock. I know you're in here, little bird.

That voice haunted my nightmares, but when I awoke, the boogeyman was still here, and reality was so much worse than the dream. I emerged from my drugged-out coma, scared out of my fucking mind, feeling like I'd been run over by a tank. I couldn't remember so much as my name, much less why I was locked away. Then, slowly, it came back to me. King said sweet things, touched me tenderly in a way only lovers did, and at first, I believed the lie...but his eyes were all wrong, dark, almost black like obsidian. There was a tattoo of a crow with an arrow in his heart splayed across this chest when it should be a lion.

He was the illusion. Not my lover, but my captor.

The heavy hand at my waist slowly stroked my stomach, sliding beneath the fabric of my dress and drawing small circles along my lower belly. I closed my eyes, willing it to be their hands, but it couldn't be. The scent of the man behind me wasn't right, the scratch of calluses in the wrong places, the cold metal of his ring.

Crowe. Danny. Nick. Crowe. Danny. Nick.

The warmth of lips pressed against my neck, and I used every part of my being to resist the urge to flinch. When I was on The Farm, I'd always been good at this part, able to easily compartmentalize. It wasn't me they were fucking, it was this other weaker version of me.

It was harder now. I'd buried that girl. Dorothy was dead, and Thea didn't know how to play this game without losing a part of herself in the process.

The worst part was knowing that I couldn't trust my memory. Flickers would come to me. King would describe an event, and it twisted from what I knew into something else. When I resisted, it was worse, so now I summoned my courage and played along. The last time he tried to dose me, I managed to talk him out of it. It had taken kissing him and putting on an award-winning performance to keep from gouging the man's eyes out.

I'd tried several times to leave the room, doing everything short of fucking him to persuade him. According to King, staying locked in here was for my own safety, same with the cuff on my wrist. In his version, I was concussed when the building collapsed, and he couldn't risk me leaving the room while I was still confused.

I knew better. Nick's blood was washed from my body. I'd scrubbed until my skin was raw, but I still felt coated in it. The trauma of his death lingered beside me like a ghost, whispering in my ear no matter how many drugs they pumped me with.

Danny's necklace was warm at the base of my neck. Whoever had initially dressed me in this absurd slip hadn't realized the true value of it. It was my ticket out of here, my one and only weapon. My fight with Albert, after the bank, taught me that I'd never overpower a man like King. He was too big, too hard, too fit for me to ever physically compete with him. What I needed was for him to show some vulnerability, something soft that I could drive my knife into.

I had to be patient, bury my rage, and play at the dutifully confused girl. King hadn't let go of me the entire night. I was certain the man didn't really sleep, but I was one step closer to the door. I just needed a little bit longer.

He pushed me onto my back, leaning over me. "I had the craziest dream." His finger toyed with the strap of my gown.

It was alarming how convincing King was, playing the role of lover effortlessly. Everything he did felt habitual. Even the casual way he pulled me into the contours of his frame as we fell asleep was like he'd done it a million times. He never pushed me farther than I allowed, though my fuzzy memories were hard to distinguish from the truth. The imprint of his touch lingered everywhere, and the flashes of his body moving with mine were hard to convince myself were purely fabricated.

King's hot breath drifted over my neck. "We were in the bank."

The fucking bank. It was always the bank and the key. He wasn't even covert about it.

"Do you remember the bank, baby?" I swallowed the urge to scream. "Do you remember the way I made you cry my name? I pushed you against the wall..." His hand slid to my ass, squeezing. "...fucked you hard, just how you like it."

A memory played, but it wasn't King's hands holding me up or his cock driving into me. *Danny* pressed me against the wall. *Tik-tock, Thea.* I closed my eyes, holding onto the memory, refusing to let him take it.

King climbed over me, fitting himself between my legs. "You sounded so sweet coming around my dick." He rocked against me. "I've missed you, baby. I've missed this. I need you to remember."

Crowe. Danny. Nick. Crowe. Danny. Nick.

Oh, I remembered the bank and how Nick looked so tortured before I entered that vault with Danny. I'd give anything to know what he was going to say. Now, I'd never get the chance. The man pressing his weight into me killed Nick. Maybe not directly, but he was definitely the one who made the call.

"I can help you remember." He dipped his head, pressing a kiss along my collar like he hadn't torn a piece of my heart out and left it back in that kitchen. With each day, the ache of loss grew. It was almost impossible to breathe beneath the pain. I wanted to slice into King's chest and show him what it was to live with a missing heart. Nick was a bastard and a liar, but he was *my* lying bastard.

"Talk to me, beautif—"

"Don't call me that," I snapped before he'd finished the word. *Fuck*. I hadn't meant that. I'd held strong for this long, but he didn't get to call me beautiful. What lay beneath him wasn't beauty; it was barely leashed carnage.

"Dorothy?" King's hands coasted over my arms, casually pinning me like I wouldn't notice I was being restrained. "Are you feeling okay? Is it the headaches? Maybe you need another dose of medicine."

Medicine. Ha. You mean, how about you prick me with that needle and send me into oblivion for a few hours, then you can try again to rewrite history and erase the only good things I've ever known in this life.

Crowe. Danny. Nick. Crowe. Danny. Nick.

I bent my leg, already hating my choice but knowing that it was better than losing what little control I had. The hem of my nightgown rose, exposing myself to him. It didn't take much. This slip was barely longer than a shirt, and I was never given any kind of underwear. Half of the time when I awoke, I was naked, having been coerced during my semi-conscious state into doing Ozma only knew. The bare skin of my thigh brushed the side of his leg. "No, I'm fine. I just meant that I don't feel beautiful."

The hand pinning my left arm dropped to my outer thigh, gripping tight enough to make me gasp. He lifted up, rotating my hips into him. Between my legs, he grew instantly harder, and I have never been more grateful for the shorts he wore.

"Is that what you want? I can make you feel beautiful, Little Bird. I can make you fly."

Or this little bird could claw your eyes out.

I pushed against his chest with my free arm, trying to create some space between us. "What I think I need is some fresh air. King...baby." The words felt like ash on my tongue. "Let's go outside. We've been holed up in this room for what feels like forever."

His grip relaxed, but his scrutinizing gaze studied mine for flaws. "I'd feel better about taking you out if you could tell me a clear memory. Tell me about the day at the bank. What did we do after we left the vault?"

"King, I..."

"How about something simpler?" He started kissing down my chest, pulling up on my dress. "Tell me where you put the key, and I'll reward you."

My stomach flipped. I'd given the vault key to Toto before she left with Ginger, but I'd be damned before I breathed a word of that to this gaslighting psycho—and I definitely didn't want whatever he was considering as a reward.

I kept my mouth shut, turning my face to the side so that I didn't have to watch what he was doing to me.

Crowe. Danny. Nick. Crowe. Danny. Nick.

King's mouth hovered over my navel. "What's the matter? You're tenser than rebar."

"Nothing. It's nothing." Think Thea. Make him believe. Make him stop.

"No, there's something. A memory? Is it those men again? I told you, baby, they aren't real. It's just your mind fracturing information." He kissed my stomach. "You feel that? This is real. You and me."

I pushed on his shoulder, rolling out from under him. "I just need a shower. Something to clear the haze of sleep."

King rose to his feet. He was massive, lying down it was easy to forget just how big the man was. I looked up at him, imagining what it would feel like to sink my dagger into his eye.

"Do you want company?"

"No." Fucking hell, the man was relentless. I pulled the bathroom door open, dragging my hand over the crow inked on his chest and gently pushing him back into the bedroom. "Maybe you can find us breakfast. I'm starving."

I closed the door to the bathroom behind me before he could answer. My back hit the wood with a thump. With both hands, I clamped them over my mouth, biting my cheeks to keep the sob clawing up my throat from exploding.

"I'll be right back, Dorothy." The handle rattled like he might try to come in. I held my breath, cursing that the door had no lock. When the brass knob went still, I let out a slow exhale. "It's going to be okay, Little Bird. You just need to learn to trust me again."

Crowe. Danny. Nick. Crowe. Danny. Nick.

-27-
CROWE

"This is crazy, even for you."

A massive gust of air tossed my hair back. I gripped the handle overlooking the hatch. Far below, a white speck sat in the middle of a black sea.

"What's the matter, Nicky? One little near-death experience and you've lost your edge?"

Nick tightened the straps of his flight suit, knitting his eyebrows in a nearly imperceptible wince. "Don't call me that." He lengthened his spine, looking down at the drop with me. I knew he must be in pain, but he didn't let it show.

Gabby just about shit a brick when he told her he was coming with me. While I didn't want him to injure himself further, I was grateful he was beside me. The wood from the table managed to do minimal damage, the worst of it being blood loss and some minor organ trauma. A half inch in either direction, and it might have been a very different scenario.

My phone call came just in time. She arrived only minutes after King left me twitching on the ground. Years of doing triage work for the family taught Gabriella to bring all kinds of supplies to the scene. Nick was pumped with fluids and blood before he'd even left the kitchen floor. She was right. Death kept rejecting the lucky bastard.

Over the next two weeks, while he recovered, Nick and I outlined our attack. Danny's original plan to approach the ship from beneath the water was good, but not feasible with only two people. It was also designed to get in and out, with the only casualty being Westin. Now, after everything she'd called down on us, her floating fortress and everyone on it would be at the bottom of the sea before we were done.

"Westin's yacht looks so small from up here. Hardly big enough to hold her ego." I regretted a lot from my past, none so much as our twisted affair. "I still think we should be doing this tandem."

"We've been over this. I'm not flying bitch." He placed a heavy hand on my shoulder. "I'm fine. Gabby packed my stitches really well."

I pulled out my phone and brought up the camera in Thea's room. Watching her hovered somewhere between punishment and obsession. After killing Orin, I cloned the signal he was using to monitor my girl. I spent hours upon hours watching her. It was the only thing that kept the darkness from overtaking what little sanity I was holding onto.

Her petite form paced in circles, worrying her hands together as she walked, the thin nightgown swaying around her thighs. King was blissfully nowhere in sight. Thank Oz. If I had to watch that stupid crow fucker put his claws on my girl again, I was going to break something. The only thing I wanted to be breaking was his spine, one vertebra at a time.

The sound of her footsteps echoed off the shiny, pristine walls. Westin loved her white tile rooms, they made a perfect canvas for blood splatter and were easy to clean. I'd instantly recognized one of the guest rooms from Westin's yacht. Although this one had been stripped down to only a bed, which King kept telling her was for her own safety. More like he'd seen her beat Eastin's face in with a snow globe and didn't want to risk any kind of a weapon being present.

"Stop torturing yourself." The contempt in Nick's voice was unmistakable.

"I still think she's faking it." I pinched the image, making her beautiful face cover the whole screen. Thea paused and looked up as if she knew I was watching. "I'm coming for you, Darling."

Pressing the phone to the pain in my chest, I rested my head against the hull of the plane. When I opened my eyes, Nick was glaring at me.

I scoffed, "Oh please, like you aren't going out of your fucking mind, too. Tell me again, why Thea was wearing *your shirt* when shit went down?"

He shrugged a shoulder. "That was before I learned what a backstabbing cunt she is."

I ground my teeth and took a deep breath, feeling the restraint pull at the edges of my jaw. "I shot Orin in the face for calling her a whore. What do you think I'll do to you for calling her a cunt?"

Nick rolled his eyes like I wasn't a legitimate threat.

I was so over his shit: the grumbling and the barely veiled insults. This time, he'd taken it too far. "I don't care that you're recovering from surgery. Do it again, and I'll send you to hell myself." I swung for him, a hard right hook aimed at his jaw. He dodged, sending my fist into the wall. "Asshole."

Nick grabbed the strap of my flight suit, spinning me into the wall. "How many times do you need to watch King fuck her before you get it through your brainless head?"

I swung with my other fist, not thinking beyond wanting to shut him up. He caught it an inch from his face.

"Fine, let's do this." He threw my hand down, releasing me with a hard push. "She used us, Crowe. You, Me, Danny. She wanted to get to The Wizard, and what did we do?"

"It wasn't like that." I pushed his shoulders, forcing him back. Fuck the scheduled drop time. I was about to shove this asshole right out of the plane. Maybe the extra airtime would help him get his priorities in line.

Nick side-stepped me, avoiding my jab and snagging my chute before I could tip over the edge. Locking his arm around my throat, he continued, "*She* locked away the emerald and *took off* with the key, Crowe. That attack on the bank, you know what it was?"

I pulled myself from his grip, readjusting the harness as I stepped away. "You, being a coward and selling us out? You're such a hypocrite."

"No. There were *three* teams that day. Three, and Westin's crew weren't the ones blowing shit apart. Does that seem familiar? Know of anyone with a fondness for explosives and unnecessary damage? It wasn't an attack. It was an extraction. King was always her escape plan."

"You don't know that."

"Don't I?" His expression was more cold and emotionless than I'd ever seen him before. Cat fucked him over, and Eastin fucked him up, but thinking Thea had double-crossed us stole his humanity. How was he so quick to believe everything we shared was a lie?

"Then why hasn't she given up the key? She's had weeks to tell him, and every time he asks, she dodges."

Flicking through the photos on my phone, I pulled up a recording. King kissing her neck. I paused it, zooming in on her expression. Her fingers were curled into a fist like she was ready for a fight. His hand was wrapped around her wrist, pinning it to the wall. Her face was turned away from King, squinting her eyes shut like she was in pain more than rapture.

I pushed the image at him. "Look at that. LOOK!"

"You kept the recording?" He shook his head, directing his eyes to anything but the screen. He might act like he wasn't in pain, but I knew it was tearing him apart. "Of course you did."

"Tell me she ever looked like that with you. She can't even bear to see what he's doing."

Still looking at the ceiling, Nick dropped his hands to his side with a long sigh, like he was admitting defeat. "Isn't it obvious, Crowe? She's playing *him*, too."

I scoffed. "Then why won't he let her out of that room? Why bring her to Westin at all?"

"Because Westin is her next target, and King's just the next idiot willing to fall for her tricks."

"Tricks? He shoots that poison into her neck, and she's a zombie for the next day at least. You should hear the toxic shit he whispers to her, the way he violates her into thinking what he's saying is real." I flipped to another still of Thea looking drugged out of her mind and then to another of her so fucking scared it made my teeth ache. "This isn't manipulation, it's rape. You're just too heartbroken to admit it."

His eyes traveled over the picture for several long seconds, throat flexing with a hard swallow. "To be heartbroken, I would need to have a heart."

A light near the hatch blinked from red to green. Nick looked down at the altimeter on his wrist, 15,000 feet. He tightened his fists, reading the words inked there. Never Again. "I'm not jumping for her. I'm going for Danny. Remember the brother she sold out? The one who didn't hesitate to rescue you when you were tied to a post. You hardly seem to care that he's trapped on that ship."

The feeds from Danny's cell weren't any easier to watch than Thea's. Westin was routinely abusing him, choosing to inflict maximum damage at the same time King was screwing Thea. The same feed I punished myself with was all he could see, projected onto the wall so he couldn't avoid it.

He looked broken. There was hardly life left in his eyes. No fight. No strength. He was nothing more than a plaything and, knowing Westin, a fail-safe if King's brainwashing stopped working.

"We have to go or we'll miss the flight window." Before I could say anything in my defense, Nick tipped sideways into the open air, plummeting toward the tiny boat below.

I looked at Thea one last time. King was back, pushing her into the door, and the glare in her eyes was murderous. She was faking it. Nick would realize it just as soon as we saw her. Securing my phone into my suit, I followed him into the black expanse.

The wind buffeted my face, pushing against my cheeks. I closed my eyes, thinking of how Thea's nose sometimes crinkled when she laughed. She hadn't once looked at King like that. There was never light in her expression, only shadows.

The haptics on my wrist buzzed. *3,000 ft.*

Ahead of me, Nick's chute was a dark silhouette against a midnight sea. I waited several seconds, savoring the adrenaline pumping like lightning in my veins.

2,500 ft.

A galaxy of stars blinked across the sky. There was a perverse beauty to flying. The world was all at once violent and still.

2,000 ft.

I yanked on the ripcord, the parachute unfurling behind me like wings. My body jerked up, forcing a choked groan from me. Fuck, I'd forgotten what that felt like. Even with how much I wanted to shake his damn head loose, I couldn't help but worry that his stitches wouldn't hold. Then again, maybe that sharp bite of pain would make him come to his senses. Unlikely.

We angled our approach to the stern of the ship. Water frothed around the hull, illuminated by the lights below the surface. The dark, graceful silhouettes of sharks glided through the water. They kept pace with the ship, no doubt expecting Westin's impulsivity to provide them with their next meal. They would be feasting well tonight. Several laser-guided defense guns tracked our approach, all set to shoot down anything unwanted.

Not for long. I unhooked the mini-launcher that I'd strapped to my leg. This was an extraordinary instrument, made to deliver only one thing: a localized EMP grenade. Normally, these only worked within a very small range, but I'd tweaked this model to deliver an electromagnetic pulse similar in scale to a nuclear blast. It would take out every electrical system in a one-mile radius. Everything from the engines to the lights would be fried, including the device strapped to Thea's wrist.

I armed the grenade and centered the sites at the base of the spinning radar system. Six simple seconds and the blast would crumple their control system like tin foil. Even if other devices managed to reboot, this ship was dead in the water.

Six.

The EMP fired with a dull pop, soaring like a small meteor towards the ship.

Five.

Several of the gunmen's heads swiveled as it went zipping past them, lodging in the metal wall above their heads.

Four.

We were close enough to hear the shouts of the security on the outer deck, "*Fire* at will!"

I couldn't help my crazed laugh as I pulled on my steering cord, making the chute dip unexpectedly to the side. At the same time, Nick maneuvered in the opposite direction. Their shots soared harmlessly between us. Bullets whirred, missing the chute entirely. I smiled at the warm buzz of victory burning through me. This was going to work.

Three.

"Head in the game, *cazzo*," he shouted, a look of devious anticipation as clear on his face as it was on mine.

Oh, my head was in the game. I was about to tear this ship apart. Nothing and no one kept me from my girl. Not King. Not Westin. There could be a hundred men waiting to take us out. It wouldn't matter.

Two.

Focusing on the deck, I memorized the layout of each person and object. Things were about to get very dark.

I'm coming for you, Darling.

One.

A sharp flare of light illuminated the entire deck in a sudden blast of sunlight before the night exploded.

"*Porca miseria!*"[1] Nick shouted. Even I was impressed by the intense force of the explosive. The blast was far more extensive and vibrant than I'd anticipated, and it worked perfectly. Lights, even the tiny LEDs blinking on weapons and watches, went dark. The hum of engines ground to a halt. The metal of the funnel imploded, pulled in by the intense magnetism set off by the grenade.

Several small fires popped to life along the electronic panels next to the doors, giving me enough light to see where I was landing. My feet hit the deck, the chute collapsing into the ocean as I released the buckles tethering me to it.

Every gun on deck crackled, like Pop Rocks of sparks igniting across their targeting circuit boards. The warm glow of heating metal lit up the faces of dozens of stunned gunmen. They crowed in pain, sounding just like the flock adorning their sleeves. All at once, they dropped their weapons in a delightful cacophony.

---

1. Holy shit!

"Oh, sorry about that." I reached forward, grabbing the closest man. "Sucks about those electronic triggers." I drove my elbow into the man's throat, dropping him to the ground and aiming my pistol at him. "Bet you wish you had any other weapon right now." I pulled the trigger, putting a bullet between his eyes. Beside me, Nick had dropped two other men. His intense expression proved precisely what I felt. *There was no mercy here.*

Only a few people approached us. Most were shouting about more immediate concerns, focusing on the people pinned with the crumpled metal and the oil leaking onto the deck from the pistons housed in the central funnel. Admittedly, I may have gone a bit overboard with the magnetic yield.

Nick drove his fist into the stomach of a gunman, followed by an uppercut, snapping the man's head back. Dipping under his shoulder, Nick heaved him overboard with a primal yell.

I knew all of that pent-up emotion would come out eventually. "Whatever happened to shooting them? You're going to pull your stitches doing that shit."

Nick straightened, flexing his fists and wiping the blood streaking them on his pants. "Yeah, well, I'm fine. The stairwell is over there." He pointed towards a metal door swinging freely with the rock of the ship. Another bonus of the EMP: all doors were now open. "Danny is on deck 3."

I looked towards the bow. Thea was that way. The lower decks were where the cells were, but the upper decks housed the living quarters. That's where we'd find her. "Thea's closer. She's not injured. She could help us with Dan—"

"I told you. I'm not here for her."

This was standing over Nonna all over again, the choice of who to save pulling me in two. Behind us, something loud boomed, the sparks igniting the oil on the deck.

"You can come with me or go after her. But I'm not wasting precious time rescuing someone who probably doesn't want to be saved."

I slowly backed away from the door. "I can't, Nick. I can't leave her behind."

Nick lowered his head, nodding slowly. "I hope you're right, for your sake."

"I hope you're wrong, for yours. I know you love her. Someday, you'll thank me for not giving up." I turned my back on him and ran towards the front of the ship.

—28—
THEA

I circled the tiny room for what felt like the millionth time. This was both the worst and best part of my day. King was called away from the room, giving me the space to breathe. It also allowed the panic to set in.

The door opened suddenly, hitting the wall with a clatter and making me jump. King stomped into the room, a fury unlike any I'd seen boiling in his eyes. Usually, he came in soft and gentle, like he was trying to tame a feral kitten. Not tonight. He pressed the panel's lock button with enough aggression I expected to see a crack in the glass.

"Wha—What's wrong?"

King dropped his gun into the dresser's top drawer, pressing his thumb to the panel and locking it. He undid his belt, wrapping it around his fist. "What's wrong?" he parroted, each syllable dripping with venom. With one hard throw, the balled-up belt flew across the room, slamming into the metal wall.

I involuntarily jumped, retreating slowly in the direction of the bathroom and what little protection that door would afford me. I always knew the day would come when he would drop the pretense.

Unbuckling his pants, he pushed them to the ground, his long cock springing free. He fisted it, giving it a firm stroke as his eyes traveled over my body.

"King?" Fuck, he was huge, all powerful muscle and hard edges, with a cock that looked like a weapon.

"What's wrong is this isn't working, and we're out of time." Long strides closed the space between us. Before I could make it to the bathroom, he wrapped his massive hand around my throat. King's fingers extended nearly the entire circumference of my neck, using his grip to push me backward until I was

245

pinned to the wall. There was pressure, not enough to restrict my breathing, but the threat made my heart pound.

"King, you're scaring me."

"Good." His hips pressed into mine, the hard line of his cock pushing into my stomach. His weight kept me from squirming beneath him. He tilted my head to the side, lips close enough to my ear that the fine hairs along my neck shifted with his breath. "Little bird, you will tell me what you did with the key to the vault." Using one leg, he forced mine apart.

"I... I... I don't remember." I put as much force as I could into my hands and pushed against his chest. He didn't shift at all. Instead, he fought against my arms, pushing down until my hands were pinned between us.

"She said we only have one more day, and then she's taking you back. Do you know what she'll do to you, to all this pretty skin?"

"Who? King, please."

"She *gave you* to me. All I had to do was find out where you stashed that key, and then you were mine." He dipped low, stealing a kiss that I didn't offer from my lips. I bit down in warning, but instead, he growled in pleasure.

"I've watched every recording multiple times. I memorized every detail. The problem is that I've been too gentle, giving you the time to accept me and waiting for you to ask for it." His free hand held up a syringe, waving it before my eyes. I focused on it like he'd just pulled a gun. It had been days since the last time he'd given me anything. I finally felt like I could trust what I was seeing and it didn't feel like I was thinking in a massive fog bubble.

"Don't." I thrashed against him, but it did nothing. I might as well have been hitting a tree.

"I've increased the hallucinogens and decreased the sedatives. No more knocking you out and starting over. We don't have time for that anymore." The pressure on my neck increased until it felt like my heart might pound straight through his hand. "But don't worry, baby. You'll drop into twilight, and while you're there, I'm going to fuck you hard, just like I know you like it."

"*No.*"

"We'll repeat this little dance over and over until mine is the only cock you remember, the only one you want. I'll keep dosing, you for as long as it takes until you tell me where the key is. You're mine, Little Bird. Accept it now or later. Either way, you will tell me what I want to know. I won't let Westin take you from me."

"I told you. I don't remember."

King's expression tightened, reading the panic in my body. "See, I think you've been lying to me. I think you remember far more than you're letting on."

"I don't. All I remember is you." I wiggled, trying to pull a leg free.

"More lies." He tilted my head to the side, exposing my neck. King's lips pressed below his hand on the exact spot he would inject me. "It's time you started giving me more than lies." The point of the needle dragged over my skin. Sweat broke out along my temple, knowing I'd never come back from this. Whatever came next, it would be the end of me.

"Please, King. Don't!" I hated the desperation in my voice. "Please!"

"Shhh. Baby. I've got you."

His soft, patronizing hush triggered something explosive in me. How many times had he said those exact words while I was too drugged to fight him off. "I'm not your baby!"

King chuckled. "There she is. I was wondering when you'd finally stop pretending."

I pulled against his grip, straining to meet his eyes. "You want to know why nothing you tried has ever worked?" King's lip curled into a sneer. "Because no amount of drugs could ever make me forget the way I loathe you."

The burning pierce of the needle radiated over my neck.

"I guess we'll find out, won't we."

I watched in terror as his thumb pushed on the plunger, that first cold wave of liquid coursing through my veins like ice. Unlike the other times, the room and everything went black, my vision disappearing in a blink. *Fuck.* The drugs never blinded before. A quiet washed through my ears, absent of the hum that vibrated all around me.

"What the fuck?" King's grip on me eased, pulling away slightly. "What happened to the power?"

A power outage was better than being blind, but the dark was smothering all the same. It took everything in me not to scream.

The electrical panel beside the door crackled with light, creating enough glow to see clearly. The latch clicked, and the metal door swung gently in its frame. OPEN.

Running on pure adrenaline and instinct, I lifted both arms in the space he'd made, bringing them down on his elbows. The needle, which we'd both nearly forgotten, crashed to the ground in a spray of glass and clear fluid. At least I hadn't taken the full dose.

My other hand yanked on my necklace. The stiletto came free, the red blade glinting in the firelight. King blinked in surprise at my sudden movement but responded too slowly to stop my upward jab. I sank the blade into the soft flesh beneath his chin, piercing the under palate of his throat. Using all of my endorphin-fueled strength, I dragged the blade down, slicing the muscle and tissue until it met his Adam's apple.

"You want the truth, King, *baby?* You could never replace them," I hissed through gritted teeth, pushing the knife in deeper. "Because you aren't half the man they are!"

I'd imagined this so many times, the look in his eyes, knowing his death was imminent, understanding he was mortal just like the rest of us.

Fuck dreams, reality was so much sweeter.

King stumbled back with a gurgle. I jerked the stiletto free and turned for the door, toward freedom.

His hand pressed against the wound while the other snagged a fist full of my hair. I screamed a feral cry of pain and frustration as he threw me to the ground. My back hit the tile hard enough to drive the air from my lungs.

"I was good to you," he coughed against the blood filling his throat. Small specks dripped onto my face as he leaned over me, kneeling on the arm holding the stiletto. "Give me that."

"You wouldn't know good if it spat in your face." I spit hard in his direction. The clear fluid landing a satisfying glob against his cheek. His nostrils flared, making the blood flow faster down his neck. King took my hand, slamming my wrist into the ground and straining at my fingers. I tightened my grip, fighting to keep hold of my only weapon while he grappled me into submission.

His face kept shifting, turning from the one I'd grown to despise into Danny's, then Nick's.

"No," I wept. Now was not the time for the drugs to start kicking in. King's jaw brushed my arm, the rough texture of his beard not matching the smooth cut of Danny's jaw. Closing my eyes so I didn't have to see them, I twisted.

King pried at my fingers, tugging on the chain tethered to the end of the dagger. Pulling my leg free, I rammed my knee upwards, crushing the soft flesh hanging between his legs.

"Bitch!" he howled, releasing my hand. I slashed forward, aiming for the cock waving in my face. The knife dragged over his groin, spraying me with a hot flow of blood. He dropped to the ground, slipping on the wet tiles. What looked like gallons of blood turned the surface from shining white to glistening crimson.

I wasn't waiting around for him to regain his strength. I took off for the door, pausing only slightly when I saw the drawer holding his gun rocking open and closed. I gave King one last look, but the man on the floor wasn't my tormentor. It was Nick, bleeding beneath the rubble.

The urge to return to him tugged at my heart, like a tether keeping me connected, but I knew. Some part of me knew that my eyes couldn't be trusted. This wasn't Nick. It was ghosts.

Quickly fastening Danny's dagger around my neck, I picked up the gun. The grip felt hot, but I palmed it, letting the burn ground me in the physical world. I didn't look back, not knowing what would be waiting for me if I did.

The hallway was pitch black, triggering every deep-rooted fear that lived in my unconscious. The expanse shifted around me like a living creature, mutating into a horde of beasts. I closed my eyes, ignoring how the banging of metal above sounded like teeth gnashing.

Fucking drugs.

This wasn't real. The people crying out for help. Crowe and Toto's screams. None of it was real. Not real. Not real. I recited it like a mantra, singing the words over and over. *Not real. Not real. Not real.*

Placing my hands on the wall, I followed it away from the room and the man who'd confused abuse with care. Feeling the hallway bend, I turned a corner and into another long corridor. At the end, the glow of moonlight shone through a window. I ran for it, slamming hard into the glass window.

With disbelief, I looked out at what lay beyond.

Ocean. Miles and miles of black sea. I'd thought all this time the swaying I felt was the lingering effects of the drug, but it wasn't. We were on a boat.

Fuck. Where was I going to go from here?

Voices echoed down the hall of several approaching men. I scanned the doors, looking for anywhere to hide. The closest one to me had a red panel, reading, Aft Stairs. I pushed it open, scanning up and down the dark stairwell. If it was a boat, maybe up would lead to a deck, and I could steal a lifeboat, or there might be somewhere to hide until we got to shore.

Gripping the handrail, I ascended toward whatever was waiting for me.

-29-
NICK

Pain was like an old friend coming to visit. I was comfortable with it, knew its boundaries and how to handle it. Or so I thought. Turns out some wounds ran deeper than others. Every time my side twinged, the burn made me think of her. Her love. Her promises. Her fucking smile. It burned like she'd stabbed me herself.

Just so there's no confusion, you're mine, Angel.

I love you.

I wish I deserved your love.

How could I have been so gullible? Again. Niccolo Chopper was many things, but gullible? Fuck, I fell for it. Just like with Cat, I laid my head on the chopping block and waited for the axe to fall with an Oz damn smile.

The terror Crowe showed me could've been faked. Maybe. The only person on screen was her. She could have been looking at anything. Where was King when that recording was made? For the fiftieth time in a week, the unbidden image of him between her thighs, tasting that sweet cunt forced its way into my thoughts. *Or stroking his cock while aiming a gun at her angelic face*, Crowe's voice whispered in my thoughts. Apparently, my conscience had a sense of humor.

No. I'd seen enough to know she wasn't forcing him off of her, and she wasn't screaming for help. A beautiful liar. I'd called her that once. I just didn't know how right I was.

It felt like having a piece of myself carved away, and not in the way Eastin had done it. This was so much worse than watching Cat get off on breaking me. A critical part of who I was had been cleaved open. I gave Thea the broken fragments of my heart, and it left with her, leaving me hollow.

The worst part was that I fucking missed her. I missed the annoying way she would bounce around a room, prattling with complete nonsense just to obliterate the silence.

My chest ached, recognizing how much we missed the airy quality of her laugh and her soft smiles when she thought no one was looking—The way being with her made me feel like I had value in this world beyond my lineage and brutality.

Cazzo.

With a single heartbeat, I'd changed. Where she'd made me feel like more, without her, there was nothing. An endless void in the shape of one small woman. This was why I tried to send her away. I'd known from the beginning she would blow my world apart... and she did, the detonation coming from the very center of my soul.

I held my side as I jogged down the stairs, the mounted light on my gun shining the way. Above me, the clatter of chaos rang out. Below, there was only a foreboding silence.

What kind of a condition would I find Danny in? Would he be broken like I was? My vision had been impaired by the fractured parts of my ocular cavity, but Danny's face was one of the few things I remembered from the day they freed me from Eastin's basement. He was covered from head to toe in blood like he'd bathed in it. The sheer number of security that he'd fought through was astounding. Nothing stopped Danny when he was motivated. Breaking into a Witcher stronghold was as good as a death sentence, but my brothers had come anyway. Now, I would save Danny, too, no matter how broken he was.

The shuffle of an approaching person turned the corner, entering the landing below me. I raised my gun, finger partially depressed on the trigger. Until I realized what I was seeing.

Thea.

I aimed the light at her, taking in the haggard details of the girl standing before me, bloody and half-naked. She lifted an arm to her eyes, shielding against the bright light.

Oz-fucking-damn, she was even more beautiful than I remembered.

"Don't shoot me. Please," her voice shook, sounding impossibly tiny for the force I knew her to be.

Despite every instinct telling me not to let her open her viperous mouth, I lowered the gun. The light bounced off the ground, illuminating the tiny space.

Finally able to see who was standing before her, recognition lifted her features, and then she brought a hand to her head—a hand holding what I now realized was a pistol.

I raised mine back into position, the pistol suddenly feeling *very fucking heavy*.

"No," the guttural sound of her voice was barely even words. "You're *not* real!" A violent tremor seized her petite frame as she backed away from me. "Fucking drugs. Fucking King."

"You can stop pretending." The words sounded as hollow as I felt.

She lifted the gun, aiming it straight at me with a steady hand despite the way the rest of her was trembling like a leaf. With that one gesture, the tiny bit of hope that I hadn't even realized I was holding onto, shattered.

"Thea, lower the gun." I descended two steps closer. If this was how I went, then I'd be damn sure I took her with me.

-30-
NICK

As I moved closer, the trembling in her bones intensified. I used to think that was because some part of me electrified her, but she was probably shaking because she was bordering on hypothermic. It was freezing in this stairwell, and all she was wearing was a blood-soaked slip.

Whose blood? Hers? King's? Had she finally double-crossed the asshole? Was she looking for a convenient exit?

"No. No." Voice breaking, she screamed, "You're *dead!*"

Dead? I paused my descent.

Tears slipped from her eyes, carving white tracks in the blood peppering her cheeks.

"You're not him. This is the drug. You died in the kitchen." She cocked the gun, the terror in her expression shifting to fury. "You killed my Nick."

I took another step forward, and she backed into the corner, moving as far from me as possible. "I won't let you drag me back to that room. I won't go." She lowered the gun to beneath her chin. "I'll kill myself before I let you touch me again."

This isn't manipulation, it's rape.

Fuck.

Suddenly, a new image forced its way into my mind—Thea pulling that trigger and her pretty features spraying against the metal walls.

"I'm not taking you anywhere." With a cautionary step back, I dropped my gun. "See, I'm lowering the gun. Now it's your turn." Thea shook her head. I was close enough to see the smaller details I'd missed before. Her normally sea-green eyes were blood-shot and glassy, with blown-out pupils that looked like doll eyes. Bruises that looked at least a week old peppered her arms and thighs, unmistakably in the shape of thumbprints.

None of it was for the benefit of the cameras. None of it was fake. None of it.

Crowe was right. *Quel fottuto coglione* was never going to let me live this down[1].

A door far below opened and closed. Thea jumped, turning towards the noise. I used the distraction to grab the pistol from her grip and immediately dropped it. It was scalding hot. The circuitry in this gun overloaded just like the ones earlier. She must have lifted it from someone, probably whoever's blood was coating her.

"How is your hand not burned?" I took it, turning it over to see angry red welts against her palm. Was she so strung out on whatever she'd been given that she didn't notice the pain? Or was she so scared that she didn't care?

"Let me go." Thea pulled against my grip, feet sliding beneath her as she tried to back away from me. "Please don't make me go."

"*Fiore Mio, sono io*. It's me, Nick."[2]

She blinked, staring up at me through wet lashes. I could see the wheels in her head turning as she processed the smaller details of my face. "Nick?" Thea reached out, putting her hands against my chest as if expecting to see them pass through me. "It's really you?"

"It's really me." I cupped her cheek, feeling like my heart was exploding within the cavity of my chest. Maybe it wasn't lost for good after all.

"I'm not dreaming?"

I shook my head, drawing her closer.

She pressed her face into my Kevlar vest, tiny sniffles shaking her against me. "But I watched you die. I saw it. I felt it. It's so hard to tell what's real and what isn't. I want this to be real. I want it so badly...but I watched you die." She

---

1. Fucking asshole was never going to let me live this down.

2. It's me.

kept repeating it, her voice becoming more distant with each word. Weeks of captivity and abuse hadn't broken her, not in the way my death had.

"Crowe saved me." I pushed on her shoulders, putting space between us so that I could see her face. For the first time in weeks, I allowed myself to take in the possibility that all my fears were false. The moment the relief hit, it was replaced with concern. Thea was willing to shoot herself over going back to King—I didn't even know what he'd been doing to her. I was so lost to my grief that I couldn't bring myself to see what Crowe saw.

"Crowe?" She looked around me and up the stairwell.

"He's on the other side of the ship, looking for you, actually."

"You're really here." She wrapped her arms around me, the trembling in her body growing more intense. "I thought you were dead. Then King tried to make me believe you weren't real, but the pain was too sharp to be fake. I knew it. I *knew* it. I'm not losing my mind because you're here."

"I'm here."

I stroked the back of her hair, dropping a kiss to her crown and taking in a deep breath. Her scent was off, mixed with blood and something else that didn't fit, something masculine. Probably King, the motherfucker.

"Where's King?" I asked, ready to tear out his throat. For Thea. For Nonna. For the hole in my fucking side.

"Hopefully dying."

I ran my hands down her arms, feeling the sticky texture of drying blood. "Dying?"

"Yeah, after I sort of cut his dick off."

"You cut his dick off?" Horror resonated in my voice. It took a special kind of fury to want to sever a man's dick.

"Well, not like *all the way* off. I just diced it up a bit." She cracked a tiny smile, and my hand involuntarily dropped to my cock. "I didn't really stick around to take inventory."

I glanced at her bare feet. "Are you okay to keep going? We have to get Danny." Not that I had a solution if she said no. I couldn't leave her here or send her up on her own. In her current state, she'd be just as likely to jump off the boat as hide in a box. Because of the EMP, Crowe and I had no way to communicate. He'd come across King and figure out what happened. Hopefully, moving directly to the rendezvous point. Which meant Thea had to come with me to get Danny.

"Danny's here?"

"He was taken from the Villa, same as you."

Overhead, the lights flickered. "Shit, that reboot is happening faster than we expected." I grabbed her arm. "We've gotta go."

The corridor holding Danny's cell was long and unexpectedly empty. The overhead lights buzzed, flickering as the systems struggled to come back to life. With each flash of light, the shadows shifted, making it impossible to miss the way Thea jumped back from them or the quiet way she kept murmuring they weren't real.

How often had Crowe said she was dosed? Daily? Was it always like this? Was she questioning the physical world when King was forcing himself on her? *Sono una testa di cazzo.*[3] A mix of rage and shame coursed through me, so potent that I could taste an acidic burn at the back of my throat.

---

3. I'm a dickhead.

The light above crackled, raining down a shower of sparks. Thea leapt away from the spray, gripping my arm like a sloth in a hurricane. *Dannazione.*[4] Every flinch she made was like the wound in my side twisted, the memory of her final kiss burning down to the bone.

Ti amo, Fiore Mio.

The cell doors were made of glass, making it easy to scan them as we passed. The locks were fried, same as the outside doors. If anyone was being held in them, they were long gone now.

"Maybe he already left with the others?" Thea suggested, peering into a cell that looked like it hadn't been cleaned in years.

"Doubtful. Westin had him chained to the wall."

I knew he was being held at the end of the hallway. Among the gifts Orin bequeathed to us were detailed notes on the current layout and the whereabouts of key players. Pulling Thea behind me, I pushed open the final door.

"Danny!" Thea hip-checked me to the side, falling to her knees before him.

He was slumped on the ground, looking more like a ragdoll than a man. If it wasn't for the way his bound hands were twitching slightly, I might have thought he was already dead.

Danny parted one tired eye. "Hey, Firecracker." His voice was barely more than a whisper, sounding like he hadn't spoken to anyone in days. The extreme dehydration wasn't helping either. I remembered what that felt like too clearly. Everyone always thought the hunger was what got to you in captivity, but it was the thirst. You eventually got used to the hollowness of your belly, but the craving for water never went away. It was enough to make you consider doing truly horrific things.

Thea blinked up at me with her large babydoll eyes, "Is this real?"

I nodded solemnly. "Unfortunately."

She lifted his head, ghosting kisses over the bruised cheekbones. "I missed you, Kitten."

Raising one eyebrow, I mouthed, "Kitten?"

---

4. Damn.

Danny rolled his head away from me, "Shut up."

Thea and her pet names. I supposed I should be grateful she wasn't running around calling me Pretty Boy.

Thea pulled on the chains binding his hands. "How do we get these off?"

"The old-fashioned way." I pulled out a lock pick. The locks on cuffs were pretty simple. Turns out, those tiny keys get misplaced all the time, so manufacturers make them relatively easy to crack.

With a quick turn, the cuffs fell to the ground. Danny flexed his hands, rotating them in circles and biting back a hiss of pain.

"It's a bit alarming how practiced you made that look." Thea kicked the chains with her bare feet.

I shrugged. "Westin once left Crowe cuffed buck ass naked—to the front gate of Ciopriani Villa."

"Naked?"

"Yeah, Crowe can be impulsive and doesn't always think through his choices. Westin was one of them."

I didn't realize just how far her jaw could drop.

"*Westin and Crowe?*"

It would be sexy as sin, if it wasn't so damn funny.

"*My Crowe* and... ugh... that's so... so..."

"Heinous," Danny offered, finally making it from the ground to his feet.

"I was going to say gross, but yeah, heinous works, too." Thea flashed a middle finger at the corner of the room...the empty corner.

I shrugged a shoulder at Danny's confused look. She could be seeing anything in that corner.

Danny wrapped Thea in his arms like he was afraid she would vanish, not caring at all about how sore he was or his injuries. "I thought I'd lost you."

"I'm here." She fought free of his grip, grasping his face and pressing a fevered kiss to his lips. "You're real."

He buried his face in her hair. "Westin told me we'd been erased, then I had to watch that dead bird fucker...the things he did. Fuck, Princess, I hope you don't remember half of it. Most of the time, you seemed drugged out of your mind."

I winced, feeling my stomach flip with sour regret. Neither Danny nor Crowe had doubted her. Not even a little. Maybe if I'd had the balls to actually watch the footage, I'd have seen what they saw: Thea being forced into playing nice.

Danny stroked her face, wiping away the tears pouring from her eyes. "Westin told me you'd never remember me."

"They tried. Sometimes it was pretty damn convincing, but I could never forget you."

"When we get home, I'm going to obliterate every trace of that man. We'll go nice and slow until you truly remember what it is to be loved."

Thea paused, pulling back to look at him clearly. "Loved?"

It felt like I was intruding. I didn't deserve to be here for this. Stepping into the hallway, I checked that we were still alone, hearing her tell him that she loved him too. It almost hurt more than thinking she'd been lying.

I love you.

I wish I deserved your love.

That was the truth. I didn't deserve her love, not after I doubted hers.

Danny shuffled into the doorway, one arm wrapped around Thea as she helped him to walk. "How do we get out of this hell hole?"

"There's an escape boat a mile out waiting for our signal." I pointed towards the open stairs. It was very possible the two of them wouldn't be able to do the seven flights back to the top deck, especially if she was supporting his weight. Danny looked like he was going to fall over any second. He needed food and water.

Ten minutes later, Thea grunted, helping Danny the final step onto the first landing. We'd never make it out at this rate. This was why Crowe should have stayed with me. Between the two of us, it would take nothing to lift him. I walked over, shoving my gun under my belt.

"You can give it to me." Thea held out her hand expectantly.

"Stop staring at the shadows like they're staring back, and then maybe we can discuss giving you a gun."

I shook my head. This was a bad decision. There seemed to be a lot of those these days.

Pushing her up the stairs, I said, "Go ahead and listen for sounds of anyone approaching."

"Do the bees count?" Thea pointed to the wall.

"What bees?" Fucking hell, tell me the girl wasn't seeing bees flying around.

"The bees in the wall. You don't hear them?"

I listened to the quiet hum. That wasn't a beehive. It was the engines starting up. "*Figlio di puttana!*[5] The EMP was supposed to take out the control panel. Come on. We need to get off this ship before it starts moving."

Danny released Thea, leaning on me as we climbed the stairs one flight at a time. The stitches in my side screamed from the added pressure, but I ignored it. The pain kept me in the present like it had hundreds of times before. My old friend.

---

5. Son of a bitch!

-31-
DANNY

After weeks of nothing but bright white light, the dark was unexpectedly unnerving. I wasn't jumping at shadows like Thea, but the darkness was disorienting. I'd begged for a respite from the light, trying to shield my eyes for any kind of reprieve. Sometimes, my chains were kept too taut to be able to cover my face, but most of the time, my jailers didn't care.

I'd been largely ignored, going days without seeing another soul. Sometimes, they'd come with food, but most of the time, they didn't. I was asked repeatedly if I knew where Thea had hidden the key. I saw her slip it to my sister as she said goodbye, but I would never place her in danger again. It didn't matter how many twisted ways Westin thought up to torture me.

Thea hadn't given up Daffodil either. That was the small thread of hope that I'd held onto. So long as she was holding out, some part of her remembered what was at stake. Some part of her would remember me.

She trudged up the stairs, peering around the corners like something from a spy movie. It was oddly adorable. It made me think of the way I could see her mouthing our names when she thought no one was looking. Seeing her perfect lips form my name was the first bit of light in my despair.

Thea stopped, spinning on her step to face us. Her eyes tightened on the space between my head and Nick's. "Ugh," she sighed, throwing her hands to her sides in exasperation and lifting her face to the ceiling. "You are the absolute worst. It's like trying to flee for my life with a giant storm cloud. Could you, for once, stop being a massive thundercunt?"

Nick's jaw dropped. "Who are you talking to?

Thea pointed between us, punctuating her words while chastising vaguely in our direction. "Like you don't know." She swiveled with a harumph and stomped up the stairs.

It took everything in me not to laugh. "Yeah, Nick, don't be a thundercunt."

His head turned to mine. "I will drop you down this shaft and leave you to drown."

"That's exactly what a thundercunt would do."

The sounds of her continued annoyance echoed around the stairwell. She clearly thought she was arguing with someone.

"King changed the drug," I whispered to Nick, hoping Thea wouldn't hear me. "He said it before the power went dark. His plan was to keep her awake but continue doping her until she accepted her new reality." I lifted my arm, pointing at the way her fingers kept moving like she was playing an invisible piano. "That twitching is new."

Shadows, dark even for this moody bastard, drifted across his expression before he shifted my weight higher on his back. "It's definitely some kind of hallucinogen, but I don't think it was a full dose. Her lucidity comes and goes."

"Whose blood is that?" I nodded at the dried blood coating her. "Tell me it's King's and that you made that motherfucker hurt."

"From what I've gathered," he confirmed. "Thea's explanations are like trying to translate for a bag of cats."

"Wait," I pushed my hand against his chest, nearly falling down the stairs in the process. "Thea broke *herself* out?" Thea was amazing. The way she never let herself stay down, refusing to tap out, was inspirational.

"She did. Crowe was headed for her, but somehow, she ended up on the opposite end of the ship, covered in blood. It took a while to convince her I wasn't a ghost."

The ship listed to one side, sending the three of us into the wall. A massive shudder trembled through the metal beneath our feet, accompanied by the unmistakable screeching noises of metal on metal.

"Is this real?" Thea looked at the walls like they might swallow her whole.

"Could be, the funnel collapse is putting strain on the internal mechanisms." Even as he said it, Nick didn't sound convinced. Whatever that sound was, it was coming from the belly of the ship. "Or, the hull. Go faster."

Like someone had left on a very, very large faucet, the rumble of water echoed up the stairwell. Nick leaned over the railing, providing me a small glimpse of the water filling up the first-floor landing.

"Faster, Princess."

Nick paused, tugging me along, balancing me on his shoulder to grasp Thea's arm. "Fiore Mio, look at me." She looked from the water already climbing the steps behind us to the top of the stairwell. "Are you with me?"

"I...yeah." Redirecting her gaze to him, she blinked her eyes rapidly. "I think so." Thea wrung her hands together, then gripped the chain at her neck like it was a lifeline. "I'm not entirely certain I can feel my face." She reached up, poking at her cheeks, and giggled. "Nevermind, there it is."

"*Siamo fottuti.*[1] Go as fast as you can. Head toward the lifeboats, there's a ladder that leads down to a loading platform. That's where Crowe will be. Find Crowe."

"Okay."

"Say it."

"Did you know the water is running?"

The frustrated bellow that erupted from him would be funny if we weren't about to drown in this stairwell.

Thea tapped his chest. "Calm down, Angel. Yelling like that will get us caught." Like scrubbing it with a cloth, her face cleared of all the confusion, morphing into her usual sarcastic grace. "I'm going to Crowe. Platform. Lifeboats. Yadda bing badda or something." Thea smiled, booping him on the nose, before loping up the stairs like she was part gazelle.

"What just happened?" I gawked at him in disbelief. "Did she just call you Angel?" Nick was as far from angelic as a man could get. Sometimes I was surprised he hadn't already sprouted horns.

---

1. We're fucked.

"Shut your mouth. Not a fucking word."

"Sorry, Angel—" The word broke out of me with a wheezing laugh.

Nick groaned. "She calls you Kitten. I'd rather be an Angel than a Kitten."

"That's not going away anytime soon. Some names stick, and that one is staying around for a long, long time. You better hope Crowe doesn't find out."

Water lapping at our heels, Nick hauled me several more flights, muttering curse words in Italian. My language skills were rusty, but I knew just about every way to cuss a mother-fucker out, and Nick was using all of them right now.

My bare feet felt like walking on knives when we couldn't outpace the water. It crept as we climbed, slowing our pace by the minute. Three floors above us, the door to the outer deck pushed open, filling the stairwell with moonlight.

"Th-thank f-fuck," I said over my shivering breath.

The lithe silhouette of Thea disappeared into the light. Knowing we were close made it easier to summon the energy to fight our way up. We'd make it out of here. Hopefully, Westin's crew were busy abandoning ship and wouldn't care about a couple of escapees.

We followed Thea into pure chaos. People were moving in every direction, and crew were lowering lifeboats, several already bobbing along the water. Thea was nowhere in sight, and I cursed Nick for sending her ahead. She was probably lost somewhere, trying to talk to a seagull.

"This way." Nick angled me towards the back of the ship. "You're going to have to try to do the ladder yourself. I can't carry you with these stitches, especially half-drenched."

"Stitches?" Thea's sobs about Nick dying played back in my head. I looked down and saw a wet splotch against the black of his jumpsuit. My own dirty shirt was stained red from where I had been pressed against him.

"Shit, you definitely shouldn't have been hauling me up here."

"It's nothing big, I was impaled a bit."

"Oh, okay, so long as it's not anything big." I made a feeble attempt to punch him in the shoulder. My fist glanced off the Kevlar arming his chest, tearing my knuckles. "You're such an asshole. You know that girl thought you were dead."

"She might have mentioned it."

"Thea cried every time she was alone. Every. Time. The least you could do is not die while trying to save her."

Nick grunted, averting his gaze like he actually felt guilty. "I'm working on it."

Up ahead, Thea's dark hair glowed bright red in the single spotlight that had come back online. She looked like an angel being bathed in the light of Ozma. Except as she leaned over the railing, her down-turned brows and the harsh set of her lips were that of horror.

"Shit. What now?"

-32-
THEA

The ratcheting sound of a gun filled my ears, even though the man pointing it was standing far below. Not just one man, many. Their guns were different than the one I'd stolen from King. These were simpler, sleeker, like the sharks circling the partially submerged platform.

"I think it best if you come down here," a tall woman in a shiny catsuit commanded. "You've left us waiting long enough." Westin Witcher swung a rope lazily in one hand. It arced slowly back and forth. My eyes followed the line, tracking it to the edge of the water.

"Fuck!" Danny's fingers dug into my hip like he feared I might leap over the banister to save the man at the end of the rope. "I guess we know where Crowe ended up."

In the back of my mind, I'd wondered why we hadn't been pursued more. Why the guards never came for me or tracked us down to Danny's cell. It would have been easy to intercept us, but I realized now that she didn't need to chase us down. We were always going to come to her.

Nick settled into my other side, cursing a long string of words as he took in what Danny and I already had. Hands bound behind him, standing atop a precarious stack of crates, was a man I'd dreamt about hundreds of times over the past few weeks. A noose was looped around his neck and strung over what looked disturbingly like a feeding hook. It was pulled taught enough to force him onto his tiptoes. I stared at the ominous hook, the crook of the metal polished to a shine from overuse. How often did you have to feed sharks to have one of these installed on your boat?

"Real?" I whispered, praying for once that this was a nightmare vision.

"It's real, Fiore Mio." Nick's hand rested over mine. "On a scale of one to ten, how lucid would you say you are right now?"

"Ship is sinking?"

"Yes."

"Crowe is strung up?"

"Yes."

I lifted my hand to the sky, where a fleet of drones was spelling out my name. "How about those giant bees circling overhead?"

Nick's hand on mine tightened. "Eh. *No.*"

"Well, two out of three isn't bad, right?"

"We're fucked," Danny groaned. "Thea's unpredictable at a ten. What do you think she's going to be like firing on only two cylinders?"

"Ah, Niccolo," Westin's voice had an uncanny ability to cut through everything like it forced the world to silence through sheer will alone. "I'm pleased to see you've retrieved my pet for me. Why don't you and Dorothy come down here for a chat? Bring the other one with you, too."

"You're a miserable, fucking bitch." Crowe's voice was tight, the rope pushing into his Adam's apple and raising the pitch, but it didn't lessen the severity of his disgust.

Westin pursed her lips, pulling the rope hard enough to make Crowe gag. "Sorry, Vincent, you'll have to repeat that." She tugged down further, causing Crowe to lose his footing, all but one toe raising off the crate's surface. Holding a hand up to her ear, she waited for a response. "Nothing? Well, that's disappointing. You always had such a way with words."

Oh, she was a dead woman.

Several long moments passed where the only movement was Crowe's toes scrabbling for purchase. Each scrape sounded like sands in an hourglass, turning the vast ocean around us into a desert wasteland. Sparkling dunes rolled towards the horizon. I looked up at the bees. The letters of my name morphed into "*Surrender*".

Fucking drugs.

Maybe King would survive, and then I could kill him again. I closed my eyes, imagining what the ship should look like, and willing my mind to catch the fuck on. Black water, grey metal, one stupidly dressed cunt, and about a dozen men with guns aimed at us. When I opened them, everything was back to normal, still horrific, but at least it was real.

"You still with me, Princess?" Danny's concern was troubling.

"Yeah. Are we going down?"

"I don't think we have much choice." Nick tilted his head to the right, where several guards were approaching, a matching set closing in from the other side.

Nick moved to the ladder first. "Thea, you come down last. I'm going to spot Danny."

"There's no need for weapons, so go ahead and dispose of them overboard for me." Westin's tone reminded me so much of Aunt Em. It was the same way she'd speak to me when I'd gotten into something I shouldn't have, and she was annoyed that she had to take the time to punish me.

Nick tossed his pistol like a frisbee, sending it straight to the bottom of the sea. He leveled a bland stare at Westin.

"And the rest." Westin's long fingernails tapped with irritation against her hip.

He slid a knife from each sleeve and one from his belt, throwing them to the deck with enough force to make them stick point down into the wood. Westin didn't look up at him, too busy inspecting her nails to give him the benefit of an audience, but she waved for him to continue all the same.

Nick huffed, pulling free two more daggers, three smaller grenades, a smoke bomb, a flare gun, and lastly, removing a small, single shot pistol from his boot. "Satisfied, cagna?"

"Are you offering?" Finally lifting her eyes to him, Westin licked her lips. The catsuit's glossy surface glistened like oil as she ran her hands over her thighs. "It's been a long time since I've had a lover who could keep up." She not so subtly lifted her long nose at Crowe.

I've never had a reason to be jealous before. Until my guys, I'd never cared enough about anything to be jealous. When Westin dragged her talons down

Crowe's stomach, all I could think was that the sharks circling the water looked mighty hungry. Truthfully, I'd pictured feeding her to the sharks several times since I'd first noticed them.

"Take your vile hands off my man." My hands bit into the railing, wishing it was her neck.

"Thea," Nick warned.

Westin lifted one corner of her mouth, palming Crowe's cock and giving it a squeeze. "Hmm. Not as firm as I remembered."

Crowe lifted a leg, driving a knee under her chin. The witch stumbled back, her high heels slipping on the metal. For a second, I thought I was going to get my feeding time wish, but she righted herself. Then turned and sank a punishing fist straight into Crowe's dick.

"Fuck...bitch," he wheezed, body falling slack against the rope and making him gurgle.

"Dorothy, I'm not a patient woman. Come down here, now, or I will start taking Vincent apart—starting with your favorite pieces first."

I pushed my tongue into my cheek, resisting the urge to call the woman out a second time. Instead, I followed Danny down the ladder, counting the rungs as I went to keep my mind steady. The last thing I needed was for one of them to mutate into a snake and bite me.

Westin strolled toward me, the stiletto points of her boots clicking against the metal surface.

Nick pushed me behind him. "That's close enough."

She rolled her eyes, and the henchman closest to Nick roughly grabbed his arm, pulling him out of her path. Nick hissed at the gun shoved into his wounded side. With an unexpected twist, he yanked free. The heavy, tattooed surface of his fist slammed into the man's face, followed by a hard kick to the sternum that sent him careening into the water.

Within seconds, a large, white-mouthed shark breached the surface, snatching the flailing man. A wave of displaced water rolled over my bare feet, sending a painful shiver up my legs. It happened so quickly that he didn't even have the chance to yell. All that was left was a small ripple of water where he had once been.

Above us, Crowe started struggling in earnest, twisting his wrists in a futile attempt to free his hands. The red tinge of blood covered the metal, dripping onto the crates below him.

Westin glared at Nick. "Do you know how hard it is to find quality guards?"

Nick rolled his shoulders back, standing nearly a full head taller than her.

"Restrain him," Westin snapped. "I'd rather not have any further interruptions." Four of Westin's men circled Nick.

"If you touch me, I can guarantee that you'll end up as shark bait, just like your friend."

"I'd listen to him," I said, keeping my eyes on Westin. She seemed bored.

Rather than make a move for him, the closest one turned and aimed his revolver at me. "Against the wall. Now."

Nick took a step back, lifting his hands. "*Tu sarai il primo a morire.*"[1]

Two others deposited a woefully weak Danny at Nick's feet.

"Ah. That's better." Westin closed the distance between us, using the time to take in the details of my haggard appearance. I could only imagine what she must think of me: blitzed eyes, covered in gore, and half-naked. Coiling a blood-soaked ringlet around her finger, she released it with a tiny bounce. "You've caused quite the stir here tonight."

"Stir?" I repeated.

"I notice King isn't with you." She looped the end of Crowe's rope around my shoulders, using it to pull me toward her. "As entertaining as this experiment has been, I had a feeling we would always end up right here. I should have pulled the trigger in the beginning, but King's proposal was such an interesting one. It's boring at the top. They never tell you that. You spend your whole life fighting your way up the ladder, but what happens after you finally make it there? I'll tell you, there's nothing here but simpering fuck wits."

---

1. You will die first.

"Maybe you're looking in the wrong direction. I've never been at the top, but I've also never had a problem finding something worth fighting for. Care for a demonstration? I'll drag your absurdly shiny ass up and down this platform."

Danny laughed, propping an arm against his knee like he was settling in for a matinee.

"Seriously, Crowe?" I looked Westin up and down with a sneer. "This bitch?"

Crowe rolled his eyes but couldn't do much more than choke and kick his foot.

Westin played with the emerald hanging between her breasts, shards of green light flaring and giving her skin a greenish hue. "Oh, sweet Dorothy, you're just like your father. He never knew when to leave well enough alone either."

A chaotic riot of emotions, bouncing between indignation and curiosity, bared their fangs. "What do you know about my father?" I took a step forward, causing the rope to fall slack against my lower back and bringing me close enough that the sweetness of her perfume encircled us. It was subtle, a complex mixture that smelled like it cost a fortune. It was like everything else about her, unnecessary.

Westin's lips curled up, not quite into a smile. A smile would imply joy. This was far more malicious, like a cat dangling the mouse by its tail. "Darren never stopped pushing, even when he was firmly beneath my boot. Maybe if he had known when to roll over, he'd still be alive today instead of at the bottom of an icy lake."

My blood thumped in my ears. I resisted the urge to claw at her perfectly blended makeup. In truth, I wanted these answers.

"Your father needed a platform, something that could guarantee the Premiership. What better way to do that than to take down the Quadrant's leading gun runners? Remove the guns, make Oz safer for all." With a girlish laugh, she gestured at all the firepower pointed at us. "Well, maybe not all the guns."

The guards laughed with her, one man firing demonstratively into the sky. I couldn't help but flinch.

"The public ate it up, especially when my father and uncle were presented as worthy sacrifices on the altar of Ozmandrian politics. Nobody cared about the children he orphaned that day or how they would survive on the streets without someone to provide for them. East and I clawed our way out of that forgotten sewer and kept climbing until all of Oz was ours." Westin grabbed my face, digging her nails into my cheeks. "That was until a meek, pathetic little girl bashed her face in with a snow globe."

Through my squished cheeks and gritted teeth, I snarled, "And I'd do it again."

Westin huffed, pushing my face away. "You're lucky I don't harbor grudges like my cousin did."

"You could have fooled me," I scoffed. "If you don't care about the past, then what was the point of that whole bullshit villain monologue?"

"Do you know how emeralds are formed?" She caressed the emerald nestled neatly between her breasts.

"Why would I know that?"

"When forgotten bits of the earth are given enough pressure, they rise to the surface, meeting the light of day and turning from useless minerals to something precious, something *envied*. I'm not going to punish you for the crimes of your parents because what I was and where I came from doesn't matter. I'm focused on the present."

"Like the key."

"Thea!" Danny yelled, jumping to his feet, his pain and exhaustion forgotten in favor of true panic for the wellbeing of his sister. The guard closest to him swung out, delivering a hard punch to his already bruised cheek.

"Shhh, you had your chance." Westin nodded at the man standing beside Danny. Without question, he gripped a rough handful of hair, ramming Danny's face straight into his knee before dropping him to the ground in a pathetic heap. Loose strands of torn hair stuck to the fresh blood dribbling over his chin and down his throat.

My face scrunched involuntarily with the sound of his nose breaking. "I'm rather partial to that face. I'd appreciate it if you stopped breaking it."

Westin rocked back on her heels, tilting her head to the side in thought. "You know, I think I might like you. I never like anyone, but you, you're practically tolerable."

"I guess that's a compliment?"

"It is. You have terrible taste in men, though." My incredulous expression must have given away my thoughts. Westin tugged on Crowe's end of the rope. "Vincent knows his way around a pussy, but he's dumber than a sack of hay." She walked right, dragging me with her. Circling her palm around Nick's strained biceps, she continued, "Niccolo has nailed the bad boy with too many tattoos persona, but he lacks finesse. There's no heart behind what he does." With a final lazy wave in Danny's general direction, she added, " And the other one is... well. He's there."

"I have a name, you stupid bitch."

"And nobody cares." Westin dragged me closer to Crowe. Sweat beaded on his brow, his throat flexing against the rope as he tried to swallow. The sapphire fire of his eyes was focused completely on me.

"Let's move this along, shall we?" Gripping Crowe's leg, she dragged him closer to the water, giving him a little push until the pole supporting his weight swiveled over the open ocean.

I screamed a feral cry, the looped bit of rope around me the only thing holding me back from jumping to save him. Crowe's feet kicked, the blood from his wrists dropping into the churning water beneath.

There was movement in my peripheral of Nick and Danny struggling against the gunmen guarding them. I couldn't hear them. All I heard was the heart-wrenching sound of Crowe's frantic motions.

"You have about three minutes before he strangles to death, less if he keeps wiggling like that." Westin slapped my face, the sting inciting more clarity than I'd felt in days. "Focus, Dorothy. The key."

"I don't fucking know, you egomaniacal cunt!" Weeks of frustration blared from me. "I can't remember. How many times do I have to say it? You scrambled my memories, pulled them apart, and reassembled them so many times that I can't tell the truth from the bullshit. You expect me to remember what I did with one small key that, at this point, I really don't give a fuck about?"

"So, that's a no?"

"It's a fuck you."

"Pity. I don't have time for games. My ship is sinking." Westin looked over her shoulder.

Crowe had stopped wriggling from his line, dead or unconscious, I didn't know. All I knew was that there was war in my heart, tearing me apart from the inside out.

"Put her in the lifeboat and dispose of them." She waved at Danny and Nick. In slow motion, I watched her hand open. The rope recoiled, whipping across the back of my legs. The shriek of fibers on metal sounding like a bowstring firing. Westin didn't even watch as Crowe's limp body dropped into the black water. Unconscious, hands bound...and circled by sharks.

A light blonde streak of hair bobbed not far below the surface, held in place by the tension of the rope tightening around my hips. The sharks bumped into his body, pushing him above the surface for a moment before he sank once more into the dark water.

I didn't stop to consider my options; instinct sent me straight to where Crowe's hair was disappearing.

Westin moved into my path. "What do yo—"

I lowered my shoulder, slamming my full weight into her stomach. My body tangled with hers as we fell, hitting the edge of the platform and rolling into the icy water. Like weights on a scale, Crowe's body flew into the air, gone before I had realized what had happened.

—33—
THEA

With each turn, the rope worked around us, growing hard and tight as it absorbed the seawater. The shock of cold assaulted my senses, clawing at my skin until it felt like I was on fire.

Tethered together, our combined weight sank fast, the spotlight on the deck quickly becoming muted and distant. My lungs already screamed for air, my eyes stinging from the salt as I tried to look around us. Westin drove an elbow into my side, somehow fighting me while also trying to extricate herself from the web binding us together. The more we struggled, the tighter the rope grew.

I wanted to scream at her to stop, or we'd both drown. It wasn't the fight or the ropes that stilled her jabs. It was the realization that her pets were circling us.

A dark silhouette bumped nose first into my leg, testing his new treat to see if it was edible. He was nearly the length of a car, heavy muscle slowly swaying from side to side. My mouth opened with a scream, a massive air bubble floating to the surface. The longer I stared at the other approaching sharks, the more I realized bits of flesh and fabric floating were from the last man who entered the water.

The vast ocean pressed down, swallowing me in its depths. My chest rapidly shook as I fought the instinct to start panting. Undiluted fear coursed through my veins. I closed my eyes, pinning down the panic as I had every time Em locked me away.

My hand went to the chain around my neck on reflex. Over the past two weeks, I'd taken to touching it whenever I felt defenseless. I wrapped my fingers around the tube, ignoring the way Westin pushed at my body. The dagger looked black in the low light.

With as much pressure as I could muster, I sawed at the rope. Fibers broke free, one small strand at a time. I said a mental thanks to Danny. If we made it out of this in one piece, he was getting the best blowjob of his life.

Another shark swam closer. His sandpaper hide was the color of wet asphalt, peppered by several long white scars. He opened his jaws wide, not aggressively but still coming for a testing bite. His lips peeled back, revealing rows upon rows of jagged teeth.

The first band of rope snapped free, cracking across the shark's snout and strafing his eye. He retreated quickly, but another was already moving in to take his place.

I shifted the knife to the band circling my hips, pushing myself to saw faster.

A muffled cry came from behind me, the water becoming hazy with a stream of fresh blood. Twisting to look over my shoulder, I watched the massive maw of a grey and white mottled shark shake vigorously. The tendons and muscles of Westin's arm and shoulder shredded beneath his razor teeth. The shark turned, opening and gnashing his jaws as he readjusted the severed arm in his mouth. A piece of black pleather floated in the water, slapping me in the face.

The stiletto dagger cut through the second band of rope, the one beneath it going slack. I wiggled, trying to push it over my hips. Westin twisted with me, tightening a smaller loop along my ankle.

She tore with her remaining hand at my shoulder, clawing at the arm that held the knife. If she wanted the dagger so badly, then she could have it. I shoved the pointed end into the first fleshy bit I could reach, her cheek. I yanked hard, the blade coming free beneath her lip. Small bubbles of air escaped with her cry until, finally, her eyes bulged, and her body convulsed against the water invading her lungs. My chest screamed in recognition of my same fate staring blankly back at me.

Beneath us, movement caught my eye. It was small at first but increasing rapidly in size. Nearly double the size of the last shark, he moved directly for us with the speed of a freight train. I pushed frantically at the rope. Westin's body, no longer fighting against mine, made the line slacken enough at my hips that I finally came free. I slithered up, pulling my legs away from the bindings.

The emerald, still hanging from her neck, winked at me. I swear I could hear it calling my name. I ripped it from her neck just as the full force of the shark rammed into us. His outer jaw brushed my stomach, and his fin rammed beneath my legs. Together, we shot vertically through the water and into the sky.

I opened my mouth, gasping and gulping in a harsh breath of air. We soared through the air, the shark's jaws growing wider. The night sky sparkled with beautiful stars. At least I was dying with one last view of freedom. I brushed my fingers through the starry field as enormous jaws clamped around Westin's limp body. The shark arched to the side, his fin knocking me clear and cartwheeling me back to earth.

The water cracked against my skin, sending a flare of pain strong enough to snap me out of the stars and back to reality. The shark landed in the water with a tidal wave splash, only inches from me. He disappeared in a flash, taking what was left of Westin's body with him.

Schools of fish swarmed, nipping at my skin and snapping up tiny bits of debris. A telltale fin sliced through the water, telling me it was only seconds until I would join Westin in the depths.

Strong hands reached under my arms, hauling me upright. I twisted, screaming, sure that a shark I hadn't seen was laying claim to the leftovers. A second set of hands pulled at my waist. Not a shark, but an Angel. Nick deposited me quickly onto the platform, all three of us falling to the floor in a heap, crushing Crowe but, more importantly, out of the range of the thousands of gnashing teeth headed for us.

The shark snapped his empty jaws, managing to come several feet onto the platform before giving up and slinking back into the darkness.

"Fuck, that was close."

Crowe's grip on my body didn't lessen. I'd watched him be nearly hanged, and he was clutching me like it was my life that had flashed before his eyes.

"Fuck. Fuck. Fuck." Was all he could say as we rocked in a wet heap against the floor.

I looked over his shoulder. What was left of Westin's men lay battered and broken across the platform. While I'd been fighting for my life beneath the surface, they'd secured ours above it.

"I have to get the flare." Nick gave me a quick kiss on the only part of me that Crowe was willing to relinquish, my elbow. Quickly ascending the ladder to where he'd dropped his small arsenal of weapons, he fired the flare high into the air. It spread bright green through the sky, exploding like a firework and returning to the water in a shower of glittering sparks.

Danny hobbled over to us. He'd looked better, but at least now he didn't look broken. His smile was wide with victory beneath bruised eyes. In the distance, the fleet of lifeboats bobbed along the water, heading towards the strip of land far against the horizon.

I held up my hand, showing him the prize I'd won. Westin's emerald swung in the spotlight, dripping water and sparkling with all it promised to give us. "I got you a present."

"What a world. Oz damn, you're amazing." Danny grabbed the side of my face, pulling me away from Crowe and planting a hard kiss on my lips. "I love you, but never fucking jump into a pit of sharks again, even to try and save this asshole."

Cold shivers wracked my body, partly from the memory of their skin scraping mine and partly from the freezing air. "I don't know that I'll ever go swimming again after that," I said through chattering teeth.

A small speedboat with an engine nearly half the size of the sleek hull rumbled over the water. As it approached, they cut the motor, making everything go silent. The pilot leaned over the side, throwing a rope to us. "Somebody order a ride?"

"Toto!" I shouted, beaming a smile at her freckled face. Pushing out of Crowe's grip, mostly, I climbed to my feet, waving wildly at my friend. Knowing that the threat of Westin was officially gone made me giddy. Although it was probably the shock and the adrenaline, or maybe it was the drugs. I didn't care what it was. I felt light. Euphoric. The stars winked down on me. Yeah, that was probably the drugs.

She looked up at the partially submerged mega-yacht and whistled. "When you guys party, you really party."

By morning, Westin's floating fortress would be a forgotten skeleton, decomposing on the ocean floor—just like her. There was a macabre satisfaction that came from knowing she'd died the same way she'd killed so many innocents. Though seeing the shark tear her body limb from limb would probably haunt my dreams for the rest of my life.

"Climb onboard. Ginger has the safe house ready for you. When I saw the boat start exploding, I told her to get a cold kit ready. I figured it couldn't hurt to be prepared for a touch of hypothermia."

Nick nodded in agreement. He wasn't shivering, but his lips were just as blue as the rest of us.

As we sailed away from the wreckage, I couldn't help but feel like we were on the verge of something massive. I didn't know what it was, but I knew things would never be the same again.

-34-
CROWE

L ove is odd. It trumps every natural reaction and makes your brain run wild. I leaned into the corner of the dark bedroom, running my hand along the rough surface of the abrasions on my throat.

You would think the first thought to go through your mind when you're being strangled to death would be fear for yourself. That the loss of air and the way the pressure makes your vision turn a hazy pink would make the panic all-consuming. There was fear, and there was panic, but as I dangled over the shark pit, it wasn't myself I was concerned for. I would never forget the way Thea screamed and the look of horror on her face.

She rolled over in bed, clutching the blanket like it was armor.

I've never felt relief like I had the moment her body breached the water. It shook me down to the marrow. I could see it in Nick, too. He leapt into the ocean the moment her red hair hit the light. He didn't care about the half dozen visible fins circling the water or the teeth heading straight for her. All that mattered was saving the girl we loved.

Now, he was avoiding her completely, and the hurt in Thea's eyes was hard to ignore.

Love is odd.

Nick would never admit it, but seeing our girl with King dusted off all those ancient feelings of betrayal. He'd been so quick to push his history with Cat onto Thea, and in the wake of the truth, he retreated into what he knew best—repression and self-denial.

Danny curled around Thea's bent form, pulling her as close as possible. He nuzzled her neck with a sleepy hum, pressing a light kiss on her shoulder before drifting back to sleep.

She held a confident face the entire ride to the hotel. It was impressive how composed she was. When we pointed her towards the shower, she insisted she needed the time alone. Concern hadn't really set in until forty minutes later when she still hadn't emerged. We found Thea in a ball on the floor of the shower, sobbing silently, her hand clamped over her mouth to muffle each gasping inhale.

Danny climbed into the water with her, clothes and all. As I watched him pull her into his lap, I couldn't help but wonder how many times she'd done this exact thing while King waited on the other side of the door. Maybe it went back farther than that. Was this how she learned to hide her pain and fear all those years under Em's watchful eyes?

It took everything in me to give them space. Seeing her broken like this made me want to level cities. All I'd ever seen from Thea was strength. Even in her weakest moments, she was still staggeringly strong. I knew why; just like Danny, I'd seen everything. I saw when she'd looked happy, believing the lie, and I was right there with her when clarity came crushing down. I wished like hell the cameras hadn't been fried in the EMP, if only so I could watch Thea finally eviscerate the bastard.

The primal instinct to run and hide her in a cave was strong. I wanted to hold her so tightly that no one would ever get to her again, but that wasn't what she needed. So instead, I went in search of a nightlight so that she didn't have to sleep in the dark.

Thea gravitated towards Danny, perhaps because he looked as broken as she felt. They held each other close, whispering about the reality they found themselves in. Danny had his own trauma to process. This was as healing for him as it was for her. They laid there for hours until exhaustion finally took them both. Hopefully, the drugs would be out of her system when she awoke.

Nick's shadow slipped into the room, silently walking to my side. "You should get some rest, too," he whispered.

I shook my head. "She looks peaceful like this."

"They both do."

I studied the dark rings around his eyes, guilt pulling at his features. "You could crawl in there with them."

Nick considered it more than I was expecting him to. "I..." He palmed the back of his neck, whispering something in Italian too low for me to understand. "I shouldn't have doubted her."

"No, you shouldn't have." I was furious with my brother, but I also understood. Losing her had killed him, even if it wasn't true. He needed to face those demons because I saw what losing him had done to Thea, and I didn't want her to lose him again. She loved him, and I loved them both.

"She deserves this..." He gestured to the bed. "She deserves better than me."

I rested my hand on his shoulder. "Better than all of us, but it isn't our choice. Thea gets to decide for herself. *That's* what she really deserves. Consider that before you make another run for it." Before he could leave, I walked from the room, closing the door behind me.

Toto was sitting in the living room, flipping slowly through an old, beat-up romance novel. The couple on the cover embraced on a beach, with the ocean crashing around them. The television was on, quietly playing the news in the background.

"Pretty sure there are no pictures in that book, but if you find any, I want to see them." I flopped onto the couch next to her with a groan. Crazy how being hanged a little could make all your joints ache so much.

Toto rolled her eyes. "He's too pretty. I can't focus on the story at all, but this..." She tossed the book onto my lap with a sigh. "...was all Ginger had."

I opened to a random page, eyes skimming over the word *member* five times before tossing it back to her. "Yeah, he seems really *pretty*. Totally distracting, what's with all that throbbing and swelling."

"Shut up. If more men read romance, there would be less dissatisfied women in the world."

"I've never had any complaints."

Toto pushed my shoulder. "That you know of."

I pushed her back, and she tipped over. I liked her. She was like the sister I'd always hoped Vanessa would've been. "Thank you, Toto. Ginger did us a solid here. This suite is probably the poshest safe house we've ever stayed in. We couldn't have done it without you."

"Eh. Ginger has more hotels than she knows what to do with, and he's my brother." Toto looked over her shoulder towards the bedrooms, noting the now closed door. "How are they doing in there?"

"Sleeping, finally. I think that's a good start."

Toto rotated, tucking her legs to sit cross-legged. "How long was he..." She picked at a bit of chipped nail polish. "What I mean is, how long has Dandy been with you?"

I debated answering. Danny needed to get his head out of his ass and have a conversation that didn't involve shouting or bossing his sister around. His story wasn't mine to tell. I settled for, "A long time. He never stopped looking for you."

She nodded. "I wondered, ya know...about what happened to them. I made out okay, as things go, but I've seen some...stuff. I always knew I was lucky."

"You should talk to him about it. Danny's an asshole, but he cares. Deep down, he's terrified of losing the people he loves. You're one of those people."

"Do you think The Wizard will keep up his end of the bargain and tell us where Daisy is?"

"I do." The Wizard didn't make a reputation for power and control by reneging on their deals.

"I can't remember what Daisy looked like. I can't even imagine what she'd look like now that she's all grown up. It feels awful to admit, but I can't remember any of them. Didi...Mom." Toto's green eyes went glossy. She tipped her head back, blinking rapidly to force back the tears. It was remarkable how similar she looked to Danny. If I squinted, they practically looked like twins.

"I can't remember my sister either." I'd never told anyone that. "My sister Vanessa died when I was young; it was how I ended up living with Nick's family. It happened slowly over time, and then, one day, I realized I couldn't picture her anymore. I try, but it changes, and her face is always sort of blurry."

"Exactly." Toto perked up. "Yes! That's exactly what it's like. When I saw Dandy in that lobby, I thought I was hallucinating. It was like looking in a mirror, but everything was wrong. We never looked alike as kids, not like Daisy and Dandy do. When they were little, Dandy wore his hair really long. People confused them all the time."

I snorted involuntarily. "Oh, that's priceless. Please tell me more."

Toto's lips quirked into a mischievous grin. "She'd make him flower crowns of daisies, and sometimes, the two of them would prank our mom by switching places. We thought it was hilarious."

"Danny wore flower crowns?" I bit on my knuckle to try and stifle my laugh. That idiot was *never* going to live this down.

"Of course. We all did."

Toto's phone blinked to life on the coffee table, chirping with an alert. Her brows knitted together in confusion. It was almost 6 A.M.. She picked it up, the uncertainty on her face growing. "It's for you."

"What?" I took the phone, puzzled. Nobody knew we were here, much less that Toto had any connection to me.

To YBR: I never doubted you. Friday, 7 P.M., Station 5, Head Shots, E.C.

"It's The Wizard. We have our meeting." How did they always know? I turned Toto's phone over, wondering if a tracker was installed in it, but that felt too pedantic for The Wizard. I could try to run a trace on the text message, but I knew it'd be pointless.

"How could he know that she already killed Westin?" Toto looked around the room like she might suddenly see cameras hidden in the corners. "It's spooky."

"We'll have to retrieve Eastin's emerald from the bank."

"I have it." Toto reached into her waistband, pulling free an old, bronze key.

"You? All this time, Thea didn't even have it." She placed it into my waiting palm. I sat back, holding the key up to the light, making emerald beams shine around the room. "I don't want to know where you were hiding this thing."

Toto winked, "Don't you?" With a laugh, she flipped the band of her leggings down, revealing a small pocket built into the elastic.

"Clever."

The phone chirped again, the ringtone sounding like a video game that I played as a kid. "Is that the warning sound from The Wheelers?" I probably hadn't heard that tone in close to a decade. "Fuck, that takes me back. Ya know, your brother used to kick my ass in that game. He always grabbed the lunch pails before me."

Don't bother with the bank. I already have Eastin's emerald.

Of course they did. Danny was going to be furious. This was exactly why he didn't want Thea to put it in the vault to begin with.

"How in the hell?" Toto picked up the phone and threw it across the room.

"Relax. There isn't a microphone or speaker in all of Ozmandria off limits to The Wizard, trust me."

"Well, that's disturbing."

The fanfare of the morning news cut over the near-silent room. *Good Morning, Emerald City. I'm Jellia Jamb. Our leading story, today marks six months since the search for Sorren Singrala began. Authorities still have no leads as to her whereabouts following the bombing of St. Ozma's Hospital.* Toto reached forward, muting the feed.

"Sorry, I like the television on in the background. Living at the Chateau, it was rarely ever quiet."

"It's fine." The smiling face of the Southern Quadrant's leader flashed on the screen, followed by bird's eye footage of the search party combing The Dark Forest, where we'd established our headquarters. I could still remember the feel of Thea that first night, her brutalized skin warm beneath my hand. She looked so small curled against the cab window as I brought her home, and changed our lives forever. I looked down at my palm. Suddenly, this living room felt so far away from where I wanted to be.

-35-
NICK

T he soft click of the door closing sounded like the tolling of death's bell. It reverberated through my bones, echoing in the beat of my heart. Whatever happened next, there was no coming back from it. Closing that door was forcing me to make a choice. Which was exactly why Crowe had done it. *Dannazione.*[1]

My brother knew if I was given the luxury of avoiding this moment, then I would never face it. I would let Thea live happily with Danny and Crowe, watching and wanting from the shadows.

Thea gasped, sucking in a sharp intake of breath, eyes flying open. Her pupils were black discs, shaking with fear. She blinked, clearing her eyes as they focused on me. The warm glow of the nightlight highlighted her features, softening their edges and making her hair glow like a bloody halo. She was so beautiful. It was hard to think about anything but wanting her. I pressed my hand to the pain tightening in the center of my chest.

"Nick?"

This was it. Whichever direction I walked, it meant the end of something. Thea pushed onto her elbow, her face scrunching tight as she tried to make sense of what she was seeing.

I looked at the closed bedroom door. If I walked through it, what we'd briefly shared would never be again. She wouldn't forgive me a second time. I wasn't even sure she'd really forgiven me for the first time.

Just so there's no confusion... You're mine.

If I went to her, it would mean living with my heart exposed. Like a live wire sparking, if I embraced it, that fire could consume us both. The what-if scenarios were endless. So many ended with one of us broken. I knew what lay beyond the door and had no idea what life would look like if I accepted the opportunity blinking up at me.

"Angel?"

I took a single step toward her. Thea pulled the covers open, a clear offer to join them. The bed was massive, more than enough space for the three of us—probably enough for Crowe, too.

I cast my eyes over her. Danny's hand was still tight to her stomach, his arm tucked tight under her breasts. The circle of red and bruising at his wrist stood out in stark contrast to her pale skin. Of course she was sleeping nude. I scrubbed a hand over my face.

The universe didn't need to provide the temptation of her rosy nipples; the memory of what they'd felt like in my mouth was imprinted on my tongue. It should make me jealous, seeing his hand pressing into her skin, knowing that she was cradled into the crook of his naked body. It didn't, though. The three of us had worked as a unit for so long that seeing them together felt natural.

The only thing that I was jealous of was how easy it was for him to let go. I jumped from a plane with zero hesitation, but the four steps separating us might as well have been an ocean.

Her lips moved with a soundless plea, "Please."

Except, when the possibility of losing her was before me, I'd leapt into the ocean without a second thought. I'd already chosen her. All that was left to do was accept what she was offering.

I grabbed the bottom of my Henley, pulling it over my head with a single decisive motion. Thea's eyes tracked the shirt as I tossed it aside. By the time they returned to me, I was already pushing one knee into the mattress. My fingers slid into her hair, pulling her mouth to mine as I rolled her back.

Against my lips, she asked, "Is this real?"

I pulled back enough to see the ring of silver in her eyes. "Loving you is the realest truth I've ever known."

Danny rolled with her, causing her weight to press into him, but I didn't care. I didn't care when his hand brushed her arm or when he pulled her hair back to place a kiss at the top of her spine, just below where my hand rested.

"Is this okay?" Danny asked, his voice still deep from sleep. He tilted her head back so that he could read her expression. "If you never wanted to be touched like this again, I would understand. *We* would understand."

My hand sprang back, recoiled by his words. I hadn't even considered that. All I wanted was to jump and let the free fall take us. *Idiota.* Forcing her down, after everything I'd gone through to become comfortable with another's touch--I knew better. The haunting sensation of that first terrible attempt to be physical with another slithered over me, making my stomach turn. Had I just forced that feeling on Thea? Fucking Idiot.

When I moved to get up, Thea's hand held me in place. Her thumb stroked the muscle of my forearm, the soft brush of her skin chasing away the memories clawing at the edges of my mind. Her huge black eyes blinked up at me, reading the lines of my face as if the trauma of my past mattered when the evidence of hers was still scattered over her perfect skin.

"I think..." Her hand traced the lines of the chained ribcage tattooed into my chest. "Nothing heals without pain...and..." She rested her hand over where she'd claimed me. "When I was with him, it was never like this. I dreamt of being with you, all of you, so many times. He tried to tell me your hands were his, but it was never right."

Thea dropped her head back, leaning her face into the crook of Danny's neck and taking a deep breath. Threading her fingers into his, she brought them to her breast. "*This* feels right. Feeling myself pressed between you—it anchors me in the present." Drawing her lips over his throat, she pressed a soft kiss to his neck. "Prove to me I'm not dreaming anymore. Give me something real."

Danny whispered into her ear. "I promise you will *never* be back in that nightmare."

Thea's leg wrapped around mine, rocking her hips against what was a shamefully hard erection, given the conversation. The skin above the piercings shifted, sending a shiver of molten heat along my spine. Fuck, I wanted her. The heat of her pussy was like a beacon. The wetness soaked through the thin fabric of my sleep pants, coating my cock.

I closed my eyes against the urge to jump on her like a rabid beast. "You're sure?" I didn't want to do something that would terrorize her, and I wasn't entirely certain King's drugs were fully out of her system, although she seemed lucid.

Arching her spine, she gripped my hair, pulling my mouth to her breast, while simultaneously pushing my pants down with her heel. I kept my eyes on her face, admiring the way her skin flushed a gorgeous shade of rose.

"You once promised to push me to the edge. Well, I'm not asking to be pushed. I'm demanding you throw me over it." Thea reached behind her, luring Danny down. His eyes flaring wide with welcome surprise.

He licked the seam of her lips, "Are you sure?"

"I need this." With a devilish grin, she added, "Do your worst, Kitten."

"Careful, Princess," Danny warned, flicking her nipple.

My jaw dropped in awe, so lost in the moment's intensity that I forgot her breast was in my mouth. My flower held Danny's gaze in challenge, daring him to push her. *This* was the Thea I'd seen in the construction yard—the fearless woman who snared my heart and refused to give it back. There wasn't even a flicker of the girl who'd been beaten down. Thea decided to take back her control, and that began right here, wedged between us.

I pulled my hand up her thigh. Thea's breathing increased, causing the rise of her full breasts to brush my jaw. *Diamine*, her skin was like velvet[2]. I hadn't realized how much I'd missed the slight tremor that increased the higher my hand raised.

My eyes met Danny's in an unspoken question. We'd passed a woman or two between us before, not as often as he had with Crowe. It was enough to know that this was far beyond anything Thea had experienced.

If she wanted to be thrown over the edge, this would do it.

---

2. Damn

"Have you ever been with two men at once?" he whispered to her, tracing the lines of her lips and sinking two fingers between them. "Do you even know what you're asking for?"

Thea's eyes narrowed on him, tongue massaging their length.

"Suck," he commanded.

Was sex between them always a game of chicken? Her cheeks dutifully hollowed, the fiery challenge in her eyes daring him to try harder. It was like watching a war unfold, each touch counting down to mutually assured destruction.

Danny groaned, "I can't wait to push my cock between these fuckable lips. Crowe told me how you sucked him off, taking him deep and swallowing him down until he came hard enough to go blind." I couldn't see what he did with his other hand, but Thea gasped, body bowing in a beautiful arch. Flushed skin lifted in offering, the definition of temptation. I wasn't one to turn down a gift, especially one as tantalizing as this.

I licked along her sternum, lingering in the valley of her breasts. Thea's broken exhale shifted to a low moan, muffled by the fingers still lodged in her mouth. Danny's elbow extended with a slow thrust. That, coupled with the way her stomach was flexing, I had a pretty good guess how he was touching her.

It made my blood feel like it was on fire. My heart thumped hard in anticipation, forcing my cock to pulse with each of her pants. Pushing her heels into my hips, her pelvis rocked in time with Danny's thrusts, the friction mutating my desire into something primal. I wanted to devour her, raw and screaming. I wanted to hear her beg for mercy and cry out in prayer.

Doubling down, Thea lifted her head. Biting his knuckles hard enough to make him hiss, she said around his fingers, "I can take it."

"You heard her." Danny pulled her head back, sinking a hard kiss on her neck that would definitely bruise.

Testing her resolve, I trailed my tongue along the curve of her abdomen before settling between her thighs. "Hold her open."

"Gladly." Hooking his knee behind hers, Danny spread her wide, causing her hips to rotate. The new angle provided me with a front-row view of what was making her moan. His index finger was two knuckles deep in her ass. The telltale sheen on the rest of his fingers told me what he'd used as lubricant.

She was wet enough that it coated her inner thighs, making her shine in welcome. I gathered the moisture on my tongue, breathing in the floral perfume and swallowing it down. It might as well have been cyanide because this would kill me. Fuck. I wanted to let it destroy me.

"More?" he asked, her legs pulling against his and going nowhere.

Thea's hips lifted in answer, chasing the motion of my tongue. I dove deeper, thrusting my tongue and sinking my face completely. Fuck breathing. Who needed to breathe when Thea was making those sounds?

Wrapping my lips around her clit, I sucked hard, letting my teeth sink slightly—finally indulging in that bite I'd been longing for. Thea's quiet whimpers finally broke. I'd replayed that sinful cry in my head for weeks. It echoed in my thoughts every time I stroked my dick, pretending that every part of me didn't belong wholly to this woman, knowing that I'd never come again to anyone but her.

The real thing was so much better. Sweat broke across her face and chest, glittering on her skin like diamonds. Thea's feet flexed, her legs shaking against Danny's. She was so fucking close. I could feel it on my tongue, taste it in the way she grew sweeter. I was torn between pulling back and drawing it out.

"Do you want Nick to make you come, Firecracker?"

I smiled against her blazing flesh, pressing a kiss to her inner thigh.

Thea panted, wiggling her hips futilely. Between my body pressing her inner leg to the mattress and Danny's immovable grip, she wasn't going anywhere but where we took her.

-36-
THEA

"I'm wondering." Danny nibbled on my earlobe, drawing it between his lips. "Which of my fingers should I replace with my cock?"

My heart skipped with anxious anticipation.

Nick lifted his head, waiting to see what I would say, but I couldn't make my brain catch up. It was still stuck on a few minutes ago when he told Danny to hold me open.

"Answer him." Nick's voice was thick with desire, its command one that made my nerves snap to attention.

My thoughts tripped over themselves, coming out in a befuddled, "Yes."

Danny's grin crept higher. Pulling the fingers from my mouth, he slid them down to cup my throat, directing my full focus on his face. He was so damn beautiful. The feral gleam in his eyes sparked, daring me to fight him.

"That wasn't a yes or no question, Princess."

I swallowed against the pressure of his hand. "It's the only answer I have."

Nick's chuckle vibrated against my thighs, sending a fresh wave of awareness tingling down to my toes. Rewarding me for my candor, he flattened his tongue against my clit with the exact amount of pressure to set my body humming.

My eyes involuntarily fluttered closed. I pressed against the hard muscles bracing me, letting myself drift with the sensation of them closing me in.

"Open your eyes," Danny demanded. "I want you with us, present for every second of what we do to you." He tilted my chin down, keeping the grip on my face firm.

The instant my eyes met Nick's, I was trapped. Helpless against their metallic pull. The raw desire staring up at me from between my thighs was intense enough to make me whimper. When I thought I'd lost him, I would have given anything to feel the weight of his gaze on me again, and now the intensity of the man between my legs was almost more than I could bear.

They held so many emotions: desire, regret, guilt...love.

Danny rested his lips against my ear, whispering, "I want you to see *who* is making you feel this way. When your body shatters, you will know exactly who it is bringing you to rapture."

Moving with slow passes of his tongue, Nick gradually ramped my body up, never once breaking eye contact with me. My nerves spun tighter and tighter. My hips rocked in time with him, chasing the feeling in hopes that he would increase the speed and give me more.

I pulled against Danny's hold on my leg. His lips drifted over my neck as he spoke, "Look how beautifully your body responds. I could stay here all night, watching you writhe for us." The finger in my ass slowly drew back, curling against something just out of reach. I wanted to scream. I was so close. Time stretched, pulling me endlessly into the moment. I could feel my release waiting for me on the edges.

"Please, more," I begged beneath my shallow pants. My head tilted against the hold Danny kept on my face. I keened, futilely trying to force the orgasm to come.

Nick chuckled, the vibration hitting my clit like the strum of a guitar.

"Danny, *please*. Nick."

"Our girl wants more, Nick. I say we give her what she's asking for." Danny pushed a second finger beside the first while Nick simultaneously slid two long fingers into my pussy.

An unintelligible set of syllables garbled from me. My body bucked against the intrusion, unsure of which direction to go. They pushed and pulled, massaging at opposite ends of the same transcendent spot. My body flooded with heat, the burn between my legs expanding to my toes in waves.

I detonated, all of the tension and fear finally leaving my body in one forceful explosion. It was a release unlike any other, leaving my soul feeling lighter.

I sucked in heaving breaths of air, my eyes losing their focus as I gazed into Danny's face.

Light poured into the room, along with an appreciative whistle. "And here I thought I was letting you rest." Crowe leaned in the doorway, his smile bright as his eyes took in the wide-open display.

"We're just getting started." Danny released me, sliding out from under us. Bending to steal a kiss, he added, "I'll be right back." His muscular ass flexed as he walked towards the bathroom, thick cock bobbing with each step. I licked my lips, thinking of the promise he'd made me, imagining what it would feel like to hold onto all that muscle while tasting him at the back of my throat.

"Oz damn, you look like you want to devour him." Crowe moved into the room, closing the door behind him, eyes glittering with predatory need.

My post-orgasm euphoria making me bold, I replied, "Because I do."

Tightening his grip on my hips, Nick groaned, "*Tocca a me adesso, Fiore Mio.*"[1] With one swift movement, he rotated us, pulling me so I was straddling him. Taking no time to acclimatize to the new position, he lined himself up and speared me all the way to the hilt.

"Holy fuck, Nick!" I pressed my palms into his chest, kicking my head back on an exhale. It felt like he just punched through my stomach to knock the air from my lungs. I could barely think beyond the feel of him stretching me, each bar rubbing with every tiny motion I made. "Warn a girl."

"I did." Unbothered, Nick rose, licking at my nipple. "*Le tue tette sono un'opera d'arte.*"[2]

"It doesn't count if I don't know what you're saying."

"They are," Crowe responded to whatever Nick had murmured, pushing the hair from my neck. "Nicky doesn't always play well with others, Beautiful."

Mouth grazing my nipple, Nick shot him a sidelong glare, "Don't call me Nicky."

---

1. Look at me, My Flower.

2. Your breasts are a work of art.

Ignoring the murder in Nick's eyes, Crowe continued, "Hearing you want to choke on another man's cock probably turns him green with envy."

With both hands around his face, I pulled Nick's mouth away from my chest. "Is that true? Does this bother you?" They'd been so concerned with my consent that I never thought to question theirs.

"Fiore Mio, I would give you anything you asked for. If you wished it, I would tear apart the world, one yellow brick at a time. Does it make me jealous to watch one of them make you come? Of course." He pumped his hips, lifting my weight and bringing me back down slowly, making sure his piercings raked over me, one at a time. My eyes fluttered when the ball at the head of his dick hit something deep. "Who wouldn't want to be the man making you look like this? That doesn't mean I don't get off on watching it happen."

Circling a hand behind my neck, he pulled me down for an indulgent kiss. I sank into the feeling, the haze of emotion and endorphins making me light-headed.

"Just don't be surprised when I'm in a hurry for my turn." Nick punched up harder, making me gasp against his rising smile.

"You're sure?" I asked, parroting his question to me earlier.

"As I've ever been." Gripping a handful of hair, he pulled me upright, turning my head to meet Crowe's eager gaze. "Now, be a good girl, and show me how well you can swallow his cock."

-37-
THEA

I cast my eyes over Crowe, noting the way his sweats clung to his hips and the outline of his dick beneath the soft fabric. Seriously, those pants were doing Ozma's work. He was downright mouthwatering.

Crooking a finger at him, I said, "Come here, Pretty Boy."

"Anything you want, Beautiful Girl." It's amazing how quickly Crowe can undress when he has an incentive.

Nick kissed my neck, laughing. "Pretty Boy. *Dovresti fargliela pagare per averti chiamato così.*"[1]

I palmed the hard line of Crowe's dick, trying not to swoon when he quirked a lazy smile that was so perfectly him.

"*Perché? È la verità, no?*"[2] Crowe's tongue rolled around the words like he was making love to them. His eyes lit up, seeing I fucking loved it.

"Why is that so hot?" I breathed, squirming against the liquid heat pooling low in my belly. Just when you thought these men couldn't be sexier, they had to go breaking out the Italian. Why was having zero idea what they were saying such a turn-on?

"*Porca puttana. Dovresti vedere quanto è bagnata adesso. Continua a parlarle.*"[3] Nick's thumb rubbed a soft circuit against my clit, sending hot shivers skittering up my spine.

Crowe grinned, drawing his thumb over my lower lip. "*Apri, dolcezza.*"[4]

Oz damn, this man. I preened beneath his gaze as he gripped my jaw, massaging the muscle as he pushed the smooth head of his cock past my lips. His dick was thick and warm, twitching in appreciation when my tongue rolled around the tip. I flexed my throat, swallowing around the urge to gag. A surge of precum coated my tongue with salty brine, and I hummed with satisfaction.

"Fuck," Crowe groaned.

Choosing evil, Nick used his hold on my hair to push me further onto Crowe's cock, his grip never loosening. My eyes watered, and my airway constricted. Fighting the urge to kick back, I relaxed my throat, took a deep breath through my nose, and swallowed against the intrusion.

"Fucking fuck, how are you so good at that?"

"You're welcome," Nick said, finally easing his hold on my hair.

There was power in the way he was nearly falling to his knees, but there was freedom in giving myself over to their control, too. I wanted both. My desire stretched like a body on the rack between strength and submission.

Gripping Crowe at the root, I swirled my tongue against his shaft. Nick's hand trailed from my hair along my side, pausing for a brief moment to palm my breast. Taking my hips in both hands, he took over our rhythm, meeting my downward motion with hard upward thrusts. I sank into the feeling one sinful second at a time.

I'd never felt more present.

The release built within me, slow push after slow push. The way Nick was touching me, his kisses hot against my skin, coupled with how Crowe looked like the entire world was here on this bed with him. There was no stopping the charge from igniting. Like an updraft tearing through a house of straw, it tore me apart, consuming me and setting my skin aflame.

"Bellissima," Crowe crooned.[5]

"She's a queen, is what she is." Danny returned, throwing something at Crowe. "Trade."

---

5. Beautiful.

He snatched the tiny bottle from the air, "Do I even want to know where you found this?"

"One very uncomfortable conversation with my sister, but it's not like hiding what's happening in here was an option. Thea's screaming like she's hoping all of the Western Quadrant can hear her."

Was I?

Crowe slid from my mouth, bending down to claim my lips in a fierce kiss. He groaned, licking the flavor from his lips. "I love that you taste like me..." He lovingly caressed my neck with the back of his hand. "...and I want nothing more than to spill down your throat, but you're going to want me hard for this next part."

"Next part?" I craned my neck, looking at Danny for some kind of indication about what he was planning.

Crowe circled behind me, crawling over Nick's spread legs. "How do you feel about taking us both at once?" He palmed the globe of my ass, squeezing. There was the snap of a bottle and cool liquid spread between my cheeks. His finger slowly stroked down, finding the sensitive rim of my ass and testing its resistance. "Do you want to feel me and Nick filling you, moving together, and becoming a part of you?" He slid his finger down, pressing in a small circle until he pushed all the way in.

Parting my lips on a strangled cry, I arched against him, my head falling onto Crowe's shoulder. Every muscle in my body tightened from the image he was painting. Nick slowly undulated beneath me, giving me a taste of what Crowe was describing. His piercings rubbed against the constant pressure of Crowe's finger. I closed my eyes, unsure if I remembered how to breathe.

"I'll make it so good for you, Darling. I promise. You'll forget about everything but how amazing it feels." He pushed further, spreading me with a second finger. Slowly pumping in and out of me in time with each of Nick's shallow thrusts. The burn radiated out, blending with the heat of his body behind me. "There will just be you, me, Nick, and Danny. The rest of the world will cease to exist."

Fuck, I wanted that. I wanted a respite from all of my insidious thoughts. My nails curled against Nick's chest, cutting small crescents into the tattooed muscle as I rolled with the way they were moving. I felt like a car trying to drive on ice, no traction, no brakes, just spinning out of control while I held on for dear life.

Nick hissed, knees bending up. "You should feel the way she's pulsing around me. I think you could get her to come just talking about it."

Crowe's free hand smoothed around my chest, palming the weight of my breast. "I need you to say the words, Gorgeous. Tell me you want this."

Want it? My body was practically screaming for him to fuck me. "Please, Crowe."

"Please? So polite." Crowe curled his fingers, pushing against where Nick's piercings stroked me. Each nerve ending started fraying one by one, leaving me quivering for more.

"Yes. Fuck, yes."

"She can do better than that," Danny said on a dark chuckle, his heavy-lidded gaze lasered straight on my tits. He prowled onto the bed, closing his mouth around my nipple and biting down.

"Danny!" I screamed, smacking the top of his head until he released my throbbing breast.

"*Cazzo!*"[6] Nick swore, reflexively bucking up. "Thea just choked my soul out through my dick. *Porca puttana.*[7] Dan, do that again."

"No." I clamped my hands over my breasts. "I swear to Oz, Danny. That's tit abuse."

Danny rose, drawing close enough to whisper in my ear. "Then do what you're told, or I'll cuff your hands behind your back and give you a reason to swear to Oz."

Holy. Filthy. Goddess. Above. The image of that dark promise.

---

6. Fuck!

7. Holy shit.

A wave of wanton heat flashed through me. How much would it take to force Danny to make good on that threat? One mouthy comment, two? My toes curled with all the delicious possibilities.

Crowe, undoubtedly hearing every seedy word, chose this moment to slide a third finger along the other two. Every thought left my mind, along with all of my breath. He stroked the thin barrier separating him from Nick's studded cock.

"*Vai a fare in culo, Vincenzo,*"[8] Nick swore through gritted teeth. "If you want me to hold out long enough for you to get balls deep, then you can't keep doing that. My restraint is already hanging by a thread."

Crowe laughed, doing it again, this time longer and with more pressure. Nick cursed, and my entire body lit up. The sensation was unreal, like being torn in two in the best possible way.

Crowe dragged his nose along my throat. "Tell me what you want, Darling Thea. Say the word, and it's yours."

"Be explicit," Danny added, dragging a chair beside the bed, directly in my line of sight.

"Tell me you want to feel my cock stretching your ass while Nick pounds that gorgeous pussy." Crowe rocked, his dick sliding between my legs in time with the slow thrust of his hand.

The image of Crowe's beautiful cock plunging into me while I stared into Nick's eyes was a fantasy I'd never allowed to take form. Maybe I was still dreaming. The heat of the men pressing into me, the strength surrounding me, the way our bodies swayed like the rolling of the ocean—it was too perfect.

This wasn't real. I'm still in the dream.

My heart rate increased, a thrum of panic taking root. I waited for the scene to disintegrate as it always did when lucidity came back to me. I shut my eyes, unable to take the heartbreak of seeing the intensity behind Nick's expression shift into King's deceitful glare. The loss this time around would break me.

A sorrowful whimper escaped me.

---

8. Fuck you, Vincenzo.

"Nick. Bring her back," Danny commanded, clutching the back of my neck and kissing me hard.

Nick gave my clit a sharp pinch, sending an instant shot of lightning into my veins and snapping me into the moment.

Danny's mouth continued to move against mine, unrelenting, even as I wailed in surprise at the sharp bite of pain. A storm of sensations clashed, leaving me suddenly very aware of every movement and breath of the men caging me. My clit throbbed. Its heat spun like a lighthouse in a storm, a beacon warning of danger and yet enticing enough to want to climb it.

My heart rate dropped, beating in time with the steady thump of Crowe's heart against my back.

"We've got you, Thea," Danny reassured, returning to his chair. "You can let go. Trust us. We won't let you drift anywhere you don't want to be. Say you want more, and you'll be feeling our touch for days. The memory will be so vivid that you'll never doubt this reality again."

"Go on, Fiore Mio. Tell them this is what you've wanted from the very beginning."

It really was, and even more overwhelming than I ever imagined.

Crowe twisted his hand, stroking a point that made my body shiver, despite the heat rolling through me in waves. How much more intense would it be when I was taking all of him?

I breathed down my nerves, finally saying the words they all wanted to hear, "I want more, Crowe. Fuck me. Make me see stars while I ride Nick into the next life. Give me everything."

"That's my girl." Crowe tilted my head back for a lazy kiss that was completely at odds with the frenetic energy coiling within me.

"I knew you'd say yes." Danny leaned back, spreading his legs wide and putting his cock on display like it was next up for auction.

Taking the bait, I asked. "What about you?"

"Trust me, Firecracker. I'm perfectly happy with this view." Squeezing the head of his dick, he ran his thumb over the seam, spreading the cum leaking from the tip in a single slow stroke. "You enjoy yourself. I'll be back."

Crowe gently pushed down on my shoulders, soothing his palm along my spine and following my hungry eyes to the pump of Danny's hand. "Do you like seeing what you do to him, to all of us?"

Nick lifted his lips to mine, hands leaving my hips to delve deep into my hair.

The deep rumble of Crowe's voice vibrated against my back. "I bet it feels powerful, like the kick of a gun. You hold our fates in your hands, Darling."

Crowe always knew exactly what I was thinking and what I needed to hear. I *did* feel powerful. They were everywhere, teasing and pulsing in time, but the power wasn't in their hands. It was in mine.

"Breathe, Thea," Nick said, drawing my lower lip between his teeth. "Things are about to get a whole lot tighter."

Replacing the fingers with the head of his cock, Crowe pushed at the ring of muscle, slowly easing in. The sensation was immediate and completely transcendent. Crowe was right. The rest of the room disappeared except for that one point of contact and the weight of Danny's eyes on us.

"That's it, Darling. Let me in."

"She can take it, Crowe. Give her mo—" I stole the end of Nick's words, claiming them with a kiss to keep from screaming. It didn't matter; an inhuman cry tore from me anyway.

"Fuck, Firecracker, you look amazing," Danny said, reverently.

Crowe pulled back, easing the rest of the way in with three smooth thrusts. A psychedelic array of colors bled into my vision, my skin prickling with awareness. I arched my spine, feeling them everywhere. I'd never felt more present. Nick's piercings, pinpointed against me, vibrating with each of his short breaths. Crowe's lips ghosted over the back of my neck, his legs sandwiching mine.

I tested the feeling, taking a large inhale that made us all collectively moan.

"Fucking hell, Nick. I forgot what all that metal felt like from this side." His forehead dropped to my shoulder, breath cooling the sweat coating my skin.

"You good up there?" Nick said, his voice tight. "Because if I don't start moving soon, I may actually pass out from lack of blood to my brain."

"How about it, Beautiful? You ready?" Crowe's large hand circled my neck, lifting me into the cage of his embrace.

"*Quanto cazzo sei sexy,*" Nick crooned.[9]

Pressing kisses along my jaw, Crowe pulled back only an inch. Even that small motion made my entire body quake. "Good?"

"Yes," I panted, shaking my head no. "It's good. Keep going."

"You're sending some mixed signals." He repeated the movement, drawing back to the tip and slowly easing forward. My entire soul moved with him. After a few more test strokes, Nick joined him, rocking in opposite directions.

He wasn't as teasing as Crowe. Nick fucked up into me with the entirety of his pent-up need. He'd held back through the entire acclimation process, and now this was the end of his restraint. Like everything he did, his motions were with brutal control.

Gripping my shoulder, Nick pushed down, raising his hips to meet mine. Air punched from my lungs, cutting off my scream. Crowe braced me from behind, holding me tightly to him as he moved. Together, we rose, allowing me to catch my breath—only for Nick to steal it again. It was easy to lose myself in the unique rhythm.

Crowe reached around, stroking my clit. "I want to feel you coming on my cock at least once before I'm spent."

Nick grunted, slamming hard in quick succession. "Don't hold back. I'm not sure how much more I have in me." He wasn't wrong. I could feel him thickening, growing impossibly harder.

"Allow me." At some point, Danny had moved closer, kneeling beside us with one leg propped on the bed. His hand came down hard on my ass, the pain blistering along my over-sensitized skin.

I fell into an unending orgasm. My muscles spasmed, intensifying when their thrusts didn't slow. With a bellow, Nick bucked up, coming hard with long strokes lashing my insides. Before Nick had finished pulsing, Crowe barreled down, finishing deep within me.

---

9. You are so fucking sexy.

Together, our bodies collapsed into an uncoordinated, twitching heap.

"You're not done, Princess."

Crowe rolled, stumbling off the bed. Danny, taking his place, flipped me off of Nick and onto my back.

"I like the sound of 'not done.'" Nick lifted onto his elbow, closing his mouth over my breast. Before my sex-addled brain could process the insanity of continuing, Danny lifted my leg over his shoulder and drove into my soaked pussy.

"Fuck, Danny." My awareness sharpened to a blade's edge. It was too much. The human body could only take so much stimulation, and mine just hit its limit. The pleasure bordered on pain. I was combusting. Electricity coursed beneath my skin, burning me from the inside out.

I screamed, tears leaking from the corners of my eyes.

"You can take it." Nick nuzzled beneath my ear, sliding his fingers down my torso to gently stroke my engorged clit. The weight of his torso pressed into my arm, pinning me in place so that I couldn't writhe away. "Don't fight against it. Give in."

Crowe sank to my other side, adding his heat to the press of Nick beside me and the unrelenting force of Danny above. It assaulted my senses from every direction. "Have you ever seen anything more beautiful?"

"Never," Nick whispered against my breast.

Diving forward, Crowe kissed me in his all-consuming way, memorizing every press of our lips and the drag of his tongue against mine. It was enough to tip me over. Like I was possessed by a demon, my spine contorted beneath the intensity of my climax. The orgasm splintered me apart until I couldn't see, couldn't hear until there was nothing but white and the sensation of floating.

"There she is," Crowe said softly.

I blinked. In the white nothing haze, my vision slowly came back. Danny lay beside me, heaving breaths just as hard as my own, his hand wrapped around mine. He lifted it, pressing a kiss to my palm. "That was fucking amazing."

"I've never seen that before. I've heard of women coming hard enough to black out, but I've never actually seen it." Crowe caressed my cheek, pushing back the hair stuck to my face. A cool cloth dragged between my thighs, icing the fire throbbing in time with my racing pulse.

"I have." Nick leaned in, kissing my neck. Each gentle peck sent out tiny waves of shivers, like ripples in a pool. "I knew you could take it." He crawled back over me, whispering into my ear, "*This* is what it feels like to fall over that edge."

-38-

DANNY

No. No. This isn't right.

Shh, Little Bird.

I flashed my eyes open, not feeling the cold tile of my cell but Thea's warm body pressed against mine. I drew in a long breath. It smelled like her, like honey and sunshine. I pressed my face into her hair. Fuck, this felt good. I said a quick prayer to whoever was listening for getting us off of that ship in one piece. My dreams were consistently a replay of my face shoved to the ground and being forced to watch that monster violating my girl.

I ran my hand over her arm, indulging in the softness of her skin.

"Don't." Thea recoiled, trembling beneath whatever nightmare was plaguing her. "Please, King, stop." Tears fell in thick streams from the corners of her eyes and pooled against my chest.

Nick's hand, which had been wrapped around her waist, lifted to her cheek. "Shhh, Fiore Mio. You're dreaming."

Propping myself on my elbow, I peered over her shoulder to the stark concern etched into his expression. "Don't say *'shh'*. It's what *he* would do whenever she didn't want him touching her." I couldn't even say King's name without wanting to put my fist through something.

"I didn't know." Nick looked devastated. *Good*.

"No, you wouldn't." I glared, knowing the truth. Crowe and Nick argued over dinner the previous night, telling Thea in no uncertain terms how Nick had spent our weeks in captivity cursing her name for betraying us. If she hadn't found him first, then Nick would have *left* her on that ship. Left her. Thea would still be living in that drug induced hell.

Because Thea was better than any of us deserved, she'd forgiven him. She was so relieved to see him breathing, she didn't care about the rest of it. That didn't mean the rest of us had. Even Toto was still pissed.

I rolled Thea toward me. Her face was scrunched, making me think of the long hours I'd spent trying to smooth away a single crease. Her arms whipped out, clawing and screaming for me to stop. It made my insides feel like they were being twisted. This time was worse because I knew in excruciating detail what was haunting her dreams.

"Hey, Hey!" Gripping her face in both hands, I whispered, "It's okay. Thea. Wake up."

Thea's eyes finally opened, tears clinging to her lashes. Her vision darted around my face, taking in the details.

"It's okay, Princess. You're safe."

She blinked several times in a gesture I now recognized was her checking to see if what she was looking at was a dream.

Nick's heavy hand gave a reassuring squeeze on her hip. "You're in the hotel room. In Emerald City."

Understanding calmed her trembling form before she collapsed into my chest, wracked with sobs. *Fuck*, I hated this part. This had happened every morning for the past week. One of the lingering effects of the drug was that she struggled coming out of the dream state. Even after waking, she'd see the ship or King anywhere she looked. After that first terrible morning, when she'd tried to slit Crowe's throat, we decided that two people needed to be with her while she slept.

Once she finally caught her breath, she asked, "At the hotel? The one Ginger got us?"

I wrapped my arms around her, wishing it would be enough to ward off the enemy I couldn't fight. "That's right."

Apparently, Ginger's connections ran deeper than she let on. A last-minute suite in the Emerald Plaza Hotel was no small feat. One day, that curly-haired minx was going to explain how she could afford every posh hotel in Ozmandria, but somehow couldn't get my sister a gig in a building that wasn't overrun by mice.

I ran my fingers through Thea's hair, her shoulders relaxing with each pass. "We've been here for the past five days."

At least Daffodil stuck around this time. She was just as eager as I was to see what The Wizard gave us. The promise of taking down The Farm and finding Daisy was almost too good. You couldn't say we didn't earn our reward. The trembling woman in my arms more than proved that.

Climbing out of bed, Nick gave Thea a withering glance. "Looks like you've got everything here." Snatching up his pants, he slipped through the door before she could register he was leaving.

"Is it Wizard day?" she said, burrowing into my chest.

"It is." I kissed the top of her head, drinking in her scent and letting it quiet the sound of Westin's slippery voice. *You'll never hold that sweet thing again, pet.*

"Look at me." I tipped her chin up. "Whatever happens, we do it together. It won't be like last time."

Thea lifted her fingers to the bridge of my nose, tracing the edge of the bandage. Most of the bruises had faded, but I still needed the brace to hold the cartilage in place. "I like it."

"Of course you do."

"It adds character to your otherwise polished features."

The gentle brush of her fingers slipped to my chin. "I miss the beard, though."

"Yeah?" I closed my eyes, tilting into her touch. "It'd be different if I'd chosen it. The beard wasn't exactly a fashion choice." The real reason I'd shaved was because I loved the way her skin felt sliding against mine when we kissed. She would drag her lips over my cheek, her breath warming my skin as she went. She probably wasn't even aware that she did it. After being kept apart for so long, I didn't want anything between us, even something as innocuous as facial hair.

"Good morning, Beautiful Girl." Crowe pushed the door open, leaping into the center of the bed with his arms extended like a superhero taking flight.

Bouncing on the mattress, Thea laughed. It was a light and airy sound, dispelling all of the heaviness from the room. Hooking her around the waist, Crowe snatched her from my arms and rolled until she was pinned beneath him.

"Hey! I was playing with that," I grumbled.

"Lunch was just delivered. Go play with that," he replied, teasing at her lips.

"Or how about you play with my fist." I slugged him in the shoulder, not that it disrupted his focus at all.

"Besides, it's after two." He pushed at the blankets, pulling them away to put each luscious curve of her body on display. "There's a shower fuck in our future, and you aren't invited. You had your turn; go brood with Nick in the kitchen."

I looked at Thea for support, but Crowe dropped to her neck, sucking hard enough to make her knees bend around him. I couldn't really complain. It was something to see how she always came back to life when he was around like he was her sun.

Crowe palmed her breasts, continuing down her body and paying tribute to each freckle along the way. "I spent a small eternity crammed into a service vent, hacking into a surprisingly complex surveillance system. I'm not saying I'm not a team player, but I haven't seen our girl in eighteen hours. I deserve a bit of quality time. "

Thea chirped with surprise, pulling up on his chin to make him look at her. "You've been counting?"

"Fucking right, I have." He surged up, planting a hard kiss on her lips before sinking back between her thighs. Thea beamed a mixture of delight and lust. It made her skin glow, and her teeth sank into the pillow of her lips.

Crowe saw it, too. Thea was resplendent. I didn't think I'd ever loved anything the way I loved this woman.

Kissing the back of her knee, Crowe continued, "We have four hours and twenty-six minutes until we have to leave for Head Shots, and I plan to make every single one of them count."

Heavy metal music thumped from behind mirrored glass. Crowe pushed the glowing button beside the door. Head Shots was a unique establishment, occupying the top four floors of Emerald City's highest tower. There was no sign or indication that anything of note lay inside except for the sounds of mayhem coming from within.

A man with green hair slicked into sharp points answered the door. He pushed his glasses down his nose, the matching green mirrored lenses reflecting back the glittering city behind us. "We're closed."

Crowe shoved his booted foot into the door. "We're on the list, it's under Scarecrowe."

The bouncer's eyes flashed, widening with recognition. He rubbed his green beard. "I thought Westin put a bounty on your head."

"She did." Crowe's voice was flat, terrifyingly devoid of emotion.

"Word was The Dead Crows cashed in. They crossed you off the leaderboard. It's all anyone around here talked about for a week."

"They did."

"You're telling me Westin let you go?"

"No," Thea pushed in front of Crowe, his hand falling to the small of her back protectively. "Westin is currently at the bottom of the ocean feeding the sharks." She propped her hands on her hips, lifting her chin with steadfast confidence. Fuck, it was hot, sending a surge of blood straight to my dick. I was definitely filing this image away for the next time one of them kicked me out of the room. The stance made the leather corset push her breasts forward, with Westin's iconic emerald centered between them. The guard's eyes instantly fell to the shimmering gem, his jaw dropping with them.

"Fucking hell." The guard stepped back, a new level of admiration in his tone. "That's it, isn't it? All those rumors about The Scarecrowe, I always thought you were one of those urban legends, but you really killed Westin Witcher."

Crowe didn't say anything, looking at Thea with enough heat to set the building on fire.

"Fuck me." Pulling his glasses all the way free of his face, his green brows rose high. "*You* killed Westin."

"Me." Thea stepped forward, her leather-clad hips swaying with each step. "I wasn't fond of the Witchers, either of them..." She patted the man on the cheek. "How about you be a doll and move aside. I have a great and terrible Wizard to meet with."

He took a step back, trailing his eyes over her ass as she passed, and not-so-subtly readjusting his cock. It was a damn fine ass, especially in those pants. Memorable, which was a problem. Em was still out there. Her attack dogs were still on Thea's scent. We didn't need this idiot bragging to all his insignificant friends about the hot piece of ass walking into the club.

I grabbed a fistful of his shirt, throwing him into the glass. "You see that?"

"Yeah," he wheezed.

I slammed him against the mirror again, slapping his face hard enough to make my palm sting. "No, you didn't."

Nick stepped beside me, pressing the flat side of his knife to the man's throat. "Breathe in her direction, mention a word of our visit, and I'll slit you from neck to nut."

"We were never here. *She* was never here. Understand?"

"Yeah. Message received. Loud and clear. I've already forgotten her."

"Smart man." I straightened his shirt, flattening the collar in an attempt to make him look a bit less rumpled.

The interior was dark, with green under-lighting along the walkways, beneath the tables, and every other fixture. The mirrored walls gave the entry area a fun house effect, which, combined with the thumping music and hazy air, made my vision swim.

Thea leaned over the railing circling the central floor, looking at the people in the network of gaming stations on the ground floor. Head Shots was a location where most of Emerald City's illicit business went down. It was more than exclusive. This club was by invitation only or as a guest of a current member.

Crowe pulled a thin tablet from his jacket pocket, flicking through the feed to see if our arrival tipped anyone off. Camera angles from every view of the club scrolled by. Like the rings of hell, each floor descended with varying layers of sin. They circled the ground floor where massive computers stood in a line, each with a gamer sitting in a leather wingback chair. The men and women at each console looked oblivious to the chaos around them.

At least this was heavily populated. Almost every corner of the club was visible; hopefully it would be enough to deter an ambush.

The massive screen, mounted to the wall, showed a live feed from one of the players below. It was a first-person shooter, and this player was positioned on the roof of an apartment building with a sniper rifle. The animation was so real that it was hard to believe what I was seeing was fake. With a flick of a button, the camera shifted to the scope, the sights tracking a man with a suit walking down the sidewalk.

"What is all of this?" Thea asked, watching the slick bodies writhing against the railing opposite us.

"Up here, it's a nightclub." I pointed to the ground floor. "Down there, a gaming den."

"And in between?"

Crowe tucked the tablet away, snagging Thea's hips and cradling them into his own. "Gambling, drugs, sex, and illicit business...not necessarily in that order."

"Come on. It's almost seven. We need to get downstairs."

-39-
THEA

We walked down the line of mega-computers. Each station had a glowing number etched into the glass. Monitors wrapped in an arc around each player, creating a 180-degree, fully immersive experience.

"It's a Battle Royale," Crowe explained, pointing at the massive screen and the marquee above it. "Last player standing gets the pot."

The leader board currently showed $15,000. Beside it was another board, gridded out with pictures and names beneath them.

"What's that list?" I pointed at the box holding my photo and the six names listed beneath it.

~~Orin Barret~~

Carron Knave

~~Scarecrowe~~

> King Avian

Marley Jacobson

Alisandra Liddell

I stopped beneath the display, scowling at the photo they'd chosen, a snapshot from a security camera. I was running through the halls of the bank. My hair was disheveled, blouse blood splattered, skirt torn, and a desperate, wild look twisting my face. I looked like an unhinged bank teller. Thick lines scored through Crowe's and Orin's names. Ignoring the shiver skittering down my spine, I held up my middle finger to the name highlighted by a big green box. "Fuck you, King."

Crowe turned, following my gaze to the list. "That's the Murder Board. Head Shots take bets on everything. When a high-end contract goes on the market, they give odds on who will make the kill. You, pretty girl, were desired mark numero uno."

"Then, why is your name on there?"

"Because I put a bid in."

"You what?" I gaped at him. First Nick, and now him. Were they all so quick to turn on me?

"Yeah, you what?" Danny parroted.

"Relax." He shrugged, "Little fish tend to keep away when big fish are swimming around. It felt like a good idea at the time." Crowe scanned the crowd above us, noting each person dancing or looking at the view from the platforms. "But if Alice is in the running...Keep your eyes open. Even I don't think I could fight her off if she realizes there's still an open contract on Thea."

Nick pulled out a rolling chair from one of the many stations, a glowing number five etched into the glass on the wall behind it.

I settled into the leather, feeling it and the music from the embedded speakers swallow me. The boys pulled up some of the stools lining the outer wall, boxing in the station on all sides.

"What now?" I said, nervously tapping my foot against the ground.

"Now we wait."

A girl with high pigtails rolled up to the booth on a pair of old-school rollerskates. Pulling a large lollipop from her cheek and gesturing with it, she asked, "Can I get you all a drink?"

"What are you, the lollipop guild?" Danny flipped open a billfold, dropping a crisp $100 bill on her tray.

Crowe raised his hand. "I wouldn't say no to a beer—"

"We'd like to ensure that we are left unbothered," Danny interjected.

"Please," I added.

The waitress gave me a tiny smirk, spinning the stick in her fingers. The candy picked up the blue overhead lighting of the room, causing it to glow. She tucked the bill into her sports bra, pushing the lollipop into her cheek. "That'll buy you ten minutes. Also, you don't want to leave him waiting." She pointed at the monitor, where a familiar floating head appeared.

"Hello, Dorothea."

Danny leaned over me. "You said in person. We didn't go through all of this to talk to a man hiding behind a screen."

I fidgeted with the emerald hanging around my neck, the stone feeling heavier with each passing second that the two stared at each other in silence.

"Fine," the modulated voice replied.

All at once, the power in the room cut. Music, lights, games, everything instantly shut down, except for Station 5. It felt like sitting in the center of a massive spotlight, with every eye on us. A collective groan came from the room, the gamers on either side of us cursing, but no one questioned it. All at once, everyone left, from the bartender to the thrupple borderline having sex in the corner.

"Happy?"

Nick and Danny pulled their guns, aiming at the chair behind us. It spun, revealing a woman in ripped jeans and a simple *'Pay no attention'* T-shirt. None of us noticed her when we walked on the floor. Her hair was pulled into two small buns, mimicked in shape by the kitty cat ears on top of the mic'd headphones. Her russet skin wasn't adorned by excessive makeup or flashy jewelry in the E.C. style. She was altogether unremarkable, except that she had obviously just cleared an entire nightclub in less than a minute.

A woman. The Wizard was a woman. Talk about a twist I didn't see coming, but of course she was. The Wizard had been holding Oz by the balls for years. Only a woman was that ruthless.

"That was spooky," Crowe said, scrolling through the camera feeds and finding them black. "Damn, you even killed the cameras *I* installed."

She ran her fingers along the ultraviolet piping on the arm of the chair. "It's cute that you thought you could actually hack my system, and I wouldn't notice."

"Your system." Danny stashed his gun, scrubbing his face with his palm. "Fuck. Of course it is."

Crowe tossed his tablet, the clatter of glass on glass loud in the now very silent club. "I wasted all that time crammed into a vent for nothing."

The Wizard crossed her legs, leaning back and holding out her palm expectantly. "I'll take that now."

I looked to Danny for confirmation. This was it; everything was about to change. I unhooked the chain, dropping the jewel into her palm. The Wizard's expression was impassive as she held the stone up to the light, turning it to inspect the intricate faceting.

She spun towards the desk, flipping open a laptop similar to the one Danny destroyed before everything went to hell in the bank. The emerald slotted into the drive beside its twin. Unwanted images ran through my mind: Eastin threading the whip through her fingers, the pendant hanging down from her slender neck as she gripped my face. The memory of her warm blood was almost sticky on my hands.

The screen came to life, lines of code scrolling faster than the eye could track.

"That's it, right?" I asked, feeling my heart pounding in my throat. "You're in?"

She ignored me, eyes continuing to scan the code flying by. After several long minutes, the type finally stopped, a single white cursor blinking at the end.

Finally, *finally*, a wide smile spread across her face, her light brown eyes flashing with victory. She spun back to face us, a small thumb drive in her hand. "Dorothea, you'll find information and current placements for Farm Assets in the—"

BANG!

A loud gunshot cut across the room, echoing off the granite floors and sleek glass walls. The monitor behind The Wizard exploded, flaring like a sparkler in the night.

Nick leapt on top of me, knocking me to the floor and covering my body with the broad expanse of his. There wasn't any more gunfire though, only that one single shot.

I pushed my way out from under Nick. We needed to have a real chat about him throwing himself in the line of fire to save me. He still had bright red scars on his back from the last time he did that.

Crowe, squatted low, helping to pull me to my feet. "You okay, beautiful?"

"Yeah, you?"

"Fine."

Danny spun in place, scanning the upper floors for where the gunman had fired from. Dozens of uniformed men, each with rifles, appeared on the deck above us. "We're sitting-fucking-ducks down here."

The gaming chair that once held Ozmandria's most illusive hacker, spun slowly in place pushed around by the shot's momentum. When it finished its slow revolution, I saw who the target had actually been, though her name had never appeared on a murder board. Slumped in the chair, the cool green lights casting a grotesque glow across her face, was The Wizard—with a bullethole perfectly centered in the middle of her forehead. Her caramel-colored eyes stared lifelessly back at me. I'd seen so many dead eyes lately the shock of this one barely registered. I didn't even scream. I just stepped back, avoiding the relatively small puddle of blood dripping from the chair.

The measured clicking of heels on granite approached. We all turned to see Gigi descending the glass staircase. She casually held a revolver, using it to flick her perfectly curled hair over her shoulder. The blonde strands looked like spun gold in the low light.

"I should have fucking known," Danny hissed.

"I told you. I *fucking* told you, but no one ever listens to me," Crowe added, his hand coming down on my shoulder to inch me backwards.

Several other men followed behind Gigi. They all wore matching suits and ID badges hanging from their coat pockets. My guess was that this was the entire Northern Syndicate.

"Do you know how hard it's been to flush out this bird? I can't tell you how long I've been waiting for this moment," Gigi said, stopping at the end of the long line of computer consoles. "I want you to know, it's nothing personal."

"Not personal? You made us take on a suicide mission just to get one hacker?" Crowe snarled.

"It's a bit more than that. Yes, we did need to take out The Wizard. That was a must." She walked over to the laptop, closing it and handing it off to a man in a uniform. He scurried up the stairs, disappearing into the dark. "We also needed access to the Witcher archives. You, Dorothea, provided an opportunity for both."

To think that I once believed she was saving me. Deep down, I knew that nobody did anything because it was the right thing to do. This was Oz.

"Tonight I caught two insurrectionists: The Wizard, legendary cyber-terrorist and his accomplice..." Gigi raised her gun aiming it straight at my heart. "Dorothea Gallant."

All three of my men started shouting at once, guns raised, threats flying—but all I could see were the red laser dots suddenly painting their bodies. This wasn't an ambush; we were sitting in the middle of an Oz damn firing squad.

"Stop! Stop!" I shouted until finally everyone looked at me. Gigi grinned like I'd done exactly what she was expecting. I hated that we were playing right into her hands.

Crowe growled, "You lay a finger on her an—"

BANG!

Blood sprayed the side of my face...and this time, I screamed.

-40-
THEA

The air tasted metallic. It hit at the back of my tongue making me feel sick, made worse by the small droplets of blood clinging to my lashes and turning my vision a cloudy pink.

Nick slammed onto his knees, immediately putting pressure to the torn flesh scarily close to Crowe's heart. Blood, nearly as black as the granite floors, poured from the wound.

Dropping beside Nick, I tore open Crowe's designer shirt, he blood-soaked fabric shredded like wet tissue beneath my hands.

"This is my fault." Frustration and fear shook my voice. Fat tears blurred his paling face. I couldn't go through losing Crowe, not after I'd lived for weeks thinking I'd lost Nick. I'd never survive it.

"Don't cry, Darling Thea." Crowe weakly brushed at my face. "Loving you was worth every second. If these are my last, at least I get to go seeing your beautiful face. It isn't all bad."

I shoved his hand away. "Shut the fuck up." I would do anything to save him. I'd tear my heart from my chest if it kept his beating. "You are *not* dying."

"Get up!" Gigi commanded, her voice flat and completely unbothered that she'd just shot a man in cold blood. My man. "Up, *Darling Thea*, or my next bullet goes in dear sweet Dandelion." Her perfectly manicured thumb cocked her gun, the mother-of-pearl grip as falsely sweet as she was.

Slowly, I rose. There were maybe fifteen steps separating us. Could I sink my stiletto into her throat before someone shot me down? Kill her the way I killed King?

"There's a good girl." Gigi smiled sweetly. "Dorothea Gallant Rosen, you are under arrest for crimes against The Quadrants, including high treason and the assassination of Eastin Witcher, Westin Witcher, Sorren Singrala, and eight of the nine members of the Northern Syndicate."

I couldn't breathe.

Gigi strode forward, picking up the remote from the desk. With only a couple of quick strokes, the big screen came back on, displaying footage of me bashing Eastin with a snow globe, tackling Westin off the ship, and boasting to the bouncer out front that I'd killed both Witchers.

"What is this bullshit?" Danny shouted.

"It would seem Dorothea Gallant has a vendetta against the Quadrants. After years of captivity with her Aunt, she planned a coup to avenge the deaths of her parents, taking out one quadrant leader at a time. Even poor Sorren, beloved by all of Oz, died when Dorothy blew up the hospital where she was undergoing extensive reconstructive therapy. Luckily, when she came for the Syndicate, I was able to detain her, so that she could answer for her crimes. Pity, that I was the only survivor, but I will be there to guide Ozmandria into a new age of peace and prosperity. A Pax Ozma."

Danny gestured around Gigi. "The Northern Syndicate is standing right there. All of them." The men beside her looked just as confused as we did.

"Yes. They are." Gigi snapped her fingers.

Thundering gunfire tore through the space, echoing in my ears long after the carnage was over. The former members of the Syndicate lay in a heap at her feet. Despite the massacre before my eyes, all I could think was that the blood pouring from Crowe's chest gave him minutes to live at best. I didn't know what to do.

"And, now, they're not." Gigi gestured to the uniformed officers, all wearing official Ozmandiran insignias. "Arrest her."

"NO!" Danny barked, moving between us.

Gigi raised her hand, and the men halted. "I have enough evidence to bury the three of you with her, but YBR has always done right by me, and I appreciate the part you played in my rise to power."

"Fuck you, you egomaniacal bitch." Danny looked like he might burn the entire skyscraper down to take her out.

Ignoring his outburst, she continued. "Niccolo..."

Nick's attention lifted from where Crowe was losing consciousness to Gigi. Fuck, his skin looked so sallow, bringing back haunting memories of when Nick had teetered on the razor's edge of death.

"Outside the lobby of this building, a mobile, fully stocked surgical unit is waiting. Vincent has—" She looked at her glittering watch, tilting her head in an exaggerated show of considering the time. "At best, four minutes to live. The elevator ride to the bottom takes two minutes and forty-five seconds. If you leave now, there is a small possibility he survives this. Small, but possible."

"Go!" I screamed. There was no question. If there was a chance, *any chance*, we had to take it. Nick looked from Crowe to me and back, the panic of indecision clear. "I swear to fucking Oz, Niccolo Ciopriani, if you don't take him to that ambulance, I will *NEVER* forgive you. Go!"

Nick gave me a heartbreaking expression, opening his mouth in what I knew was an argument.

"GO!" I repeated, my voice breaking beneath the strain of my command. "Please, Angel, don't make me lose him the way I lost you. Go."

"Fuck!" Nick lifted Crowe into his arms and over his shoulder, wincing from the pain in his side that I knew wasn't fully healed yet. When the elevator doors closed, I breathed a sigh of relief.

"Then there were two. It's a shame Nick took a whole minute to decide. I hate to say it, Dorothea, but I don't like poor Vincent's chances."

"Fuck you." I shook with rage.

"Now, that wasn't very nice. After all, I did save your life once." I leapt at the woman who would dare take one of my men from me. Gigi raised her gun, not even flinching. Danny wrapped a strong arm around my waist, heaving me back.

He lowered his mouth to my ear, "Choose your moment, Firecracker. You go after her now, and all that will happen is you get another one of us shot."

343

Gigi leaned down to The Wizard, prying the memory stick from the dead girl's hand.

"Fuck," Danny cursed under his breath. He was hoping, just like I had, that perhaps Gigi hadn't realized what The Wizard was about to hand over, but of course she had.

"I'll give you a choice, Danny."

Danny's eyes were locked on the hand holding the drive, but he lifted his chin defiantly. "There is no choice. I'm with Thea. I go where she goes, and she's going with me out that door."

"See, that's the thing. She's not. The only place our Dorothea is going, is to the Emerald City Detention Center, where she will be tried and executed for treason."

"I will never allow that to happen."

"You say that, but you haven't seen what's behind door number three." Gigi held up the remote, pushing a couple buttons to make the big screen come back on. "Not only can I confidently say Dorothea is leaving with me. I can also tell you where some other important women are headed."

Spread fifteen feet across the screen was an arrest warrant for Daffodil Kalidah.

"The Emerald City Plaza has a fabulous view of the park. It's always so beautiful this time of year."

"You leave her out of this," Danny growled.

"I debated on sending her to jail with Dorothea. But, I owe a favor to a mutual acquaintance." She flipped to a transfer of custody paper. One name in particular standing out: *Sylvan Deveaux.* "Detestable man. He doesn't hunt with guns or knives, you know. He likes to kill his prey with his bare hands. Turns out he was rather fond of your other sister. The dead one. What was her name?"

Beside me, hands still wrapped around my waist, Danny trembled. His fingers ground into my stomach in a painful attempt to hold himself back.

She flicked a button. Didi's autopsy report and photos appeared on screen, the same ones The Wizard gave us in a show of good faith. "That's right, Dahlia. She was so pretty, too."

I glared at Gigi like the fire of my wrath might vaporize her. "One day, you're going to wake up with a knife in your face, and you'll know I put it there."

Gigi lifted an unbelieving eyebrow. "Go home, and sweet Daffodil won't find her way into Sylvan's hands." Gigi changed slides, but it wasn't Daffodil staring back. A woman who could be Danny's twin scowled at the camera. She looked nearly the same age as us, so this picture couldn't have been very old.

"Daisy." I saw the exact moment Danny's will broke. It was like parts of him turned to ash, flaking away one bit at a time. His hand gripped mine, and he fell to his knees. "She's alive?"

"I think that depends on what you choose." Gigi tossed the memory stick at his knees, bending over to whisper in his ear, "This is the part where you leave."

Danny stared at the drive like it was a snake. His grip on my hand tightened, even as he leaned forward to pick up the small bit of plastic off the ground.

He didn't look at me, instead he clenched the drive into a tight fist. "I'm sorry, Princess. I have to."

I didn't blame him, not really, but it didn't make the hurt of his admission sting any less.

"I'm coming back for you."

Guards surged forward, tearing me from his grip. I struggled, kicking at them as they forced me to my knees, pinning my hands behind my back.

"Go, Danny," I said softly, refusing to let Gigi see the way my heart was crumbling.

"I'll be back, Thea."

Whatever happens, we do it together. It won't be like last time.

I shouldn't have looked up. Seeing the desperation in his liquid-green eyes made this so much harder. He shook as he took my face in the briefest of kisses. "I love you."

"Go." Tears fell from my eyes, mixing into the streaks of Crowe's blood still painting the ground.

Danny slowly climbed to his feet, ambling towards the elevators. He paused before Gigi, his hands in fists at his side. "This isn't over. Thea's a better person than anyone in this room. She deserves better than this."

Gigi nodded. "This is Oz, Dandelion. People rarely get what they deserve. Haven't you learned? There are no happy endings here."

Danny walked onto the elevator. As the doors closed, he vowed, "Not for you, there isn't."

-EPILOGUE-
AUNT EM

I drove my knife down, a watery trickle of blood spilling over the edges of the blade as I sawed into the flesh. My mouth watered in eager anticipation.

"Good afternoon, Emerald City. I'm Jellia Jamb. Our live coverage of the trial of the century continues."

The television mounted to the wall had been playing Dorothy's trial for the past week. It was becoming such prime entertainment that I didn't want to miss a second of it. Naturally, I had televisions mounted into each room of my quarters, ensuring I never had to.

"It was merely one month ago that Dorothea Gallant Rosen attempted her coup to overthrow the Quadrants."

I highly doubted that. Dorothy was many things, but ambitious was not one of them. That bullshit story about wanting revenge was almost laughable. There was no way that girl knew enough about her parents to want to avenge anything.

No, this had been a brilliant plan for Gigi to ascend as sole ruler of Ozmandria. Maybe the rest of the nation was buying her story of survival and capture of the infamous Dorothy Gallant, but I wasn't.

Holding my goblet aloft, a server poured a cabernet almost as red as the buttered steak before me. I told the cook to prepare something special the moment the jury went to deliberate.

Celebrations deserved feasts.

Not that I cared what Gigi was up to. My business would thrive either way. I didn't need fame when I could have the fortune. Overturning of government meant more overlooked areas of the country. It would only make it easier for Cyclone Shipping to operate. Gigi was doing me a favor.

"We've just received word that the jury has emerged from their chambers, having already reached a verdict in record time. We're going live to the courtroom now."

I giggled, kicking my feet with a jubilance I hadn't felt since I was a girl. This was it. Dorothy would be executed, and finally, everything the Gallants owned would be mine.

The camera panned to Dorothy. She looked terrible. I smiled into my wine. Dark rings circled her eyes; maybe she'd been crying. Wouldn't that be lovely? Her skin blanched when the judge smacked the gavel, calling everyone to order.

"Mr. Foreman, have you reached a verdict?"

A portly man rose, straightening his tie before he spoke. *"We have, your honor."*

"Dorothea Gallant Rosen, please rise."

Dorothy stood, her red jumpsuit making her look even paler. Her eyes darted around the room like she was looking for someone. Probably one of those useless men she was gallivanting around Oz with.

"On the charge of high treason, how do you find the defendant?"

"Ms. Rosen." My assistant knocked on the door, entering without being given permission.

"Not now! They're about to read the verdict."

· *"We find the defendan—"*

"Em."

"No." If I missed the reading of this verdict, I would remove his impertinent tongue.

"This is urgent."

"Guilty." The sounds of a riled courtroom erupted. People screamed for retribution, demanding Dorothy's death in medieval fashion.

"What?!" I snarled, gesturing at the close-up of the tears pouring down Dorothy's cheeks. "What could possibly be worth interrupting this?"

"There are some people here to speak with you."

"Send them away. I'm obviously busy right now."

My phone rang, the shrill chirp of the ringtone making me jump. Was the entire world out to destroy this moment for me? After another second, the phone silenced, having sent whoever was on the line to voicemail.

"Em, these aren't the kind of people you can send away."

On the television, the judge banged his gavel, trying to wrangle the unruly courtroom into silence. Slowly the chamber settled down, everyone eager for sentencing.

The phone trilled again, and when I ignored it, the damn thing rang a third time. My accountant's name flashed on the screen.

Flicking it open, I snapped, "What?!"

"Dorothy Gallant Rosen, for crimes against the Quadrants, high treason, and the deaths of Eastin Witcher, Westin Wit—"

My accountant's panicked voice nearly shrieked over the line, "There are people here. I tried to stop them, but Em—"

The door to the dining room slammed open against the wall. Four uniformed officers and one man in a crisp black suit pushed into the room.

"Sorren Singrala, Aaron Edvardson..."

My eyes went wide, recognizing the head of Ozmandria's secret service, Sebastian Charles. This man was as close to a second as Gigi had.

The voice over the phone continued, "They're taking everything. Em, are you hearing me? Everything!"

I rose to my feet, ending the call and setting the phone beside my plate. "Hello, Sebastian."

"Emily." He gave a curt nod. "By order of the Queen, all assets belonging to Dorothea Gallant Rosen have been seized by the Ozmandrian state."

"The Queen?" I scoffed, tipping my head back in disbelief. That bitch. Of course she would wipe the existing system and set herself up as the one and only monarch.

"You have been sentenced to death by beheading."

Beheading? That was unexpected and perhaps a bit barbaric, but who was I to judge?

"Execution is set for one week's time. May Ozma have mercy on your soul."

"No!" Dorothy screamed, *"I didn't do anything wrong. It's her! This is all her."* She climbed over the partition, making a run for the door and driving her elbows into anyone standing in her way. Wrists still bound, her fingertips brushed the door handle when a uniformed officer pulled a taser. The electrified barbs easily dropped her to the ground. I couldn't even revel in the way she twitched against the parquet floor because all I could think was "seized by the state." He couldn't mean everything.

"It's a shame." He nodded at the television, a limp Dorothy being dragged out of the room. "If this had happened a year ago, Cyclone Shipping would still be under your aegis." He handed me a piece of folded paper. "As it stands, you have thirty days to vacate the premises. All accounts have been frozen, and Cyclone Shipping is to cease operations immediately. All properties are to be cleared of personal items, or they will be sold at auction."

After everything I'd done to help her with this bid for power, this was how Gigi repaid me? My steak and wine turned in my stomach. What was once a victory celebration now felt a lot like a last meal.

I had one week to figure out a way to seize back control before my niece lost her head, and I lost everything.

One. Week.

End of Book 2

Thea and the boys of YBR will be back for the conclusion of Dark Oz, <u>No Place Like Home</u>, coming May 31, 2024. Preorder it on Amazon now.

To get all the sneak peeks and information on the next book, be sure to sign up for Geneva's newsletter.
www.genevamonroeauthor.com

You can also get in on the conversation at Geneva Monroe's Pretty St@bby Readers on Facebook.

If you enjoyed this book, I would be extremely grateful for a review. Reviews make an incredible impact for indie authors.
Thank you for reading.

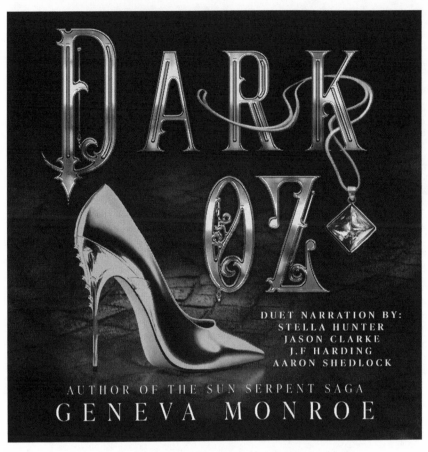

The dark world of Ozmandria is coming to audio.

Live the story again. Performed in DUET NARRATION by:

Stella Hunter as Thea Rosen

Jason Clarke as Nick Chopper

J.F. Harding as Vincent Crowe

Aaron Shedlock – Dandelion Kalidah

Coming Spring 2024

Oh hey! Before you sharpen your pitchforks, remember I'm following Frank's roadmap... and it's dark. Sure, I may have diverged a *bit* at the end there, but at least I didn't drop Nick down a ravine.

The plan all along was to make this book be Nick's journey, coming to terms with his past and accepting how he feels about Thea. I didn't anticipate how much I would love being in his head. The conflict rooted deep within him was so complicated. I loved diving into the tender soul wrapped in so many layers of damage that he appears heartless–to the point that he's convinced himself of it..Then, our girl storms into his life, proving everything he thought was a lie. My editor described him as the mafia Mr. Darcy, and I love that concept. It fits Nick so well. He loves her so deeply, and he hates that she's brought that out in him when he was comfortable with the man he'd become. Not happy, mind you, but comfortable.

For as soft as Nick is at his core, Crowe is hard. His fight has always been suppressing the darkness. He talked about it in book one, but I knew I wanted to see The Scarecrowe come out to play. It was fun letting the rougher bit of Crowe show. Hopefully, Nick got him to the ground floor in time so that we can see more of Crowe's brand of justice.

In No Place Like Home: Dark Oz Book 3, we'll see the conclusion of YBR's story. For all the people out there rooting for Dandelion—Look, I know you're angry with him. Again. But hear me out– he didn't really have a choice. He was never gonna fight his way out of that pit. The person you're really angry at is Gigi. So feel free to direct all your anger her way because that bitch has been orchestrating the whole thing from the beginning...going way farther back than anyone realizes. The point is: Danny will get his moment. There's a lot of baggage that he needs to unpack. He and Thea both have some trauma to work through. There's just that pesky issue of a death sentence to deal with. Am I above killing a main character? Probably not. Will I? That's the real question.

As always, thank you for reading. I'll be back soon.

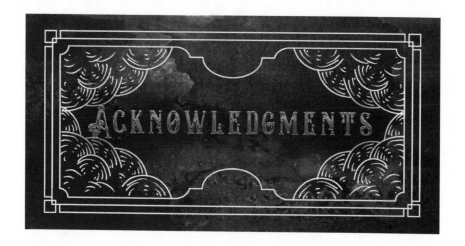

I will forever thank my husband first. Without his help and support, there is no way I would have the time or ability to finish one book in a year, much less three.

Thank you to my editor and friend, Sierra Cassidy. You're the first person I come to with my crazy ideas, and you're always there to hear me out, even at two in the morning.

Reanna Breaux, I'll never forget how you were the first person to take a chance on my writing. Your eagle eyes make my books shine. I will always be grateful for you...p.s. please forgive me for Nonna.

Thank you to my beta team: Jessica Jordan, Sarah Konieczny, Erica Karwoski, Megan Hannon Visger, Lauren Levendusky, and Andi McClane. You guys are seriously the best. This manuscript wouldn't be half as good without you and your feedback.

Lauren and Erica, thank you for keeping my head on straight and our reader group interesting. I love that I can count on you both to keep me going.

Alessia Quaranta, I don't want there to be a day when we don't share late-night stories about Italy. One day, we'll make salsa together and it will be the highlight of my year. I adore you. Thank you for lending me your insight and your stories. I hope I did you and your Nonna proud.

Lastly, to the kickass readers in my reader group. My self-proclaimed aunties. You make the long nights worth it. I hope you loved this book as much as I loved writing it for you.

All my love,

Gen

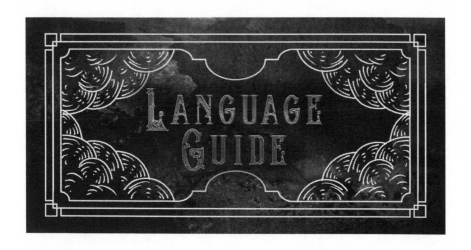

I probably should have subtitled this: *How to swear like an Italian.* Not to disappoint, there are some swoony lines later in the book. Turns out, death and danger make Nick surprisingly poetic.

Chapter 1

Però cazzo - But damn

Chapter 6

Cazzo - Fucker
  Niente - Nothing

Chapter 7

Fottuti idioti- Stupid fuckers

Chapter 8

Cazzo- fucker
Diamine- damn
Idiota- idiot

Chapter 9

Leone - Lion
Cazzo - Fuck
Coglione di merda - Fucking idiot
Cagna - Bitch

Chapter 10

Siamo cambiati tutti - We all have.
Ciao, cugino! - Hello, Cousin!
Chi non muore es rivede. - Who doesn't die, sees each other again. (In English this is similar in feeling to saying, "Look what the cat dragged in.")
Ma che bel bocconcino. - What a nice little treat.
Stronzo- Asshole
Fratello- brother
Ehilà, Leone, come va? - Hey, Lion, how's it going?

Chapter 11

Zio - Uncle

   Carina - Sweetheart

   bellezza - Lovely

   A domani, papà - Until tomorrow, father.

   Not turtle, stronzo, tortura - Not turtle, asshole, torture.

   quella cazzo di strada - that fucking road

Chapter 12

guardami- look at me

   Sei così bella - You look so beautiful like this

Chapter 13

stronzetto - little shit

   Bravissima - very well done

Chapter 14

Porca miseria. Sei così dolce che mi è venuto il mal di denti - Damn, you're so sweet my teeth ache

   Fragolina - Little strawberry

   Levati dai coglioni! - Get the fuck out.

   fratello - brother

Chapter 15

Mannaggia santissima, Gesù bambino! Ma porca miseria, mi hai fatto venire un cazzo di colpo! Come cazzo ti è venuto in mente! - "Holy spirits, baby jesus! Fucking hell, you gave me a fucking fright! What the fuck were you thinking!"

"Ciao, Nonna."- Hey, Grandma

Ciao, Nonna? E me lo dici così? Sono passati cinque anni, Nicco. Cinque! Ciao, nonna un cavolo!" - "Ciao, Nonna? And you say it just like that? It's been five years, Nicco. Five! Ciao, nonna my arse!"

Perchè non sei venuto prima a salutare nonna tua? - "Why haven't you come sooner to say hi to your nonna?"

quell'idiota - that idiot

calma - calm down

"Un nome così bello per una ragazza altrettanto bella. I vostri bambini saranno degli angioletti." - A beautiful name for a girl that's just as beautiful. Your babies are going to be little angels."

Bambini - babies

I figli sono pezzi di cuore - children are pieces of your heart

Topolino- little mouse

E poi lo sai che questa è la MIA cucina - And you know that this is MY kitchen afterall

Oggi devo fare la salsa!- I have to make tomato sauce today!

E se non la faccio io la salsa non la fa nessuno. – And if I don't make salsa no one will!

è tutto fresco - it's all fresh

Angioletto - little angel

Chapter 16

Perfetto. - Perfect
  Pronto - Hello
  stronzi - assholes
  Certo - of course

Chapter 17

Quando parli con me, devi farlo con rispetto! - You will speak to me with respect.

Te n'è fregato qualcosa - Did you care

Chapter 18

Ma porca puttana! - Fucking hell.

Mi ricordi cosa significa sentirsi vivo. - You remind me what it is to be alive.

Come il fragore delle onde che si infrangono sulla riva. - Like the roar of waves crashing on the shore.

Sei la scintilla che ha messo a FUOCO la mia anima - You are the spark that ignited my soul

Tutto e nulla. – Everything and nothing

Chapter 19

Sei così bella. - You are so beautiful

E ancora, e ancora - and again and again.

Splendida - wonderful

Miseriaccia - bloody hell

Vediamo se riuscirai a camminare quando avrò finito con te. - We'll see if you'll be able to walk once I'm done with you.

Chapter 21

Ti amo. - *I love you.*
Cazzo! – Fuck!

Chapter 22

Mi sei mancato, amore di nonna - I missed you, my love.

Grazie per avermi accolto nella tua famiglia - thank you for making me part of your family.

Chapter 23

Va bene. Va bene, ho capito. - Fine. Fine, I understand.

Vaffanculo! - Fuck off

Chapter 27

Porca miseria! – Holy shit!

Chapter 30

Quel fottuto coglione - Fucking asshole

sono io. - It's me.

Sono una testa di cazzo. - I'm a dickhead

Dannazione - damn

Figlio di puttana! - Son of a Bitch!

Chapter 31

Siamo fottuti - we are fucked

Chapter 32

Tu sarai il primo a morire - You will die first.

Chapter 35

Dannazione - damn

Diamine - damn

Chapter 36

Tocca a me adesso, Fiore Mio - My turn, Fiore Mio
Le tue tette sono un'opera d'arte Your breasts are a work of art

Chapter 37

Dovresti fargliela pagare per averti chiamato così - You should make her pay for calling you that.

Perché? È la verità, no? - Why? It's true, isn't it?

Porca puttana. Dovresti vedere quanto è bagnata adesso. Continua a parlarle. - Holy shit! You should feel how wet she just got. Keep talking to her.

Apri, dolcezza - Open, sweet thing.

Bellissima - Beautiful

Cazzo - Fuck

Porca puttana - holy shit

Vai a fare in culo- fuck you

Quanto cazzo sei sex - you are so fucking sexy

I'm off to find the Wizard, and I'm not going to let anyone stand in my way...

Not my vicious Aunt Em, who wants me dead because I tried to expose her human trafficking ring. Not Westin Witcher, who is seeking payback after I killed her cousin. And especially not the dangerous group of smugglers running Yellow Brick Taxi.

I'm at their mercy to get me to the Emerald City, and I'm under no illusions about my unlikely heroes. Hiding beneath Crowe's protective act is a violent past, and Danny may behave like a king, except he's really a coward. While Nick is just heartless.

I'll sacrifice whatever it takes to meet the Wizard and convince him to give me a new life outside of Oz. Plus, I have the ultimate bargaining chip—the emerald I stole from Eastin Witcher.

I just have to make it there alive first...

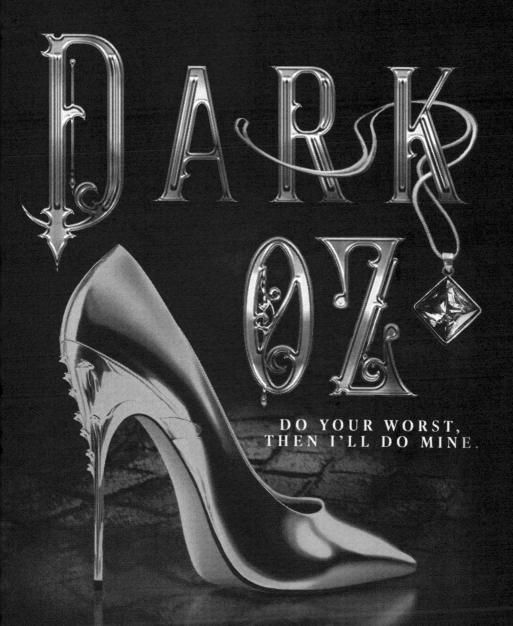

DARK OZ

DO YOUR WORST,
THEN I'LL DO MINE.

AUTHOR OF THE SUN SERPENT SAGA

GENEVA MONROE

A cursed kingdom.
A Fire Singer seeking vengeance.
And a prince who is not what he seems...

Under the silks of her circus troupe's tent, Elyria Solaris dances with fire. She disguises her gift as showmanship, but longs for answers about why she has a power no one else possesses.

Somewhere in the city of never-ending night, Prince Cal is looking for the girl who burns the brightest. Only she can stop the horror inflicted on his kingdom by a sadistic lord who controls the minds of his victims.

When Cal spies Elyria, he knows without a doubt that she is the most beautifully dangerous thing he has ever seen. More importantly, she's the Fire Draken he's been waiting his whole life to find.

Moments after Cal serendipitously enters Elyria's life, a loved one's gruesome death sets her on the path of vengeance. Cal will do anything to protect his people, including lying to Elyria about who he really is and promising her the answers that she seeks.

But if Elyria trusts the undeniable spark between them, could it turn out to be the one fire she is unable to tame?

49659502R00231